Samuel Beckett:

The Complete Short Prose,

1929–1989

Samuel Beckett:

The Complete Short Prose,

1929–1989

Edited and with an Introduction and Notes by

S. E. Gontarski

GROVE PRESS
New York

First Love originally written in French (1945): *Premier amour* © Les Éditions de Minuit 1970; *Stories and Texts for Nothing (The Expelled, The Calmative, The End,* and *Texts for Nothing I–XIII)* originally written in French: (1945–1950) *Nouvelles et Textes pour rien (L'Expulsé, Le Calmant, La Fin et Textes pour rien I–XIII)* © Les Éditions de Minuit 1955; *The Image* originally written in French (1958): *L'Image* © Les Éditions de Minuit 1988; *Enough* originally written in French (1965): *Assez* © Les Éditions de Minuit 1966; *Imagination Dead Imagine* originally written in French (1965): *Imagination morte imaginez* © Les Éditions de Minuit 1965; *Ping* originally written in French (1965): *Bing* © Les Éditions de Minuit 1966; *Lessness* originally written in French (1968): *Sans* © Les Éditions de Minuit 1969; *The Lost Ones* originally written in French (1969): *Le dépeupleur* © Les Éditions de Minuit 1970; *For to End Yet Again* originally written in French (1975): *Pour finir encore* in *Pour finir encore et autres foirades* © Les Éditions de Minuit 1976; *Fizzles* 1, 2, 3, 4, 5, 6 originally written in French (1972–1975): *Foirades* in *Pour finir encore et autres foirades* © Les Éditions de Minuit 1976; *The Cliff* originally written in French (1975): *La falaise* © Les Éditions de Minuit (1991).

Published simultaneously in Canada
Printed in the United States of America

FIRST EDITION

Library of Congress Cataloging-in-Publication Data

Beckett, Samuel, 1906–1989
   [Prose works]
   Samuel Beckett, the complete short prose, 1929–1989 / edited and with an introduction and notes by S. E. Gontarski.—1st ed.
   Includes bibliographical references.
   ISBN 0-8021-1577-2
   I. Gontarski, S. E.   II. Title
PR6003.E282A6   1995   848'.91409—dc20   95-13074

Design by Laura Hammond Hough

Grove Press
841 Broadway
New York, NY 10003

10 9 8 7 6 5 4 3 2 1

Contents

Introduction

From Unabandoned Works: Samuel Beckett's Short Prose

WHILE SHORT FICTION was a major creative outlet for Samuel Beckett, it has heretofore attracted only a minor readership. Such neglect is difficult to account for, given that Beckett wrote short fiction for the entirety of his creative life and his literary achievement and innovation are as apparent in the short works as in his more famous novels and plays, if succinctly so. Christopher Ricks, for one, has suggested that the 1946 short story "The End" is "the best possible introduction to Beckett's fiction,"[1] and writing in the *Irish Times* (11 March 1995), literary editor John Banville has called "First Love" "the most nearly perfect short story ever written." Yet few anthologists of short fiction, and in particular of the Irish short story, include Beckett's work. Beckett's stories have instead often been treated as anomalous or aberrant, a species so alien to the tradition of short fiction that critics are still struggling to assess not only what they mean—if indeed they "mean" at all—but what they are: stories or novels, prose or poetry, rejected fragments or completed tales. William Trevor has justified his exclusion of Beckett from *The Oxford Book of Irish Short Stories* (1989) by asserting that, like his countrymen Shaw and O'Casey, Beckett "conveyed [his] ideas more skillfully in another medium" (p. xvi). But to see Beckett as fundamentally a dramatist who wrote some narratives is seriously to distort his literary achievement. Beckett himself considered his prose fiction "the important writing."[2] The omission is all the more curious given that Beckett's short pieces exemplify Trevor's characterization of the genre as "the distillation of an essence." Beckett distilled essences for some sixty years, and through that process novels were often reduced to stories, stories pared to fragments, first abandoned then unabandoned and "completed" through the act of publication. When that master of the Irish short story Frank O'Connor noted that "there is something in the short story at its most characteristic[—]something we do not often find in the novel—an intense awareness of human loneliness,"[3] he could have been writing directly about Beckett's short prose. As Beckett periodically confronted first the difficulties then the impossibility of sustaining and shaping longer works, as his aesthetic preoccupations grew more contractive than expansive, short prose became his principal narrative form—the distillate of longer fiction as well as the testing ground for occasional longer works—and the theme of "human loneliness" pervades it.

Beckett's own creative roots, furthermore, were set deep in the tradition of Irish storytelling that Trevor valorizes, "the immediacy of the spoken word," particularly that of the Irish *seanchaí*. Although self-consciously experimental, self-referential, and often mannered, Beckett's short fiction is never wholly divorced from the culturally pervasive traditions of Irish storytelling. Even when his subject is the absence of subject, the story the impossibility of stories, its form the disintegration of form, Beckett's short prose can span the gulf between the more fabulist strains of Irish storytelling and the aestheticized experimental narratives of European modernism, of which Beckett was a late, if formative, part. Self-conscious and aesthetic as they often are, Beckett's stories gain immeasurably from oral presentation, performance, and so they have attracted theater artists who, like Joseph Chaikin, have adapted the stories to the stage or who, like Billie Whitelaw and Barry McGovern, have simply read them in public performance.

Much of Beckett's short prose inhabits the margins between prose and poetry, between narrative and drama, and finally between completion and incompletion. The short work "neither" has routinely been published with line breaks suggestive of poetry, but when British publisher John Calder was about to gather "neither" in the *Collected Poems*, Beckett resisted because he considered it a prose work, a short story. Calder relates the incident in a letter to the *Times Literary Supplement* (24–30 August 1990): He had "originally intended to put ["neither"] in the *Collected Poems*. We did not do so, because Beckett at the last moment said that it was not a poem and should not be there" (p. 895). The work is here printed for the first time corrected (q.v. "A Note on the Texts") and without line breaks, the latter to reinforce the fact that at least Beckett considered "neither" a prose work.

"From an Abandoned Work," furthermore, was initially published as a theater piece by the British publisher Faber and Faber after it was performed on the BBC Third Programme on 14 December 1957 by Patrick Magee. Although "From an Abandoned Work" is now generally anthologized with Beckett's short fiction, Faber collected it among four theater works in *Breath and Other Shorts* (1971). That grouping, of course, punctuated its debut as a piece *for* performance.[4] It might be argued, then, that "From an Abandoned Work" could as well be anthologized with Beckett's theater writings. It is no less "dramatic," after all, than "A Piece of Monologue," with which it shares a titular admission of fragmentation. Even as Beckett expanded the boundaries of short fiction, often by contracting the form, his stories retained that oral, performative quality of their Irish roots. Many an actor has discovered that even Beckett's most intractable fictions, like *Texts for Nothing, Enough,* or *Stirrings Still,* share ground with theater and so maintain an immediacy in performance that makes them accessible to a broad audience.

With the exception, then, of *More Pricks Than Kicks,* which with its single, unifying character, Belacqua Shuah, is as much a novel as a collection of stories,[5] and the 1933 coda to that collection, "Echo's Bones," which Beckett wrote as the novel's tailpiece but which was rejected first by the publisher, Chatto and Windus, then by Beckett himself for subsequent editions, and most recently by the Beckett Estate for this collection, this anthology gathers the entire output of Beckett's short fiction from his first published story, "Assumption," which appeared in *transition* magazine in 1929 when he was twenty-three years old, to his last, which were produced nearly sixty years later, shortly before his death. In failing health and stirring little from his Paris flat, Beckett demonstrated that there were creative stirrings still, the title he gave three related short tales dedicated to his friend and longtime American publisher, Barney Rosset. In between, Beckett used short fiction to rescue what was in 1932 a failed and abandoned novel, *Dream of Fair to Middling Women,* salvaging two discrete segments of that unfinished and only recently published (1992) work as short fiction, adding eight fresh, if fairly conventional, tales (or chapters) to fill out *More Pricks Than Kicks* (1934), a work whose title alone, although biblical in origin, ensured its scandalous reception and eventual banning in Ireland. In 1945–46 Beckett turned to short fiction to launch "the French venture," producing four *nouvelles:* "Premier Amour" ("First Love"), "L'Expulsé" ("The Expelled"), "Le Calmant" ("The Calmative"), and "La Fin" or "Suite" ("The End"). These stories, "the very first writing in French,"[6] seemed to have tapped a creative reservoir, for a burst of writing followed: two full-length plays, *Eleuthéria* and *En attendant Godot (Waiting for Godot),* and a "trilogy" of novels, *Molloy, Malone meurt (Malone Dies), L'Innommable (The Unnamable).* When the frenetic creativity of that period began to flag, Beckett turned afresh to short fiction in his struggle to "go on," producing thirteen brief tales grouped under a title adapted from the phrase conductors use for that ghost measure which sets the orchestra's tempo. The conductor calls his silent gesture a "measure for nothing"; Beckett called his prose stutterings *Texts for Nothing*. For Beckett these tales "express the failure to implement the last words of *L'Innommable:* 'il faut continuer, je vais continuer' "[7] ["I can't go on, I'll go on"].

By the 1940s Beckett had apparently abandoned the literary use of his native tongue. Writing to George Reavey about "a book of short stories," Beckett noted on 15 December 1946, "I do not think I shall write very much in English in the future."[8] But early in 1954 Beckett's American publisher, Barney Rosset, suggested that he return to English: "I have been wondering if you would not get almost the freshness of turning to doing something in English which you must have gotten when you first seriously took to writing in French."[9] Shortly thereafter, Beckett began a new English novel, which he first abandoned then published in 1958 as "From an Abandoned Work." In a transcription of the story, a fair copy made as a gift for a friend, Beckett appended a note on its provenance: "This text was written 1954 or 1955. It was the first text written directly in English since *Watt* (1945)."[10] Almost a decade intervened between "From an Abandoned Work" and Beckett's next major impasse, a novel tentatively entitled *Fancy Dying*, portions of which, in French and English (with German translations of both), were published as "Faux Départs" to launch a new German literary journal, *Karsbuch* in 1965.[11] That abandoned novel (q.v. Appendix II) developed into *All Strange Away* (where although "Fancy is her only hope," "Fancy dead") and its sibling, *Imagination Dead Imagine*, but was the impetus for several other *Residua* as well. Although these works were apparently distillations of a longer work, Beckett's British publisher treated the 1,500-word *Imagination Dead Imagine* as a completed novel, issuing it separately in 1965 with the following gloss: "The present work was conceived as a novel, and in spite of its brevity, remains a novel, a work of fiction from which the author has removed all but the essentials, having first imagined them and created them. It is possibly the shortest novel ever published."

In between Beckett completed an impressive array of theater work, including *Fin de partie (Endgame)* (1957), *Krapp's Last Tape* (1958), *Happy Days* (1961), and *Play* (1964), and another extended prose work, *Comment c'est (How It Is)*, itself first abandoned, then "unabandoned" in 1960. A fragment was published separately as "L'Image" in the journal *X* in December 1959. The English version, "The Image," is here published for the first time in a new translation by Edith Fournier (q.v. "Notes on the Texts"). Another segment of *How It Is* was published as "From an Unabandoned Work" in *Evergreen Review* in 1960.[12] For the next three decades, the post–*How It Is* period, Beckett would write, in French and English, denuded tales in the manner of *All Strange Away*, stories that focused on a single, often static image "ill seen" and consequently "ill said," *Residua* that resulted from the continued impossibility of long fiction. As the titles of two of Beckett's late stories suggest, these are tales "Heard in the Dark," stories that were themselves early versions of the novel *Company*. And in a note accompanying the French manuscript of "Bing," translated into English first as "Pfft" but quickly revised to the equally onomatopoetic "Ping," Beckett noted: " 'Bing' may be regarded as the result or miniaturization of 'Le Dépeupleur' abandoned because of its intractable complexities." Abandoned in 1966, *Le Dépeupleur* was also unabandoned, "completed" in 1970, and translated as *The Lost Ones* in 1971. Throughout this period Beckett managed to turn apparent limitations, impasses, rejections into aesthetic triumphs. Adapting the aesthetics of two architects, Mies van der Rohe's "less is more" and Adolf Loos's "ornament is a crime," Beckett set out to expunge "ornament," to write "less," to remove "all but the essentials" from his art, to distill his essences and so develop his own astringent, desiccated, monochromatic minimalism, miniaturizations, the "minima" he alluded to in the "fizzle" called "He is barehead." As Beckett's fiction developed from the pronominal unity of the four *nouvelles* through the disembodied voices of the *Texts for Nothing* toward the voiceless bodies of *All Strange Away* and its evolutionary descendant *Imagination Dead Imagine*, he continued his ontological exploration of being in narrative and finally being as narrative, producing in the body of the text the text as body. If the *Texts for Nothing* suggest the dispersal of character and the subsequent writing beyond the body, *All Strange Away* signaled a refiguration, the body's return, its textualization, the body as voiceless, static object, or the object of text, unnamed except for a series of geometric signifiers, being as mathematical formulae. The subject of these late tales is less the secret recesses of the repressed subconscious or the imagination valorized by Romantic poets and painters than the dispersed, post-Freudian ego, voice as alien other. As the narrator of "Fizzle 2," "Horn came always," suggests, "It is in the outer space, not to be confused with the other [inner space or the Other?], that such images develop."

Despite such dehumanized immobility, these figures (one hesitates to call them characters) and their chronologically earlier disembodied voices retain a direct and fundamental dramatic quality of which Beckett was fully aware. Despite occasional protestations to the contrary, Beckett encouraged directors eager to stage his prose and developed several thematically revealing stage adaptations of his short narratives. When the American director Joseph Chaikin wrote for permission to stage *Stories and Texts for Nothing*, for example, Beckett encouraged him in a letter of 26 April 1980 to mount a single *Text*, for which he proposed a simple, precise staging: a single figure, "[s]eated. Head in hands. Nothing else. Face invisible. Dim spot. Speech hesitant. Mike for audibility." Beckett wrote again on 1 August 1980 developing his adaptation:

> Curtain up on speechless author (A) still or moving or alternately. Silence broken by recorded voice (V) speaking opening of text. A takes over. Breaks down. V again. A again. So on. Till text completed piecemeal. Then spoken through, more or less hesitantly, by A alone.
>
> Prompt not always successful, i.e., not regular alternation VAVA. Sometimes: Silence, V, silence, V again, A. Or even three prompts before A can speak.
>
> A does not repeat, but takes over where V leaves off.
>
> V: not necessarily A's voice. Nor necessarily the same throughout. Different voices, 3 or 4, male and female, might be used for V. Perhaps coming to A from different quarters.
>
> Length of prompt (V) and take over (A) as irregular as you like.
>
> V may stop, A break down, at any point of sentence.

Chaikin ultimately rejected Beckett's staging, preferring his own vision of a medley of texts, and Beckett conceded in a letter of 5 September 1980, "The method I suggest is only valid for a single text. The idea was to caricature the labour of composition. If you prefer extracts from a number of texts you will need a different approach." Chaikin finally chose another, more "theatrical" approach, but Beckett's adaptation of his story remains astonishing, a dramatic foregrounding of the mysterious voices, external to the perceiving part of self. What is caricatured in Beckett's adaptation is at least the Romantic notion of creativity, the artist's agonized communion with his own pure, uncorrupted, inner being, consciousness, or imagination. In Beckett's vision the author figure "A" has at least an unnamed collaborator, an external Other. "A" is as much audience to the emerging artwork as its instigator, as he folds the voices of Others, origins unknown, into his own.

Shivaun O'Casey, daughter of dramatist Sean O'Casey, worked with Beckett to dramatize *From an Abandoned Work,* and Beckett likewise detailed a staging for her. O'Casey's initial impulse was to mount the work on the analogy of *Play,* but Beckett resisted. "I think the spotlight face presentation would be wrong here." He went on to offer an alternative that separated speaker from spoken: "The face is irrelevant. I feel also that no form of monologue technique will work for this text and that it should somehow be presented as a document for which the speaker is not responsible." Beckett's outline is as follows:

> Moonlight. Ashcan a little left of centre. Enter man left, limp-ing, with stick, shadowing in paint general lighting along [*sic*]. Advances to can, raises lid, pushes about inside with crook of stick, inspects and rejects (puts back in can) an unidentifiable refuse, fishes out finally tattered ms. or copy of FAAW, reads aloud standing "Up bright and early that day, I was young then, feeling awful and out—" and a little further in silence, lowers text, stands motionless, finally closes ashcan, sits down on it, hooks stick round neck, and reads text through from beginning, i.e., including what he had read standing. Finishes, sits a mo-ment motionless, gets up, replaces text in ashcan and limps off right. Breathes with maximum authenticity, only effect to be sought in [*sic*] slight hesitation now and then in places where most effective, due to strangeness of text and imperfect light and state of ms.[13]

In such an adaptation the narrative offered to the audience is, as Beckett says, separated from the stage character, who is then only an ac-cidental protagonist in the drama, more messenger, say, than character. It was a form of staging that Beckett preferred for most of his prose, a compromise between an unadorned stage reading and a full, theatrical adaptation where characters and not just the text are represented on the stage. When the American theatrical group Mabou Mines requested permission through Jean Reavey to stage *The Lost Ones*, Beckett approved at first only a "straight reading." In rehearsals, however, the work developed into a complex, environmental adaptation with a naked actor "demonstrating" the text with a host of miniature figures. Beckett's comment on the adaptation was finally, "Sounds like a crooked straight reading to me."[14] With O'Casey, Beckett resisted the resurrection of a dramatic structure he himself had by then rejected, the monologue, a form he developed in prose with the four *nouvelles* in 1947 and adapted to the stage with *Krapp's Last Tape* in 1958. The monologue form embraced an ideology of concrete presence, a single coherent being (or a unified ego or, in literary terms, a unified character), an idea with which Beckett was increasingly uncomfortable (witness the tapes themselves in *Krapp's Last Tape*) and all pretense to which was finally abandoned in the "trilogy" and the subsequent *Texts for Nothing*. In the theater Beckett gave full voice to that disintegration of character and the fragmentation of monologue in *Not I* and with the incorporeal, ghostly figure of May in *Footfalls*. When consulted about stagings of his prose, Beckett invariably rejected, as he did with Shivaun O'Casey, adaptations that posited a unity of character and narrative that the monologue form suggests. When I prepared with him stagings of first his novella *Company* and then the story "First Love," he offered possibilities almost identical to those for Chaikin and O'Casey respectively.[15] The central question to Beckett's dramatization of "First Love," for instance, was how to break up an unrelieved reading of the text, again discovered in a rubbish heap:

> The reading can be piecemealed by all kinds of business—such as returning it to bin (on which he sits to read)—exiting and returning to read to the end—looking feverishly for a flea or other vermin—chewing a crust—getting up to piss in a corner with back modestly to audience—etc. etc. making the poor best of a hopeless job.[16]

Actors, then, have intuited what literary critics have too often failed to articulate, that even Beckett's most philosophical and experimental short fictions have an immediacy and emotional power, "the immediacy of the spoken voice," which makes them accessible to a broad audience and places them firmly within a tradition of Irish storytelling.

Beckett's first short stories, "Assumption," "A Case in a Thousand," "Text," and "Sedendo et Quiescendo,"[17] however, retain the rhetorical ornament and psychological probing characteristic of much high modernism. These stories, the latter two fragments of a then-abandoned novel, are finally uncharacteristic of the narrative diaspora Beckett would eventually develop, but they are central to understanding its creative genesis. Beckett's first two stories, for instance, were written as if he were still preoccupied with literary models. In the first case Beckett seems to have been reading too many of Baudelaire's translations of Poe; in the second, too much Sigmund Freud. But it was with such derivative short fiction that Beckett launched a literary career in 1929, less than a year after having arrived in Paris, in Eugene Jolas's journal of experimental writing, *transition*. Jolas was in the midst of championing James Joyce's *Finnegans Wake* by publishing not only excerpts from the *Work in Progress* but essays about it as well. Beckett had impressed Joyce enough that he was offered the opportunity to write an essay comparing Joyce to three of Joyce's favorite Italian writers, Dante, Bruno, and Vico, for a volume of essays defining and defending the *Work in Progress*. Jolas (and evidently Joyce himself, for the essay would not have appeared without Joyce's approval) thought enough of the essay to reprint it in *transition*. Along with the essay, Jolas accepted a short story from Beckett, "Assumption," which opens with the sort of paradox that would eventually become Beckett's literary signature, "He could have shouted and could not."

The story details the fate of a young, anguished "artist" who struggles to retain and restrain "that wild rebellious surge that aspired violently towards realization in sound." The silent, unnamed protagonist, however, commands a "remarkable faculty of whispering the turmoil down." He can silence "the most fiercely oblivious combatant" with a gesture, with "all but imperceptible twitches of impatience." He develops as well an aesthetic that separates Beauty from Prettiness. The latter merely proceeds "comfortably up the staircase of sensation, and sit[s] down mildly on the topmost stair to digest our gratification." More powerful are sensations generated when "[w]e are taken up bodily and pitched breathless on the peak of a sheer crag: which is the pain of Beauty." The remainder of "Assumption" develops just such an aesthetic of pain, which echoes the German Romanticism Beckett never quite purged from his art. As the artist struggles to restrain the animal voice that "tore at his throat as he choked it back in dread and sorrow," an unnamed Woman enters. She flatters and finally seduces the artist manqué, and "SO [sic] each evening in contemplation and absorption of this woman, he lost part of his essential animality." After he is seduced, "spent with extasy [sic]," the dammed "stream of whispers" explodes in "a great storm of sound." The story ends with the sort of epiphany that Beckett would recycle in the final line of "Dante and the Lobster": "They found her caressing his wild dead hair." "Assumption" works through (and finally against) the image of a Promethean artist: "Thus each night he died and was God [the Assumption of the title?], each night revived and was torn, torn and battered with increasing grievousness. . . ." But whether the artist transcends the worldly through this experience to unite with something like the Idea, or pure essence, transcends Schopenhauer's world of representation to achieve the pure will, or whether the title refers simply to the arrogance of such desire may be the crux of the story. The protagonist's romantic agony (in both senses of that phrase) may simply describe postcoital depression, and so travesty the belabored agonies of a would-be artist.

When Beckett came to publish another story in *transition* in March 1932, he selected an excerpt from the stalled novel *Dream of Fair to Middling Women*, which he called "Sedendo et Quiescendo" (but which appeared as "Sedendo et Quiesciendo"). The story includes a sonnet from the protagonist, Belacqua Shuah, to his lover, the Smeraldina, which developed the same sort of yearning for transcendence and union with the "Eternally, irrevocably one" evident in "Assumption." The means to this end was to "be consumed and fused in the white heat / Of her sad finite essence. . . ." In the sonnet the speaker claims that he "cannot be whole . . . unless I be consumed," which consumption provides the climax to "Assumption." The parallels between story and sonnet extend to the recycling of imagery and phrasing: "One with the birdless, cloudless, colourless skies" (untitled sonnet to the Smeraldina); "he hungered to be irretrievably engulfed in the light of eternity, one with the birdless cloudless colourless skies" ("Assumption"). Even the image of the "blue flower" reappears: "Belacqua . . . inscribed to his darling blue flower some of the finest Night of May hiccupsobs that ever left a fox's paw sneering and rotting in a snaptrap" ("Sedendo et Quiescendo"); "He was released, acheived [sic], the blue flower, Vega, GOD . . ." ("Assumption").

Beckett's fourth published story, "A Case in a Thousand," appeared in *Bookman* in August 1934 along with his critical article "Recent

Irish Poetry," the latter, however, signed with the pseudonym Andrew Belis. "A Case in a Thousand" features one Dr. Nye, who "belonged to the sad men." Physician though he is, Dr. Nye "cannot save" himself. He is called in on a case of surgeon Bor who had operated on the tubercular glands of a boy named Bray, who had then taken a turn for the worse. "Dr. Nye found a rightsided empyema," and then another on the left. He discovered as well that the boy's mother, who has been barred from the hospital excepting an hour's visit in the morning and another in the evening but who maintains a day-long vigil on the hospital grounds until her appointed visiting hour, is actually Nye's "old nurse," who on their meeting reminds him that he was " 'always in a great hurry so you could grow up and marry me.' " Mrs. Bray, however, "did not disclose the trauma at the root of this attachment." There are then at least two patients in this story, the Bray boy and Dr. Nye. As the boy's condition worsens and a decision about another operation must be made, the doctor regresses, "took hold of the boy's wrist, stretched himself all along the edge of the bed and entered the kind of therapeutic trance that he reserved for such happily rare dilemmas." At that moment Mrs. Bray "saw him as she could remember him," that is, as the boy she had nursed. The young Bray does not survive the operation, but after the funeral the mother resumes her vigil outside the hospital as if her child were still alive—as in a sense he is. When Nye appears, "she related a matter connected with his earliest years, so trivial and intimate that it need not be enlarged on here, but from the elucidation of which Dr. Nye, that sad man, expected great things." The undisclosed incident, at once a "trauma at the root of this attachment" and an incident so "trivial and intimate that it need not be enlarged on here," is at the root of the story as well. The matter is certainly sexual, particularly Oedipal, and at least one critic, J. D. O'Hara, has surmised that the "trivial and intimate" incident involves the young Nye's curiosity about female anatomy, in particular whether or not women have penises. Dr. Nye's nurse may have answered the question by anatomical demonstration, and the unexpected disclosure may have left the young Nye impotent, which condition would help explain why as an adult Nye was "one of the sad men." The "Case in a Thousand," then, is not (or not only) the young boy's empyema but Nye's disorder, impotence perhaps, as well.

Thereafter, Beckett returned to his stalled and incomplete novel, *Dream of Fair to Middling Women.* Having published two excerpts as separate stories, "Text" and "Sedendo et Quiescendo," he now cannibalized two of its more detachable pieces, "A Wet Night" and "The Smeraldina's Billet-Doux," retaining the protagonist, Belacqua Shuah, to develop an episodic novel, *More Pricks Than Kicks*, whose lead story, "Dante and the Lobster," was published separately in *This Quarter* in December 1932. (The story "Yellow" was also published separately in *New World Writing* but not until November 1956, twenty-two years after the publication of the novel.)

Beckett's subsequent venture into short fiction began just after the second World War, after the writing of *Watt*, when he produced four stories in his adopted language. Originally, all four of the French stories were scheduled for publication by Beckett's first French publisher, Bordas, which had published his translation of *Murphy*. But Bordas dropped plans to issue *Mercier et Camier* and *Quatre Nouvelles* when sales of the French *Murphy* proved disastrous. Subsequently, Beckett suppressed for a time the French novel and one of the stories. The remaining three *nouvelles* of 1946 were finally published in France by Les Editions de Minuit (1955) and in the U.S. by Grove Press (1967) in combination with thirteen *Texts for Nothing* ("First Love" being published separately only in 1970). Although conjoined, the two sets of stories remained very separate in Beckett's mind, as he explained to Joseph Chaikin. Beckett resisted Chaikin's theatrical mixing of the stories, noting that *"Stories* and *Texts for Nothing* are two very different matters, the former the beginning of the French venture, the latter in the doldrums that followed the 'trilogy.' "When Chaikin persisted, arguing that *Stories and Texts for Nothing* could all be read as tales for "nothing," Beckett corrected him by return post: "Have only now realized ambiguity of title. What I meant to say was *Stories. Followed by Texts for Nothing."*

The four stories, "First Love," "The Expelled," "The Calmative," and "The End," written before, almost in anticipation of, the "trilogy" of novels, and the thirteen *Texts for Nothing* form the bookends to Beckett's great creative period, which has memorably been dubbed the "siege in the room" and which in some regards was anticipated by the final two paragraphs of "Assumption." The "trilogy" seems almost embedded within the *Stories and Texts for Nothing*, as Beckett's first two full-length plays, *Eleuthéria* and *En attendant Godot (Waiting for Godot)*, are embedded within the novels, the plays written, as Beckett confessed, "in search of respite from the wasteland of prose" he had been writing in

1948–49. In fact, the unnamed narrator of this four-story sequence, almost always suddenly and inexplicably expelled from the security of a shelter, an ejection that mimics the birth trauma, anticipates the eponymous Molloy, even in the postmortem story "The Calmative," and remains a theme through *Fizzles*, where in "For to end yet again," "the expelled falls headlong down." In these four stories what has been and continued to be one of Beckett's central preoccupations developed in its full complexity: the psychological, ontological, narratological bewilderment at the inconsistency, the duality of the human predicament, the experience of existence. On the one side is the post-Medieval tradition of humanism, which develops through the Renaissance into the rationality of the Enlightenment. Its ideology buttresses the capacity of humanity to know and adapt to the mechanism of the universe and understand humanity's place in the scheme. This is the world of the schoolroom and laboratory, the world of mathematics and proportion, the world of Classical symmetry, of the pensum. For Beckett's narrators, the punctum, the lived, sentient experience of existence, the being in the world, punctures and deflates that humanistic tradition, the empiricism of the classroom, although the latter never loses its appeal and is potentially a source of comfort (although it apparently destroys Watt). The opening of "The Expelled," for instance, focuses not on the trauma of rejection and forcible ejection but on the difficulty of counting the stairs down which the narrator has, presumably, already been dispatched. There is little resentment here at the injustice of having been ejected from some place like a home. The focus of injustice in Beckett is almost never local, civil, or social, but cosmic, the injustice of having been born, after which one finds one's consolations where one may—in mathematics, say. As the protagonist of "Heard in the Dark 2" (and *Company*) suggests, "Simple sums you find a help in times of trouble. A haven. . . . Even still in the timeless dark you find figures a comfort." The experience of living is dark, mysterious, inexplicable, chthonic, in many respects Medieval but without the absolution of a benign deity. Such a dissociation had preoccupied Beckett in his earlier work, chiefly in *Dream of Fair to Middling Women*, *Murphy*, *Watt*, and the long poem "Whoroscope," through the philosophical meditations of the seventeenth-century philosopher and mathematician René Descartes, that is, in terms of the conflict between mind (pensum) and body (punctum), although Schopenhauer's division of the world in terms of the will and its representations is never very far from the foreground. Here the hormonal surges in even a spastic body like Murphy's conspire against the idealism and serenity of mind (or soul or spirit). But in the four *Stories* Beckett went beyond Descartes and descended further into the inchoate subconscious of existence, rationality, and civilization, beyond even the Freudian Eros and the Schopenhauerian Will into the more Jungian Collective Unconscious of the race, and the four separate narrators (or the single collective narrator called "I") of these *Stories* confront those primeval depths with little sense of horror, shame, or judgment. The stories retain an unabashedly Swiftian misanthropy: "The living wash in vain, in vain perfume themselves, they stink" ("First Love"). In "The Expelled" grotesqueries acquire comic effect even as they disclose psychoanalytic enigmas: "They never lynch children, babies, no matter what they do they are whitewashed in advance. I personally would lynch them with the utmost pleasure." The theme will resurface in the 1957 radio play *All that Fall* when Dan Rooney asks wife Maddy, "Did you ever wish to kill a child. . . . Nip some young doom in the bud." This is depersonalized humanity sunk in on itself: "It is not my wish to labour these antinomies, for we are, needless to say, in a skull, but I have no choice but to add the following few remarks. All the mortals I saw were alone and as if sunk in themselves" ("The Calmative"). It is a descent, most often into an emblematic skull, from which Beckett's fiction, long or short, will never emerge. The image anticipates not only the skullscapes of the "trilogy," but the dehumanized, dystopic tale *The Lost Ones,* and what is generally called the post–*How It Is* prose. Such a creative descent into "inner space," into the unconscious, had been contemplated by Beckett at least since the earliest stages of *Watt.* In the notebook and subsequent typescript versions of the novel, Beckett noted, "the unconscious mind! What a subject for a short story." "The Expelled" seems a fulfillment of that wish to plumb "perhaps deep down in those palaeozoic profounds, midst mammoth Old Red Sandstone phalli and Carboniferous pudenda . . . into the pre-uterine . . . the agar-agar . . . impossible to describe."[18]

But while character names may shift in the four stories (Lulu, for instance, becomes Anna in "First Love") the narrating consciousness, the "I" of these stories, remains more or less cogent, intact, coherent, psychologically and narratologically whole, and at least pronominally namable. And something like representable external reality still exists, even as it is folded in on itself and therefore inseparable from the consciousness perceiving it. Writing subsequently three interrelated and sequential novels dubbed the "trilogy," Beckett continued to probe the "pre-uterine." It is a period during which Beckett pushed beyond recognizable external reality and discrete literary characters, replacing them with something like naked consciousness or pure being (living or dead is not always clear) and a plethora of voices.

The *Texts for Nothing* are then, as Beckett tried to explain to Chaikin, a major leap beyond the four *Stories*. To use the current historical markers, they represent a leap from Modernism to Post-Modernism, from interior voices to exterior voices, from internality to externality. Beckett's fragments are in fact no longer "completed" stories but shards, aperçus of a continuous unfolding narrative, glimpses at a never to be complete being (narrative). The *Texts for Nothing* would redefine at least Beckett's short fiction, if not the possibilities of the short story itself, as narrative per se was finally discarded (as it was for the most part in the "trilogy" of novels), replaced by attempts of consciousness to perceive, comprehend, or create first a life, then a more or less stable, static image, an essence, failing at the latter no less often than at the former. "No need of a story," says one of the voices, "a story is not compulsory, just a life, that's the mistake I made, one of the mistakes, to have wanted a story for myself, whereas life alone is enough" (*Text* IV). The struggle of the protean narrators of the four *Stories* and the three novels was to create a narrative to capture or reflect, to represent at least a segment of a life in a work of art—that struggle has been abandoned with the *Texts for Nothing*. If "life," and so story, assumes character, the voice has made yet another mistake, for the coherent entity that in literature we call "character" is itself disbursed amid a plurality of disembodied voices and echoes whose distinctions are unclear and whose sources are unknowable. The disembodied voice captivated Beckett from his earliest creative years when he took the image of Echo as the literary emblem for his first collection of poems, *Echo's Bones*. Echo, an Oread or mountain nymph, pined away for the love of Narcissus until all that remained of her was her voice. *Texts for Nothing* could as easily be called *Echo's Bones* as well, and from there on Beckett would never again create anything like literary characters save for an unnamed (even unnamable) narrator straining to see images and hear sounds, almost always echoes—bodiless voices or later voiceless bodies, origins unknown. In Beckett's tribute to painter and friend Bram van Velde, the *témoignage* "La Falaise" ("The Cliff," published here in a translation by Edith Fournier), the window through which the observing "you" views the cliff both separates him from and joins him to the cliff in a process that blends perception and imagination. In these late works the artist figures inhabit a no-man's-land, "an unspeakable [because unnamable?] home" in "neither," which is neither wholly self nor wholly other. In theatrical adaptations of his prose, Beckett retained such paradoxes of self by insisting on the separation of character and narrative, and such separation was evident in almost every stage adaptation of his prose works that he himself had a hand in. These, then, are the limitations, the necessary incoherence and fragmentation within which the writer is obliged to work in the post-Auschwitz era in order to convey the punctum, the experience of living in the world: "I'm here, that's all I know, and that it's still not me, it's of that the best has to be made" (*Text* III). Because of such an impasse, narrative (at least as we've known and expected it, even amid the more experimental Modernists) "can't go on," and yet somehow is obliged to "go on." How it goes on is in fits, sputters, and not so much starts as re-starts, in imaginative ventures doomed to failure. As it had been in *The Unnamable*, all pretense to artistic completion was abandoned even in the titles of these later works to suggest not only that the individual works are themselves incomplete, unfinished, but that completion is beyond human experience. The thirteen *Texts for Nothing* are merely numbered, for instance, and Beckett went on to write stories with titles like "Lessness," "From an Abandoned Work," *Fizzles* (*foirades* in French), and *Residua*. But these tales are no more unfinished works of art than those paintings by Matisse that retain raw, unpainted canvas.

What one is left with after the *Texts for Nothing* is "nothing," incorporeal consciousness perhaps, into which Beckett plunged afresh in English in the early 1950s to produce a tale rich in imagery but short on external coherence. "From an Abandoned Work" deals with three days in the life of the unnamed narrator, an old man recalling his childhood. That childhood was as uneventful as it was loveless, except, perhaps, for words, which "have been my only loves, not many."[19] The father died when the narrator was young, and he lived with his mother until she died. The narrator's life is ordered by the daily journey and return: "in the morning out from home and in the evening back home again." He had taken long walks with his father, and those have continued even after the father's death. His motion, however, is directionless, "I have never in my life been on my way anywhere, but simply on my way." In contrast to his own patterned motion, he retains, "Great love in [his] heart for all things still and rooted." There is, however, a great deal of hostility in the parental relationship: "ah my father and mother, to think they are probably in paradise, they were so good. Let me go to hell, that's all I ask, and go on cursing them there, and them looking down and hear me, that might take some shine off their bliss." In fact, his admission that he may have killed his father, "as well as [his] mother," suggests a consciousness permeated with guilt. The events of the days grow more bizarre. There is "the white horse and white mother in the window." Another day, "I was set on and pursued by a family or tribe of stoats." The narrator, moreover, experiences inexplicable periods of rage: "The next thing I was up in the bracken lashing out with my stick making the drops fly and cursing, filthy language, the same over and over, I hope nobody heard me." The most comprehensive reading of this enigmatic text is one offered by J. D. O'Hara in which he sees the word "work" of the title as referring not to a work of art, the story itself, but to a session of psychotherapy. Freud often spoke of his therapy sessions, for instance, as working through psychological problems. What is abandoned for O'Hara, then, is not a narrative or story, which is in this reading complete, but the therapy, which is never completed and so abandoned. The emotional tensions are never resolved, the anxiety never relieved, the personality never integrated. For O'Hara:

> the protagonist has divided his feelings for his parents into love
> and hatred, has expressed that hatred to us while concealing it
> from the world, and has repressed his love and displaced it into
> a love of words, of animals, of this earth, etc. In all this he has
> expressed his love of self while expressing his hatred of that self
> by youthful punishment in the walks, by future punishment in
> hell, and by present punishment among the rocks, isolated from
> all humans.

It took almost a decade for Beckett to put such psychological strangeness away. When he returned to short fiction in the early 1960s it was to reshape the remains of aborted longer fiction yet again, a work tentatively entitled *Fancy Dead*, a short excerpt of which, in French and English, was published in 1965 as "Faux Départs." The work suggests, however, less a false start than a major aesthetic shift, a rejection of the journey motif and structure (incipient in *Murphy* and *Watt* and fully developed in "First Love" and the fiction through "From an Abandoned Work"), a return to which might have signaled the death of creative imagination: "Out of the door and down the road in the old hat and coat like after the war, no, not that again." Instead, Beckett (or the narrator) announced a new literary preoccupation, "A closed space five foot square by six high, try for him there" in which he would conduct exercises in human origami, all with a rechristened pronoun through which to tell his story, "last person." For the opening of "All Strange Away" Beckett would delete the first three words of the sentence above, but "A closed space" ("Closed place" opens "Fizzle 5") would come close to describing the creative terrain that Beckett's short fiction would thereafter explore. And if an impasse were reached in such imaginative spelunking, the light (of imagination?) go out, "no matter, start again, another place, someone in it. . . ."

The British novelist David Lodge's analysis of one of Beckett's "closed space" tales, "Ping" ("Bing" in French), originally a segment of *Le Dépeupleur (The Lost Ones)*, is a cogent reading of this cryptic tale, and so of much of Beckett's late prose: "I suggest that 'Ping' is the rendering of the consciousness of a person confined in a small, bare, white room, a person who is evidently under extreme duress, and probably at the last gasp of life."[20] Such is what passes for plot in Beckett's late prose, and Lodge goes on to suggest that:

> "Ping" seems to record the struggles of an expiring consciousness to find some meaning in a situation which offers no purchase to the mind or to sensation. The consciousness makes repeated, feeble efforts to assert the possibility of colour, movement, sound, memory, another person's presence, only to fall back hopelessly into the recognition of colourlessness, paralysis, silence, oblivion, solitude.

Lodge struggles to situate "Ping" within a more or less traditional, realistic frame: an expiring consciousness in search of meaning. The questions that Lodge defers, however, are the narratological ones: Who is the figure to whom all is "known"? By whom is the image described "never seen"?; to whom is it repeatedly "invisible"? Certainly not the reader, to whom even these white-on-white images are strikingly visible, for the reader, like the narrator, sees them clearly if fleetingly in his mind's eye through the imaginative construct we call literature, fiction. The figure described, the narrator hints, is "perhaps not alone," and so the possibility exists of others, whose perceptions fail as well. Although the story lines of the late tales are fairly simple, as Lodge suggests, narratologically they are more complex. The reader's focus is not only on a figure in a closed space, but on another figure and a narrator imagining them. We have, then, not just the psychologically complex but narratologically transparent image of a self imagining itself, but a self imagining itself imagining itself, often suspecting that it is being imagined itself.

In these late tales the mysterious narrator is often recorded in the midst of the fiction-making process. Beckett's subject here is, therefore, less the objects perceived and recorded, a process, of necessity, "ill seen" and so "ill said," but the human imagination. In his seminal study, *The Sense of an Ending: Studies in the Theory of Fiction*, critic Frank Kermode quotes Hans Vaihinger on the human impulse of fiction making; fictions are "mental structures. The psyche weaves this or that thought out of itself; for the mind is invention; under the compulsion of necessity [in Beckett, the "obligation to express"], stimulated by the outer world, it discovers the store of contrivances hidden within itself."[21] Beckett's late short fiction, the post–*How It Is* prose, constitutes a record of those discoveries, and so the late work may have more in common with that of American poet Wallace Stevens than with any of the writers of short fiction.

Such then is the rarefied world of Beckett's late short fiction, from "All Strange Away" to *Stirrings Still,* short tales that in fundamental ways are almost indistinguishable from the late novels—as the late prose is almost indistinguishable from the late theater. Despite his early insistence on keeping "our genres more or less distinct,"[22] Beckett seemed in this later phase of his work to have stretched beyond such limitations, beyond generic boundaries to examine the diaphanous membrane separating inside from outside, perception from imagination, self from others, narrative from experience, "neither" wholly the one nor wholly the other. Despite such psychological and philosophical flux, an almost frustrating thematic irresolution, the literary oscillation between waves and particles, these stories retain a direct dramatic and poetic simplicity as if they had been spoken into a tape recorder. Taken together, Beckett's short prose pieces not only outline his development as an artist, but suggest as well Beckett's own view of his art, that it is all part of a continuous process, a series. Writing to George Reavey on 8 July 1948, for instance, Beckett noted, "I am now retyping, for rejection by the publishers, *Malone Meurt* [*Malone Dies*], the last I hope of the series Murphy, Watt, Mercier & Camier, Molloy, not to mention the 4 Nouvelles & Eleuthéria."[23] That series did not, of course, end with *Malone Meurt*. It continued for another forty years to *Stirrings Still*. The post–*How It Is* stories were just the latest in a series whose end was only Beckett's own. In these generically androgynous stories Beckett produced a series of literary hermaphrodites that echo one another (and the earlier work as well) like reverberations in a skull. Taken together the stories suggest the intertextual weave of a collaboration between Rorschach and Escher.

S. E. GONTARSKI
Dunedin, New Zealand

Notes

1. "Mr Artesian," *The Listener* (3 August 1967): 148–49. Reprinted in *Samuel Beckett: The Critical Heritage*, ed. by Lawrence Graver and Raymond Federman (London: Routledge & Kegan Paul, 1979), 286–291.

2. *No Symbols Where None Intended: A Catalogue of Books, Manuscripts, and Other Material Relating to Samuel Beckett in the Collection of the Humanities Research Center*, Selected and described by Carlton Lake (Austin, TX: Humanities Research Center, 1984), 133.

3. *The Lonely Voice: A Study of the Short Story* (New York: Harper & Row [Harper Colophon Books], 1985), 19.

4. The work finally seems to have wound up anthologized with Beckett's prose via an exchange between publishers. The dramaticule "Come and Go" was originally published in the U.K. by John Calder, to whom the work is dedicated. Faber has subsequently published "Come and Go" in anthologies of Beckett's drama, and Calder published "From an Abandoned Work" in anthologies of Beckett's prose.

   Beckett's short story "Lessness" was also performed on the BBC, on 25 February 1971 with Donal Donnelly, Leonard Fenton, Denys Hawthorne, Patrick Magee, and Harold Pinter.

5. Even Beckett's earliest critics like Dylan Thomas referred to *More Pricks Than Kicks* as a novel; see *New English Weekly* (17 March 1938): 454–55.

6. Letter to American publisher Barney Rosset dated 11 February 1954.

7. *Ibid.*

8. *No Symbols Where None Intended*, 81.

9. Rosset letter to Samuel Beckett, 5 February 1954.

10. *No Symbols Where None Intended*, 90.

11. A reference to this abandoned work appears in "Why Actors Are Fascinated by Beckett's Theater," *The Times* (27 January 1965): 14: "Mr. Beckett is at present finishing a novel called *Fancy Dying*, and also writing a play"—the latter presumably *Play*. The source of the information is apparently Jack MacGowran, who was not only playing in *Endgame* at the time but also preparing a one-man performance of Beckett's prose writings, which became *Beginning to End*.

12. "From an Unabandoned Work," *Evergreen Review* 4.14 (September–October 1960): 58–65.

13. Deirdre Bair, *Samuel Beckett* (New York: Harcourt Brace Jovanovich, 1978) 578.

14. *No Symbols Where None Intended*, 140.

15. For further discussion of adaptation of Beckett's prose to the stage see my "*Company* for Company: Androgyny and Theatricality in Samuel Beckett's Prose," *Beckett's Later Fiction and Drama: Texts for Company*, ed. James Acheson and Kateryna Arthur (London: Macmillan Press, 1987), 193–202.

16. Samuel Beckett letter to the editor dated 12 September 1986.

17. The title alludes to Dante's *Purgatorio*, "Sedendo et quiescendo anima efficitur prudens" (roughly, sitting quietly the soul acquires wisdom).

18. Cited by Chris Ackerley, "Fatigue and Disgust: The Addenda to *Watt*," *Samuel Beckett Today/Aujourd'hui: Beckett in the 1990s* II: 179.

19. Some twenty-two years later, directing his play *Footfalls* in Germany, Beckett returned to this theme as he told the actress playing May, "Words are as food for this poor girl. . . . They are her best friends" (Walter D. Asmus, "Rehearsal Notes for the German Premiere of Samuel Beckett's *That Time* and *Footfalls*," *On Beckett: Essays and Criticism*, ed. by S. E. Gontarski [New York: Grove Press, Inc., 1986], 339).

20. "Some Ping Understood," *Encounter* (February 1968): 85–89. Reprinted in *Samuel Beckett: The Critical Heritage*, 291–301. The original publication of the essay, however,

contains line numberings to the original publication of "Ping" in *Encounter* 28.2 (February 1967): 25–26.

21. Hans Vaihinger from *The Philosophy of As If*, cited in Kermode (New York: Oxford University Press, 1979), 40.

22. This oft-quoted letter to Barney Rosset of 27 August 1957 objects to a staging of *All that Fall*. Beckett's full wording is: "If we can't keep our genres more or less distinct, or extricate them from the confusion that has them where they are, we might as well go home and lie down." Beckett subsequently authorized several stage versions of *All that Fall*.

23. *No Symbols Where None Intended*, 53.

Samuel Beckett:

The Complete Short Prose,

1929–1989

Assumption

HE COULD HAVE shouted and could not. The buffoon in the loft swung steadily on his stick and the organist sat dreaming with his hands in his pockets. He spoke little, and then almost husk- ily, with the low-voiced timidity of a man who shrinks from ar- gument, who can reply confidently to Pawn to King's fourth, but whose faculties are frozen into bewildered suspension by Pawn to Rook's third, of the unhappy listener who will not face a clash with the vulgar, uncultivated, terribly clear and personal ideas of the unread intelligenzia. He indeed was not such a man, but his voice was of such a man; and occasionally, when he chanced to be interested in a discussion whose noisy violence would have been proof against most resonant interruption of the beautifully banal kind, he would exercise his remarkable faculty of whisper- ing the turmoil down. This whispering down, like all explosive feats of the kind, was as the apogee of a Vimy Light's parabola, commanding undeserved attention because of its sudden bril- liance. The actual imposition of silence by an agent that drifted off itself into silence a few tables away was merely the easy cli- max of a long series of subtle preparations: all but imperceptible twitches of impatience, smiles artistically suppressed, a swift af- fection of uninterested detachment, all finely produced and thrown into the heat of the conflict, so that the most fiercely oblivious combatant could not fail to be neatly and intolerably irritated. Then, when his work had been done and an angry lull was imminent, he whispered. As with all artists, this casting of an effect in the teeth of his audience was the least difficult part of his business; he had been working hard for the last half-hour, and no one had seen him; that long chain of inspired gesture had been absorbed unconsciously by every being within the wide orbit of his control, and accepted as normal and spontaneous. To avoid the expansion of the commonplace is not enough; the highest art reduces significance in order to obtain that inexplicable bombshell perfection. Before no supreme manifestation of Beauty do we proceed comfortably up a staircase of sensation, and sit down mildly on the topmost stair to digest our gratification: such is the pleasure of Prettiness. We are taken up bodily and pitched breathless on the peak of a sheer crag: which is the pain of Beauty. Just as the creative artist must be partly illusionist, our whispering prestidigitator was partly artist. A member of the Browning Society would say that he played on the souls of men as on an instrument; a unanimist, that he imposed his personality on a group. But we must be careful not to imply that the least apostolic fervour coloured what was at its worst the purely utilitarian contrivance of a man who wished to gain himself a hearing, and at its best an amused experiment in applied psychology.

   In the silence of his room he was afraid, afraid of that wild rebellious surge that aspired violently towards realization in sound. He felt its implacable caged resentment, its longing to be released in one splendid drunken scream and fused with the cosmic discord. Its struggle for divinity was as real as his own, and as futile. He wondered if the Power which, having denied him the conscious completion of the meanest mongrel, bade him forget his fine imperfection beside it in the gutter, ever trembled at the force of his revolt. Meanwhile that flesh-locked sea of silence achieved a miserable consummation in driblets of sound, as each falling leaf saps the painful vigour of a tree in a cruelly windless autumn. The process was absurd, extravagantly absurd, like boiling an egg over a bonfire. But in his case it was not a willful extravagance; he felt compassion as well as fear; he dreaded lest his prisoner should escape, he longed that it might escape; it tore at his throat and he choked it back in dread and sorrow. Fear breeds fear: he began to have a horror of unexpected pain, of sleep, of anything that might remove the involuntary inhibition. He drugged himself that he might sleep heavily, silently; he scarcely left his room, scarcely spoke, thus denying even that rare transmutation to the rising tossing soundlessness that seemed now to rend his whole being with the violence of its effort. He felt he was losing, playing into the hands of the enemy by the very severity of his restrictions. By damming the stream of whispers he had raised the level of the flood, and he knew the day would come when it could no longer be denied. Still he was silent, in silence listening for the first murmur of the torrent that must destroy him. At this moment the Woman came to him. . . .

He was listening in the dusk when she came, listening so intently that he did not hear her enter. From the door she spoke to him, and he winced at the regularity of her clear, steady speech. It was the usual story, vulgarly told: admiration for his genius, sympathy with his suffering, only a woman could understand. . . . He clenched his hands in a fury against the enormous impertinence of women, their noisy intrusive curious enthusiasm, like the spontaneous expression of admiration bursting from American hearts before Michelangelo's tomb in Santa Croce. The voice droned on, wavered, stopped. He sketched a tired gesture of acceptation, and prepared to withdraw once more within that terrifying silent immobility. She turned on the light and advanced carelessly into the room. An irruption of demons would not have scattered his intentness so utterly. She sat down before him at the table, and leaned forward with her jaws in the cups of her hands. He looked at her venomously, and was struck in spite of himself by the extraordinary pallor of her lips, of which the lower protruded slightly and curled upwards contemptuously to compress the upper, resulting in a faintly undershot local sensuality which went strangely with the extreme cold purity stretching sadly from the low broad brow to the closed nostrils. He thought of George Meredith and recovered something of his calm. The eyes were so deeply set as to be almost cavernous; the light falling on the cheekbones threw them back into a misty shadow. In daylight they were strange, almost repulsive, deriving a pitiless penetration from the rim of white showing naturally above the green-flecked pupil. Now as she leaned forward beneath the light, they were pools of obscurity. She wore a close-fitting hat of faded green felt: he thought he had never seen such charming shabbiness. . . . When at last she went away he felt that something had gone out from him, something he could not spare, but still less could grudge, something of the desire to live, something of the unreasonable tenacity with which he shrank from dissolution. So each evening, in contemplation and absorption of this woman, he lost a part of his essential animality: so that the water rose, terrifying him. Still he fought on all day, hopelessly, mechanically, only relaxing with twilight, to listen for her coming to loosen yet another stone in the clumsy dam set up and sustained by him, frightened and corruptible. Until at last, for the first time, he was unconditioned by the Satanic dimensional Trinity, he was released, achieved, the blue flower, Vega, GOD. . . . After a timeless parenthesis he found himself alone in his room, spent with ecstasy, torn by the bitter loathing of that which he had condemned to the humanity of silence. Thus each night he died and was God, each night revived and was torn, torn and battered with increasing grievousness, so that he hungered to be irretrievably engulfed in the light of eternity, one with the birdless cloudless colourless skies, in infinite fulfillment.

Then it happened. While the woman was contemplating the face that she had overlaid with death, she was swept aside by a great storm of sound, shaking the very house with its prolonged, triumphant vehemence, climbing in a dizzy, bubbling scale, until, dispersed, it fused into the breath of the forest and the throbbing cry of the sea.

They found her caressing his wild dead hair.

Sedendo et Quiescendo

DOWN YOU GET now and step around. Two hours menopause. Drag your coffin my lord. Half a day and I'll be with. HIER! The bright beer goes like water through the nearsighted Frankfort porter. In Perpignan exiled dream-Dantes screaming in the planetrees and freezing the sun with peacock feathers and at last at least a rudimentary black swan with the bloodbeak and HIC! for the bladderjerk of the little Catalan postman. Oh who can hold a fire in his hand by thinking on the frosty Caucasus. Here oh here oh art thou pale with weariness. I hope yes after a continental third-class insomnia among the reluctantly military philologists asleep and armed as to nasals and dentals. Laughter. Ten Pfenigs in such a dainty slot gives the la I am bound to concede and releases the appropriate tonic for the waning lust-affair. Moderate strength rings the bell. I don't believe it. Così fan tutte with the magic flute. Even in the Xmas holidays. Half a day and I'll be in.

Up to time then after this little railway-station rectification she advanced up the railway-platform like a Gozzi-Epstein, being careful not to lose the platform ticket that yet ten Pfenigs cost had, insisting on the Garden of Eden in Mammy's furcoat, scarcely suggesting within the mild aphrodisiac of cheap loose black leather Russian boots legs that even flexed nervously in black stockings stretched to the absolute limit of intensity and viewed from a certain very special Blickpunkt against a very special quality of hard light during a period of oestruation were not alas reasonably exciting. The truly tremendous bowl of the hips (frequent and easy) breaking out and away from the waistroot (she won't need no Lupercus) like a burdocked bulb of Ruffino and the two great melons of the buttocks received an almost Rhineline from the dark peltsheath. Sheath within sheath and the missing sword. Not forgetting this was the suit he had bought for next to nothing from a lefthanded indivisible individual, with a charitable desire to justify his fatigue he forced his right hand down past the craggy coxa (almost a woman's basin in these trousers) into the glairy gallant depths and fished up a fifty. A cigarette quick for the cheekbones and the ticket handy there in the breast of my reefer and the heavy valise to snatch him skilfully detached and extenuated into the loveglue and a smoke after that was nearly as good as in the Maison du Café.

"At last!"

"Beloved!"

"Taxi!" Vie de taxi. Je t'adore à l'égal.

Carry your coffin my lord. Männer. Moving east to the segregation of the sexes. Ausgang on the right. Rule of the road. Lady on right arm. Nonsens unique. Astuce. All the same sleep on right side. Gentle reader don't overlook will you the fact that he celebrated the signing of the armistice with a pubic lanugo and

BELACQUA

we'll call him and no indolent virgin is his sister (indolent virgin!) and he doesn't much care whether he plays the tinkle-tinkle of a fourhander or not but he won't facing the keyboard observe the rule of the road (a megalomaniac you see with his head in his thighs as a general rule) so we ask you to humour what of course

naturally looks merely like so much intestinal incohesion, remember he belongs to the costermonger times of a pale and ar-
dent generation, pray that he'll let a few sighs out of him ere it's
too late and speedy promotion from the Godbirds. And the lady
that even in this very short and public space of time and notwithstanding that fur has no conductive properties of the appropriate kind worth speaking of has succeeded in transmitting
certain unexpectedly stimulating sensations to her young visitor,
what shall we call her. What name would you suggest? I'm rather
inclined myself to think

SMERALDINA-RIMA

and anything that comes in handy for short. He handed her into
the cab of the Wagen with its charming deep Bluepoint zoster
and spoke an address confidently to the chauffeur who but a moment previously had thought to light a cigarette and who now
naturally was in no humour to start his engine and set off but
was not slow to yield to the promising accent of the young tour-
ist whose heavy fibre case he hoisted vigorously on board on his
left beside him and clipping the yet intact Ova between his rub-
bery helix and hypertrophied mastoid process gratified in his di-
alogue doubtless his nearest colleagues with what no doubt was a
passionate Hessian epigram, set his machine angrily in motion,
suffering with a kind of hopeless interest the refracted deport-
ment of his clients. Down the cobbled avenue then of bitter
Xmas trees, trembling in many and many a shadowy stasis between tram and sidewalk, the superb Wagen ran towards the
spire that eliminates in impeccable imperial alignment the now
dim height of Hercules and the meagre cascade sullen and abandoned dropping, what there was of it and because it bloody well
had to, down the choked channel of Hohenzollern rocaille,
snowclad, upon the castle. Blocus sentimental. Belacqua took her
hand and drew it down upon the skirted, nearly the thighjoy
through the fingers, and all the same he enquires:

"Where did you get the hat?" A glaucous helmethat.

"Do you like it?"

"Very nice do you?"

"Oh I don't know do you?" Snotgasp of reliefhilarity in honour of private joke.

"It goes with the ring." He turned over the hand and looked at the warts. Two dwindling warts in the shadow of the Mount of Venus. Warts in the valley of the shadow of.

"Your warts are better." Ostentatiously he dropped his mouth upon the place. She squeezed the Giudecca of her palm against the centre of distribution, nailing his cheekbones with thumb and index. In the rue Delambre with a silk handkerchief did he not staunch the vomitdribble of a littérateur deaddrunk and cornuted what's more into the bargain on Pernod and Pickmeup? How often had he not denied all knowledge of Hernani? Poor Hamlet rolling his belly waxes and tapers the spike of his navelthread for the red waistcoat. The beadlust. By no thinking shall he consume that enterprise, by no new thoughts shall he be altogether released from the postulate of his undertaking. Fast in the black sand.

Let me off the tutti chords now and tell me frankly shutting your eyes like Rouletabille what you think of my erotic sostenutino. Crémieux hold your saliva and you Curtius, I have a note somewhere on Anteros I believe, in fact I seem to remember I once wrote a poem (Nth. Gt. George's St. diphthong Captain Duncan if you please) on him or to him cogged from the lecherous laypriest's Magic Ode and if I don't forget I'll have the good taste to use the little duckydiver as a kind of contrapuntal compensation do you comprehend me and in deference to your Pisan penchants for literary stress and strain. Well really you know and in spite of the haricot skull and a tendency to use up any odds and ends of pigment that might possibly be left over she was the living spit he thought of Madonna Lucrezia del Fede.

SAMUEL BECKETT: THE COMPLETE SHORT PROSE, 1929–1989

Ne suis-je point pâle? Suis-je belle? Certainly pale and belle my pale belle Braut with a winter skin like an old sail in the wind. The root and the source between and behind the little athletic or esthetic bit of a birdnose was indeed I assure you a constant source of delight and astonishment, when his solitude was not peopled and justified and beautified and even his sociability by a cold in the head, to his forefinger pad and nail, rubbing and plumbing and boring it just as for many years he polished his glasses (ecstasy of attrition!) or suffered the shakes and gracenote strangulations and enthrottlements of the Winkelmusik of Szopen or Pichon or Chopinek or Chopinetto or whoever it was embraced her heartily as sure as my name is Fred, dying all his life (thank you Mr. Auber) on a sickroom talent (thank you Mr. Field) and a Kleinmeister's Leidenschaftsucherei (thank you Mr. Beckett), or crossed the Seine or the Tolka or the Pegnitz or the Fulda as the case might be and it never for one single solitary instant occurring to me that he was on all such and similar occasions (which we are sorry to say lack of space obliges us regretfully to exclude from this chronicle) indulging in and pandering to the vilest and basest excesses of sublimation of a certain kind. The wretched little wet rag of an upperlip, pugnozzling up and back in a kind of a duck or a cobra sneer to the nostrils, was happily to some extent mollified and compensated by the full firm undershot priapism of underlip and chin, a signal recovery to say the least and a reaffirmation of the promise of sentimental vehemence already so gothically declamatory in the wedgehead of the strapping girl. From time to time she literally only had to lift off her casco to be a birdface and to have put Mr. John Kissmearse and Orchids in mind of his Perpetually Succourful Lady as she positively must have appeared on two probationary occasions: *primo,* pinned, there's no other word for it, to her loggia by the shining sage-femme: *secundo,* confined, by Thermidor, in the interests of her armpits, to her bathroom, shamed in mind, yes, and yet—grieving for the doomed olives. Well I must say and no offence intended, that class of egoterminal immaculate quackery and dupery gives me the sick properly. No, whatever she was she wasn't that kind. I suppose I'm entitled to say she looked like a parrot in a Pieta, a pietra serena parrot. On occasions that is. Not in the helmet of salvation I need hardly point out. By Jove when I look back and think how chaste was the passion of mutual attraction that juxtaposed those two young people in the first instance. It's out of the question to give you any idea of the reverence with which they—how shall I say?—*clave* the one to the other in an ecstasy and an agony of mystical adhesion. Yessir! An ecstasy and an agony! A sentimental coagulum, sir, that biggers descruption. Don't I know for a positive fact that the unhappy Belacqua (Bollocky, though it's hardly the time or the place for that, to his friends) separated from his sweet Vega by two channels and 29 hours third-class if he went over Ostend, tossing and turning and tightening the slender white cords of his nervi nervorum with the frogs' and the corncrakes' Chinese chromatism, muting the long fever of the midos and the dolas in a scorching a piacere, inscribed to his darling blue flower some of the finest Night of May hiccupsobs that ever left a fox's paw sneering and rotting in a snaptrap. For example:

> *At last I find in my confusèd soul,*
> *Dark with the dark flame of the cypresses,*
> *The certitude that I cannot be whole,*
> *Consummate, finally achieved, unless*
> *I be consumed and fused in the white heat*
> *Of her sad finite essence, so that none*
> *Shall sever us who are at last complete,*
> *Eternally, irrevocably one,*
> *One with the birdless cloudless colourless skies,*

One with the bright purity of the fire
Of which we are and for which we must die
A strange exalted death and be entire,
Like two merged stars, intolerably bright,
Conjoined in One and in the Infinite!

Lilly Neary has a lovely Gee and her poor Paddy got his B.A. and by the holy fly I wouldn't recommend you to ask me what class of a tree they were under when he put his hand on her and enjoyed that. The thighjoy through the fingers. What does she want for her thighbeauty? A bitch-melba and a long long come before breakfast, toast and. Keycold Lucrece the chaste and the castaway in the cruel tights and Christ the useful culmination, footpounds through the fingers. No, more—more?—other than that to my bright agenesia. No no don't admire that. No but I thought perhaps honeysuckle round the cradle, custard and nutmeg on my grave, and the Eingang? Then he reddied his nose with the hand that came off her. Christ that was fine too. I wouldn't look at your Haus Albrecht Dürer, Adam Kraft my iron buck virgin. No smoking in the torture-chamber. Not really you don't mean to tell me well well! Now the thin little sandy the others do the streets but I go and dien in the, furchtbar, all of a sudden with tears, now I must go and dien in the, the others do the streets but I go and dien in the, furchtbar, find a hotel, take a Wagen, no?, aufwiedersehen, write, to hell with you, strive for your stout little hoffentlich ballbearing bastardpimp, I'll spend the night in the station without the Benedictina, my old bald darling, you slip in and dien, your room stinks of spunksweat, I won't kiss your playful hand, dass heisst spielen, my dolorific nymphae and a tic douleureux in my imperforate hymen, what's the Deutsch for randy, my dirty little hungry bony vulture of a whorchen away up first floor Burgwards over the stream, I'll send you a Schein when I have a Schwips. No f—— smoking in the

f—— Folterzimmer. I had to ask her sister and she closed me
the vowel. I wonder did I do well to leave my notes at home, in
39 under the east wind, weind please. Well then when he'd
picked his nose for a little bit and the thighs there Gott sei dank
up he rose didn't he and left her playing there against the oak
before the ash oh don't infuriate me don't bother me, let me pay
let me buy you was, eat my little Augen Celeryice, didn't he, and
wandered uphill and downdale like the cat and the mouse in
business together or the Marienkind. No no I *won't* say everything, I *won't* tell you everything. No but surely now you see
what he am? See! Heiliger Brahmaputra! A hedgecreeper! A
peeping Tom in bicycle clips! I once said that otherwise. Well
then up he rose and apprehended without passion round and
about the weekend brushwood foothill copulations. Yes indeed
of course you're right it'd be hard for you to understand my
meaning, you see he led a fairly small fleshy maiden I might have
said Jungfrau into the wood I might have said Wald and creeped
and peeped at the Sabbath fornications instead of. Oh did I do
right to leave my notes at home! So then after another little bit
he came back through the leaves and stood looking with his
tongue in his cheek instead of.

J'aime et je veux pââlir. Livid rapture of a Zurbaran St.
Onan. Schwindsucht and pollution in a tunnel in de Thebaid.
Strange exalted death! Plus précieuse que la vie, the dirty dog!
But right enough all the same what more miserable than the miserable being who commiserates not himself, caesura, with a new
grief grieves not for his grief, is not worn by a double sorrow,
drowns not in ken of shore. Who said that? Turned he hath the
audacious soul, turned he hath and turned again upon back sides
and belly, like Miss Florence on the mattress while Virgil and
Sordello, yet all was painful. As an herpetic spider (do you
recognise the style?) hath he consumed away. He dared to grow
wild with his shadowy love and he daily watered by daily littles

the ground under his face and beerbibbing did not lay siege to his spirit and he was continent and he was not sustenant and many of his months have since run out with him the pestilent person to take him from behind his crooked back and set him before his ulcerous gob in the boiling over of his fornications and in chambering and wantonness and in deafness and death and bitter and blind bawling against the honey what honey bloody well you know the honey and in canvassing and getting and weltering in filth and scratching off the scabies of lust. All on a mild scale of course, don't be misled, Paterson's Camp Coffee is the Best, perhaps I let my pen run away with me, don't for a moment imagine Bollocky's down the drain, of course he's got a bit wasted that was bound to happen and his feet have gone to bits and his bitch of a heart knocks hell out of his bosom three or four nights a week and to make a long story short Lucy and Jude are kept going pretty well from dawn to dark with his shingles and his graphospasmus and his weeping eczema and his general condition, but for all that we'll all agree I feel sure that there's a long call from feeling a bit slack and run down to lying senseless in a deathsweat. Here we are. Out we get. Step around. Thank you. You put on the light. Up we go. Out of step. Randygasp of ruthilarity in honour of private joke. Here we are. There they are. Hello. Great to be here. Grand to be here. Same old Wohnung. Wonderful to be here. Prosit. God bless. Lav on the left. Won't be a sec. Mind the bike. Mind the skis. Beschissenes Dasein beschissenes Dasein Augenblick bitte beschissenes Dasein Augenblickchen bitte beschissenes.

Text

COME COME and cull me bonny bony doublebed cony swiftly my springal and my thin Kerry twingle-twangler comfort my days of roses days of beauty week of redness with mad shame to my lips of shame to my shamehill for the newest news the shemost of shenews is I'm lust-belepered and unwell oh I'd rather be a sparrow for my puckfisted coxcomb bird to bird and branch or a coalcave with goldy veins for my wicked doty's potystick trimly to besom gone the hartshorn and the cowslip wine gone and the lettuce nibbled up nibbled up and gone nor the last beauty day of the red time opened its rose and struck with its thorn oh I'm all of a gallimaufry or a salady salmafundi singly and single to bed she said I'll have no toadspit about this house and whose quab was I I'd like to know that from my cheerfully cornuted Dublin landloper and whose foal hackney mare toeing the line like a Viennese Taubchen take my tip and clap a padlock on your Greek galligaskins before I'm quick and living in hope and glad to go snacks with my twingle-twangler and grow grow into the earth mother of whom clapdish and foreshop.

A Case in a Thousand

SURGEON BOR OPERATED with the utmost success on a boy called Bray who had been brought to him suffering from tubercular glands in the neck, since when the boy showed an unfathomable tendency to sink, and did in fact begin to sink. Surgeon Bor shrugged his shoulders without rancour and called in his physician, Dr. Nye, young but most eminent.

Dr. Nye belonged to the sad men, but not to the extent of accepting, in the blank way the most of them do, this condition as natural and proper. He looked upon it as a disorder. He stood still before the window of his consulting-room, his right hand opening and closing the jigger button of his jacket, his left hand playing with the small change in his trouser pocket. He felt the afternoon light, glistening now between showers, like a high frequency shampoo on his face. Children throughout the locality had been waiting angrily for the rain to stop, so that they might go out to play. Without warning a proposition sprang up in his mind: Myself I cannot save. He sat down on the couch, still tossed from the last patient. After a while he lay down on it. The distant furious crying of a child, the light fading and then the rain again, his heart that knocked and misfired for no reason known to the medical profession, these and a compound of minor disturbances began to exhaust his mind and senses. In the absence of the feet of some other person, he thought, the meditative life has little to recommend it. His distress was interrupted by Surgeon Bor, on the telephone.

Dr. Nye found a rightsided empyema. He stood with Surgeon Bor at the end window of the long ward and looked out. Canal, bridge, lock and bright hoarding composed the scene. Three groups had gathered, one on the bridge and one on either bank, to watch a barge pass through the lock. Detached from the far group, paying no heed to the manoeuvre, holding up an umbrella as though oblivious of the fine interval, a large woman stood looking up at the hospital.

"Mrs. Bray," said Surgeon Bor.

Sister came up to tell Surgeon Bor he was wanted.

"Tell Dr. Nye the Mother Bray saga," he said and went away.

Already the barge was working clear of the dock. The group on the bridge had crossed over to the other parapet, with the result, most pleasing to Dr. Nye, that where formerly he had seen their faces, now he enjoyed a clear view of their buttocks, male and female. The groups on the banks had passed out of sight under the bridge. Mrs. Bray's umbrella was still open, but reposing now on her hat and bosom, so that both her arms were free to dangle. Thus partially eclipsed she kept watch. Dr. Nye watched the long line of buttocks, sister watched Dr. Nye.

"She would come first thing in the morning," said sister, "and stay all day till she was put out last thing. Not saying anything, only watching the boy. The same when the doctor came, she wouldn't say anything, only watch his face. Then the other patients began to complain and the nurses said she was upsetting the ward. So we had to tell her she could only have an hour in the morning and another in the evening. So there she stands now the best part of the day, watching the window and waiting for it to be time to come up."

Dr. Nye did not feel there was anything he wanted particularly to say in reply to all this.

"God knows she was quiet enough," said sister, "and no trouble, only she got on the nurses' nerves some way."

Dr. Nye mumbled something smart about her no doubt being widowed and he her only child.

"Well, then, she's married," said sister, "and has a family down in Tuam."

"Then it is as I feared," said Dr. Nye. "The woman is my old nurse."

"Oh, doctor," said sister, "what a coincident!"

The barge had passed on its way, the fine interval was drawing to an end, the buttocks had dispersed, only Mrs. Bray had suffered no change. The handle of the umbrella, carved in bog-oak to represent a bird, rose and fell. Dr. Nye planted himself before her. Sister called out to the nurses to come and look. "It's his old nanny," she cried.

Mrs. Bray, when she learned who he was and who he had been, lowered, as though in deference, her umbrella. He was troubled to find that of the woman whom as baby and small boy he had adored, nothing remained but the strawberry mottle of the nose and the breath smelling heavily of clove and peppermint. He took her arm and they walked up and down, to and fro between the bridge and her station. The conversation turned first on her son. "He has turned the corner," said Dr. Nye, but did not make it clear in what direction. Then it passed to the good old days. "Yes," said Mrs. Bray, "you were always in a great hurry to grow up so's you could marry me," but did not disclose the trauma at the root of this attachment. On the bridge they parted, Dr. Nye to visit an old schoolfellow professionally, Mrs.

Bray to move over to the hospital steps, for it was nearly her time.

A nurse let a loud giggle. "Did you see him kiss her?" she said. "Why wouldn't he kiss her?" said sister, "and she his old nanny."

The boy developed an empyema on the left side, so now he had two, and they put a screen round his bed. One good result of this was that the mother could be with him all day. She neither spoke to him nor touched him; it was not even certain that she saw him, though she kept her face turned steadfastly in his direction. She made no attempt to draw Dr. Nye when he came, but was content to watch his face, and this not so much in order to learn what he was thinking as in the hope of recognising him as the creature she had once cared. There was always something he wanted to ask her with reference to the good old days, but he felt it was neither the time nor the place, and this feeling grew steadily stronger. One day, when he had made an end of his examination, instead of departing without comment as he always had done, he sat down on the edge of the bed. The point had been reached when he must decide whether to operate at once or hold his hand a little longer. It was a decision that lay outside the scope of his science, because from the strictly pathological point of view there was as much to be urged on the one side as there was on the other. Nevertheless it had to be made, and at once, and by him. He took hold of the boy's wrist, stretched himself all along the edge of the bed and entered the kind of therapeutic trance that he reserved for such happily rare dilemmas.

Mrs. Bray, noting the expression, at once aghast and rapt, that overcame his face, was moved in a number of ways: to trouble, at such dissolution of feature; to gratification that at last she saw him as she could remember him; to shame, as the memory grew defined; to embarrassment, as though she were intruding on a privacy or a face asleep. She forced herself to look at her son instead. Then, very sensibly, she closed her eyes altogether.

Sister peeped round the corner of the screen and surveyed the tableau. As soon as it began to show signs of coming to life she advanced with great heartiness, craving loudly to be of service. She received no encouragement, not the slightest. She went, having seen what she had seen.

Little by little Dr. Nye reintegrated his pathological outlook. He sat up on the bed, without releasing the boy's wrist however. He stood up and laid the hand gently on the breastbone. Exasperated by the inaptness of this arrangement he looked sharply at Mrs. Bray, whose mild and baffled gaze, as though she had seen nothing, had resumed operations. No doubt it was his duty to make known to her the decision that had been reached, but he really could not bear another moment of her presence. If only he had a box of peppermint creams to leave with her. Mrs. Bray again closed her eyes as she felt the imposition too pregnant for words of his hand on the crown of her hat (which nothing could ever induce her to leave off), the rapid flutter of his fingers down her cheek, the ineffable chuck to her dewlap. Feeling nothing further, she opened them. She was alone. She turned her face towards her son.

Surgeon Bor operated, the boy's lung collapsed and he died. Mrs. Bray suddenly found her tongue and thanked Dr. Nye for all he had done. Dr. Nye tried hard to recapture the sensation which as a medical student he had experienced when a baby died under his hand, just as he had it nicely spitted for a lumbar puncture. He succeeded up to a point. The blush gathered together like a wave in his entrails, sweeping aloft and breaking in his heart—this much at least he was permitted to re-enact. He realised that she had quite done thanking him, also that he could not hope to reproduce that profound blush in her honour, yet somehow he did not seem able to get away from her. So they remained together for a time in silence, making great efforts to speak their minds. Then they gave it up and parted.

Dr. Nye took a short holiday at the seaside, towards the end of which he received a letter from Surgeon Bor, with a post-script to the effect that Mrs. Bray was back at her old games. Dr. Nye had supposed her back in Tuam. He took the first train up to town and went straight to the hospital.

"What do you mean," he said to Surgeon Bor, "back at her old games?"

Surgeon Bor turned to sister.

"Has she come on duty yet?" he said.

Sister looked at her watch.

"She should be due any minute now," she said.

They went up to the long ward and stood at the end window. There was no sign of Mrs. Bray. But before long she came into view, carrying the umbrella and a shooting-stick. This she opened and plunged into the earth of the towing-path. Then she sat down and cocked up her face at the hospital.

"Ever since the funeral," said sister.

Dr. Nye set out on his rounds. At one o'clock the news came through that Mrs. Bray, having eaten an orange, was walking up and down between the bridge and the stick; a little later, that she was again in position; finally, about lighting-up time, that she was making ready to go. Dr. Nye dropped what he was doing, happily nothing very important, and hastened out to intercept her. On the bridge they met face to face. They moved into a recess in the parapet out of the noise, they leaned out over the water.

"There's something I've been wanting to ask you," he said, looking at the water where it flowed out of the shadow of the bridge.

She replied, also looking down at the water:

"I wonder would that be the same thing I've been wanting to tell you ever since that time you stretched out on his bed."

There was a silence, she waiting for him to ask, he for her to tell.

"Can't you go on?" he said.

Thereupon she related a matter connected with his earliest years, so trivial and intimate that it need not be enlarged on here, but from the elucidation of which Dr. Nye, that sad man, expected great things.

"Thank you very much," he said, "that was what I was wondering."

They watched the water flowing out of the shadow a little longer, then she said she must be going. Dr. Nye took a box out of his pocket.

"I brought you a few peppermint creams," he said.

So they parted, Mrs. Bray to go and pack up her things and the dead boy's things, Dr. Nye to carry out Wasserman's test on an old schoolfellow.

First Love

I ASSOCIATE, rightly or wrongly, my marriage with the death of my father, in time. That other links exist, on other levels, between these two affairs, is not impossible. I have enough trouble as it is in trying to say what I think I know.

I visited, not so long ago, my father's grave, that I do know, and noted the date of his death, of his death alone, for that of his birth had no interest for me, on that particular day. I set out in the morning and was back by night, having lunched lightly in the graveyard. But some days later, wishing to know his age at death, I had to return to the grave, to note the date of his birth. These two limiting dates I then jotted down on a piece of paper, which I now carry about with me. I am thus in a position to affirm that I must have been about twenty-five at the time of my marriage. For the date of my own birth, I repeat, my own birth, I have never forgotten, I never had to note it down, it remains graven in my memory, the year at least, in figures that life will not easily erase. The day itself comes back to me, when I put my mind to it, and I often celebrate it, after my fashion, I don't say each time it comes back, for it comes back too often, but often.

Personally I have no bone to pick with graveyards, I take

the air there willingly, perhaps more willingly than elsewhere, when take the air I must. The smell of corpses, distinctly perceptible under those of grass and humus mingled, I do not find unpleasant, a trifle on the sweet side perhaps, a trifle heady, but how infinitely preferable to what the living emit, their feet, teeth, armpits, arses, sticky foreskins and frustrated ovules. And when my father's remains join in, however modestly, I can almost shed a tear. The living wash in vain, in vain perfume themselves, they stink. Yes, as a place for an outing, when out I must, leave me my graveyards and keep—you—to your public parks and beautyspots. My sandwich, my banana, taste sweeter when I'm sitting on a tomb, and when the time comes to piss again, as it so often does, I have my pick. Or I wander, hands clasped behind my back, among the slabs, the flat, the leaning and the upright, culling the inscriptions. Of these I never weary, there are always three or four of such drollery that I have to hold on to the cross, or the stele, or the angel, so as not to fall. Mine I composed long since and am still pleased with it, tolerably pleased. My other writings are no sooner dry than they revolt me, but my epitaph still meets with my approval. There is little chance unfortunately of its ever being reared above the skull that conceived it, unless the State takes up the matter. But to be unearthed I must first be found, and I greatly fear those gentlemen will have as much trouble finding me dead as alive. So I hasten to record it here and now, while there is yet time:

> *Hereunder lies the above who up below*
> *So hourly died that he lived on till now.*

The second and last or rather latter line limps a little perhaps, but that is no great matter, I'll be forgiven more than that when I'm forgotten. Then with a little luck you hit on a genuine interment, with real live mourners and the odd relict trying to throw herself into the pit. And nearly always that charming business with the dust, though in my experience there is nothing less dusty than holes of this type, verging on muck for the most part, nor anything particularly powdery about the deceased, unless he happened to have died, or she, by fire. No matter, their little gimmick with the dust is charming. But my father's yard was not amongst my favourites. To begin with it was too remote, way out in the wilds of the country on the side of a hill, and too small, far too small, to go on with. Indeed it was almost full, a few more widows and they'd be turning them away. I infinitely preferred Ohlsdorf, particularly the Linne section, on Prussian soil, with its nine hundred acres of corpses packed tight, though I knew no one there, except by reputation the wild animal collector Hagenbeck. A lion, if I remember right, is carved on his monument, death must have had for Hagenbeck the countenance of a lion. Coaches ply to and fro, crammed with widows, widowers, orphans and the like. Groves, grottoes, artificial lakes with swans, offer consolation to the inconsolable. It was December, I had never felt so cold, the eel soup lay heavy on my stomach, I was afraid I'd die, I turned aside to vomit, I envied them.

But to pass on to less melancholy matters, on my father's death I had to leave the house. It was he who wanted me in the house. He was a strange man. One day he said, Leave him alone, he's not disturbing anyone. He didn't know I was listening. This was a view he must have often voiced, but the other times I wasn't by. They would never let me see his will, they simply said he had left me such a sum. I believed then and still believe he had stipulated in his will that I be left the room I had occupied in his lifetime and for food to be brought me there, as hitherto. He may even have given this the force of condition precedent. Presumably he liked to feel me under his roof, otherwise he would not have opposed my eviction. Perhaps he merely pitied me. But somehow I think not. He should have left me the entire house, then I'd have been all right, the others too for that matter, I'd have summoned them and said, Stay, stay by all means, your home is here. Yes, he was properly had, my poor father, if his purpose was really to go on protecting me from beyond the tomb. With regard to the money it is only fair to say they gave it to me without delay, on the very day following the inhumation. Perhaps they were legally bound to. I said to them, Keep this money and let me live on here, in my room, as in Papa's lifetime. I added, God rest his soul, in the hope of melting them. But they refused. I offered to place myself at their disposal, a few hours every day, for the little odd maintenance jobs every dwelling requires, if it is not to crumble away. Pottering is still just possible, I don't know why. I proposed in particular to look after the hothouse. There I would have gladly whiled away the hours, in the heat, tending the tomatoes, hyacinths, pinks and seedlings. My father and I alone, in that household, understood tomatoes. But they refused. One day, on my return from stool, I found my room locked and my belongings in a heap before the door. This will give you some idea how constipated I was, at this juncture. It was, I am now convinced, anxiety constipation. But was I genuinely constipated? Somehow I think not. Softly, softly. And yet I must have been, for how otherwise account for those long, those cruel sessions in the necessary house? At such times I never read, any more than at other times, never gave way to revery or meditation, just gazed dully at the almanac hanging from a nail before my eyes, with its chromo of a bearded stripling in the midst of sheep, Jesus no doubt, parted the cheeks with both hands and strained, heave! ho! heave! ho!, with the motions of one tugging at the oar, and only one thought in my mind, to be back in my room and flat on my back again. What can that have been but constipation? Or am I confusing it with diarrhoea? It's all a muddle in my head, graves and nuptials and the different varieties of motion. Of my scanty belongings they had made a little heap, on the floor, against the door. I can still see that little heap, in the kind of recess full of shadow between the landing and my room. It was in this narrow space, guarded on three sides only, that I had to change, I mean exchange my dressing-gown and night-gown for my travelling costume, I mean shoes, socks, trousers, shirt, coat, greatcoat and hat, I can think of nothing else. I tried other doors, turning the knobs and pushing, or pulling, before I left the house, but none yielded. I think if I'd found one open I'd have barricaded myself in the room, nothing less than gas would have dislodged me. I felt the house crammed as usual, the usual pack, but saw no one. I imagined them in their various rooms, all bolts drawn, every sense on the alert. Then the rush to the window, each holding back a little, hidden by the curtain, at the sound of the street door closing behind me, I should have left it open. Then the doors fly open and out they pour, men, women and children, and the voices, the sighs, the smiles, the hands, the keys in the hands, the blessed relief, the precautions rehearsed, if this then that, but if that then this, all clear and joy in every heart, come let's eat, the fumigation can wait. All imagination to be sure, I was already on my way, things may have passed quite differently, but who cares how things pass, provided they pass. All those lips that had kissed me, those hearts that had loved me (it is with the heart one loves, is it not, or am I confusing it with something else?), those hands that had played with mine and those minds that had almost made their own of me! Humans are truly strange. Poor Papa, a nice mug he must have felt that day if he could see me, see us, a nice mug on my account I mean. Unless in his great disembodied wisdom he saw further than his son whose corpse was not yet quite up to scratch.

But to pass on to less melancholy matters, the name of the woman with whom I was soon to be united was Lulu. So at least she assured me and I can't see what interest she could have had in lying to me, on this score. Of course one can never tell.

She also disclosed her family name, but I've forgotten it. I should have made a note of it, on a piece of paper, I hate to forget a proper name. I met her on a bench, on the bank of the canal, one of the canals, for our town boasts two, though I never knew which was which. It was a well situated bench, backed by a mound of solid earth and garbage, so that my rear was covered. My flanks too, partially, thanks to a pair of venerable trees, more than venerable, dead, at either end of the bench. It was no doubt these trees one fine day, aripple with all their foliage, that had sown the idea of a bench, in someone's fancy. To the fore, a few yards away, flowed the canal, if canals flow, don't ask me, so that from that quarter too the risk of surprise was small. And yet she surprised me. I lay stretched out, the night being warm, gazing up through the bare boughs interlocking high above me, where the trees clung together for support, and through the drifting cloud, at a patch of starry sky as it came and went. Shove up, she said. My first movement was to go, but my fatigue, and my having nowhere to go, dissuaded me from acting on it. So I drew back my feet a little way and she sat. Nothing more passed between us that evening and she soon took herself off, without another word. All she had done was sing, beneath her breath as to herself, and without the words fortunately, some old folk songs, and so disjointedly, skipping from one to another and finishing none, that even I found it strange. The voice, though out of tune, was not unpleasant. It breathed of a soul too soon wearied ever to conclude, that perhaps least arse-aching soul of all. The bench itself was soon more than she could bear and as for me, one look had been enough for her. Whereas in reality she was a most tenacious woman. She came back next day and the day after and all went off more or less as before. Perhaps a few words were exchanged. The next day it was raining and I felt in security. Wrong again. I asked her if she was resolved to disturb me every evening. I disturb you? she said. I felt her eyes on me. They can't have seen much, two eyelids at the most, with a hint of nose and brow, darkly, because of the dark. I thought we were easy, she said. You disturb me, I said, I can't stretch out with you there. The collar of my greatcoat was over my mouth and yet she heard me. Must you stretch out? she said. The mistake one makes is to speak to people. You have only to put your feet on my knees, she said. I didn't wait to be asked twice, under my miserable calves I felt her fat thighs. She began stroking my ankles. I considered kicking her in the cunt. You speak to people about stretching out and they immediately see a body at full length. What mattered to me in my dispeopled kingdom, that in regard to which the disposition of my carcass was the merest and most futile of accidents, was supineness in the mind, the dulling of the self and of that residue of execrable frippery known as the non-self and even the world, for short. But man is still today, at the age of twenty-five, at the mercy of an erection, physically too, from time to time, it's the common lot, even I was not immune, if that may be called an erection. It did not escape her naturally, women smell a rigid phallus ten miles away and wonder, How on earth did he spot me from there? One is no longer oneself, on such occasions, and it is painful to be no longer oneself, even more painful if possible than when one is. For when one is one knows what to do to be less so, whereas when one is not one is any old one irredeemably. What goes by the name of love is banishment, with now and then a postcard from the homeland, such is my considered opinion, this evening. When she had finished and my self been resumed, mine own, the mitigable, with the help of a brief torpor, it was alone. I sometimes wonder if that is not all invention, if in reality things did not take quite a different course, one I had no choice but to forget. And yet her image remains bound, for me, to that of the bench, not the bench by day, nor yet the bench by night, but the bench at evening, in such sort that to speak of the bench, as it appeared to me at evening, is to speak of her, for me. That proves nothing, but there is nothing I wish to prove. On the subject of the bench by day no words need be wasted, it never knew me, gone before morning and never back till dusk. Yes, in the daytime I foraged for food and marked down likely cover. Were you to inquire, as undoubtedly you itch, what I had done with the money my father had left me, the answer would be I had done nothing with it but leave it lie in my pocket. For I knew I would not be always young, and that summer does not last for ever either, nor even autumn, my mean soul told me so. In the end I told her I'd had enough. She disturbed me exceedingly, even absent. Indeed she still disturbs me, but no worse now than the rest. And it matters nothing to me now, to be disturbed, or so little, what does it mean, disturbed, and what would I do with myself if I wasn't? Yes, I've changed my system, it's the winning one at last, for the ninth or tenth time, not to mention not long now, not long till curtain down, on disturbers and disturbed, no more tattle about that, all that, her and the others, the shitball and heaven's high halls. So you don't want me to come any more, she said. It's incredible the way they repeat what you've just said to them, as if they risked faggot and fire in believing their ears. I told her to come just the odd time. I didn't understand women at that period. I still don't for that matter. Nor men either. Nor animals either. What I understand best, which is not saying much, are my pains. I think them through daily, it doesn't take long, thought moves so fast, but they are not only in my thought, not all. Yes, there are moments, particularly in the afternoon, when I go all syncretist, à la Reinhold. What equilibrium! But even them, my pains, I understand ill. That must come from my not being all pain and nothing else. There's the rub. Then they recede, or I, till they fill me with amaze and wonder, seen from a better planet. Not often, but I ask no more. Catch-cony life! To be nothing but pain, how that would simplify matters! Omnidolent! Impious dream. I'll tell them to you some day none the less, if I think of it, if I can, my strange pains, in detail, distinguishing between the different kinds, for the sake of clarity, those of the mind, those of the heart or emotional conative, those of the soul (none prettier than these) and finally those of the frame proper, first the inner or latent, then those affecting the surface, beginning with the hair and scalp and moving methodically down, without haste, all the way down to the feet beloved of the corn, the cramp, the kibe, the bunion, the hammer toe, the nail ingrown, the fallen arch, the common blain, the club foot, duck foot, goose foot, pigeon foot, flat foot, trench foot and other curiosities. And I'll tell by the same token, for those kind enough to listen, in accordance with a system whose inventor I forget, of those instants when, neither drugged, nor drunk, nor in ecstasy, one feels nothing. Next of course she desired to know what I meant by the odd time, that's what you get for opening your mouth. Once a week? Once in ten days? Once a fortnight? I replied less often, far less often, less often to the point of no more if she could, and if she could not the least often possible. And the next day (what is more) I abandoned the bench, less I must confess on her account than on its, for the site no longer answered my requirements, modest though they were, now that the air was beginning to strike chill, and for other reasons better not wasted on cunts like you, and took refuge in a deserted cowshed marked on one of my forays. It stood in the corner of a field richer on the surface in nettles than in grass and in mud than in nettles, but whose subsoil was perhaps possessed of exceptional qualities. It was in this byre, littered with dry and hollow cowclaps subsiding with a sigh at the poke of my finger, that for the first time in my life, and I would not hesitate to say the last if I had not to husband my cyanide, I had to contend with a feeling which gradually assumed, to my dismay, the dread name of love. What constitutes the charm of our country, apart of course from its scant population, and this without help of the meanest contraceptive, is that all is derelict, with the sole exception of history's ancient faeces. These are ardently sought after, stuffed and carried in procession. Wherever nauseated time has dropped a nice fat turd you will find our patriots, sniffing it up on all fours, their faces on fire. Elysium of the roofless. Hence my happiness at last. Lie down, all seems to say, lie down and stay down. I see no connexion between these remarks. But that one exists, and even more than one, I have little doubt, for my part. But what? Which? Yes, I loved her, it's the name I gave, still give alas, to what I was doing then. I had nothing to go by, having never loved before, but of course had heard of the thing, at home, in school, in brothel and at church, and read romances, in prose and verse, under the guidance of my tutor, in six or seven languages, both dead and living, in which it was handled at length. I was therefore in a position, in spite of all, to put a label on what I was about when I found myself inscribing the letters of Lulu in an old heifer pat or flat on my face in the mud under the moon trying to tear up the nettles by the roots. They were giant nettles some full three foot high, to tear them up assuaged my pain, and yet it's not like me to do that to weeds, on the contrary, I'd smother them in manure if I had any. Flowers are a different matter. Love brings out the worst in man and no error. But what kind of love was this, exactly? Love-passion? Somehow I think not. That's the priapic one, is it not? Or is this a different variety? There are so many, are there not? All equally if not more delicious, are they not? Platonic love, for example, there's another just occurs to me. It's disinterested. Perhaps I loved her with a platonic love? But somehow I think not. Would I have been tracing her name in old cowshit if my love had been pure and disinterested? And with my devil's finger into the bargain, which I then sucked. Come now! My thoughts were all of Lulu, if that doesn't give you some idea nothing will. Anyhow I'm sick and tired of this name Lulu, I'll give her another, more like her, Anna for example, it's not more like her but no matter. I thought of Anna then, I who had learnt to think of nothing, nothing except my pains, a quick think through, and of what steps to take not to perish off-hand of hunger, or cold, or shame, but never on any account of living beings as such (I wonder what that means) whatever I may have said, or may still say, to the contrary or otherwise, on this subject. But I have always spoken, no doubt always shall, of things that never existed, or that existed if you insist, no doubt always will, but not with the existence I ascribe to them. Kepis, for example, exist beyond a doubt, indeed there is little hope of their ever disappearing, but personally I never wore a kepi. I wrote somewhere, They gave me . . . a hat. Now the truth is they never gave me a hat, I have always had my own hat, the one my father gave me, and I have never had any other hat than that hat. I may add it has followed me to the grave. I thought of Anna then, long long sessions, twenty minutes, twenty-five minutes and even as long as half an hour daily. I obtain these figures by the addition of other, lesser figures. That must have been my way of loving. Are we to infer from this I loved her with that intellectual love which drew from me such drivel, in another place? Somehow I think not. For had my love been of this kind would I have stooped to inscribe the letters of Anna in time's forgotten cowpats? To divellicate urtica *plenis manibus*? And felt, under my tossing head, her thighs to bounce like so many demon bolsters? Come now! In order to put an end, to try and put an end, to this plight, I returned one evening to the bench, at the hour she had used to join me there. There was no sign of her and I waited in vain. It was December already, if not January, and the cold was seasonable, that is to say reasonable, like all that is seasonable. But one is the hour of the dial, and another that of changing air and sky, and another yet again the heart's. To this thought, once back in the straw, I owed an excellent night. The next day I was earlier to the bench, much earlier, night having barely fallen, winter night, and yet too late, for she was there already, on the bench, under the boughs tinkling with rime, her back to the frosted mound, facing the icy water. I told you she was a highly tenacious woman. I felt nothing. What interest could she have in pursuing me thus? I asked her, without sitting down, stumping to and fro. The cold had embossed the path. She replied she didn't know. What could she see in me, would she kindly tell me that at least, if she could. She replied she couldn't. She seemed warmly clad, her hands buried in a muff. As I looked at this muff, I remember, tears came to my eyes. And yet I forget what colour it was. The state I was in then! I have always wept freely, without the least benefit to myself, till recently. If I had to weep this minute I could squeeze till I was blue, I'm convinced not a drop would fall. The state I am in now! It was things made me weep. And yet I felt no sorrow. When I found myself in tears for no apparent reason it meant I had caught sight of something unbeknownst. So I wonder if it was really the muff that evening, if it was not rather the path, so iron hard and bossy as perhaps to feel like cobbles to my tread, or some other thing, some chance thing glimpsed below the threshold, that so unmanned me. As for her, I might as well never have laid eyes on her before. She sat all huddled and muffled up, her head sunk, the muff with her hands in her lap, her legs pressed tight together, her heels clear of the ground. Shapeless, ageless, almost lifeless, it might have been anything or anyone, an old woman or a little girl. And the way she kept on saying, I don't know, I can't. I alone did not know and could not. Is it on my account you came? I said. She managed yes to that. Well here I am, I said. And I? Had I not come on hers? Here we are, I said. I sat down beside her but sprang up again immediately as though scalded. I longed to be gone, to know if it was over. But before going, to be on the safe side, I asked her to sing me a song. I thought at first she was going to refuse, I mean simply not sing, but no, after a moment she began to sing and sang for some time, all the time the same song it seemed to me, without change of attitude. I did not know the song, I had never heard it before and shall never hear it again. It had something to do with lemon trees, or orange trees, I forget, that is all I remember, and for me that is no mean feat, to remember it had something to do with lemon trees, or orange trees, I forget, for of all the other songs I have ever heard in my life, and I have heard plenty, it being apparently impossible, physically impossible short of being deaf, to get through this world, even my way, without hearing singing, I have retained nothing, not a word, not a note, or so few words, so few notes, that, that what, that nothing, this sentence has gone on long enough. Then I started to go and as I went I heard her singing another song, or perhaps more verses of the same, fainter and fainter the further I went, then no more, either because she had come to an end or because I was gone too far to hear her. To have to harbour such a doubt was something I preferred to avoid, at that period. I lived of course in doubt, on doubt, but such trivial doubts as this, purely somatic as some say, were best cleared up without delay, they could nag at me like gnats for weeks on end. So I retraced my steps a little way and stopped. At first I heard nothing, then the voice again, but only just, so faintly did it carry. First I didn't hear it, then I did, I must therefore have begun hearing it, at a certain point, but no, there was no beginning, the sound emerged so softly from the silence and so resembled it. When the voice ceased at last I approached a little nearer, to make sure it had really ceased and not merely been lowered. Then in despair, saying, No knowing, no knowing, short of being beside her, bent over her, I turned on my heel and went, for good, full of doubt. But some weeks later, even more dead than alive than usual, I returned to the bench, for the fourth or fifth time since I had abandoned it, at roughly the same hour, I mean roughly the same sky, no, I don't mean that either, for it's always the same sky and never the same sky, what words are there for that, none I know, period. She wasn't there, then suddenly she was, I don't know how, I didn't see her come, nor hear her, all ears and eyes though I was. Let us say it was raining, nothing like a change, if only of weather. She had her umbrella up, naturally, what an outfit. I asked if she came every evening. No, she said, just the odd time. The bench was soaking wet, we paced up and down, not daring to sit. I took her arm, out of curiosity, to see if it would give me pleasure, it gave me none, I let it go. But why these particulars. To put off the evil hour. I saw her face a little clearer, it seemed normal to me, a face like millions of others. The eyes were crooked, but I didn't know that till later. It looked neither young nor old, the face, as though stranded between the vernal and the sere. Such ambiguity I found difficult to bear, at that period. As to whether it was beautiful, the face, or had once been beautiful, or could conceivably become beautiful, I confess I could form no opinion. I had seen faces in photographs I might have found beautiful had I known even vaguely in what beauty was supposed to consist. And my father's face, on his death-bolster, had seemed to hint at some form of aesthetics relevant to man. But the faces of the living, all grimace and flush, can they be described as objects? I admired in spite of the dark, in spite of my fluster, the way still or scarcely flowing water reaches up, as though athirst, to that falling from the sky. She asked if I would like her to sing something. I replied no, I would like her to say something. I thought she would say she had nothing to say, it would have been like her, and so was agreeably surprised when she said she had a room, most agreeably surprised, though I suspected as much. Who has not a room? Ah I hear the clamour. I have two rooms, she said. Just how many rooms do you have? I said. She said she had two rooms and a kitchen. The premises were expanding steadily, given time she would remember a bathroom. Is it two rooms I heard you say? I said. Yes, she said. Adjacent? I said. At last conversation worthy of the name. Separated by the kitchen, she said. I asked her why she had not told me before. I must have been beside myself, at this period. I did not feel easy when I was with her, but at least free to think of something else than her, of the old trusty things, and so little by little, as down steps towards a deep, of nothing. And I knew that away from her I would forfeit this freedom.

There were in fact two rooms, separated by a kitchen, she had not lied to me. She said I should have fetched my things. I explained I had no things. It was at the top of an old house, with a view of the mountains for those who cared. She lit an oil-lamp. You have no current? I said. No, she said, but I have running water and gas. Ha, I said, you have gas. She began to undress. When at their wit's end they undress, no doubt the wisest course. She took off everything, with a slowness fit to enflame an elephant, except her stockings, calculated presumably to bring my concupiscence to the boil. It was then I noticed the squint. Fortunately she was not the first naked woman to have crossed my path, so I could stay, I knew she would not explode. I asked to see the other room which I had not yet seen. If I had seen it already I would have asked to see it again. Will you not undress? she said. Oh you know, I said, I seldom undress. It was the truth, I was never one to undress indiscriminately. I often took off my boots when I went to bed, I mean when I composed myself (composed!) to sleep, not to mention this or that outer garment according to the outer temperature. She was therefore obliged, out of common savoir faire, to throw on a wrap and light me the way. We went via the kitchen. We could just as well have gone via the corridor, as I realized later, but we went via the kitchen, I don't know why, perhaps it was the shortest way. I surveyed the room with horror. Such density of furniture defeats imagination. Not a doubt, I must have seen that room somewhere. What's

this? I cried. The parlour, she said. The parlour! I began putting
out the furniture through the door to the corridor. She watched,
in sorrow I suppose, but not necessarily. She asked me what I
was doing. She can't have expected an answer. I put it out piece
by piece, and even two at a time, and stacked it all up in the
corridor, against the outer wall. There were hundreds of pieces,
large and small, in the end they blocked the door, making egress
impossible, and *a fortiori* ingress, to and from the corridor. The
door could be opened and closed, since it opened inwards, but
had become impassable. To put it mildly. At least take off your
hat, she said. I'll treat of my hat some other time perhaps. Finally
the room was empty but for a sofa and some shelves fixed to the
wall. The former I dragged to the back of the room, near the
door, and next day took down the latter and put them out, in
the corridor, with the rest. As I was taking them down, strange
memory, I heard the word fibrome, or brone, I don't know
which, never knew, never knew what it meant and never had the
curiosity to find out. The things one recalls! and records! When
all was in order at last I dropped on the sofa. She had not raised
her little finger to help me. I'll get sheets and blankets, she said.
But I wouldn't hear of sheets. You couldn't draw the curtain? I
said. The window was frosted over. The effect was not white,
because of the night, but faintly luminous none the less. This
faint cold sheen, though I lay with my feet towards the door, was
more than I could bear. I suddenly rose and changed the position
of the sofa, that is to say turned it round so that the back, hitherto against the wall, was now on the outside and consequently
the front, or way in, on the inside. Then I climbed back, like a
dog into its basket. I'll leave you the lamp, she said, but I begged
her to take it with her. And suppose you need something in the
night, she said. She was going to start quibbling again, I could
feel it. Do you know where the convenience is? she said. She was
right, I was forgetting. To relieve oneself in bed is enjoyable at

the time, but soon a source of discomfort. Give me a chamber-pot, I said. But she did not possess one. I have a close-stool of sorts, she said. I saw the grandmother on it, sitting up very stiff and grand, having just purchased it, pardon, picked it up, at a charity sale, or perhaps won it in a raffle, a period piece, and now trying it out, doing her best rather, almost wishing someone could see her. That's the idea, procrastinate. Any old recipient, I said, I don't have the flux. She came back with a kind of sauce-pan, not a true saucepan for it had no handle, it was oval in shape with two lugs and a lid. My stewpan, she said. I don't need the lid, I said. You don't need the lid? she said. If I had needed the lid she would have said, You need the lid? I drew this utensil down under the blanket, I like something in my hand when sleeping, it reassures me, and my hat was still wringing. I turned to the wall. She caught up the lamp off the mantelpiece where she had set it down, that's the idea, every particular, it flung her waving shadow over me, I thought she was off, but no, she came stooping down towards me over the sofa back. All family possessions, she said. I in her shoes would have tiptoed away, but not she, not a stir. Already my love was waning, that was all that mattered. Yes, already I felt better, soon I'd be up to the slow descents again, the long submersions, so long denied me through her fault. And I had only just moved in! Try and put me out now, I said. I seemed not to grasp the meaning of these words, nor even hear the brief sound they made, till some seconds after having uttered them. I was so unused to speech that my mouth would sometimes open, of its own accord, and vent some phrase or phrases, grammatically unexceptionable but entirely devoid if not of meaning, for on close inspection they would reveal one, and even several, at least of foundation. But I heard each word no sooner spoken. Never had my voice taken so long to reach me as on this occasion. I turned over on my back to see what was going on. She was smiling. A little later she went away, taking the lamp with her. I heard her steps in the kitchen and then the door of her room close behind her. Why behind her? I was alone at last, in the dark at last. Enough about that. I thought I was all set for a good night, in spite of the strange surroundings, but no, my night was most agitated. I woke next morning quite worn out, my clothes in disorder, the blanket likewise, and Anna beside me, naked naturally. One shudders to think of her exertions. I still had the stewpan in my grasp. It had not served. I looked at my member. If only it could have spoken! Enough about that. It was my night of love.

Gradually I settled down, in this house. She brought my meals at the appointed hours, looked in now and then to see if all was well and make sure I needed nothing, emptied the stewpan once a day and did out the room once a month. She could not always resist the temptation to speak to me, but on the whole gave me no cause to complain. Sometimes I heard her singing in her room, the song traversed her door, then the kitchen, then my door, and in this way won to me, faint but indisputable. Unless it travelled by the corridor. This did not greatly incommode me, this occasional sound of singing. One day I asked her to bring me a hyacinth, live, in a pot. She brought it and put it on the mantelpiece, now the only place in my room to put things, unless you put them on the floor. Not a day passed without my looking at it. At first all went well, it even put forth a bloom or two, then it gave up and was soon no more than a limp stem hung with limp leaves. The bulb, half clear of the clay as though in search of oxygen, smelt foul. She wanted to remove it, but I told her to leave it. She wanted to get me another, but I told her I didn't want another. I was more seriously disturbed by other sounds, stifled giggles and groans, which filled the dwelling at certain hours of the night, and even of the day. I had given up thinking of her, quite given up, but still I needed silence, to live my life. In vain I tried to listen to such reasonings as that air is made to carry the clamours of the world, including inevitably much groan and giggle, I obtained no relief. I couldn't make out if it was always the same gent or more than one. Lovers' groans are so alike, and lovers' giggles. I had such horror then of these paltry perplexities that I always fell into the same error, that of seeking to clear them up. It took me a long time, my lifetime so to speak, to realize that the colour of an eye half seen, or the source of some distant sound, are closer to Giudecca in the hell of unknowing than the existence of God, or the origins of protoplasm, or the existence of self, and even less worthy than these to occupy the wise. It's a bit much, a lifetime, to achieve this consoling conclusion, it doesn't leave you much time to profit by it. So a fat lot of help it was when, having put the question to her, I was told they were clients she received in rotation. I could obviously have got up and gone to look through the keyhole. But what can you see, I ask you, through holes the likes of those? So you live by prostitution, I said. We live by prostitution, she said. You couldn't ask them to make less noise? I said, as if I believed her. I added, Or a different kind of noise. They can't help but yap and yelp, she said. I'll have to leave, I said. She found some old hangings in the family junk and hung them before our doors, hers and mine. I asked her if it would not be possible, now and then, to have a parsnip. A parsnip! she cried, as if I had asked for a dish of sucking Jew. I reminded her that the parsnip season was fast drawing to a close and that if, before it finally got there, she could feed me nothing but parsnips I'd be grateful. I like parsnips because they taste like violets and violets because they smell like parsnips. Were there no parsnips on earth violets would leave me cold and if violets did not exist I would care as little for parsnips as I do for turnips, or radishes. And even in the present state of their flora, I mean on this planet where parsnips and violets contrive to coexist, I could do without both with the utmost ease, the uttermost ease. One day she had the impudence to announce she was with child, and four or five months gone into the bargain, by me of all people! She offered me a side view of her belly. She even undressed, no doubt to prove she wasn't hiding a cushion under her skirt, and then of course for the pure pleasure of undressing. Perhaps it's just wind, I said, by way of consolation. She gazed at me with her big eyes whose colour I forget, with one big eye rather, for the other seemed riveted on the remains of the hyacinth. The more naked she was the more cross-eyed. Look, she said, stooping over her breasts, the haloes are darkening already. I summoned up my remaining strength and said, Abort, abort, and they'll blush like new. She had drawn back the curtain for a clear view of all her rotundities. I saw the mountain, impassible, cavernous, secret, where from morning to night I'd hear nothing but the wind, the curlews, the clink like distant silver of the stone-cutters' hammers. I'd come out in the daytime to the heather and gorse, all warmth and scent, and watch at night the distant city lights, if I chose, and the other lights, the lighthouses and lightships my father had named for me, when I was small, and whose names I could find again, in my memory, if I chose, that I knew. From that day forth things went from bad to worse, to worse and worse. Not that she neglected me, she could never have neglected me enough, but the way she kept plaguing me with *our* child, exhibiting her belly and breasts and saying it was due any moment, she could feel it lepping already. If it's lepping, I said, it's not mine. I might have been worse off than I was, in that house, that was certain, it fell short of my ideal naturally, but I wasn't blind to its advantages. I hesitated to leave, the leaves were falling already, I dreaded the winter. One should not dread the winter, it too has its bounties, the snow gives warmth and deadens the tumult and its pale days are soon over. But I did not yet know, at that time, how tender the earth can be for those who have only her and how many graves in her giving, for the living. What finished me was the birth. It woke me up. What that infant must have been going through! I fancy she had a woman with her, I seemed to hear steps in the kitchen, on and off. It went to my heart to leave a house without being put out. I crawled out over the back of the sofa, put on my coat, greatcoat and hat, I can think of nothing else, laced up my boots and opened the door to the corridor. A mass of junk barred my way, but I scrabbled and barged my way through it in the end, regardless of the clatter. I used the word marriage, it was a kind of union in spite of all. Precautions would have been superfluous, there was no competing with those cries. It must have been her first. They pursued me down the stairs and out into the street. I stopped before the house door and listened. I could still hear them. If I had not known there was crying in the house I might not have heard them. But knowing it I did. I was not sure where I was. I looked among the stars and constellations for the Wains, but could not find them. And yet they must have been there. My father was the first to show them to me. He had shown me others, but alone, without him beside me, I could never find any but the Wains. I began playing with the cries, a little in the same way as I had played with the song, on, back, on, back, if that may be called playing. As long as I kept walking I didn't hear them, because of the footsteps. But as soon as I halted I heard them again, a little fainter each time, admittedly, but what does it matter, faint or loud, cry is cry, all that matters is that it should cease. For years I thought they would cease. Now I don't think so any more. I could have done with other loves perhaps. But there it is, either you love or you don't.

Translated by the author

Stories (from *Stories and Texts for Nothing*)
The Expelled

THERE WERE NOT many steps. I had counted them a thousand times, both going up and coming down, but the figure has gone from my mind. I have never known whether you should say one with your foot on the sidewalk, two with the following foot on the first step, and so on, or whether the sidewalk shouldn't count. At the top of the steps I fell foul of the same dilemma. In the other direction, I mean from top to bottom, it was the same, the word is not too strong. I did not know where to begin nor where to end, that's the truth of the matter. I arrived therefore at three totally different figures, without ever knowing which of them was right. And when I say that the figure has gone from my mind, I mean that none of the three figures is with me any more, in my mind. It is true that if I were to find, in my mind, where it is certainly to be found, one of these figures, I would find it and it alone, without being able to deduce from it the other two. And even were I to recover two, I would not know the third. No, I would have to find all three, in my mind, in order to know all three. Memories are killing. So you must not think of certain things, of those that are dear to you, or rather you must think of them, for if you don't there is the danger of finding them, in your mind, little by little. That is to say, you must think of them for a while, a good while, every day several times a day, until they sink forever in the mud. That's an order.

After all it is not the number of steps that matters. The important thing to remember is that there were not many, and that I have remembered. Even for the child there were not many, compared to other steps he knew, from seeing them every day, from going up them and coming down, and from playing on them at knucklebones and other games the very names of which he has forgotten. What must it have been like then for the man I had overgrown into?

The fall was therefore not serious. Even as I fell I heard the door slam, which brought me a little comfort, in the midst of my fall. For that meant they were not pursuing me down into the street, with a stick, to beat me in full view of the passers-by. For if that had been their intention they would not have shut the door, but left it open, so that the persons assembled in the vestibule might enjoy my chastisement and be edified. So, for once, they had confined themselves to throwing me out and no more about it. I had time, before coming to rest in the gutter, to conclude this piece of reasoning.

Under these circumstances nothing compelled me to get up immediately. I rested my elbow on the sidewalk, funny the things you remember, settled my ear in the cup of my hand and began to reflect on my situation, notwithstanding its familiarity. But the sound, fainter but unmistakable, of the door slammed again, roused me from my reverie, in which already a whole landscape was taking form, charming with hawthorn and wild roses, most dreamlike, and made me look up in alarm, my hands flat on the sidewalk and my legs braced for flight. But it was merely my hat sailing towards me through the air, rotating as it came. I caught it and put it on. They were most correct, according to their god. They could have kept this hat, but it was not theirs, it was mine, so they gave it back to me. But the spell was broken.

How describe this hat? And why? When my head had attained I shall not say its definitive but its maximum dimensions, my father said to me, Come, son, we are going to buy your hat, as though it had pre-existed from time immemorial in a pre-established place. He went straight to the hat. I personally had no say in the matter, nor had the hatter. I have often wondered if my father's purpose was not to humiliate me, if he was not jealous of me who was young and handsome, fresh at least, while he was already old and all bloated and purple. It was forbidden me, from that day forth, to go out bareheaded, my pretty brown hair blowing in the wind. Sometimes, in a secluded street, I took it off and held it in my hand, but trembling. I was required to brush it morning and evening. Boys my age with whom, in spite of everything, I was obliged to mix occasionally, mocked me. But I said to myself, It is not really the hat, they simply make merry at the hat because it is a little more glaring than the rest, for they have no finesse. I have always been amazed at my contemporaries' lack of finesse, I whose soul writhed from morning to night, in the mere quest of itself. But perhaps they were simply being kind, like those who make game of the hunchback's big nose. When my father died I could have got rid of this hat, there was nothing more to prevent me, but not I. But how describe it? Some other time, some other time.

I got up and set off. I forget how old I can have been. In what had just happened to me there was nothing in the least memorable. It was neither the cradle nor the grave of anything whatever. Or rather it resembled so many other cradles, so many other graves, that I'm lost. But I don't believe I exaggerate when I say that I was in the prime of life, what I believe is called the full possession of one's faculties. Ah yes, them I possessed all right. I crossed the street and turned back towards the house that had just ejected me, I who never turned back when leaving. How beautiful it was! There were geraniums in the windows. I have brooded over geraniums for years. Geraniums are artful customers, but in the end I was able to do what I liked with them. I have always greatly admired the door of this house, up on top of its little flight of steps. How describe it? It was a massive green door, encased in summer in a kind of green and white striped housing, with a hole for the thunderous wrought-iron knocker and a slit for letters, this latter closed to dust, flies and tits by a brass flap fitted with springs. So much for that description. The door was set between two pillars of the same colour, the bell being on that to the right. The curtains were in unexceptionable taste. Even the smoke rising from one of the chimney-pots seemed to spread and vanish in the air more sorrowful than the neighbours', and bluer. I looked up at the third and last floor and saw my window outrageously open. A thorough cleansing was in full swing. In a few hours they would close the window, draw the curtains and spray the whole place with disinfectant. I knew them. I would have gladly died in that house. In a sort of vision I saw the door open and my feet come out.

I wasn't afraid to look, for I knew they were not spying on me from behind the curtains, as they could have done if they had wished. But I knew them. They had all gone back into their dens and resumed their occupations.

And yet I had done them no harm.

I did not know the town very well, scene of my birth and of my first steps in this world, and then of all the others, so many that I thought all trace of me was lost, but I was wrong. I went out so little! Now and then I would go to the window, part the curtains and look out. But then I hastened back to the depths of the room, where the bed was. I felt ill at ease with all this air about me, lost before the confusion of innumerable prospects. But I still knew how to act at this period, when it was absolutely necessary. But first I raised my eyes to the sky, whence cometh our help, where there are no roads, where you wander freely, as in a desert, and where nothing obstructs your vision, wherever you turn your eyes, but the limits of vision itself. When I was younger I thought life would be good in the middle of a plain and went to the Lüneburg heath. With the plain in my head I went to the heath. There were other heaths far less remote, but a voice kept saying to me, It's the Lüneburg heath you need. The element lüne must have had something to do with it. As it turned out the Lüneburg heath was most unsatisfactory, most unsatisfactory. I came home disappointed, and at the same time relieved. Yes, I don't know why, but I have never been disappointed, and I often was in the early days, without feeling at the same time, or a moment later, an undeniable relief.

I set off. What a gait. Stiffness of the lower limbs, as if nature had denied me knees, extraordinary splaying of the feet to right and left of the line of march. The trunk, on the contrary, as if by the effect of a compensatory mechanism, was as flabby as an old ragbag, tossing wildly to the unpredictable jolts of the pelvis. I have often tried to correct these defects, to stiffen my bust, flex my knees and walk with my feet in front of one another, for I had at least five or six, but it always ended in the same way, I mean with a loss of equilibrium, followed by a fall. A man must walk without paying attention to what he's doing, as he sighs, and when I walked without paying attention to what I was doing I walked in the way I have just described, and when I began to pay attention I managed a few steps of creditable execution and then fell. I decided therefore to be myself. This carriage is due, in my opinion, in part at least, to a certain leaning from which I have never been able to free myself completely and which left its stamp, as was only to be expected, on my impressionable years, those which govern the fabrication of character, I refer to the period which extends, as far as the eye can see, from the first totterings, behind a chair, to the third form, in which I concluded my studies. I had then the deplorable habit, having pissed in my trousers, or shat there, which I did fairly regularly early in the morning, about ten or half past ten, of persisting in going on and finishing my day as if nothing had happened. The very idea of changing my trousers, or of confiding in mother, who goodness knows asked nothing better than to help me, was unbearrable, I don't know why, and till bedtime I dragged on with burning and stinking between my little thighs, or sticking to my bottom, the result of my incontinence. Whence this wary way of walking, with the legs stiff and wide apart, and this desperate rolling of the bust, no doubt intended to put people off the scent, to make them think I was full of gaiety and high spirits, without a care in the world, and to lend plausibility to my explanations concerning my nether rigidity, which I ascribed to hereditary rheumatism. My youthful ardour, in so far as I had any, spent itself in this effort, I became sour and mistrustful, a little before my time, in love with hiding and the prone position. Poor juvenile solutions, explaining nothing. No need then for caution, we may reason on to our heart's content, the fog won't lift.

The weather was fine. I advanced down the street, keeping as close as I could to the sidewalk. The widest sidewalk is never wide enough for me, once I set myself in motion, and I hate to inconvenience strangers. A policeman stopped me and said, The street for vehicles, the sidewalk for pedestrians. Like a bit of Old Testament. So I got back on the sidewalk, almost apologetically, and persevered there, in spite of an indescribable jostle, for a good twenty steps, till I had to fling myself to the ground to avoid crushing a child. He was wearing a little harness, I remember, with little bells, he must have taken himself for a pony, or a Clydesdale, why not. I would have crushed him gladly, I loathe children, and it would have been doing him a service, but I was afraid of reprisals. Everyone is a parent, that is what keeps you from hoping. One should reserve, on busy streets, special tracks for these nasty little creatures, their prams, hoops, sweets, scooters, skates, grandpas, grandmas, nannies, balloons and balls, all their foul little happiness in a word. I fell then, and brought down with me an old lady covered with spangles and lace, who must have weighed about sixteen stone. Her screams soon drew a crowd. I had high hopes she had broken her femur, old ladies break their femur easily, but not enough, not enough. I took advantage of the confusion to make off, muttering unintelligible oaths, as if I were the victim, and I was, but I couldn't have proved it. They never lynch children, babies, no matter what they do they are whitewashed in advance. I personally would lynch them with the utmost pleasure, I don't say I'd lend a hand, no, I am not a violent man, but I'd encourage the others and stand them drinks when it was done. But no sooner had I begun to reel on than I was stopped by a second policeman, similar in all respects to the first, so much so that I wondered whether it was not the same one. He pointed out to me that the sidewalk was for every one, as if it was quite obvious that I could not be assimilated to that category. Would you like me, I said, without thinking for a single moment of Heraclitus, to get down in the gutter? Get down wherever you want, he said, but leave some room for others. If you can't bloody well get about like every one else, he said, you'd do better to stay at home. It was exactly my feeling. And that he should attribute to me a home was no small satisfaction. At that moment a funeral passed, as sometimes happens. There was a great flurry of hats and at the same time a flutter of countless fingers. Personally if I were reduced to making the sign of the cross I would set my heart on doing it right, nose, navel, left nipple, right nipple. But the way they did it, slovenly and wild, he seemed crucified all of a heap, no dignity, his knees under his chin and his hands anyhow. The more fervent stopped dead and muttered. As for the policeman, he stiffened to attention, closed his eyes and saluted. Through the windows of the cabs I caught a glimpse of the mourners conversing with animation, no doubt scenes from the life of their late dear brother in Christ, or sister. I seem to have heard that the hearse trappings are not the same in both cases, but I never could find out what the difference consists in. The horses were farting and shitting as if they were going to the fair. I saw no one kneeling.

But with us the last journey is soon done, it is in vain you quicken your pace, the last cab containing the domestics soon leaves you behind, the respite is over, the bystanders go their ways, you may look to yourself again. So I stopped a third time, of my own free will, and entered a cab. Those I had just seen pass, crammed with people hotly arguing, must have made a strong impression on me. It's a big black box, rocking and swaying on its springs, the windows are small, you curl up in a corner, it smells musty. I felt my hat grazing the roof. A little later I leant forward and closed the windows. Then I sat down again with my back to the horse. I was dozing off when a voice made me start, the cabman's. He had opened the door, no doubt despairing of making himself heard through the window. All I saw was his moustache. Where to? he said. He had climbed down from his seat on purpose to ask me that. And I who thought I was far away already. I reflected, searching in my memory for the name of a street, or a monument. Is your cab for sale? I said. I added, Without the horse. What would I do with a horse? But what would I do with a cab? Could I as much as stretch out in it? Who would bring me food? To the Zoo, I said. It is rare for a capital to be without a Zoo. I added, Don't go too fast. He laughed. The suggestion that he might go too fast to the Zoo must have amused him. Unless it was the prospect of being cabless. Unless it was simply myself, my own person, whose presence in the cab must have transformed it, so much so that the cabman, seeing me there with my head in the shadows of the roof and my knees against the window, had wondered perhaps if it was really his cab, really a cab. He hastens to look at his horse, and is reassured. But does one ever know oneself why one laughs? His laugh in any case was brief, which suggested I was not the joke. He closed the door and climbed back to his seat. It was not long then before the horse got under way.

Yes, surprising though it may seem, I still had a little money at this time. The small sum my father had left me as a gift, with no restrictions, at his death, I still wonder if it wasn't stolen from me. Then I had none. And yet my life went on, and even in the way I wanted, up to a point. The great disadvantage of this condition, which might be defined as the absolute impossibility of all purchase, is that it compels you to bestir yourself. It is rare, for example, when you are completely penniless, that you can have food brought to you from time to time in your retreat. You are therefore obliged to go out and bestir yourself, at least one day a week. You can hardly have a home address under these circumstances, it's inevitable. It was therefore with a certain delay that I learnt they were looking for me, for an affair concerning me. I forget through what channel. I did not read the newspapers, nor do I remember having spoken with anyone during these years, except perhaps three or four times, on the subject of food. At any rate, I must have had wind of the affair one way or another, otherwise I would never have gone to see the lawyer, Mr. Nidder, strange how one fails to forget certain names, and he would never have received me. He verified my identity. That took some time. I showed him the metal initials in the lining of my hat, they proved nothing but they increased the probabilities. Sign, he said. He played with a cylindrical ruler, you could have felled an ox with it. Count, he said. A young woman, perhaps venal, was present at this interview, as a witness no doubt. I stuffed the wad in my pocket. You shouldn't do that, he said. It occurred to me that he should have asked me to count before I signed, it would have been more in order. Where can I reach you, he said, if necessary? At the foot of the stairs I thought of something. Soon after I went back to ask him where this money came from, adding that I had a right to know. He gave me a woman's name that I've forgotten. Perhaps she had dandled me on her knees while I was still in swaddling clothes and there had been some lovey-dovey. Sometimes that suffices. I repeat, in swaddling clothes, for any later it would have been too late, for lovey-dovey. It is thanks to this money then that I still had a little. Very little. Divided by my life to come it was negligible, unless my conjectures were unduly pessimistic. I knocked on the partition beside my hat, right in the cabman's back if my calculations were correct. A cloud of dust rose from the upholstery. I took a stone from my pocket and knocked with the stone, until the cab stopped. I noticed that, unlike most vehicles, which slow down before stopping, the cab stopped dead. I waited. The whole cab shook. The cabman, on his high seat, must have been listening. I saw the horse as with my eyes of flesh. It had not lapsed into the drooping attitude of its briefest halts, it remained alert, its ears pricked up. I looked out of the window, we were again in motion. I banged again on the partition, until the cab stopped again. The cabman got down cursing from his seat. I lowered the window to prevent his opening the door. Faster, faster. He was redder than ever, purple in other words. Anger, or the rushing wind. I told him I was hiring him for the day. He replied that he had a funeral at three o'clock. Ah the dead. I told him I had changed my mind and no longer wished to go to the Zoo. Let us not go to the Zoo, I said. He replied that it made no difference to him where we went, provided it wasn't too far, because of his beast. And they talk to us about the specificity of primitive peoples' speech. I asked him if he knew of an eating-house. I added, You'll eat with me. I prefer being with a regular customer in such places. There was a long table with two benches of exactly the same length on either side. Across the table he spoke to me of his life, of his wife, of his beast, then again of his life, of the atrocious life that was his, chiefly because of his character. He asked me if I realized what it meant to be out of doors in all weathers. I learnt there were still some cabmen who spent their day snug and warm inside their cabs on the rank, waiting for a customer to come and rouse them. Such a thing was possible in the past, but nowadays other methods were necessary, if a man was to have a little laid up at the end of his days. I described my situation to him, what I had lost and what I was looking for. We did our best, both of us, to understand, to explain. He understood that I had lost my room and needed another, but all the rest escaped him. He had taken it into his head, whence nothing could ever dislodge it, that I was looking for a furnished room. He took from his pocket an evening paper of the day before, or perhaps the day before that again, and proceeded to run through the advertisements, five or six of which he underlined with a tiny pencil, the same that hovered over the likely outsiders. He underlined no doubt those he would have underlined if he had been in my shoes, or perhaps those concentrated in the same area, because of his beast. I would only have confused him by saying that I could tolerate no furniture in my room except the bed, and that all the other pieces, and even the very night table, had to be removed before I would consent to set foot in it. About three o'clock we roused the horse and set off again. The cabman suggested I climb up beside him on the seat, but for some time already I had been dreaming of the inside of the cab and I got back inside. We visited, methodically I hope, one after another, the addresses he had underlined. The short winter's day was drawing to a close. It seems to me sometimes that these are the only days I have ever known, and especially that most charming moment of all, just before night wipes them out. The addresses he had underlined, or rather marked with a cross, as common people do, proved fruitless one by one, and one by one he crossed them out with a diagonal stroke. Later he showed me the paper, advising me to keep it safe so as to be sure not to look again where I had already looked in vain. In spite of the closed windows, the creaking of the cab and the traffic noises, I heard him singing, all alone aloft on his seat. He had preferred me to a funeral, this was a fact which would endure forever. He sang, *She is far from the land where her young hero,* those are the only words I remember. At each stop he got down from his seat and helped me down from mine. I rang at the door he directed me to and sometimes I disappeared inside the house. It was a strange feeling, I remember, a house all about me again, after so long. He waited for me on the sidewalk and helped me climb back into the cab. I was sick and tired of this cabman. He clambered back to his seat and we set off again. At a certain moment there occurred this. He stopped. I shook off my torpor and made ready to get down. But he did not come to open the door and offer me his arm, so that I was obliged to get down by myself. He was lighting the lamps. I love oil lamps, in spite of their having been, with candles, and if I except the stars, the first lights I ever knew. I asked him if I might light the second lamp, since he had already lit the first himself. He gave me his box of matches, I swung open on its hinges the little convex glass, lit and closed at once, so that the wick might burn steady and bright, snug in its little house, sheltered from the wind. I had this joy. We saw nothing, by the light of these lamps, save the vague outlines of the horse, but the others saw them from afar, two yellow glows sailing slowly through the air. When the equipage turned an eye could be seen, red or green as the case might be, a bossy rhomb as clear and keen as stained glass.

After we had verified the last address the cabman suggested bringing me to a hotel he knew where I would be comfortable. That makes sense, cabman, hotel, it's plausible. With his recommendation I would want for nothing. Every convenience, he said, with a wink. I place this conversation on the sidewalk, in front of the house from which I had just emerged. I remember, beneath the lamp, the flank of the horse, hollow and damp, and on the handle of the door the cabman's hand in its woollen glove. The roof of the cab was on a level with my neck. I suggested we have a drink. The horse had neither eaten nor drunk all day. I mentioned this to the cabman, who replied that his beast would take no food till it was back in the stable. If it ate anything whatever, during work, were it but an apple or a lump of sugar, it would have stomach pains and colics that would root it to the spot and might even kill it. That was why he was compelled to tie its jaws together with a strap whenever for one reason or another he had to let it out of his sight, so that it would not have to suffer from the kind hearts of the passers-by. After a few drinks the cabman invited me to do his wife and him the honour of spending the night in their home. It was not far. Recollecting these emotions, with the celebrated advantage of tranquility, it seems to me he did nothing else, all that day, but turn about his lodging. They lived above a stable, at the back of a yard. Ideal location, I could have done with it. Having presented me to his wife, extraordinarily full-bottomed, he left us. She was manifestly ill at ease, alone with me. I could understand her, I don't stand on ceremony on these occasions. No reason for this to end or go on. Then let it end. I said I would go down to the stable and sleep there. The cabman protested. I insisted. He drew his wife's attention to the pustule on top of my skull, for I had removed my hat out of civility. He should have that removed, she said. The cabman named a doctor he held in high esteem who had rid him of an induration of the seat. If he wants to sleep in the stable, said his wife, let him sleep in the stable. The cabman took the lamp from the table and preceded me down the stairs, or rather ladder, which descended to the stable, leaving his wife in the dark. He spread a horse blanket on the ground in a corner on the straw and left me a box of matches in case I needed to see clearly in the night. I don't remember what the horse was doing all this time. Stretched out in the dark I heard the noise it made as it drank, a noise like no other, the sudden gallop of the rats and above me the muffled voices of the cabman and his wife as they criticized me. I held the box of matches in my hand, a big box of safety matches. I got up during the night and struck one. Its brief flame enabled me to locate the cab. I was seized, then abandoned, by the desire to set fire to the stable. I found the cab in the dark, opened the door, the rats poured out, I climbed in. As I settled down I noticed that the cab was no longer level, it was inevitable, with the shafts resting on the ground. It was better so, that allowed me to lie well back, with my feet higher than my head on the other seat. Several times during the night I felt the horse looking at me through the window and the breath of its nostrils. Now that it was unharnessed it must have been puzzled by my presence in the cab. I was cold, having forgotten to take the blanket, but not quite enough to go and get it. Through the window of the cab I saw the window of the stable, more and more clearly. I got out of the cab. It was not so dark now in the stable, I could make out the manger, the rack, the harness hanging, what else, buckets and brushes. I went to the door but couldn't open it. The horse didn't take its eyes off me. Don't horses ever sleep? It seemed to me the cabman should have tied it, to the manger for example. So I was obliged to leave by the window. It wasn't easy. But what is easy? I went out head first, my hands were flat on the ground of the yard while my legs were still thrashing to get clear of the frame. I remember the tufts of grass on which I pulled with both hands, in my effort to extricate myself. I should have taken off my greatcoat and thrown it through the window, but that would have meant thinking of it. No sooner had I left the yard than I thought of something. Weakness. I slipped a banknote in the match box, went back to the yard and placed the box on the sill of the window through which I had just come. The horse was at the window. But after I had taken a few steps in the street I returned to the yard and took back my banknote. I left the matches, they were not mine. The horse was still at the window. I was sick and tired of this cabhorse. Dawn was just breaking. I did not know where I was. I made towards the rising sun, towards where I thought it should rise, the quicker to come into the light. I would have liked a sea horizon, or a desert one. When I am abroad in the morning I go to meet the sun, and in the evening, when I am abroad, I follow it, till I am down among the dead. I don't know why I told this story. I could just as well have told another. Perhaps some other time I'll be able to tell another. Living souls, you will see how alike they are.

—*Translated by Richard Seaver in collaboration with the author*

The Calmative

I DON'T KNOW when I died. It always seemed to me I died old, about ninety years old, and what years, and that my body bore it out, from head to foot. But this evening, alone in my icy bed, I have the feeling I'll be older than the day, the night, when the sky with all its lights fell upon me, the same I had so often gazed on since my first stumblings on the distant earth. For I'm too frightened this evening to listen to myself rot, waiting for the great red lapses of the heart, the tearings at the caecal walls, and for the slow killings to finish in my skull, the assaults on unshakable pillars, the fornications with corpses. So I'll tell myself a story, I'll try and tell myself another story, to try and calm myself, and it's there I feel I'll be old, old, even older than the day I fell, calling for help, and it came. Or is it possible that in this story I have come back to life, after my death? No, it's not like me to come back to life, after my death.

What possessed me to stir when I wasn't with anybody? Was I being thrown out? No, I wasn't with anybody. I see a kind of den littered with empty tins. And yet we are not in the country. Perhaps it's just ruins, a ruined folly, on the skirts of the town, in a field, for the fields come right up to our walls, their walls, and the cows lie down at night in the lee of the ramparts. I have changed refuge so often, in the course of my rout, that now I can't tell between dens and ruins. But there was never any city but the one. It is true you often move along in a dream, houses and factories darken the air, trams go by and under your feet wet from the grass there are suddenly cobbles. I only know the city of my childhood, I must have seen the other, but unbelieving. All I say cancels out, I'll have said nothing. Was I hungry itself? Did the weather tempt me? It was cloudy and cool, I insist, but not to the extent of luring me out. I couldn't get up at the first attempt, nor let us say at the second, and once up, propped against the wall, I wondered if I could go on, I mean up, propped against the wall. Impossible to go out and walk. I speak as though it all happened yesterday. Yesterday indeed is recent, but not enough. For what I tell this evening is passing this evening, at this passing hour. I'm no longer with these assassins, in this bed of terror, but in my distant refuge, my hands twined together, my head bowed, weak, breathless, calm, free, and older than I'll have ever been, if my calculations are correct. I'll tell my story in the past none the less, as though it were a myth, or an old fable, for this evening I need another age, that age to become another age in which I became what I was.

But little by little I got myself out and started walking with short steps among the trees, oh look, trees! The paths of other days were rank with tangled growth. I leaned against the trunks to get my breath and pulled myself forward with the help of boughs. Of my last passage no trace remained. They were the perishing oaks immortalized by d'Aubigné. It was only a grove. The fringe was near, a light less green and kind of tattered told me so, in a whisper. Yes, no matter where you stood, in this little wood, and were it in the furthest recess of its poor secrecies, you saw on every hand the gleam of this pale light, promise of God knows what fatuous eternity. Die without too much pain, a little, that's worth your while. Under the blind sky close with your own hands the eyes soon sockets, then quick into carrion not to mislead the crows. That's the advantage of death by drowning, one of the advantages, the crabs never get there too soon. But here a strange thing, I was no sooner free of the wood at last, having crossed unminding the ditch that girdles it, than thoughts came to me of cruelty, the kind that smiles. A lush pasture lay before me, nonsuch perhaps, who cares, drenched in evening dew or recent rain. Beyond this meadow to my certain knowledge a path, then a field and finally the ramparts, closing the prospect. Cyclopean and crenellated, standing out faintly against a sky scarcely less sombre, they did not seem in ruins, viewed from mine, but were, to my certain knowledge. Such was the scene offered to me, in vain, for I knew it well and loathed it. What I saw was a bald man in a brown suit, a comedian. He was telling a funny story about a fiasco. Its point escaped me. He used the word snail, or slug, to the delight of all present. The women seemed even more entertained than their escorts, if that were possible. Their shrill laughter pierced the clapping and, when this had subsided, broke out still here and there in sudden peals even after the next story had begun, so that part of it was lost. Perhaps they had in mind the reigning penis sitting who knows by their side and from that sweet shore launched their cries of joy towards the comic vast, what a talent. But it's to me this evening something has to happen, to my body as in myth and metamorphosis, this old body to which nothing ever happened, or so little, which never met with anything, loved anything, wished for anything, in its tarnished universe, except for the mirrors to shatter, the plane, the curved, the magnifying, the minifying, and to vanish in the havoc of its images. Yes, this evening it has to be as in the story my father used to read to me, evening after evening, when I was small, and he had all his health, to calm me, evening after evening, year after year it seems to me this evening, which I don't remember much about, except that it was the adventures of one Joe Breem, or Breen, the son of a lighthouse-keeper, a strong muscular lad of fifteen, those were the words, who swam for miles in the night, a knife between his teeth, after a shark, I forget why, out of sheer heroism. He might have simply told me the story, he knew it by heart, so did I, but that wouldn't have calmed me, he had to read it to me, evening after evening, or pretend to read it to me, turning the pages and explaining the pictures that were of me already, evening after evening the same pictures till I dozed off on his shoulder. If he had skipped a single word I would have hit him, with my little fist, in his big belly bursting out of the old cardigan and unbuttoned trousers that rested him from his office canonicals. For me now the setting forth, the struggle and perhaps the return, for the old man I am this evening, older than my father ever was, older than I shall ever be. I crossed the meadow with little stiff steps at the same time limp, the best I could manage. Of my last passage no trace remained, it was long ago. And the little bruised stems soon straighten up again, having need of air and light, and as for the broken their place is soon taken. I entered the town by what they call the Shepherds' Gate without having seen a soul, only the first bats like flying crucifixions, nor heard a sound except my steps, my heart in my breast and then, as I went under the arch, the hoot of an owl, that cry at once so soft and fierce which in the night, calling, answering, through my little wood and those nearby, sounded in my shelter like a tocsin. The further I went into the city the more I was struck by its deserted air. It was lit as usual, brighter than usual, although the shops were shut. But the lights were on in their windows with the object no doubt of attracting customers and prompting them to say, I say, I like that, not dear either, I'll come back tomorrow, if I'm still alive. I nearly said, Good God it's Sunday. The trams were running, the buses too, but few, slow, empty, noiseless, as if under water. I didn't see a single horse! I was wearing my long green greatcoat with the velvet collar, such as motorists wore about 1900, my father's, but that day it was sleeveless, a vast cloak. But on me it was still the same great dead weight, with no warmth to it, and the tails swept the ground, scraped it rather, they had grown so stiff, and I so shrunken. What would, what could happen to me in this empty place? But I felt the houses packed with people, lurking behind the curtains they looked out into the street or, crouched far back in the depths of the room, head in hands, were sunk in dream. Up aloft my hat, the same as always, I reached no further. I went right across the city and came to the sea, having followed the river to its mouth. I kept saying, I'll go back, unbelieving. The boats at anchor in the harbour, tied up to the jetty, seemed no less numerous than usual, as if I knew anything about what was usual. But the quays were deserted and there was no sign or stir of arrival or departure. But all might change from one moment to the next and be transformed like magic before my eyes. Then all the bustle of the people and things of the sea, the masts of the big craft gravely rocking and of the small more jauntily, I insist, and I'd hear the gulls' terrible cry and perhaps the sailors' cry. And I might slip unnoticed aboard a freighter outward bound and get far away and spend far away a few good months, perhaps even a year or two, in the sun, in peace, before I died. And without going that far it would be a sad state of affairs if in that unscandalizable throng I couldn't achieve a little encounter that would calm me a little, or exchange a few words with a navigator for example, words to carry away with me to my refuge, to add to my collection. I waited sitting on a kind of topless capstan, saying, The very capstans this evening are out of order. And I gazed out to sea, out beyond the breakwaters, without sighting the least vessel. I could see lights flush with the water. And the pretty beacons at the harbour mouth I could see too, and others in the distance, flashing from the coast, the islands, the headlands. But seeing still no sign or stir I made ready to go, to turn away sadly from this dead haven, for there are scenes that call for strange farewells. I had merely to bow my head and look down at my feet, for it is in this attitude I always drew the strength to, how shall I say, I don't know, and it was always from the earth, rather than from the sky, notwithstanding its reputation, that my help came in time of trouble. And there, on the flagstone, which I was not focussing, for why focus it, I saw haven afar, where the black swell was most perilous, and all about me storm and wreck. I'll never come back here, I said. But when with a thrust of both hands against the the rim of the capstan I heaved myself up I found facing me a young boy holding a goat by a horn. I sat down again. He stood there silent looking at me without visible fear or revulsion. Admittedly the light was poor. His silence seemed natural to me, it befitted me as the elder to speak first. He was barefoot and in rags. Haunter of the waterfront he had stepped aside to see what the dark hulk could be abandoned on the quayside. Such was my train of thought. Close up to me now with his little guttersnipe's eye there could be no doubt left in his mind. And yet he stayed. Can this base thought be mine? Moved, for after all that is what I must have come out for, in a way, and with little expectation of advantage from what might follow, I resolved to speak to him. So I marshalled the words and opened my mouth, thinking I would hear them. But all I heard was a kind of rattle, unintelligible even to me who knew what was intended. But it was nothing, mere speechlessness due to long silence, as in the wood that darkens the mouth of hell, do you remember, I only just. Without letting go of his goat he moved right up against me and offered me a sweet out of a twist of paper such as you could buy for a penny. I hadn't been offered a sweet for eighty years at least, but I took it eagerly and put it in my mouth, the old gesture came back to me, more and more moved since that is what I wanted. The sweets were stuck together and I had my work cut out to separate the top one, a green one, from the others, but he helped me and his hand brushed mine. And a moment later as he made to move away, hauling his goat after him, with a great gesticulation of my whole body I motioned him to stay and I said, in an impetuous murmur, Where are you off to, my little man, with your nanny? The words were hardly out of my mouth when for shame I covered my face. And yet they were the same I had tried to utter but a moment before. Where are you off to, my little man, with your nanny! If I could have blushed I would have, but there was not enough blood left in my extremities. If I had had a penny in my pocket I would have given it to him, for him to forgive me, but I did not have a penny in my pocket, nor anything resembling it. Nothing that could give pleasure to a little unfortunate at the mouth of life. I suspect I had nothing with me but my stone, that day, having gone out as it were without premeditation. Of his little person I was fated to see no more than the black curly hair and the pretty curve of the long bare legs all muscle and dirt. And the hand, so fresh and keen, I would not forget in a hurry either. I looked for better words to say to him, I found them too late, he was gone, oh not far, but far. Out of my life too he went without a care, not one of his thoughts would ever be for me again, unless perhaps when he was old and, delving in his boyhood, would come upon that gallows night and hold the goat by the horn again and linger again a moment by my side, with who knows perhaps a touch of tenderness, even of envy, but I have my doubts. Poor dear dumb beasts, how you will have helped me. What does your daddy do? that's what I would have said to him if he had given me the chance. Soon they were no more than a single blur which if I hadn't known I might have taken for a young centaur. I was nearly going to have the goat dung, then pick up a handful of the pellets so soon cold and hard, sniff and even taste them, no, that would not help me this evening. I say this evening as if it were always the same evening, but are there two evenings? I went, intending to get back as fast as I could, but it would not be quite empty-handed, repeating, I'll never come back here. My legs were paining me, every step would gladly have been the last, but the glances I darted towards the windows, stealthily, showed me a great cylinder sweeping past as though on rollers on the asphalt. I must indeed have been moving fast, for I overhauled more than one pedestrian, there are the first men, without extending myself, I who in the normal way was left standing by cripples, and then I seemed to hear the foot-falls die behind me. And yet each little step would gladly have been the last. So much so that when I emerged on a square I hadn't noticed on the way out, with a cathedral looming on the far side, I decided to go in, if it was open, and hide, as in the Middle Ages, for a space. I say cathedral, it may not have been, I don't know, all I know is it would vex me in this story that as-pires to be the last, to have taken refuge in a common church. I remarked the Saxon Stützenwechsel. Charming effect, but it didn't charm me. The brilliantly lit nave appeared deserted. I walked round it several times without seeing a soul. They were hiding perhaps, under the choir-stalls, or dodging behind the pillars, like woodpeckers. Suddenly close to where I was, and without my having heard the long preliminary rumblings, the organ began to boom. I sprang up from the mat on which I lay before the altar and hastened to the far end of the nave as if on my way out. But it was a side aisle and the door I disappeared through was not the exit. For instead of being restored to the night I found myself at the foot of a spiral staircase which I began to climb at top speed, mindless of my heart, like one hotly pursued by a homicidal maniac. This staircase faintly lit by I know not what means, slits perhaps, I mounted panting as far as the projecting gallery in which it culminated and which, sepa-rated from the void by a cynical parapet, encompassed a smooth round wall capped by a little dome covered with lead or verdigrised copper, phew, if that's not clear. People must have come here for the view, those who fall die on the way. Flattening myself against the wall I started round, clockwise. But I had hardly gone a few steps when I met a man revolving in the other direction, with the utmost circumspection. How I'd love to push him, or him to push me, over the edge. He gazed at me wild-eyed for a moment and then, not daring to pass me on the parapet side and surmising correctly that I would not relinquish the wall just to oblige him, abruptly turned his back on me, his head rather, for his back remained glued to the wall, and went back the way he had come so that soon there was nothing left of him but a left hand. It lingered a moment, then slid out of sight. All that remained to me was the vision of two burning eyes starting out of their sockets under a check cap. Into what nightmare thingness am I fallen? My hat flew off, but did not get far thanks to the string. I turned my head towards the staircase and lent an eye. Nothing. Then a little girl came into view followed by a man holding her by the hand, both pressed against the wall. He pushed her into the stairway, disappeared after her, turned and raised towards me a face that made me recoil. I could only see his bare head above the top step. When they were gone I called. I completed in haste the round of the gallery. No one. I saw on the horizon, where sky, sea, plain and mountain meet, a few low stars, not to be confused with the fires men light, at night, or that go alight alone. Enough. Back in the street I tried to find my way in the sky, where I knew the Bears so well. If I had seen someone I would have stopped him to ask, the most ferocious aspect would not have daunted me. I would have said, touching my hat, Pardon me your honour, the Shepherds' Gate for the love of God. I thought I could go no further, but no sooner had the impetus reached my legs than on I went, believe it or not, at a very fair pace. I wasn't returning empty-handed, not quite, I was taking back with me the virtual certainty that I was still of this world, of that world too, in a way. But I was paying the price. I would have done better to spend the night in the cathedral, on the mat before the altar, I would have continued on my way at first light, or they would have found me stretched out in the rigor of death, the genuine bodily article, under the blue eyes fount of so much hope, and put me in the evening papers. But suddenly I was descending a wide street, vaguely familiar, but in which I could never have set foot, in my lifetime. But soon realizing I was going downhill I turned about and set off in the other direction. For I was afraid if I went downhill of returning to the sea where I had sworn never to return. When I say I turned about I mean I wheeled round in a wide semi-circle without slowing down, for I was afraid if I stopped of not being able to start again, yes, I was afraid of that too. And this evening too I dare not stop. I was struck more and more by the contrast between the brightly lit streets and their deserted air. To say it distressed me, no, but I say it all the same, in the hope of calming myself. To say there was no one abroad, no, I would not go that far, for I remarked a number of shapes, male and female, strange shapes, but not more so than usual. As to what hour it might have been I had no idea, except that it must have been some hour of the night. But it might have been three or four in the morning just as it might have been ten or eleven in the evening, depending no doubt on whether one wondered at the scarcity of passers-by or at the extraordinary radiance shed by the street-lamps and traffic-lights. For at one or other of these no one could fail to wonder, unless he was out of his mind. Not a single private car, but admittedly from time to time a public vehicle, slow sweep of light silent and empty. It is not my wish to labour these antinomies, for we are needless to say in a skull, but I have no choice but to add the following few remarks. All the mortals I saw were alone and as if sunk in themselves. It must be a common sight, but mixed with something else I imagine. The only couple was two men grappling, their legs intertwined. I only saw one cyclist! He was going the same way as I was. All were going the same way as I was, vehicles too, I have only just realized it. He was pedalling slowly in the middle of the street, reading a newspaper which he held with both hands spread open before his eyes. Every now and then he rang his bell without interrupting his reading. I watched him recede till he was no more than a dot on the horizon. Suddenly a young woman perhaps of easy virtue, dishevelled and her dress in disarray, darted across the street like a rabbit. That is all I had to add. But here a strange thing, yet another, I had no pain whatever, not even in my legs. Weakness. A good night's nightmare and a tin of sardines would restore my sensitivity. My shadow, one of my shadows, flew before me, dwindled, slid under my feet, trailed behind me the way shadows will. This degree of opacity appeared to me conclusive. But suddenly ahead of me a man on the same side of the street and going the same way, to keep harping on the same thing lest I forget. The distance between us was considerable, seventy paces at least, and fearing he might escape me I quickened my step with the result I swept forward as if on rollers. This is not me, I said, let us make the most of it. Finding myself in an instant a bare ten paces in his rear I slowed down so as not to burst in on him and so heighten the aversion my person inspired even in its most abject and obsequious attitudes. And a moment later, keeping humbly in step with him, Excuse me your honour, the Shepherds' Gate for the love of God! At close quarters he appeared normal apart from that air already noted of ebbing inward. I drew a few steps ahead, turned, cringed, touched my hat and said, The right time for mercy's sake! I might as well not have existed. But what about the sweet? A light! I cried. Given my need of help I can't think why I did not bar his path. I couldn't have, that's all, I couldn't have touched him. Seeing a stone seat by the kerb I sat down and crossed my legs, like Walther. I must have dozed off, for the next thing was a man sitting beside me. I was still taking him in when he opened his eyes and set them on me, as if for the first time, for he shrank back unaffectedly. Where did you spring from? he said. To hear myself addressed again so soon impressed me greatly. What's the matter with you? he said. I tried to look like one with whom that only is the matter which is native to him. Forgive me your honour, I said, gingerly lifting my hat and rising a fraction from the seat, the right time for the love of God! He said a time, I don't remember which, a time that explained nothing, that's all I remember, and did not calm me. But what time could have done that? Oh I know, I know, one will come that will. But in the meantime? What's that you said? he said. Unfortunately I had said nothing. But I wriggled out of it by asking him if he could help me find my way which I had lost. No, he said, for I am not from these parts and if I am sitting on this slab it is because the hotels were full or would not let me in, I have no opinion. But tell me the story of your life, then we'll see. My life! I cried. Why yes, he said, you know, that kind of—what shall I say? He brooded for a time, no doubt trying to think of what life could well be said to be a kind. In the end he went on, testily, Come now, everyone knows that. He jogged me in the ribs. No details, he said, the main drift, the main drift. But as I remained silent he said, Shall I tell you mine, then you'll see what I mean. The account he then gave was brief and dense, facts, without comment. That's what I call a life, he said, do you follow me now? It wasn't bad, his story, positively fairy-like in places. But that Pauline, I said, are you still with her? I am, he said, but I'm going to leave her and set up with another, younger and plumper. You travel a lot, I said. Oh widely, widely, he said. Words were coming back to me, and the way to make them sound. All that's a thing of the past for you no doubt, he said. Do you think of spending some time among us? I said. This sentence struck me as particularly well turned. If it's not a rude question, he said, how old are you? I don't know, I said. You don't know! he cried. Not exactly, I said. Are thighs much in your thoughts, he said, arses, cunts and environs? I didn't follow. No more erections naturally, he said. Erections? I said. The penis, he said, you know what the penis is, there, between the legs. Ah that! I said. It thickens, lengthens, stiffens and rises, he said, does it not? I assented, though they were not the terms I would have used. That is what we call an erection, he said. He pondered, then exclaimed, Phenomenal! No? Strange right enough, I said. And there you have it all, he said. But what will become of her? I said. Who? he said. Pauline, I said. She will grow old, he said with tranquil assurance, slowly at first, then faster and faster, in pain and bitterness, pulling the devil by the tail. The face was not full, but I eyed it in vain, it remained clothed in its flesh instead of turning all chalky and channelled as with a gouge. The very vomer kept its cushion. It is true discussion was always bad for me. I longed for the tender nonsuch, I would have trodden it gently, with my boots in my hand, and for the shade of my wood, far from this terrible light. What are you grinning and bearing? he said. He held on his knees a big black bag, like a midwife's I imagine. It was full of glittering phials. I asked him if they were all alike. Oho no, he said, for every taste. He took one and held it out to me, saying, One and six. What did he want? To sell it to me? Proceeding on this hypothesis I told him I had no money. No money! he cried. All of a sudden his hand came down on the back of my neck, his sinewy fingers closed and with a jerk and a twist he had me up against him. But instead of dispatching me he began to murmur words so sweet that I went limp and my head fell forward in his lap. Between the caressing voice and the fingers rowelling my neck the contrast was striking. But gradually the two things merged in a devastating hope, if I dare say so, and I dare. For this evening I have nothing to lose that I can discern. And if I have reached this point (in my story) without anything having changed, for if anything had changed I think I'd know, the fact remains I have reached it, and that's something, and with nothing changed, and that's something too. It's no excuse for rushing matters. No, it must cease gently, as gently cease on the stairs the steps of the loved one, who could not love and will not come back, and whose steps say so, that she could not love and will not come back. He suddenly shoved me away and showed me the phial again. There you have it all, he said. It can't have been the same all as before. Want it? he said. No, but I said yes, so as not to vex him. He proposed an exchange. Give me your hat, he said. I refused. What vehemence! he said. I haven't a thing, I said. Try in your pockets, he said. I haven't a thing, I said, I came out without a thing. Give me a lace, he said. I refused. Long silence. And if you gave me a kiss, he said finally. I knew there were kisses in the air. Can you take off your hat? he said. I took it off. Put it back, he said, you look nicer with it on. I put it back. Come on, he said, give me a kiss and let there be an end to it. Did it not occur to him I might turn him down? No, a kiss is not a bootlace, he must have seen from my face that all passion was not quite spent. Come, he said. I wiped my mouth in its tod of hair and advanced it towards his. Just a moment, he said. My mouth stood still. You know what a kiss is? he said. Yes yes, I said. If it's not a rude question, he said, when was your last? Some time ago, I said, but I can still do them. He took off his hat, a bowler, and tapped the middle of his forehead. There, he said, and there only. He had a noble brow, white and high. He leaned forward, closing his eyes. Quick, he said. I pursed up my lips as mother had taught me and brought them down where he had said. Enough, he said. He raised his hand to the spot, but left the gesture unfinished and put on his hat. I turned away and looked across the street. It was then I noticed we were sitting opposite a horse-butcher's. Here, he said, take it. I had forgotten.

He rose. Standing he was quite short. One good turn, he said, with radiant smile. His teeth shone. I listened to his steps die away. How tell what remains? But it's the end. Or have I been dreaming, am I dreaming? No no, none of that, for dream is nothing, a joke, and significant what is worse. I said, Stay where you are till day breaks, wait sleeping till the lamps go out and the streets come to life. But I stood up and moved off. My pains were back, but with something untoward which prevented my wrapping them round me. But I said, Little by little you are coming to. From my gait alone, slow, stiff and which seemed at every step to solve a stato-dynamic problem never posed before, I would have been known again, if I had been known. I crossed over and stopped before the butcher's. Behind the grille the curtains were drawn, rough canvas curtains striped blue and white, colours of the Virgin, and stained with great pink stains. They did not quite meet in the middle, and through the chink I could make out the dim carcasses of the gutted horses hanging from hooks head downwards. I hugged the walls, famished for shadow. To think that in a moment all will be said, all to do again. And the city clocks, what was wrong with them, whose great chill clang even in my wood fell on me from the air? What else? Ah yes, my spoils. I tried to think of Pauline, but she eluded me, gleamed an instant and was gone, like the young woman in the street. So I went in the atrocious brightness, bedded in my old flesh, straining towards an issue and passing them by to left and right and my mind panting after this and that and always flung back to where there was nothing. I succeeded however in fastening briefly on the little girl, long enough to see her a little more clearly than before, so that she wore a kind of bonnet and clasped in her hand a book, of common prayer perhaps, and to try and have her smile, but she did not smile, but vanished down the staircase without having yielded me her little face. I had to stop. At first nothing, then little by little, I mean rising up out of the silence till suddenly no higher, a kind of massive murmur coming perhaps from the house that was propping me up. That reminded me that the houses were full of people, besieged, no, I don't know. When I stepped back to look at the windows I could see, in spite of shutters, blinds and muslins, that many of the rooms were lit. The light was so dimmed by the brilliancy flooding the boulevard that short of knowing or suspecting it was not so one might have supposed everyone sleeping. The sound was not continuous, but broken by silences possibly of consternation. I thought of ringing at the door and asking for shelter and protection till morning. But suddenly I was on my way again. But little by little, in a slow swoon, darkness fell about me. I saw a mass of bright flowers fade in an exquisite cascade of paling colours. I found myself admiring, all along the housefronts, the gradual blossoming of squares and rectangles, casement and sash, yellow, green, pink, according to the curtains and blinds, finding that pretty. Then at last, before I fell, first to my knees, as cattle do, then on my face, I was in a throng. I didn't lose consciousness, when I lose consciousness it will not be to recover it. They paid no heed to me, though careful not to walk on me, a courtesy that must have touched me, it was what I had come out for. It was well with me, sated with dark and calm, lying at the feet of mortals, fathom deep in the grey of dawn, if it was dawn. But reality, too tired to look for the right word, was soon restored, the throng fell away, the light came back and I had no need to raise my head from the ground to know I was back in the same blinding void as before. I said, Stay where you are, down on the friendly stone, or at least indifferent, don't open your eyes, wait for morning. But up with me again and back on the way that was not mine, on uphill along the boulevard. A blessing he was not waiting for me, poor old Breem, or Breen. I said, The sea is east, it's west I must go, to the left of north. But in vain I raised without hope my eyes to the sky to look for the Bears. For the light I stepped in put out the stars, assuming they were there, which I doubted, remembering the clouds.

Translated by the author

The End

THEY CLOTHED ME and gave me money. I knew what the money was for, it was to get me started. When it was gone I would have to get more, if I wanted to go on. The same for the shoes, when they were worn out I would have to get them mended, or get myself another pair, or go on barefoot, if I wanted to go on. The same for the coat and trousers, needless to say, with this difference, that I could go on in my shirtsleeves, if I wanted. The clothes—shoes, socks, trousers, shirt, coat, hat—were not new, but the deceased must have been about my size. That is to say, he must have been a little shorter, a little thinner, for the clothes did not fit me so well in the beginning as they did at the end, the shirt especially, and it was many a long day before I could button it at the neck, or profit by the collar that went with it, or pin the tails together between my legs in the way my mother had taught me. He must have put on his Sunday best to go to the consultation, perhaps for the first time, unable to bear it any longer. Be that as it may the hat was a bowler, in good shape. I said, Keep your hat and give me back mine. I added, Give me back my greatcoat. They replied that they had burnt them, together with my other clothes. I understood then that the end was near, at least fairly near. Later on I tried to exchange this hat for a cap, or

78

a slouch which could be pulled down over my face, but without much success. And yet I could not go about bare-headed, with my skull in the state it was. At first this hat was too small, then it got used to me. They gave me a tie, after long discussion. It seemed a pretty tie to me, but I didn't like it. When it came at last I was too tired to send it back. But in the end it came in useful. It was blue, with kinds of little stars. I didn't feel well, but they told me I was well enough. They didn't say in so many words that I was as well as I would ever be, but that was the implication. I lay inert on the bed and it took three women to put on my trousers. They didn't seem to take much interest in my private parts which to tell the truth were nothing to write home about, I didn't take much interest in them myself. But they might have passed some remark. When they had finished I got up and finished dressing unaided. They told me to sit on the bed and wait. All the bedding had disappeared. It made me angry that they had not let me wait in the familiar bed, instead of leaving me standing in the cold, in these clothes that smelt of sulphur. I said, You might have left me in the bed till the last moment. Men all in white came in with mallets in their hands. They dismantled the bed and took away the pieces. One of the women followed them out and came back with a chair which she set before me. I had done well to pretend I was angry. But to make it quite clear to them how angry I was that they had not left me in my bed, I gave the chair a kick that sent it flying. A man came in and made a sign to me to follow him. In the hall he gave me a paper to sign. What's this, I said, a safe-conduct? It's a receipt, he said, for the clothes and money you have received. What money? I said. It was then I received the money. To think I had almost departed without a penny in my pocket. The sum was not large, compared to other sums, but to me it seemed large. I saw the familiar objects, companions of so many bearable hours. The stool, for example, dearest of all. The long afternoons together, waiting for it to be time for bed. At times I felt its wooden life invade me, till I myself became a piece of old wood. There was even a hole for my cyst. Then the window pane with the patch of frosting gone, where I used to press my eye in the hour of need, and rarely in vain. I am greatly obliged to you, I said, is there a law which prevents you from throwing me out naked and penniless? That would damage our reputation in the long run, he replied. Could they not possibly keep me a little longer, I said, I could make myself useful. Useful, he said, joking apart you would be willing to make yourself useful? A moment later he went on, If they believed you were really willing to make yourself useful they would keep you, I am sure. The number of times I had said I was going to make myself useful, I wasn't going to start that again. How weak I felt! Perhaps, I said, they would consent to take back the money and keep me a little longer. This is a charitable institution, he said, and the money is a gift you receive when you leave. When it is gone you will have to get more, if you want to go on. Never come back here whatever you do, you would not be let in. Don't go to any of our branches either, they would turn you away. Exelmans! I cried. Come come, he said, and anyway no one understands a tenth of what you say. I'm so old, I said. You are not so old as all that, he said. May I stay here just a little longer, I said, till the rain is over? You may wait in the cloister, he said, the rain will go on all day. You may wait in the cloister till six o'clock, you will hear the bell. If anyone challenges you, you need only say you have permission to shelter in the cloister. Whose name will I give? I said. Weir, he said.

I had not been long in the cloister when the rain stopped and the sun came out. It was low and I reckoned it must be getting on for six, considering the season. I stayed there looking through the archway at the sun as it went down behind the cloister. A man appeared and asked me what I was doing. What do you want? were the words he used. Very friendly. I replied that I had Mr. Weir's permission to stay in the cloister till six o'clock. He went away, but came back immediately. He must have spoken to Mr. Weir in the interim, for he said, You must not loiter in the cloister now the rain is over.

Now I was making my way through the garden. There was that strange light which follows a day of persistent rain, when the sun comes out and the sky clears too late to be of any use. The earth makes a sound as of sighs and the last drops fall from the emptied cloudless sky. A small boy, stretching out his hands and looking up at the blue sky, asked his mother how such a thing was possible. Fuck off, she said. I suddenly remembered I had not thought of asking Mr. Weir for a piece of bread. He would surely have given it to me. I had as a matter of fact thought of it during our conversation in the hall, I had said to myself, Let us first finish our conversation, then I'll ask. I knew well they would not keep me. I would gladly have turned back, but I was afraid one of the guards would stop me and tell me I would never see Mr. Weir again. That might have added to my sorrow. And anyway I never turned back on such occasions.

In the street I was lost. I had not set foot in this part of the city for a long time and it seemed greatly changed. Whole buildings had disappeared, the palings had changed position, and on all sides I saw, in great letters, the names of tradesmen I had never seen before and would have been at a loss to pronounce. There were streets where I remembered none, some I did remember had vanished and others had completely changed their names. The general impression was the same as before. It is true I did not know the city very well. Perhaps it was quite a different one. I did not know where I was supposed to be going. I had the great good fortune, more than once, not to be run over. My appearance still made people laugh, with that hearty jovial laugh so good for the health. By keeping the red part of the sky as much as possible on my right hand I came at last to the river. Here all seemed at first sight more or less as I had left it. But if I had looked more closely I would doubtless have discovered many changes. And indeed I subsequently did so. But the general appearance of the river, flowing between its quays and under its bridges, had not changed. Yes, the river still gave the impression it was flowing in the wrong direction. That's all a pack of lies I feel. My bench was still there. It was shaped to fit the curves of the seated body. It stood beside a watering trough, gift of a Mrs. Maxwell to the city horses, according to the inscription. During the short time I rested there several horses took advantage of this monument. The iron shoes approached and the jingle of the harness. Then silence. That was the horse looking at me. Then the noise of pebbles and mud that horses make when drinking. Then the silence again. That was the horse looking at me again. Then the pebbles again. Then the silence again. Till the horse had finished drinking or the driver deemed it had drunk its fill. The horses were uneasy. Once, when the noise stopped, I turned and saw the horse looking at me. The driver too was looking at me. Mrs. Maxwell would have been pleased if she could have seen her trough rendering such services to the city horses. When it was night, after a tedious twilight, I took off my hat which was paining me. I longed to be under cover again, in an empty place, close and warm, with artificial light, an oil lamp for choice, with a pink shade for preference. From time to time someone would come to make sure I was all right and needed nothing. It was long since I had longed for anything and the effect on me was horrible.

In the days that followed I visited several lodgings, without much success. They usually slammed the door in my face, even when I showed my money and offered to pay a week in advance, or even two. It was in vain I put on my best manners, smiled and spoke distinctly, they slammed the door in my face before I could even finish my little speech. It was at this time I perfected a method of doffing my hat at once courteous and discreet, neither servile nor insolent. I slipped it smartly forward, held it a second poised in such a way that the person addressed could not see my skull, then slipped it back. To do that naturally, without creating an unfavorable impression, is no easy matter. When I deemed that to tip my hat would suffice, I naturally did no more than tip it. But to tip one's hat is no easy matter either. I subsequently solved this problem, always fundamental in time of adversity, by wearing a kepi and saluting in military fashion, no, that must be wrong, I don't know, I had my hat at the end. I never made the mistake of wearing medals. Some landladies were in such need of money that they let me in immediately and showed me the room. But I couldn't come to an agreement with any of them. Finally I found a basement. With this woman I came to an agreement at once. My oddities, that's the expression she used, did not alarm her. She nevertheless insisted on making the bed and cleaning the room once a week, instead of once a month as I requested. She told me that while she was cleaning, which would not take long, I could wait in the area. She added, with a great deal of feeling, that she would never put me out in bad weather. This woman was Greek, I think, or Turkish. She never spoke about herself. I somehow got the idea she was a widow or at least that her husband had left her. She had a strange accent. But so had I with my way of assimilating the vowels and omitting the consonants.

Now I didn't know where I was. I had a vague vision, not a real vision, I didn't see anything, of a big house five or six stories high, one of a block perhaps. It was dusk when I got there and I did not pay the same heed to my surroundings as I might have done if I had suspected they were to close about me. And by then I must have lost all hope. It is true that when I left this house it was a glorious day, but I never look back when leaving. I must have read somewhere, when I was small and still read, that it is better not to look back when leaving. And yet I sometimes did. But even without looking back it seems to me I should have seen something when leaving. But there it is. All I remember is my feet emerging from my shadow, one after the other. My shoes had stiffened and the sun brought out the cracks in the leather.

I was comfortable enough in this house, I must say. Apart from a few rats I was alone in the basement. The woman did her best to respect our agreement. About noon she brought me a big tray of food and took away the tray of the previous day. At the same time she brought me a clean chamber-pot. The chamber-pot had a large handle which she slipped over her arm, so that both her hands were free to carry the tray. The rest of the day I saw no more of her except sometimes when she peeped in to make sure nothing had happened to me. Fortunately I did not need affection. From my bed I saw the feet coming and going on the sidewalk. Certain evenings, when the weather was fine and I felt equal to it, I fetched my chair into the area and sat looking up into the skirts of the women passing by. Once I sent for a crocus bulb and planted it in the dark area, in an old pot. It must have been coming up to spring, it was probably not the right time for it. I left the pot outside, attached to a string I passed through the window. In the evening, when the weather was fine, a little light crept up the wall. Then I sat down beside the window and pulled on the string to keep the pot in the light and warmth. That can't have been easy, I don't see how I managed it. It was probably not the right thing for it. I manured it as best I could and pissed on it when the weather was dry. It may not have been the right thing for it. It sprouted, but never any flowers, just a wilting stem and a few chlorotic leaves. I would have liked to have a yellow crocus, or a hyacinth, but there, it was not to be. She wanted to take it away, but I told her to leave it. She wanted to buy me another, but I told her I didn't want another. What lacerated me most was the din of the newspaper boys. They went pounding by every day at the same hours, their heels thudding on the sidewalk, crying the names of their papers and even the headlines. The house noises disturbed me less. A little girl, unless it was a little boy, sang every evening at the same hour, somewhere above me. For a long time I could not catch the words. But hearing them day after day I finally managed to catch a few. Strange words for a little girl, or a little boy. Was it a song in my head or did it merely come from without? It was a sort of lullaby, I believe. It often sent me to sleep, even me. Sometimes it was a little girl who came. She had long red hair hanging down in two braids. I didn't know who she was. She lingered awhile in the room, then went away without a word. One day I had a visit from a policeman. He said I had to be watched, without explaining why. Suspicious, that was it, he told me I was suspicious. I let him talk. He didn't dare arrest me. Or perhaps he had a kind heart. A priest too, one day I had a visit from a priest. I informed him I belonged to a branch of the reformed church. He asked me what kind of clergyman I would like to see. Yes, there's that about the reformed church, you're lost, it's unavoidable. Perhaps he had a kind heart. He told me to let him know if I needed a helping hand. A helping hand! He gave me his name and explained where I could reach him. I should have made a note of it.

One day the woman made me an offer. She said she was in urgent need of cash and that if I could pay her six months in advance she would reduce my rent by one fourth during that period, something of that kind. This had the advantage of saving six weeks' (?) rent and the disadvantage of almost exhausting my small capital. But could you call that a disadvantage? Wouldn't I stay on in any case till my last penny was gone, and even longer, till she put me out? I gave her the money and she gave me a receipt.

One morning, not long after this transaction, I was awakened by a man shaking my shoulder. It could not have been much past eleven. He requested me to get up and leave his house immediately. He was most correct, I must say. His surprise, he said, was no less than mine. It was his house. His property. The Turkish woman had left the day before. But I saw her last night, I said. You must be mistaken, he said, for she brought the keys to my office no later than yesterday afternoon. But I just paid her six months' rent in advance, I said. Get a refund, he said. But I don't even know her name, I said, let alone her address. You don't know her name? he said. He must have thought I was lying. I'm sick, I said, I can't leave like this, without any notice. You're not so sick as all that, he said. He offered to send for a taxi, even an ambulance if I preferred. He said he needed the room immediately for his pig which even as he spoke was catching cold in a cart before the door and no one to look after him but a stray urchin whom he had never set eyes on before and who was probably busy tormenting him. I asked if he couldn't let me have another place, any old corner where I could lie down long enough to recover from the shock and decide what to do. He said he could not. Don't think I'm being unkind, he added. I could live here with the pig, I said, I'd look after him. The long months of peace, wiped out in an instant! Come now, come now, he said, get a grip on yourself, be a man, get up, that's enough. After all it was no concern of his. He had really been most patient. He must have visited the basement while I was sleeping.

I felt weak. Perhaps I was. I stumbled in the blinding light. A bus took me into the country. I sat down in a field in the sun. But it seems to me that was much later. I stuck leaves under my hat, all the way round, to make a shade. The night was cold. I wandered for hours in the fields. At last I found a heap of dung. The next day I started back to the city. They made me get off three buses. I sat down by the roadside and dried my clothes in the sun. I enjoyed doing that. I said to myself, There's nothing more to be done now, not a thing, till they are dry. When they were dry I brushed them with a brush, I think a kind of curry-comb, that I found in a stable. Stables have always been my salvation. Then I went to the house and begged a glass of milk and a slice of bread and butter. They gave me everything except the butter. May I rest in the stable? I said. No, they said. I still stank, but with a stink that pleased me. I much preferred it to my own which moreover it prevented me from smelling, except a waft now and then. In the days that followed I took the necessary steps to recover my money. I don't know exactly what happened, whether I couldn't find the address, or whether there was no such address, or whether the Greek woman was unknown there. I ransacked my pockets for the receipt, to try and decipher the name. It wasn't there. Perhaps she had taken it back while I was sleeping. I don't know how long I wandered thus, resting now in one place, now in another, in the city and in the country. The city had suffered many changes. Nor was the country as I remembered it. The general effect was the same. One day I caught sight of my son. He was striding along with a briefcase under his arm. He took off his hat and bowed and I saw he was as bald as a coot. I was almost certain it was he. I turned round to gaze after him. He went bustling along on his duck feet, bowing and scraping and flourishing his hat left and right. The insufferable son of a bitch.

One day I met a man I had known in former times. He lived in a cave by the sea. He had an ass that grazed winter and summer, over the cliffs, or along the little tracks leading down to the sea. When the weather was very bad this ass came down to the cave of his own accord and sheltered there till the storm was past. So they had spent many a night huddled together, while the wind howled and the sea pounded on the shore. With the help of this ass he could deliver sand, sea-wrack, and shells to the townsfolk, for their gardens. He couldn't carry much at a time, for the ass was old and small and the town was far. But in this way he earned a little money, enough to keep him in tobacco and matches and to buy a piece of bread from time to time. It was during one of these excursions that he met me, in the suburbs. He was delighted to see me, poor man. He begged me to go home with him and spend the night. Stay as long as you like, he said. What's wrong with your ass? I said. Don't mind him, he said, he doesn't know you. I reminded him that I wasn't in the habit of staying more than two or three minutes with anyone and that the sea did not agree with me. He seemed deeply grieved to hear it. So you won't come, he said. But to my amazement I got up on the ass and off we went, in the shade of the red chestnuts springing from the sidewalk. I held the ass by the mane, one hand in front of the other. The little boys jeered and threw stones, but their aim was poor, for they only hit me once, on the hat. A policeman stopped us and accused us of disturbing the peace. My friend replied that we were as nature had made us, the boys too were as nature had made them. It was inevitable, under these conditions, that the peace should be disturbed from time to time. Let us continue on our way, he said, and order will soon be restored throughout your beat. We followed the quiet, dustwhite inland roads with their hedges of hawthorn and fuchsia and their footpaths fringed with wild grass and daisies. Night fell. The ass carried me right to the mouth of the cave, for in the dark I could not have found my way down the path winding steeply to the sea. Then he climbed back to his pasture.

I don't know how long I stayed there. The cave was nicely arranged, I must say. I treated my crablice with salt water and seaweed, but a lot of nits must have survived. I put compresses of seaweed on my skull, which gave me great relief, but not for long. I lay in the cave and sometimes looked out at the horizon. I saw above me a vast trembling expanse without islands or promontories. At night a light shone into the cave at regular intervals. It was here I found the phial in my pocket. It was not broken, for the glass was not real glass. I thought Mr. Weir had confiscated all my belongings. My host was out most of the time. He fed me on fish. It is easy for a man, a proper man, to live in a cave, far from everybody. He invited me to stay as long as I liked. If I preferred to be alone he would gladly prepare another cave for me further on. He would bring me food every day and drop in from time to time to make sure I was all right and needed nothing. He was kind. Unfortunately I did not need kindness. You wouldn't know of a lake dwelling? I said. I couldn't bear the sea, its splashing and heaving, its tides and general convulsiveness. The wind at least sometimes stops. My hands and feet felt as though they were full of ants. This kept me awake for hours on end. If I stayed here something awful would happen to me, I said, and a lot of good that would do me. You'd get drowned, he said. Yes, I said, or jump off the cliff. And to think I couldn't live anywhere else, he said, in my cabin in the mountains I was wretched. Your cabin in the mountains? I said. He repeated the story of his cabin in the mountains, I had forgotten it, it was as though I were hearing it for the first time. I asked him if he still had it. He replied he had not seen it since the day he fled from it, but that he believed it was still there, a little decayed no doubt. But when he urged me to take the key I refused, saying I had other plans. You will always find me here, he said, if you ever need me. Ah people. He gave me his knife.

What he called his cabin in the mountains was a sort of wooden shed. The door had been removed, for firewood, or for some other purpose. The glass had disappeared from the window. The roof had fallen in at several places. The interior was divided, by the remains of a partition, into two unequal parts. If there had been any furniture it was gone. The vilest acts had been committed on the ground and against the walls. The floor was strewn with excrements, both human and animal, with condoms and vomit. In a cowpad a heart had been traced, pierced by an arrow. And yet there was nothing to attract tourists. I noticed the remains of abandoned nosegays. They had been greedily gathered, carried for miles, then thrown away, because they were cumbersome or already withered. This was the dwelling to which I had been offered the key.

The scene was the familiar one of grandeur and desolation.

Nevertheless it was a roof over my head. I rested on a bed of ferns, gathered at great labour with my own hands. One day I couldn't get up. The cow saved me. Goaded by the icy mist she came in search of shelter. It was probably not the first time. She can't have seen me. I tried to suck her, without much success. Her udder was covered with dung. I took off my hat and, summoning all my energy, began to milk her into it. The milk fell to the ground and was lost, but I said to myself, No matter, it's free. She dragged me across the floor, stopping from time to time only to kick me. I didn't know our cows too could be so inhuman. She must have recently been milked. Clutching the dug with one hand I kept my hat under it with the other. But in the end she prevailed. For she dragged me across the threshold and out into the giant streaming ferns, where I was forced to let go.

As I drank the milk I reproached myself with what I had done. I could no longer count on this cow and she would warn the others. More master of myself I might have made a friend of her. She would have come every day, perhaps accompanied by other cows. I might have learnt to make butter, even cheese. But I said to myself, No, all is for the best.

Once on the road it was all downhill. Soon there were carts, but they all refused to take me up. In other clothes, with another face, they might have taken me up. I must have changed since my expulsion from the basement. The face notably seemed to have attained its climacteric. The humble, ingenuous smile would no longer come, nor the expression of candid misery, showing the stars and the distaff. I summoned them, but they would not come. A mask of dirty old hairy leather, with two holes and a slit, it was too far gone for the old trick of please your honour and God reward you and pity upon me. It was disastrous. What would I crawl with in future? I lay down on the side of the road and began to writhe each time I heard a cart approaching. That was so they would not think I was sleeping or resting. I tried to groan, Help! Help! But the tone that came out was that of polite conversation. My hour was not yet come and I could no longer groan. The last time I had cause to groan I had groaned as well as ever, and no heart within miles of me to melt. What was to become of me? I said to myself, I'll learn again. I lay down across the road at a narrow place, so that the carts could not pass without passing over my body, with one wheel at least, or two if there were four. But the day came when, looking round me, I was in the suburbs, and from there to the old haunts it was not far, beyond the stupid hope of rest or less pain.

So I covered the lower part of my face with a black rag and went and begged at a sunny corner. For it seemed to me my eyes were not completely spent, thanks perhaps to the dark glasses my tutor had given me. He had given me the *Ethics* of Geulincx. They were a man's glasses, I was a child. They found him dead, crumpled up in the water closet, his clothes in awful disorder, struck down by an infarctus. Ah what peace. The *Ethics* had his name (Ward) on the fly-leaf, the glasses had belonged to him. The bridge, at the time I am speaking of, was of brass wire, of the kind used to hang pictures and big mirrors, and two long black ribbons served as wings. I wound them round my ears and then down under my chin where I tied them together. The lenses had suffered, from rubbing in my pocket against each other and against the other objects there. I thought Mr. Weir had confiscated all my belongings. But I had no further need of these glasses and used them merely to soften the glare of the sun. I should never have mentioned them. The rag gave me a lot of trouble. I got it in the end from the lining of my greatcoat, no, I had no greatcoat now, of my coat then. The result was a grey rag rather than a black, perhaps even chequered, but I had to make do with it. Till afternoon I held my face raised towards the southern sky, then towards the western till night. The bowl gave me a lot of trouble. I couldn't use my hat because of my skull. As for holding out my hand, that was quite out of the question. So I got a tin and hung it from a button of my greatcoat, what's the matter with me, of my coat, at pubis level. It did not hang plumb, it leaned respectfully towards the passer-by, he had only to drop his mite. But that obliged him to come up close to me, he was in danger of touching me. In the end I got a bigger tin, a kind of big tin box, and I placed it on the sidewalk at my feet. But people who give alms don't much care to toss them, there's something contemptuous about this gesture which is repugnant to sensitive natures. To say nothing of their having to aim. They are prepared to give, but not for their gift to go rolling under the passing feet or under the passing wheels, to be picked up perhaps by some undeserving person. So they don't give. There are those, to be sure, who stoop, but generally speaking people who give alms don't much care to stoop. What they like above all is to sight the wretch from afar, get ready their penny, drop it in their stride and hear the God bless you dying away in the distance. Personally I never said that, nor anything like it, I wasn't much of a believer, but I did make a noise with my mouth. In the end I got a kind of board or tray and tied it to my neck and waist. It jutted out just at the right height, pocket height, and its edge was far enough from my person for the coin to be bestowed without danger. Some days I strewed it with flowers, petals, buds and that herb which men call fleabane, I believe, in a word whatever I could find. I didn't go out of my way to look for them, but all the pretty things of this description that came my way were for the board. They must have thought I loved nature. Most of the time I looked up at the sky, but without focussing it, for why focus it? Most of the time it was a mixture of white, blue and grey, and then at evening all the evening colours. I felt it weighing softly on my face, I rubbed my face against it, one cheek after the other, turning my head from side to side. Now and then to rest my neck I dropped my head on my chest. Then I could see the board in the distance, a haze of many colours. I leaned against the wall, but without nonchalance, I shifted my weight from one foot to the other and my hands clutched the lapels of my coat. To beg with your hands in your pockets makes a bad impression, it irritates the workers, especially in winter. You should never wear gloves either. There were guttersnipes who swept away all I had earned, under cover of giving me a coin. It was to buy sweets. I unbuttoned my trousers discreetly to scratch myself. I scratched myself in an upward direction, with four nails. I pulled on the hairs, to get relief. It passed the time, time flew when I scratched myself. Real scratching is superior to masturbation, in my opinion. One can masturbate up to the age of seventy, and even beyond, but in the end it becomes a mere habit. Whereas to scratch myself properly I would have needed a dozen hands. I itched all over, on the privates, in the bush up to the navel, under the arms, in the arse, and then patches of eczema and psoriasis that I could set raging merely by thinking of them. It was in the arse I had the most pleasure. I stuck my forefinger up to the knuckle. Later, if I had to shit, the pain was atrocious. But I hardly shat any more. Now and then a flying machine flew by, sluggishly it seemed to me. Often at the end of the day I discovered the legs of my trousers all wet. That must have been the dogs. I personally pissed very little. If by chance the need came on me a little squirt in my fly was enough to relieve it. Once at my post I did not leave it till nightfall. I had no appetite, God tempered the wind to me. After work I bought a bottle of milk and drank it in the evening in the shed. Better still, I got a little boy to buy it for me, always the same, they wouldn't serve me, I don't know why. I gave him a penny for his pains. One day I witnessed a strange scene. Normally I didn't see a great deal. I didn't hear a great deal either. I didn't pay attention. Strictly speaking I wasn't there. Strictly speaking I believe I've never been anywhere. But that day I must have come back. For some time past a sound had been scarifying me. I did not investigate the cause, for I said to myself, It's going to stop. But as it did not stop I had no choice but to find out the cause. It was a man perched on the roof of a car and haranguing the passers-by. That at least was my interpretation. He was bellowing so loud that snatches of his discourse reached my ears. Union . . . brothers . . . Marx . . . capital . . . bread and butter . . . love. It was all Greek to me. The car was drawn up against the kerb, just in front of me, I saw the orator from behind. All of a sudden he turned and pointed at me, as at an exhibit. Look at this down and out, he vociferated, this leftover. If he doesn't go down on all fours, it's for fear of being impounded. Old, lousy, rotten, ripe for the muckheap. And there are a thousand like him, worse than him, ten thousand, twenty thousand—. A voice, Thirty thousand. Every day you pass them by, resumed the orator, and when you have backed a winner you fling them a farthing. Do you ever think? The voice, God forbid. A penny, resumed the orator, tup-pence—. The voice, Thruppence. It never enters your head, resumed the orator, that your charity is a crime, an incentive to slavery, stultification and organized murder. Take a good look at this living corpse. You may say it's his own fault. Ask him if it's his own fault. The voice, Ask him yourself. Then he bent forward and took me to task. I had perfected my board. It now consisted of two boards hinged together, which enabled me, when my work was done, to fold it and carry it under my arm. I liked doing little odd jobs. So I took off the rag, pocketed the few coins I had earned, untied the board, folded it and put it under my arm. Do you hear me, you crucified bastard! cried the orator. Then I went away, although it was still light. But generally speaking it was a quiet corner, busy but not overcrowded, thriving and well-frequented. He must have been a religious fanatic, I could find no other explanation. Perhaps he was an escaped lunatic. He had a nice face, a little on the red side.

I did not work every day. I had practically no expenses. I even managed to put a little aside, for my very last days. The days I did not work I spent lying in the shed. The shed was on a private estate, or what had once been a private estate, on the riverside. This estate, the main entrance to which opened on a narrow, dark and silent street, was enclosed with a wall, except of course on the river front, which marked its northern boundary for a distance of about thirty yards. From the last quays beyond the water the eyes rose to a confusion of low houses, wasteland, hoardings, chimneys, steeples and towers. A kind of parade ground was also to be seen, where soldiers played football all the year round. Only the ground-floor windows—no, I can't. The estate seemed abandoned. The gates were locked and the paths were overgrown with grass. Only the ground-floor windows had shutters. The others were sometimes lit at night, faintly, now one, now another. At least that was my impression. Perhaps it was reflected light. In this shed, the day I adopted it, I found a boat, upside down. I righted it, chocked it up with stones and pieces of wood, took out the thwarts and made my bed inside. The rats had difficulty in getting at me, because of the bulge of the hull. And yet they longed to. Just think of it, living flesh, for in spite of everything I was still living flesh. I had lived too long among rats, in my chance dwellings, to share the dread they inspire in the vulgar. I even had a soft spot in my heart for them. They came with such confidence towards me, it seemed without the least repugnance. They made their toilet with catlike gestures. Toads at evening, motionless for hours, lap flies from the air. They like to squat where cover ends and open air begins, they favour thresholds. But I had to contend now with water rats, exceptionally lean and ferocious. So I made a kind of lid with stray boards. It's incredible the number of boards I've come across in my lifetime, I never needed a board but there it was, I had only to stoop and pick it up. I liked doing little odd jobs, no, not particularly, I didn't mind. It completely covered the boat, I'm referring again to the lid. I pushed it a little towards the stern, climbed into the boat by the bow, crawled to the stern, raised my feet and pushed the lid back towards the bow till it covered me completely. But what did my feet push against? They pushed against a cross bar I nailed to the lid for that purpose, I liked these little odd jobs. But it was better to climb into the boat by the stern and pull back the lid with my hands till it completely covered me, then push it forward in the same way when I wanted to get out. As holds for my hands I planted two spikes just where I needed them. These little odds and ends of carpentry, if I may so describe it, carried out with whatever tools and material I chanced to find, gave me a certain pleasure. I knew it would soon be the end, so I played the part, you know, the part of—how shall I say, I don't know. I was comfortable enough in this boat, I must say. The lid fitted so well I had to pierce a hole. It's no good closing your eyes, you must leave them open in the dark, that is my opinion. I am not speaking of sleep, I am speaking of what I believe is called waking. In any case, I slept very little at this period, I wasn't sleepy, or I was too sleepy, I don't know, or I was afraid, I don't know. Flat then on my back I saw nothing except, dimly, just above my head, through the tiny chinks, the grey light of the shed. To see nothing at all, no, that's too much. I heard faintly the cries of the gulls ravening about the mouth of the sewer near by. In a spew of yellow foam, if my memory serves me right, the filth gushed into the river and the slush of birds above screaming with hunger and fury. I heard the lapping of water against the slip and against the bank and the other sound, so different, of open wave, I heard it too. I too, when I moved, felt less boat than wave, or so it seemed to me, and my stillness was the stillness of eddies. That may seem impossible. The rain too, I often heard it, for it often rained. Sometimes a drop, falling through the roof of the shed, exploded on me. All that composed a rather liquid world. And then of course there was the voice of the wind or rather those, so various, of its playthings. But what does it amount to? Howling, soughing, moaning, sighing. What I would have liked was hammer strokes, bang bang bang, clanging in the desert. I let farts to be sure, but hardly ever a real crack, they oozed out with a sucking noise, melted in the mighty never. I don't know how long I stayed there. I was very snug in my box, I must say. It seemed to me I had grown more independent of recent years. That no one came any more, that no one could come any more to ask me if I was all right and needed nothing, distressed me then but little. I was all right, yes, quite so, and the fear of getting worse was less with me. As for my needs, they had dwindled as it were to my dimensions and become, if I may say so, of so exquisite a quality as to exclude all thought of succour. To know I had a being, however faint and false, outside of me, had once had the power to stir my heart. You become unsociable, it's inevitable. It's enough to make you wonder sometimes if you are on the right planet. Even the words desert you, it's as bad as that. Perhaps it's the moment when the vessels stop communicating, you know, the vessels. There you are still between the two murmurs, it must be the same old song as ever, but Christ you wouldn't think so. There were times when I wanted to push away the lid and get out of the boat and couldn't, I was so indolent and weak, so content deep down where I was. I felt them hard upon me, the icy, tumultuous streets, the terrifying faces, the noises that slash, pierce, claw, bruise. So I waited till the desire to shit, or even to piss, lent me wings. I did not want to dirty my nest! And yet it sometimes happened, and even more and more often. Arched and rigid I edged down my trousers and turned a little on my side, just enough to free the hole. To contrive a little kingdom, in the midst of the universal muck, then shit on it, ah that was me all over. The excrements were me too, I know, I know, but all the same. Enough, enough, the next thing I was having visions, I who never did, except sometimes in my sleep, who never had, real visions, I'd remember, except perhaps as a child, my myth will have it so. I knew they were visions because it was night and I was alone in my boat. What else could they have been? So I was in my boat and gliding on the waters. I didn't have to row, the ebb was carrying me out. Anyway I saw no oars, they must have taken them away. I had a board, the remains of a thwart perhaps, which I used when I came too close to the bank, or when a pier came bearing down on me or a barge at its moorings. There were stars in the sky, quite a few. I didn't know what the weather was doing, I was neither cold nor warm and all seemed calm. The banks receded more and more, it was inevitable, soon I saw them no more. The lights grew fainter and fewer as the river widened. There on the land men were sleeping, bodies were gathering strength for the toil and joys of the morrow. The boat was not gliding now, it was tossing, buffeted by the choppy waters of the bay. All seemed calm and yet foam was washing aboard. Now the sea air was all about me, I had no other shelter than the land, and what does it amount to, the shelter of the land, at such a time. I saw the beacons, four in all, including a lightship. I knew them well, even as a child I had known them well. It was evening, I was with my father on a height, he held my hand. I would have liked him to draw me close with a gesture of protective love, but his mind was on other things. He also taught me the names of the mountains. But to have done with these visions I also saw the lights of the buoys, the sea seemed full of them, red and green, and to my surprise even yellow. And on the slopes of the mountain, now rearing its unbroken bulk behind the town, the fires turned from gold to red, from red to gold. I knew what it was, it was the gorse burning. How often I had set a match to it myself, as a child. And hours later, back in my home, before I climbed into bed, I watched from my high window the fires I had lit. That night then, all aglow with distant fires, on sea, on land and in the sky, I drifted with the currents and the tides. I noticed that my hat was tied, with a string I suppose, to my buttonhole. I got up from my seat in the stern and a great clanking was heard. That was the chain. One end was fastened to the bow and the other round my waist. I must have pierced a hole beforehand in the floor-boards, for there I was down on my knees prying out the plug with my knife. The hole was small and the water rose slowly. It would take a good half hour, everything included, barring accidents. Back now in the stern-sheets, my legs stretched out, my back well propped against the sack stuffed with grass I used as a cushion, I swallowed my calmative. The sea, the sky, the mountains and the islands closed in and crushed me in a mighty systole, then scattered to the uttermost confines of space. The memory came faint and cold of the story I might have told, a story in the likeness of my life, I mean without the courage to end or the strength to go on.

Translated by Richard Seaver in collaboration with the author

Texts for Nothing

1

SUDDENLY, NO, AT LAST, long last, I couldn't any more, I couldn't go on. Someone said, You can't stay here. I couldn't stay there and I couldn't go on. I'll describe the place, that's unimportant. The top, very flat, of a mountain, no, a hill, but so wild, so wild, enough. Quag, heath up to the knees, faint sheep-tracks, troughs scooped deep by the rains. It was far down in one of these I was lying, out of the wind. Glorious prospect, but for the mist that blotted out everything, valleys, loughs, plain and sea. How can I go on, I shouldn't have begun, no, I had to begin. Someone said, perhaps the same, What possessed you to come? I could have stayed in my den, snug and dry, I couldn't. My den, I'll describe it, no, I can't. It's simple, I can do nothing any more, that's what you think. I say to the body, Up with you now, and I can feel it struggling, like an old hack foundered in the street, struggling no more, struggling again, till it gives up. I say to the head, Leave it alone, stay quiet, it stops breathing, then pants on worse than ever. I am far from all that wrangle, I shouldn't bother with it, I need nothing, neither to go on nor to stay where I am, it's truly all one to me, I should turn away from it all, away from the body, away from the head, let them work it out between them, let them cease, I can't, it's I would have to cease. Ah yes, we seem to be more than one, all deaf, not even, gathered together for life. Another said, or the same, or the first, they all have the same voice, the same ideas, All you had to do was stay at home. Home. They wanted me to go home. My dwelling-place. But for the mist, with good eyes, with a telescope, I could see it from here. It's not just tiredness, I'm not just tired, in spite of the climb. It's not that I want to stay here either. I had heard tell, I must have heard tell of the view, the distant sea in hammered lead, the so-called golden vale so often sung, the double valleys, the glacial loughs, the city in its haze, it was all on every tongue. Who are these people anyway? Did they follow me up here, go before me, come with me? I am down in the hole the centuries have dug, centuries of filthy weather, flat on my face on the dark earth sodden with the creeping saffron waters it slowly drinks. They are up above, all round me, as in a graveyard. I can't raise my eyes to them, what a pity, I wouldn't see their faces, their legs perhaps, plunged in the heath. Do they see me, what can they see of me? Perhaps there is no one left, perhaps they are all gone, sickened. I listen and it's the same thoughts I hear, I mean the same as ever, strange. To think in the valley the sun is blazing all down the ravelled sky. How long have I been here, what a question, I've often wondered. And often I could answer, An hour, a month, a year, a century, depending on what I meant by here, and me, and being, and there I never went looking for extravagant meanings, there I never much varied, only the here would sometimes seem to vary. Or I said, I can't have been here long, I wouldn't have held out. I hear the curlews, that means close of day, fall of night, for that's the way with curlews, silent all day, then crying when the darkness gathers, that's the way with those wild creatures and so short-lived, compared with me. And that other question I know so well too, What possessed you to come? unanswerable, so that I answered, To change, or, It's not me, or, Chance, or again, To see, or again, years of great sun, Fate, I feel that other coming, let it come, it won't catch me napping. All is noise, unending suck of black sopping peat, surge of giant ferns, heathery gulfs of quiet where the wind drowns, my life and its old jingles. To change, to see, no, there's no more to see, I've seen it all, till my eyes are blear, nor to get away from harm, the harm is done, one day the harm was done, the day my feet dragged me out that must go their ways, that I let go their ways and drag me here, that's what possessed me to come. And what I'm doing, all-important, breathing in and out and saying, with words like smoke, I can't go, I can't stay, let's see what happens next. And in the way of sensation? My God I can't complain, it's himself all right, only muffled, like buried in snow, less the warmth, less the drowse, I can follow them well, all the voices, all the parts, fairly well, the cold is eating me, the wet too, at least I presume so, I'm far. My rheumatism in any case is no more than a memory, it hurts me no more than my mother's did, when it hurt her. Eye ravening patient in the haggard vulture face, perhaps it's carrion time. I'm up there and I'm down here, under my gaze, foundered, eyes closed, ear cupped against the sucking peat, we're of one mind, all of one mind, always were, deep down, we're fond of one another, we're sorry for one another, but there it is, there's nothing we can do for one another. One thing at least is certain, in an hour it will be too late, in half-an-hour it will be night, and yet it's not, not certain, what is not certain, absolutely certain, that night prevents what day permits, for those who know how to go about it, who have the will to go about it, and the strength, the strength to try again. Yes, it will be night, the mist will clear, I know my mist, for all my distraction, the wind freshen and the whole night sky open over the mountain, with its lights, including the Bears, to guide me once again on my way, let's wait for night. All mingles, times and tenses, at first I only had been here, now I'm here still, soon I won't be here yet, toiling up the slope, or in the bracken by the wood, it's larch, I don't try to understand, I'll never try to understand any more, that's what you think, for the moment I'm here, always have been, always shall be, I won't be afraid of the big words any more, they are not big. I don't remember coming, I can't go, all my little company, my eyes are closed and I feel the wet humus harsh against my cheek, my hat is gone, it can't be gone far, or the wind has swept it away, I was attached to it. Sometimes it's the sea, other times the mountains, often it was the forest, the city, the plain too, I've flirted with the plain too, I've given myself up for dead all over the place, of hunger, of old age, murdered, drowned, and then for no reason, of tedium, nothing like breathing your last to put new life in you, and then the rooms, natural death, tucked up in bed, smothered in household gods, and always muttering, the same old mutterings, the same old stories, the same old questions and answers, no malice in me, hardly any, stultior stultissimo, never an imprecation, not such a fool, or else it's gone from mind. Yes, to the end, always muttering, to lull me and keep me company, and all ears always, all ears for the old stories, as when my father took me on his knee and read me the one about Joe Breem, or Breen, the son of a lighthouse keeper, evening after evening, all the long winter through. A tale, it was a tale for children, it all happened on a rock, in the storm, the mother was dead and the gulls came beating against the light, Joe jumped into the sea, that's all I remember, a knife between his teeth, did what was to be done and came back, that's all I remember this evening, it ended happily, it began unhappily and it ended happily, every evening, a comedy, for children. Yes, I was my father and I was my son, I asked myself questions and answered as best I could, I had it told to me evening after evening, the same old story I knew by heart and couldn't believe, or we walked together, hand in hand, silent, sunk in our worlds, each in his worlds, the hands forgotten in each other. That's how I've held out till now. And this evening again it seems to be working,

I'm in my arms, I'm holding myself in my arms, without much tenderness, but faithfully, faithfully. Sleep now, as under that ancient lamp, all twined together, tired out with so much talking, so much listening, so much toil and play.

Translated by the author

2

ABOVE IS THE LIGHT, the elements, a kind of light, sufficient to see by, the living find their ways, without too much trouble, avoid one another, unite, avoid the obstacles, without too much trouble, seek with their eyes, close their eyes, halting, without halting, among the elements, the living. Unless it has changed, unless it has ceased. The things too must still be there, a little more worn, a little even less, many still standing where they stood in the days of their indifference. Here you are under a different glass, not long habitable either, it's time to leave it. You are there, there it is, where you are will never long be habitable. Go then, no, better stay, for where would you go, now that you know? Back above? There are limits. Back in that kind of light. See the cliffs again, be again between the cliffs and the sea, reeling shrinking with your hands over your ears, headlong, innocent, suspect, noxious. Seek, by the excessive light of night, a demand commensurate with the offer, and go to ground empty-handed at the old crack of day. See Mother Calvet again, creaming off the garbage before the nightmen come. She must still be there. With her dog and her skeletal baby-buggy. What could be more endurable? She wavered through the night, a kind of trident in her hand, muttering and ejaculating, Your highness! Your honour! The dog tottered on its hind-legs begging, hooked its paws over the rim of the can and snouted round with her in the muck. It got in her way, she cursed it for a lousy cur and let it have its way. There's a good memory. Mother Calvet. She knew what she liked, perhaps even what she would have liked. And beauty, strength, intelligence, the latest, daily, action, poetry, all one price for one and all. If only it could be wiped from knowledge. To have suffered under that miserable light, what a blunder. It let nothing show, it would have gone out, nothing terrible, nothing showed, of the true affair, it would have snuffed out. And now here, what now here, one enormous second, as in Paradise, and the mind slow, slow, nearly stopped. And yet it's changing, something is changing, it must be in the head, slowly in the head the ragdoll rotting, perhaps we're in a head, it's as dark as in a head before the worms get at it, ivory dungeon. The words too, slow, slow, the subject dies before it comes to the verb, words are stopping too. Better off then than when life was babble? That's it, that's it, the bright side. And the absence of others, does that count for so little? Pah others, that's nothing, others never inconvenienced anyone, and there must be a few here too, other others, invisible, mute, what does it matter. It's true you hid from them, hugged their walls, true, you miss that here, you miss the derivatives, here it's pure ache, pah you were saying that above and you a living mustard-plaster. So long as the words keep coming nothing will have changed, there are the old words out again. Utter, there's nothing else, utter, void yourself of them, here as always, nothing else. But they are failing, true, that's the change, they are failing, that's bad, bad. Or it's the dread of coming to the last, of having said all, your all, before the end, no, for that will be the end, the end of all, not certain. To need to groan and not be able, Jesus, better ration yourself, watch out for the genuine death-pangs, some are deceptive, you think you're home, start howling and revive, health-giving howls, better be silent, it's the only method, if you want to end, not a word but smiles, end rent with stifled imprecations, burst with speechlessness, all is possible, what now? Perhaps above it's summer, a summer Sunday, Mr. Joly is in the belfry, he has wound up the clock, now he's ringing the bells. Mr. Joly. He had only one leg and a half. Sunday. It was folly to be abroad. The roads were crawling with them, the same roads so often kind. Here at least none of that, no talk of a creator and nothing very definite in the way of a creation. Dry, it's possible, or wet, or slime, as before matter took ill. Is this stuff air that permits you to suffocate still, almost audibly at times, it's possible, a kind of air. What exactly is going on, exactly, ah old xanthic laugh, no, farewell mirth, good riddance, it was never droll. No, but one more memory, one last memory, it may help, to abort again. Piers pricking his oxen o'er the plain, no, for at the end of the furrow, before turning to the next, he raised his eyes to the sky and said, Bright again too early. And sure enough, soon after, the snow. In other words the night was black, when it fell at last, but no, strange, it wasn't, in spite of the buried sky. The way was long that led back to the den, over the fields, a winding way, it must still be there. When it comes to the top of the cliff it springs, some might think blindly, but no, wilily, like a goat, in hairpin zigzags towards the shore. Never had the sea so thundered from afar, the sea beneath the snow, though superlatives have lost most of their charm. The day had not been fruitful, as was only natural, considering the season, that of the very last leeks. It was none the less the return, to what no matter, the return, unscathed, always a matter for wonder. What happened? Is that the question? An encounter? Bang! No. Level with the farm of the Graves brothers a brief halt, opposite the lamplit window. A glow, red, afar, at night, in winter, that's worth having, that must have been worth having. There, it's done, it ends there, I end there. A far memory, far from the last, it's possible, the legs seem to be still working. A pity hope is dead. No. How one hoped above, on and off. With what diversity.

Translated by the author

3

LEAVE, I was going to say leave all that. What matter who's speaking, someone said what matter who's speaking. There's going to be a departure, I'll be there, I won't miss it, it won't be me, I'll be here, I'll say I'm far from here, it won't be me, I won't say anything, there's going to be a story, someone's going to try and tell a story. Yes, no more denials, all is false, there is no one, it's understood, there is nothing, no more phrases, let us be dupes, dupes of every time and tense, until it's done, all past and done, and the voices cease, it's only voices, only lies. Here, depart from here and go elsewhere, or stay here, but coming and going. Start by stirring, there must be a body, as of old, I don't deny it, no more denials, I'll say I'm a body, stirring back and forth, up and down, as required. With a cluther of limbs and organs, all that is needed to live again, to hold out a little time, I'll call that living, I'll say it's me, I'll get standing, I'll stop thinking, I'll be too busy, getting standing, staying standing, stirring about, holding out, getting to tomorrow, tomorrow week, that will be ample, a week will be ample, a week in spring, that puts the jizz in you. It's enough to will it, I'll will it, will me a body, will me a head, a little strength, a little courage, I'm starting now, a week is soon served, then back here, this inextricable place, far from the days, the far days, it's not going to be easy. And why, come to think, no no, leave it, no more of that, don't listen to it all, don't say it all, it's all old, all one, once and for all. There you are now on your feet, I give you my word, I swear they're yours, I swear it's mine, get to work with your hands, palp your skull, seat of the understanding, without which nix, then the rest, the lower regions, you'll be needing them, and say what you're like, have a guess, what kind of man, there has to be a man, or a woman, feel between your legs, no need of beauty, nor of vigour, a week's a short stretch, no one's going to love you, don't be alarmed. No, not like that, too sudden, I gave myself a start. And to start with stop palpitating, no one's going to kill you, no one's going to love you and no one's going to kill you, perhaps you'll emerge in the high depression of Gobi, you'll feel at home there. I'll wait for you here, no, I'm alone, I alone am, this time it's I must go. I know how I'll do it, I'll be a man, there's nothing else for it, a kind of man, a kind of old tot, I'll have a nanny, I'll be her sweet pet, she'll give me her hand, to cross over, she'll let me loose in the Green, I'll be good, I'll sit quiet as a mouse in a corner and comb my beard, I'll tease it out, to look more bonny, a little more bonny, if only it could be like that. She'll say to me, Come, doty, it's time for bye-bye. I'll have no responsibility, she'll have all the responsibility, her name will be Bibby, I'll call her Bibby, if only it could be like that. Come, ducky, it's time for yum-yum. Who taught me all I know, I alone, in the old wanderyears, I deduced it all from nature, with the help of an all-in-one, I know it's not me, but it's too late now, too late to deny it, the knowledge is there, the bits and scraps, flickering on and off, turn about, winking on the storm, in league to fool me. Leave it and go, it's time to go, to say so anyway, the moment has come, it's not known why. What matter how you describe yourself, here or elsewhere, fixed or mobile, without form or oblong like man, in the dark or the light of the heavens, I don't know, it seems to matter, it's not going to be easy. And if I went back to where all went out and on from there, no, that would lead nowhere, never led anywhere, the memory of it has gone out too, a great flame and then blackness, a great spasm and then no more weight or traversable space. I tried throwing me off a cliff, collapsing in the street in the midst of mortals, that led nowhere, I gave up. Take the road again that cast me up here, then retrace it, or follow it on, wise advice. That's so that I'll never stir again, dribble on here till time is done, murmuring every ten centuries, It's not me, it's not true, it's not me, I'm far. No no, I'll speak now of the future, I'll speak in the future, as when I used to say, in the night, to myself, Tomorrow I'll put on my dark blue tie, with the yellow stars, and put it on, when night was past. Quick quick before I weep. I'll have a crony, my own vintage, my own bog, a fellow warrior, we'll relive our campaigns and compare our scratches. Quick quick. He'll have served in the navy, perhaps under Jellicoe, while I was potting at the invader from behind a barrel of Guinness, with my arquebuse. We have not long, that's the spirit, in the present, not long to live, it's our positively last winter, halleluiah. We wonder what will carry us off in the end. He's gone in the wind, I in the prostate rather. We envy each other, I envy him, he envies me, occasionally. I catheterize myself, unaided, with trembling hand, bent double in the public pisshouse, under cover of my cloak, people take me for a dirty old man. He waits for me to finish, sitting on a bench, coughing up his guts, spitting into a snuffbox which no sooner overflows than he empties it in the canal, out of civic-mindedness. We have well deserved of our motherland, she'll get us into the Incurables before we die. We spend our life, it's ours, trying to bring together in the same instant a ray of sunshine and a free bench, in some oasis of public verdure, we've been seized by a love of nature, in our sere and yellow, it belongs to one and all, in places. In a choking murmur he reads out to me from the paper of the day before, he had far far better been the blind one. The sport of kings is our passion, the dogs too, we have no political opinions, simply limply republican. But we also have a soft spot for the Windsors, the Hanoverians, I forget, the Hohenzollerns is it. Nothing human is foreign to us, once we have digested the racing news. No, alone, I'd be better off alone, it would be quicker. He'd nourish me, he had a friend a pork-butcher, he'd ram the ghost back down my gullet with black pudding. With his consolations, allusions to cancer, recollections of imperishable raptures, he'd prevent discouragement from sapping my foundations. And I, instead of concentrating on my own horizons, which might have enabled me to throw them under a lorry, would let my mind be taken off them by his. I'd say to him, Come on, gunner, leave all that, think no more about it, and it's I would think no more about it, besotted with brotherliness. And the obligations! I have in mind particularly the appointments at ten in the morning, hail rain or shine, in front of Duggan's, thronged already with sporting men fevering to get their bets out of harm's way before the bars open. We were, there we are past and gone again, so much the better, so much the better, most punctual I must say. To see the remains of Vincent arriving in sheets of rain, with the brave involuntary swagger of the old tar, his head swathed in a bloody clout and a glitter in his eye, was for the acute observer an example of what man is capable of, in his pursuit of pleasure. With one hand he sustained his sternum, with the heel of the other his spinal column, as if tempted to break into a hornpipe, no, that's all memories, last shifts older than the flood. See what's happening here, where there's no one, where nothing happens, get something to happen here, someone to be here, then put an end to it, have silence, get into silence, or another sound, a sound of other voices than those of life and death, of lives and deaths everyone's but mine, get into my story in order to get out of it, no, that's all meaningless. Is it possible

I'll sprout a head at last, all my very own, in which to brew poisons worthy of me, and legs to kick my heels with, I'd be there at last, I could go at last, it's all I ask, no, I can't ask anything. Just the head and the two legs, or one, in the middle, I'd go hopping. Or just the head, nice and round, nice and smooth, no need of lineaments, I'd go rolling, downhill, almost a pure spirit, no, that wouldn't work, all is uphill from here, the leg is unavoidable, or the equivalent, perhaps a few annular joints, contractile, great ground to be covered with them. To set out from Duggan's door, on a spring morning of rain and shine, not knowing if you'll ever get to evening, what's wrong with that? It would be so easy. To be bedded in that flesh or in another, in that arm held by a friendly hand, and in that hand, without arms, without hands, and without soul in those trembling souls, through the crowd, the hoops, the toy balloons, what's wrong with that? I don't know, I'm here, that's all I know, and that it's still not me, it's of that the best has to be made. There is no flesh anywhere, nor any way to die. Leave all that, to want to leave all that, not knowing what that means, all that, it's soon said, soon done, in vain, nothing has stirred, no one has spoken. Here, nothing will happen here, no one will be here, for many a long day. Departures, stories, they are not for tomorrow. And the voices, wherever they come from, have no life in them.

Translated by the author

4

WHERE WOULD I GO, if I could go, who would I be, if I could be, what would I say, if I had a voice, who says this, saying it's me? Answer simply, someone answer simply. It's the same old stranger as ever, for whom alone accusative I exist, in the pit of my inexistence, of his, of ours, there's a simple answer. It's not with thinking he'll find me, but what is he to do, living and bewildered, yes, living, say what he may. Forget me, know me not, yes, that would be the wisest, none better able than he. Why this sudden affability after such desertion, it's easy to understand, that's what he says, but he doesn't understand. I'm not in his head, nowhere in his old body, and yet I'm there, for him I'm there, with him, hence all the confusion. That should have been enough for him, to have found me absent, but it's not, he wants me there, with a form and a world, like him, in spite of him, me who am everything, like him who is nothing. And when he feels me void of existence it's of his he would have me void, and vice versa, mad, mad, he's mad. The truth is he's looking for me to kill me, to have me dead like him, dead like the living. He knows all that, but it's no help his knowing it, I don't know it, I know nothing. He protests he doesn't reason and does nothing but reason, crooked, as if that could improve matters. He thinks words fail him, he thinks because words fail him he's on his way to my speechlessness, to being speechless with my speechlessness, he would like it to be my fault that words fail him, of course words fail him. He tells his story every five minutes, saying it is not his, there's cleverness for you. He would like it to be my fault that he has no story, of course he has no story, that's no reason for trying to foist one on me. That's how he reasons, wide of the mark, but wide of what mark, answer us that. He has me say things saying it's not me, there's profundity for you, he has me who say nothing say it's not me. All that is truly crass. If at least he would dignify me with the third person, like his other figments, not he, he'll be satisfied with nothing less than me, for his me. When he had me, when he was me, he couldn't get rid of me quick enough, I didn't exist, he couldn't have that, that was no kind of life, of course I didn't exist, any more than he did, of course it was no kind of life, now he has it, his kind of life, let him lose it, if he wants to be in peace, with a bit of luck. His life, what a mine, what a life, he can't have that, you can't fool him, ergo it's not his, it's not him, what a thought, treat him like that, like a vulgar Molloy, a common Malone, those mere mortals, happy mortals, have a heart, land him in that shit, who never stirred, who is none but me, all things considered, and what things, and how considered, he had only to keep out of it. That's how he speaks, this evening, how he has me speak, how he speaks to himself, how I speak, there is only me, this evening, here, on earth, and a voice that makes no sound because it goes towards none, and a head strewn with arms laid down and corpses fighting fresh, and a body, I nearly forgot. This evening, I say this evening, perhaps it's morning. And all these things, what things, all about me, I won't deny them any more, there's no sense in that any more. If it's nature perhaps it's trees and birds, they go together, water and air, so that all may go on, I don't need to know the details, perhaps I'm sitting under a palm. Or it's a room, with furniture, all that's required to make life comfortable, dark, because of the wall outside the window. What am I doing, talking, having my figments talk, it can only be me. Spells of silence too, when I listen, and hear the local sounds, the world sounds, see what an effort I make, to be reasonable. There's my life, why not, it is one, if you like, if you must, I don't say no, this evening. There has to be one, it seems, once there is speech, no need of a story, a story is not compulsory, just a life, that's the mistake I made, one of the mistakes, to have wanted a story for myself, whereas life alone is enough. I'm making progress, it was time, I'll learn to keep my foul mouth shut before I'm done, if nothing foreseen crops up. But he who somehow comes and goes, unaided from place to place, even though nothing happens to him, true, what of him? I stay here, sitting, if I'm sitting, often I feel sitting, sometimes standing, it's one or the other, or lying down, there's another possibility, often I feel lying down, it's one of the three, or kneeling. What counts is to be in the world, the posture is immaterial, so long as one is on earth. To breathe is all that is required, there is no obligation to ramble, or receive company, you may even believe yourself dead on condition you make no bones about it, what more liberal regimen could be imagined, I don't know, I don't imagine. No point under such circumstances in saying I am somewhere else, someone else, such as I am I have all I need to hand, for to do what, I don't know, all I have to do, there I am on my own again at last, what a relief that must be. Yes, there are moments, like this moment, when I seem almost restored to the feasible. Then it goes, all goes, and I'm far again, with a far story again, I wait for me afar for my story to begin, to end, and again this voice cannot be mine. That's where I'd go, if I could go, that's who I'd be, if I could be.

Translated by the author

5

I'M THE CLERK, I'm the scribe, at the hearings of what cause I know not. Why want it to be mine, I don't want it. There it goes again, that's the first question this evening. To be judge and party, witness and advocate, and he, attentive, indifferent, who sits and notes. It's an image, in my helpless head, where all sleeps, all is dead, not yet born, I don't know, or before my eyes, they see the scene, the lids flicker and it's in. An instant and then they close again, to look inside the head, to try and see inside, to look for me there, to look for someone there, in the silence of quite a different justice, in the toils of that obscure assize where to be is to be guilty. That is why nothing appears, all is silent, one is frightened to be born, no, one wishes one were, so as to begin to die. One, meaning me, it's not the same thing, in the dark where I will in vain to see there can't be any willing. I could get up, take a little turn, I long to, but I won't. I know where I'd go, I'd go into the forest, I'd try and reach the forest, unless that's where I am, I don't know where I am, in any case I stay. I see what it is, I seek to be like the one I seek, in my head, that my head seeks, that I bid my head seek, with its probes, within itself. No, don't pretend to seek, don't pretend to think, just be vigilant, the eyes staring behind the lids, the ears straining for a voice not from without, were it only to sound an instant, to tell another lie. I hear, that must be the voice of reason again, that the vigil is in vain, that I'd be better advised to take a little turn, the way you manoeuvre a tin soldier. And no doubt it's the same voice answers that I can't, I who but a moment ago seemed to think I could, unless it's old shuttlecock sentiment chiming in, full stop, got all that. Why did Pozzo leave home, he had a castle and retainers. Insidious question, to remind me I'm in the dock. Sometimes I hear things that seem for a moment judicious, for a moment I'm sorry they are not mine. Then what a relief, what a relief to know I'm mute for ever, if only it didn't distress me. And deaf, it seems to me sometimes that deaf I'd be less distressed, at being mute, listen to that, what a relief not to have that on my conscience. Ah yes, I hear I have a kind of conscience, and on top of that a kind of sensibility, I trust the orator is not forgetting anything, and without ceasing to listen or drive the old quill I'm afflicted by them, I heard, it's noted. This evening the session is calm, there are long silences when all fix their eyes on me, that's to make me fly off my hinges, I feel on the brink of shrieks, it's noted. Out of the corner of my eye I observe the writing hand, all dimmed and blurred by the—by the reverse of farness. Who are all these people, gentlemen of the long robe, according to the image, but according to it alone, there are others, there will be others, other images, other gentlemen. Shall I never see the sky again, never be free again to come and go, in sunshine and in rain, the answer is no, all answer no, it's well I didn't ask anything, that's the kind of extravagance I envy them, till the echoes die away. The sky, I've heard—the sky and earth, I've heard great accounts of them, now that's pure word for word, I invent nothing. I've noted, I must have noted many a story with them as setting, they create the atmosphere. Between

them where the hero stands a great gulf is fixed, while all about
they flow together more and more, till they meet, so that he finds
himself as it were under glass, and yet with no limit to his movements in all directions, let him understand who can, that is no
part of my attributions. The sea too, I am conversant with the
sea too, it belongs to the same family, I have even gone to the
bottom more than once, under various assumed names, don't
make me laugh, if only I could laugh, all would vanish, all what,
who knows, all, me, it's noted. Yes, I see the scene, I see the
hand, it comes creeping out of shadow, the shadow of my head,
then scurries back, no connexion with me. Like a little creepy
crawly it ventures out an instant, then goes back in again, the
things one has to listen to, I say it as I hear it. It's the clerk's
hand, is he entitled to the wig, I don't know, formerly perhaps.
What do I do when silence falls, with rhetorical intent, or denot-
ing lassitude, perplexity, consternation, I rub to and fro against
my lips, where they meet, the first knuckle of my forefinger, but
it's the head that moves, the hand rests, it's to such details the
liar pins his hopes. That's the way this evening, tomorrow will
be different, perhaps I'll appear before the council, before the
justice of him who is all love, unforgiving and justly so, but subject to strange indulgences, the accused will be my soul, I prefer
that, perhaps someone will ask pity for my soul, I mustn't miss
that, I won't be there, neither will God, it doesn't matter, we'll be
represented. Yes, it can't be much longer now, I haven't been
damned for what seems an eternity, yes, but sufficient unto the
day, this evening I'm the scribe. This evening, it's always evening,
always spoken of as evening, even when it's morning, it's to make
me think night is at hand, bringer of rest. The first thing would
be to believe I'm there, if I could do that I'd lap up the rest,
there'd be none more credulous than me, if I were there. But I
am, it's not possible otherwise, just so, it's not possible, it

doesn't need to be possible. It's tiring, very tiring, in the same breath to win and lose, with concomitant emotions, one's heart is not of stone, to record the doom, don the black cap and collapse in the dock, very tiring, in the long run, I'm tired of it, I'd be tired of it, if I were me. It's a game, it's getting to be a game, I'm going to rise and go, if it's not me it will be someone, a phantom, long live all our phantoms, those of the dead, those of the living and those of those who are not born. I'll follow him, with my sealed eyes, he needs no door, needs no thought, to issue from this imaginary head, mingle with air and earth and dissolve, little by little, in exile. Now I'm haunted, let them go, one by one, let the last desert me and leave me empty, empty and silent. It's they murmur my name, speak to me of me, speak of a me, let them go and speak of it to others, who will not believe them either, or who will believe them too. Theirs all these voices, like a rattling of chains in my head, rattling to me that I have a head. That's where the court sits this evening, in the depths of that vaulty night, that's where I'm clerk and scribe, not understanding what I hear, not knowing what I write. That's where the council will be tomorrow, prayers will be offered for my soul, as for that of one dead, as for that of an infant dead in its dead mother, that it may not go to Limbo, sweet thing theology. It will be another evening, all happens at evening, but it will be the same night, it too has its evenings, its mornings and its evenings, there's a pretty conception, it's to make me think day is at hand, disperser of phantoms. And now birds, the first birds, what's this new trouble now, don't forget the question-mark. It must be the end of the session, it's been calm, on the whole. Yes, that's sometimes the way, there are suddenly birds and all goes silent, an instant. But the phantoms come back, it's in vain they go abroad, mingle with the dying, they come back and slip into the coffin, no bigger than a matchbox, it's they have taught me all I know, about things above, and all I'm said to know about me, they

want to create me, they want to make me, like the bird the birdi-
kin, with larvae she fetches from afar, at the peril—I nearly said
at the peril of her life! But sufficient unto the day, those are other
minutes. Yes, one begins to be very tired, very tired of one's toil,
very tired of one's quill, it falls, it's noted.

Translated by the author

6

HOW ARE THE INTERVALS filled between these apparitions? Do my keepers snatch a little rest and sleep before setting about me afresh, how would that be? That would be very natural, to enable them to get back their strength. Do they play cards, the odd rubber, bowls, to recruit their spirits, are they entitled to a little recreation? I would say no, if I had a say, no recreation, just a short break, with something cold, even though they should not feel inclined, in the interests of their health. They like their work, I feel it in my bones! No, I mean how filled for me, they don't come into this. Wretched acoustics this evening, the merest scraps, literally. The news, do you remember the news, the latest news, in slow letters of light, above Piccadilly Circus, in the fog? Where were you standing, in the doorway of the little tobacconist's closed for the night on the corner of Glasshouse Street was it, no, you don't remember, and for cause. Sometimes that's how it is, in a way, the eyes take over, and the silence, the sighs, like the sighs of sadness weary with crying, or old, that suddenly feels old and sighs for itself, for the happy days, the long days, when it cried it would never perish, but it's far from common, on the whole. My keepers, why keepers, I'm in no danger of stirring an inch, ah I see, it's to make me think I'm a prisoner, frantic with corporeality, rearing to get out and away. Other times it's male nurses, white from head to foot, even their shoes are white, and then it's another story, but the burden is the same. Other times it's like ghouls, naked and soft as worm, they grovel round me gloating on the corpse, but I have no more success dead than dying. Other times it's great clusters of bones, dangling and knocking with a clatter of castanets, it's clean and gay like coons, I'd join them with a will if it could be here and now, how is it nothing is ever here and now? It's varied, my life is varied, I'll never get anywhere. I know, there is no one here, neither me nor anyone else, but some things are better left unsaid, so I say nothing. Elsewhere perhaps, by all means, elsewhere, what elsewhere can there be to this infinite here? I know, if my head could think I'd find a way out, in my head, like so many others, and out of worse than this, the world would be there again, in my head, with me much as in the beginning. I would know that nothing had changed, that a little resolution is all that is needed to come and go under the changing sky, on the moving earth, as all along the long summer days too short for all the play, it was known as play, if my head could think. The air would be there again, the shadows of the sky drifting over the earth, and that ant, that ant, oh most excellent head that can't think. Leave it, leave it, nothing leads to anything, nothing of all that, my life is varied, you can't have everything, I'll never get anywhere, but when did I? When I laboured, all day long and let me add, before I forget, part of the night, when I thought that with perseverance I'd get at me in the end? Well look at me, a little dust in a little nook, stirred faintly this way and that by breath straying from the lost without. Yes, I'm here for ever, with the spinners and the dead flies, dancing to the tremor of their meshed wings, and it's well pleased I am, well pleased, that it's over and done with, the puffing and panting after me up and down their Tempe of tears. Sometimes a butterfly comes, all warm from the flowers, how weak it is, and quick dead, the wings crosswise, as when resting, in the sun, the scales grey. Blot, words can be blotted and the mad thoughts they invent, the nostalgia for that slime where the Eternal breathed and his son wrote, long after, with divine idiotic finger, at the feet of the adulteress, wipe it out, all you have to do is say you said nothing and so say nothing again. What can have become then of the tissues I was, I can see them no more, feel them no more, flaunting and fluttering all about and inside me, pah they must be still on their old prowl somewhere, passing themselves off as me. Did I ever believe in them, did I ever believe I was there, somewhere in that ragbag, that's more the line, of inquiry, perhaps I'm still there, as large as life, merely convinced I'm not. The eyes, yes, if these memories are mine, I must have believed in them an instant, believed it was me I saw there dimly in the depths of their glades. I can see me still, with those of now, sealed this long time, staring with those of then, I must have been twelve, because of the glass, a round shaving-glass, double-faced, faithful and magnifying, staring into one of the others, the true ones, true then, and seeing me there, imagining I saw me there, lurking behind the bluey veils, staring back sightlessly, at the age of twelve, because of the glass, on its pivot, because of my father, if it was my father, in the bathroom, with its view of the sea, the lightships at night, the red harbour light, if these memories concern me, at the age of twelve, or at the age of forty, for the mirror remained, my father went but the mirror remained, in which he had so greatly changed, my mother did her hair in it, with twitching hands, in another house, with no view of the sea, with a view of the mountains, if it was my mother, what a refreshing whiff of life on earth. I was, I was, they say in Purgatory, in Hell too, admirable singulars, admirable assurance.

Plunged in ice up to the nostrils, the eyelids caked with frozen tears, to fight all your battles o'er again, what tranquillity, and know there are no more emotions in store, no, I can't have heard aright. How many hours to go, before the next silence, they are not hours, it will not be silence, how many hours still, before the next silence? Ah to know for sure, to know that this thing has no end, this thing, this thing, this farrago of silence and words, of silence that is not silence and barely murmured words. Or to know it's life still, a form of life, ordained to end, as others ended and will end, till life ends, in all its forms. Words, mine was never more than that, than this pell-mell babel of silence and words, my viewless form described as ended, or to come, or still in progress, depending on the words, the moments, long may it last in that singular way. Apparitions, keepers, what childishness, and ghouls, to think I said ghouls, do I as much as know what they are, of course I don't, and how the intervals are filled, as if I didn't know, as if there were two things, some other thing besides this thing, what is it, this unnamable thing that I name and name and never wear out, and I call that words. It's because I haven't hit on the right ones, the killers, haven't yet heaved them up from that heart-burning glut of words, with what words shall I name my unnamable words? And yet I have high hopes, I give you my word, high hopes, that one day I may tell a story, hear a story, yet another, with men, kinds of men as in the days when I played all regardless or nearly, worked and played. But first stop talking and get on with your weeping, with eyes wide open that the precious liquid may spill freely, without burning the lids, or the crystalline humour, I forget, whatever it is it burns. Tears, that could be the tone, if they weren't so easy, the true tone and tenor at last. Besides not a tear, not one, I'd be in greater danger of mirth, if it wasn't so easy. No, grave, I'll be grave, I'll close my ears, close my mouth and be grave. And when they open again it may be to hear a story, tell a story, in the true sense of the words, the word hear, the word tell, the word story, I have high hopes, a little story, with living creatures coming and going on a habitable earth crammed with the dead, a brief story, with night and day coming and going above, if they stretch that far, the words that remain, and I've high hopes, I give you my word.

Translated by the author

7

DID I TRY EVERYTHING, ferret in every hold, secretly, silently, patiently, listening? I'm in earnest, as so often, I'd like to be sure I left no stone unturned before reporting me missing and giving up. In every hold, I mean in all those places where there was a chance of my being, where once I used to lurk, waiting for the hour to come when I might venture forth, tried and trusty places, that's all I meant when I said in every hold. Once, I mean in the days when I still could move, and feel myself moving, painfully, barely, but unquestionably changing position on the whole, the trees were witness, the sands, the air of the heights, the cobblestones. This tone is promising, it is more like that of old, of the days and nights when in spite of all I was calm, treading back and forth the futile road, knowing it short and easy seen from Sirius, and deadly calm at the heart of my frenzies. My question, I had a question, ah yes, did I try everything, I can see it still, but it's passing, lighter than air, like a cloud, in moonlight, before the skylight, before the moon, like the moon, before the skylight. No, in its own way, I know it well, the way of an evening shadow you follow with your eyes, thinking of something else, yes, that's it, the mind elsewhere, and the eyes too, if the truth were known, the eyes elsewhere too. Ah if there must be speech at least none from the heart, no, I have only one desire, if I have it still. But another thing, before the ones that matter, I have just time, if I make haste, in the trough of all this time just time. Another thing, I call that another thing, the old thing I keep on not saying till I'm sick and tired, revelling in the flying instants, I call that revelling, now's my chance and I talk of revelling, it won't come back in a hurry if I remember right, but come back it must with its riot of instants. It's not me in any case, I'm not talking of me, I've said it a million times, no point in apologizing again, for talking of me, when there's X, that paradigm of human kind, moving at will, complete with joys and sorrows, perhaps even a wife and brats, forebears most certainly, a carcass in God's image and a contemporary skull, but above all endowed with movement, that's what strikes you above all, with his likeness so easy to take and his so instructive soul, that really, no, to talk of oneself, when there's X, no, what a blessing I'm not talking of myself, enough vile parrot I'll kill you. And what if all this time I had not stirred hand or foot from the third-class waiting-room of the South-Eastern Railway Terminus, I never dared wait first on a third class ticket, and were still there waiting to leave, for the south-east, the south rather, east lay the sea, all along the track, wondering where on earth to alight, or my mind absent, elsewhere. The last train went at twenty-three thirty, then they closed the station for the night. What thronging memories, that's to make me think I'm dead, I've said it a million times. But the same return, like the spokes of a turning wheel, always the same, and all alike, like spokes. And yet I wonder, whenever the hour returns when I have to wonder that, if the wheel in my head turns, I wonder, so given am I to thinking with my blood, or if it merely swings, like a balance-wheel in its case, a minute to and fro, seeing the immensity to measure and that heads are only wound up once, so given am I to thinking with my breath. But tut there I am far again from that terminus and its pretty neo-Doric colonnade, and far from that heap of flesh, rind, bones and bristles waiting to depart it knows not where, somewhere south, perhaps asleep, its ticket between finger and thumb for the sake of appearances, or let fall to the ground in the great limpness of sleep, perhaps dreaming it's in heaven, alit in heaven, or better still the dawn, waiting for the dawn and the joy of being able to say, I've the whole day before me, to go wrong, to go right, to calm down, to give up, I've nothing to fear, my ticket is valid for life. Is it there I came to a stop, is that me still waiting there, sitting up stiff and straight on the edge of the seat, knowing the dangers of laisser-aller, hands on thighs, ticket between finger and thumb, in that great room dim with the platform gloom as dispensed by the quarter-glass self-closing door, locked up in those shadows, it's there, it's me. In that case the night is long and singularly silent, for one who seems to remember the city sounds, confusedly, sunk now to a single sound, the impossible confused memory of a single confused sound, lasting all night, swelling, dying, but never for an instant broken by a silence the like of this deafening silence. Whence it should follow, but does not, that the third-class waiting-room of the South-Eastern Railway Terminus must be struck from the list of places to visit, see above, centuries above, that this lump is no longer me and that search should be made elsewhere, unless it be abandoned, which is my feeling. But not so fast, all cities are not eternal, that of this pensum is perhaps among the dead, and the station in ruins where I sit waiting, erect and rigid, hands on thighs, the tip of the ticket between finger and thumb, for a train that will never come, never go, natureward, or for day to break behind the locked door, through the glass black with the dust of ruin. That is why one must not hasten to conclude, the risk of error is too great. And to search for me elsewhere, where life persists, and me there, whence all life has withdrawn, except mine, if I'm alive, no, it would be a loss of time. And personally, I hear it said, personally I have no more time to lose, and that that will be all for this evening, that night is at hand and the time come for me too to begin.

Translated by the author

8

ONLY THE WORDS break the silence, all other sounds have ceased. If I were silent I'd hear nothing. But if I were silent the other sounds would start again, those to which the words have made me deaf, or which have really ceased. But I am silent, it sometimes happens, no, never, not one second. I weep too without interruption. It's an unbroken flow of words and tears. With no pause for reflection. But I speak softer, every year a little softer. Perhaps. Slower too, every year a little slower. Perhaps. It is hard for me to judge. If so the pauses would be longer, between the words, the sentences, the syllables, the tears, I confuse them, words and tears, my words are my tears, my eyes my mouth. And I should hear, at every little pause, if it's the silence I say when I say that only the words break it. But nothing of the kind, that's not how it is, it's for ever the same murmur, flowing unbroken, like a single endless word and therefore meaningless, for it's the end gives the meaning to words. What right have you then, no, this time I see what I'm up to and put a stop to it, saying, None, none. But get on with the stupid old threne and ask, ask until you answer, a new question, the most ancient of all, the question were things always so. Well I'm going to tell myself something (if I'm able), pregnant I hope with promise for the future, namely that I begin to have no very clear recollection of how things were before (I was!), and by before I mean elsewhere, time has turned into space and there will be no more time, till I get out of here. Yes, my past has thrown me out, its gates have slammed behind me, or I burrowed my way out alone, to linger a moment free in a dream of days and nights, dreaming of me moving, season after season, towards the last, like the living, till suddenly I was here, all memory gone. Ever since nothing but fantasies and hope of a story for me somehow, of having come from somewhere and of being able to go back, or on, somehow, some day, or without hope. Without what hope, haven't I just said, of seeing me alive, not merely inside an imaginary head, but a pebble sand to be, under a restless sky, restless on its shore, faint stirs day and night, as if to grow less could help, ever less and less and never quite be gone. No truly, no matter what, I say no matter what, hoping to wear out a voice, to wear out a head, or without hope, without reason, no matter what, without reason. But it will end, a desinence will come, or the breath fail better still, I'll be silence, I'll know I'm silence, no, in the silence you can't know, I'll never know anything. But at least get out of here, at least that, no? I don't know. And time begin again, the steps on the earth, the night the fool implores at morning and the morning he begs at evening not to dawn. I don't know, I don't know what all that means, day and night, earth and sky, begging and imploring. And I can desire them? Who says I desire them, the voice, and that I can't desire anything, that looks like a contradiction, it may be for all I know. Me, here, if they could open, those little words, open and swallow me up, perhaps that is what has happened. If so let them open again and let me out, in the tumult of light that sealed my eyes, and of men, to try and be one again. Or if I'm guilty let me be forgiven and graciously authorized to expiate, coming and going in passing time, every day a little purer, a little deader. The mistake I make is to try and think, even the way I do, such as I am I shouldn't be able, even the way I do. But whom can I have offended so grievously, to be punished in this inexplicable way, all is inexplicable, space and time, false and inexplicable, suffering and tears, and even the old convulsive cry, It's not me, it can't be me. But am I in pain, whether it's me or not, frankly now, is there pain? Now is here and here there is no frankness, all I say will be false and to begin with not said by me, here I'm a mere ventriloquist's dummy, I feel nothing, say nothing, he holds me in his arms and moves my lips with a string, with a fish-hook, no, no need of lips, all is dark, there is no one, what's the matter with my head, I must have left it in Ireland, in a saloon, it must be there still, lying on the bar, it's all it deserved. But that other who is me, blind and deaf and mute, because of whom I'm here, in this black silence, helpless to move or accept this voice as mine, it's as him I must disguise myself till I die, for him in the meantime do my best not to live, in this pseudo-sepulture claiming to be his. Whereas to my certain knowledge I'm dead and kicking above, somewhere in Europe probably, with every plunge and suck of the sky a little more overripe, as yesterday in the pump of the womb. No, to have said so convinces me of the contrary, I never saw the light of day, any more than he, ah if no were content to cut yes's throat and never cut its own. Watch out for the right moment, then not another word, is that the only way to have being and habitat? But I'm here, that much at least is certain, it's in vain I keep on saying it, it remains true. Does it? It's hard for me to judge. Less true and less certain in any case than when I say I'm on earth, come into the world and assured of getting out, that's why I say it, patiently, variously, trying to vary, for you never know, it's perhaps all a question of hitting on the right aggregate.

So as to be here no more at last, to have never been here, but all this time above, with a name like a dog to be called up with and distinctive marks to be had up with, the chest expanding and contracting unaided, panting towards the grand apnoea. The right aggregate, but there are four million possible, nay probable, according to Aristotle, who knew everything. But what is this I see, and how, a white stick and an ear-trumpet, where, Place de la République, at pernod time, let me look closer at this, it's perhaps me at last. The trumpet, sailing at ear level, suddenly resembles a steam-whistle, of the kind thanks to which my steamers forge fearfully through the fog. That should fix the period, to the nearest half-century or so. The stick gains ground, tapping with its ferrule the noble bassamento of the United Stores, it must be winter, at least not summer. I can also just discern, with a final effort of will, a bowler hat which seems to my sorrow a sardonic synthesis of all those that never fitted me and, at the other extremity, similarly suspicious, a complete pair of brown boots lacerated and gaping. These insignia, if I may so describe them, advance in concert, as though connected by the traditional human excipient, halt, move on again, confirmed by the vast show windows. The level of the hat, and consequently of the trumpet, hold out some hope for me as a dying dwarf or at least hunchback. The vacancy is tempting, shall I enthrone my infirmities, give them this chance again, my dream infirmities, that they may take flesh and move, deteriorating, round and round this grandiose square which I hope I don't confuse with the Bastille, until they are deemed worthy of the adjacent Père Lachaise or, better still, prematurely relieved trying to cross over, at the hour of night's young thoughts. No, the answer is no. For even as I moved, or when the moment came, affecting beyond all others, to hold out my hand, or hat, without previous song, or any other form of concession to self-respect, at the terrace of a café, or in the mouth of the underground, I would know it was not me, I would know I was here, begging in another dark, another silence, for another alm, that of being or of ceasing, better still, before having been. And the hand old in vain would drop the mite and the old feet shuffle on, towards an even vainer death than no matter whose.

Translated by the author

9

IF I SAID, There's a way out there, there's a way out somewhere, the rest would come. What am I waiting for then, to say it? To believe it? And what does that mean, the rest? Shall I answer, try to answer, or go on as though I had asked nothing? I don't know, I can't know beforehand, nor after, nor during, the future will tell, some future instant, soon, or late, I won't hear, I won't understand, all dies so fast, no sooner born. And the yeses and noes mean nothing in this mouth, no more than sighs it sighs in its toil, or answers to a question not understood, a question unspoken, in the eyes of a mute, an idiot, who doesn't understand, never understood, who stares at himself in a glass, stares before him in the desert, sighing yes, sighing no, on and off. But there is reasoning somewhere, moments of reasoning, that is to say the same things recur, they drive one another out, they draw one another back, no need to know what things. It's mechanical, like the great colds, the great heats, the long days, the long nights, of the moon, such is my conviction, for I have convictions, when their turn comes round, then stop having them, that's how it goes, it must be supposed, at least it must be said, since I have just said it. The way out, this evening it's the turn of the way out, isn't it like a duo, or a trio, yes, there are moments when it's like that, then they pass and it's not like that any more, never was like that, is like nothing, no resemblance with anything, of no interest. What variety and at the same time what monotony, how varied it is and at the same time how, what's the word, how monotonous. What agitation and at the same time what calm, what vicissitudes within what changelessness. Moments of hesitation not so much rare as frequent, if one had to choose, and soon overcome in favour of the old crux, on which at first all depends, then much, then little, then nothing. That's right, wordshit, bury me, avalanche, and let there be no more talk of any creature, nor of a world to leave, nor of a world to reach, in order to have done, with worlds, with creatures, with words, with misery, misery. Which no sooner said, Ah, says I, punctually, if only I could say, There's a way out there, there's a way out somewhere, then all would be said, it would be the first step on the long travellable road, destination tomb, to be trod without a word, tramp tramp, little heavy irrevocable steps, down the long tunnels at first, then under the mortal skies, through the days and nights, faster and faster, no, slower and slower, for obvious reasons, and at the same time faster and faster, for other obvious reasons, or the same, obvious in a different way, or in the same way, but at a different moment of time, a moment earlier, a moment later, or at the same moment, there is no such thing, there would be no such thing, I recapitulate, impossible. Would I know where I came from, no, I'd have a mother, I'd have had a mother, and what I came out of, with what pain, no, I'd have forgotten, what is it makes me say that, what is it makes me say this, whatever it is makes me say all, and it's not certain, not certain the way the mother would be certain, the way the tomb would be certain, if there was a way out, if I said there was a way out, make me say it, demons, no, I'll ask for nothing. Yes, I'd have a mother, I'd have a tomb, I wouldn't have come out of here, one doesn't come out of here, here are my tomb and mother, it's all here this evening, I'm dead and getting born, without having ended, helpless to begin, that's my life. How reasonable it is and what am I complaining of? Is it because I'm no longer slinking to and fro before the graveyard, saying, God grant I'm buriable before the curtain drops, is that my grievance, it's possible. I was well inspired to be anxious, wondering on what score, and I asked myself, as I came and went, on what score I could possibly be anxious, and found the answer and answered, saying, It's not me, I haven't yet appeared, I haven't yet been noticed, and saying further, Oh yes it is, it's me all right, and ceasing to be what is more, then quickening my step, so as to arrive before the next onslaught, as though it were on time I trod, and saying further, and so forth. I can scarcely have gone unperceived, all this time, and yet you wouldn't have thought so, that I didn't go unperceived. I don't refer to the spoken salutation, I'd have been the first to be perturbed by that, almost as much as by the bow, kiss or handshake. But the other signs, irrepressible, with which the fellow-creature unwillingly betrays your presence, the shudders and wry faces, nothing of that nature either it would seem, except possibly on the part of certain hearse-horses, in spite of their blinkers and strict funereal training, but perhaps I flatter myself. Truly I can't recall a single face, proof positive that I was not there, no, proof of nothing. But the fact that I was not molested, can I have remained insensible to that? Alas I fear they could have subjected me to the most gratifying brutalities, I won't go so far as to say without my knowledge, but without my being encouraged, as a result, to feel myself there rather than elsewhere. And I may well have spent one half of my life in the prisons of their Arcady, purging the delinquencies of the other half, all unaware of any break or lull in my problematic patrolling, unconstrained, before the gates of the graveyard. But what if weary of seeing me relieve myself, of seeing me resume, after each forced vacation, my beat before the gates of the graveyard, what if finally they had plucked up heart and slightly stressed their blows, just enough to confer death, without any mutilation of the corpse, there, at the gates of the graveyard, where that very morning I had reappeared, no sooner set at large, and resumed by old offence, to and fro, with step now slow and now precipitate, like that of the conspirator Catilina plotting the ruin of the fatherland, saying, It's not me, yes, it's me, and further, There's a way out there, no no, I'm getting mixed, I must be getting mixed, confusing here and there, now and then, just as I confused them then, the here of then, the then of there, with other spaces, other times, dimly discerned, but not more dimly than now, now that I'm here, if I'm here, and no longer there, coming and going before the graveyard, perplexed. Or did I end up by simply sitting down, with my back to the wall, all the long night before me when the dead lie waiting, on the beds where they died, shrouded or coffined, for the sun to rise? What am I doing now, I'm trying to see where I am, so as to be able to go elsewhere, should occasion arise, or else simply to say, You have merely to wait till they come and fetch you, that's my impression at times. Then it goes and I see it's not that, but something else, difficult to grasp, and which I don't grasp, or which I do grasp, it depends, and it comes to the same, for it's not that either, but something else, some other thing, or the first back again, or still the same, always the same thing proposing itself to my perplexity, then disappearing, then proposing itself again, to my perplexity still unsated, or momentarily dead, of starvation. The graveyard, yes, it's there I'd return, this evening it's there, borne by my words, if I could get out of here, that is to say if I could say, There's a way out there, there's a way out somewhere, to know exactly where would be a mere matter of time, and patience, and sequency of thought, and felicity of expression. But the body, to get there with, where's the body? It's a minor point, a minor point. And I have no doubts, I'd get there somehow, to the way out, sooner or later, if I could say, There's a way out there, there's a way out somewhere, the rest would come, the other words, sooner or later, and the power to get there, and the way to get there, and pass out, and see the beauties of the skies, and see the stars again.

Translated by the author

10

GIVE UP, but it's all given up, it's nothing new, I'm nothing new. Ah so there was something once, I had something once. It may be thought there was, so long as it's known there was not, never anything, but giving up. But let us suppose there was not, that is to say let us suppose there was, something once, in a head, in a heart, in a hand, before all opened, emptied, shut again and froze. This is most reassuring, after such a fright, and emboldens me to go on, once again. But there is not silence. No, there is utterance, somewhere someone is uttering. Inanities, agreed, but is that enough, is that enough, to make sense? I see what it is, the head has fallen behind, all the rest has gone on, the head and its anus the mouth, or else it has gone on alone, all alone on its old prowls, slobbering its shit and lapping it back off the lips like in the days when it fancied itself. But the heart's not in it any more, nor is the appetite what it was. So home to roost it comes among my other assets, home yet again, and no trickery involved, that old past ever new, ever ended, ever ending, with all its hidden treasures of promise for tomorrow, and of consolation for today. And I'm in good hands again, they hold my head from behind, intriguing detail, as at the hairdresser's, the forefingers close my eyes, the middle fingers my nostrils, the thumbs stop up my ears, but imperfectly, to enable me to hear, but imperfectly, while the four remaining make merry with my jaws and tongue, to enable me to suffocate, but imperfectly, and to utter, for my good, what I must utter, for my future good, well-known ditty, and in particular to observe without delay, speaking of the passing moment, that worse have been known to pass, that it will pass in time, a mere moment of respite which but for this first aid might have proved fatal, and that one day I shall know again that I once was, and roughly who, and how to go on, and speak unaided, nicely, about number one and his pale imitations. And it is possible, just, for I must not be too affirmative at this stage, it would not be in my interest, that other fingers, quite a different gang, other tentacles, that's more like it, other charitable suckers, waste no more time trying to get it right, will take down my declarations, so that at the close of the interminable delirium, should it ever resume, I may not be reproached with having faltered. This is awful, awful, at least there's that to be thankful for. And perhaps beside me, and all around, other souls are being licked into shape, souls swooned away, or sick with over-use, or because no use could be found for them, but still fit for use, or fit only to be cast away, pale imitations of mine. Or has it knelled here at last for our committal to flesh, as the dead are committed to the ground, in the hour of their death at last, and at the place where they die, to keep the expenses down, or for our reassignment, souls of the stillborn, or dead before the body, or still young in the midst of the ruins, or never come to life through incapacity or for some other reason, or the immortal type, there must be a few of them too, whose bodies were always wrong, but patience there's a true one in pickle, among the unborn hordes, the true sepulchral body, for the living have no room for a second. No, no souls, or bodies, or birth, or life, or death, you've got to go on without any of that junk, that's all dead with words, with excess of words, they can say nothing else, they say there is nothing else, that here it's that and nothing else, but they won't say it eternally, they'll find some other nonsense, no matter what, and I'll be able to go on, no, I'll be able to stop, or start, another guzzle of lies but piping hot, it will last my time, it will be my time and place, my voice and silence, a voice of silence, the voice of my silence. It's with such prospects they exhort you to have patience, whereas you are patient, and calm, somehow somewhere calm, what calm here, ah that's an idea, say how calm it is here, and how fine I feel, and how silent I am, I'll start right away, I'll say what calm and silence, which nothing has ever broken, nothing will ever break, which saying I don't break, or saying I'll be saying, yes, I'll say all that tomorrow, yes, tomorrow evening, some other evening, not this evening, this evening it's too late, too late to get things right, I'll go to sleep, so that I may say, hear myself say, a little later, I've slept, he's slept, but he won't have slept, or else he's sleeping now, he'll have done nothing, nothing but go on, doing what, doing what he does, that is to say, I don't know, giving up, that's it, I'll have gone on giving up, having had nothing, not being there.

Translated by the author

11

WHEN I THINK, no, that won't work, when come those who knew me, perhaps even know me still, by sight of course, or by smell, it's as though, it's as if, come on, I don't know, I shouldn't have begun. If I began again, setting my mind to it, that sometimes gives good results, it's worth trying, I'll try it, one of these days, one of these evenings, or this evening, why not this evening, before I disappear, from up there, from down here, scattered by the everlasting words. What am I saying, scattered, isn't that just what I'm not, just what I'm not, I was wandering, my mind was wandering, just the very thing I'm not. And it's still the same old road I'm trudging, up yes and down no, towards one yet to be named, so that he may leave me in peace, be in peace, be no more, have never been. Name, no, nothing is namable, tell, no, nothing can be told, what then, I don't know, I shouldn't have begun. Add him to the repertory, there we have it, and execute him, as I execute me, one dead bar after another, evening after evening, and night after night, and all through the days, but it's always evening, why is that, why is it always evening, I'll say why, so as to have said it, have it behind me, an instant. It's time that can't go on at the hour of the serenade, unless it's dawn, no, I'm not in the open, I'm under the ground, or in my body somewhere, or in another body, and time devours on, but not me, there we have it, that's why it's always evening, to let me have the best to look forward to, the long black night to sleep in, there, I've answered, I've answered something. Or it's in the head, like a minute time switch, a second time switch, or it's like a patch of sea, under the passing lighthouse beam, a passing patch of sea under the passing beam. Vile words to make me believe I'm here, and that I have a head, and a voice, a head believing this, then that, then nothing more, neither in itself, nor in anything else, but a head with a voice belonging to it, or to others, other heads, as if there were two heads, as if there were one head, or headless, a headless voice, but a voice. But I'm not deceived, for the moment I'm not deceived, for the moment I'm not there, nor anywhere else what is more, neither as head, nor as voice, nor as testicle, what a shame, what a shame I'm not appearing anywhere as testicle, or as cunt, those areas, a female pubic hair, it sees great sights, peeping down, well, there it is, can't be helped, that's how it is. And I let them say their say, my words not said by me, me that word, that word they say, but say in vain. We're getting on, getting on, and when come those who knew me, quick quick, it's as though, no, premature. But peekaboo here I come again, just when most needed, like the square root of minus one, having terminated my humanities, this should be worth seeing, the livid face stained with ink and jam, caput mortuum of a studious youth, ears akimbo, eyes back to front, the odd stray hair, foaming at the mouth, and chewing, what is it chewing, a gob, a prayer, a lesson, a little of each, a prayer got by rote in case of emergency before the soul resigns and bubbling up all arsy-versy in the old mouth bereft of words, in the old head done with listening, there I am old, it doesn't take long, a snotty old nipper, having terminated his humanities, in the two-stander urinal on the corner of the Rue d'Assas was it, with the leak making the same gurgle as sixty years ago, my favourite because of the encouragement like mother hissing to baby on pot, my brow glued to the partition among the graffiti, straining against the prostate, belching up Hail Marys, buttoned as to the fly, I invent nothing, through absent-mindedness, or exhaustion, or insouciance, or on purpose, to promote priming, I know what I mean, or one-armed, better still, no arms, no hands, better by far, as old as the world and no less hideous, amputated on all sides, erect on my trusty stumps, bursting with old piss, old prayers, old lessons, soul, mind and carcass finishing neck and neck, not to mention the gobchucks, too painful to mention, sobs made mucus, hawked up from the heart, now I have a heart, now I'm complete, apart from a few extremities, having terminated their humanities, then their career, and with that not in the least pretentious, making no demands, rent with ejaculations, Jesus, Jesus. Evenings, evenings, what evenings they were then, made of what, and when was that, I don't know, made of friendly shadows, friendly skies, of time cloyed, resting from devouring, until its midnight meats, I don't know, any more than then, when I used to say, from within, or from without, from the coming night or from under the ground, Where am I, to mention only space, and in what semblance, and since when, to mention also time, and till when, and who is this clot who doesn't know where to go, who can't stop, who takes himself for me and for whom I take myself, anything at all, the old jangle. Those evenings then, but what is this evening made of, this evening now, that never ends, in whose shadows I'm alone, that's where I am, where I was then, where I've always been, it's from them I spoke to myself, spoke to him, where has he vanished, the one I saw then, is he still in the street, it's probable, it's possible, with no voice speaking to him, I don't speak to him any more, I don't speak to me any more, I have no one left to speak to, and I speak, a voice speaks that can be none but mine, since there is none but me. Yes, I have lost him and he has lost me, lost from view, lost from hearing, that's what I wanted, is it possible, that I wanted that, wanted this, and he, what did he want, he wanted to stop, perhaps he has stopped, I have stopped, but I never stirred, perhaps he is dead, I am dead, but I never lived. But he moved, proof of animation, through those evenings, moving too, evenings with an end, evenings with a night, never saying a word, unable to say a word, not knowing where to go, unable to stop, listening to my cries, hearing a voice crying that it was no kind of life, as if he didn't know, as if the allusion was to his, which was a kind of one, there's the difference, those were the days, I didn't know where I was, nor in what semblance, nor since when, nor till when, whereas now, there's the difference, now I know, it's not true, but I say it just the same, there's the difference, I'm saying it now, I'll say it soon, I'll say it in the end, then end, I'll be free to end, I won't be any more, it won't be worth it any more, it won't be necessary any more, it won't be possible any more, but it's not worth it now, it's not necessary now, it's not possible now, that's how the reasoning runs. No, something better must be found, a better reason, for this to stop, another word, a better idea, to put in the negative, a new no, to cancel all the others, all the old noes that buried me down here, deep in this place which is not one, which is merely a moment for the time being eternal, which is called here, and in this being which is called me and is not one, and in this impossible voice, all the old noes dangling in the dark and swaying like a ladder of smoke, yes, a new no, that none says twice, whose drop will fall and let me down, shadow and babble, to an absence less vain than inexistence. Oh I know it won't happen like that, I know that nothing will happen, that nothing has happened and that I'm still, and particularly since the day I could no longer believe it, what is called flesh and blood somewhere above in their gonorrhoeal light, cursing myself heartily. And that is why, when comes the hour of those who knew me, this time it's going to work, when comes the hour of those who knew me, it's as though I were among them, that is what I had to say, among them watching me approach, then watching me recede, shaking my head and saying, Is it really he, can it possibly be he, then moving on in their company along a road that is not mine and with every step takes me further from that other not mine either, or remaining alone where I am, between two parting dreams, knowing none, known of none, that finally is what I had to say, that is all I can have had to say, this evening.

Translated by the author

12

IT'S A WINTER NIGHT, where I was, where I'm going, remembered,
imagined, no matter, believing in me, believing it's me, no, no
need, so long as the others are there, where, in the world of the
others, of the long mortal ways, under the sky, with a voice, no,
no need, and the power to move, now and then, no need either,
so long as the others move, the true others, but on earth, beyond
all doubt on earth, for as long as it takes to die again, wake again,
long enough for things to change here, for something to change,
to make possible a deeper birth, a deeper death, or resurrection
in and out of this murmur of memory and dream. A winter
night, without moon or stars, but light, he sees his body, all the
front, part of the front, what makes them light, this impossible
night, this impossible body, it's me in him remembering, remembering the true night, dreaming of the night without morning,
and how will he manage tomorrow, to endure tomorrow, the
dawning, then the day, the same as he managed yesterday, to endure yesterday. Oh I know, it's not me, not yet, it's a veteran,
inured to days and nights, but he forgets, he thinks of me, more
than is wise, and it's a far cry to morning, perhaps it has time
never to dawn at last. That's what he says, with his voice soon to
leave him, perhaps tonight, and he says, How light it is, how

shall I manage tomorrow, how did I manage yesterday, pah it's the end, it's a far cry to morning, and who's this speaking in me, and who's this disowning me, as though I had taken his place, usurped his life, that old shame that kept me from living, the shame of my living that kept me from living, and so on, muttering, the old inanities, his chin on his heart, his arms dangling, sagging at the knees, in the night. Will they succeed in slipping me into him, the memory and dream of me, into him still living, aren't I there already, wasn't I always there, like a stain of remorse, is that my night and contumacy, in the dungeons of this moribund, and from now till he dies my last chance to have been, and who is this raving now, pah there are voices everywhere, ears everywhere, one who speaks saying, without ceasing to speak, Who's speaking?, and one who hears, mute, uncomprehending, far from all, and bodies everywhere, bent, fixed, where my prospects must be just as good, just as poor, as in this firstcomer. And none will wait, he no more than the others, none ever waited to die for me to live in him, so as to die with him, but quick quick all die, saying, Quick quick let us die, without him, as we lived, before it's too late, lest we won't have lived. And this other now, obviously, what's to be said of this latest other, with his babble of homeless mes and untenanted hims, this other without number or person whose abandoned being we haunt, nothing. There's a pretty three in one, and what a one, what a no one. So, I'm supposed to say now, it's the moment, so that's the earth, these expiring vitals set aside for me which no sooner taken over would be set aside for another, many thanks, and here the laugh, the long silent guffaw of the knowing nonexister, at hearing ascribed to him such pregnant words, confess you're not the man you were, you'll end up riding a bicycle. That's the accountants' chorus, opining like a single man, and there are more to come, all the peoples of the earth would not suffice, at the end of the billions you'd need a god, unwitnessed witness of witnesses, what a blessing it's all down the drain, nothing ever as much as begun, nothing ever but nothing and never, nothing ever but lifeless words.

Translated by the author

13

WEAKER STILL the weak old voice that tried in vain to make me, dying away as much as to say it's going from here to try elsewhere, or dying down, there's no telling, as much as to say it's going to cease, give up trying. No voice ever but it in my life, it says, if speaking of me one can speak of life, and it can, it still can, or if not of life, there it dies, if this, if that, if speaking of me, there it dies, but who can the greater can the less, once you've spoken of me you can speak of anything, up to the point where, up to the time when, there it dies, it can't go on, it's been its death, speaking of me, here or elsewhere, it says, it murmurs. Whose voice, no one's, there is no one, there's a voice without a mouth, and somewhere a kind of hearing, something compelled to hear, and somewhere a hand, it calls that a hand, it wants to make a hand, or if not a hand something somewhere that can leave a trace, of what is made, of what is said, you can't do with less, no, that's romancing, more romancing, there is nothing but a voice murmuring a trace. A trace, it wants to leave a trace, yes, like air leaves among the leaves, among the grass, among the sand, it's with that it would make a life, but soon it will be the end, it won't be long now, there won't be any life, there won't have been any life, there will be silence, the air quite still that trembled once an instant, the tiny flurry of dust quite settled. Air, dust, there is no air here, nor anything to make dust, and to speak of instants, to speak of once, is to speak of nothing, but there it is, those are the expressions it employs. It has always spoken, it will always speak, of things that don't exist, or only exist elsewhere, if you like, if you must, if that may be called existing. Unfortunately it is not a question of elsewhere, but of here, ah there are the words out at last, out again, that was the only chance, get out of here and go elsewhere, go where time passes and atoms assemble an instant, where the voice belongs perhaps, where it sometimes says it must have belonged, to be able to speak of such figments. Yes, out of here, but how when here is empty, not a speck of dust, not a breath, the voice's breath alone, it breathes in vain, nothing is made. If I were here, if it could have made me, how I would pity it, for having spoken so long in vain, no, that won't do, it wouldn't have spoken in vain if I were here, and I wouldn't pity it if it had made me, I'd curse it, or bless it, it would be in my mouth, cursing, blessing, whom, what, it wouldn't be able to say, in my mouth it wouldn't have much to say, that had so much to say in vain. But this pity, all the same, it wonders, this pity that is in the air, though no air here for pity, but it's the expression, it wonders should it stop and wonder what pity is doing here and if it's not hope gleaming, another expression, evilly among the imaginary ashes, the faint hope of a faint being after all, human in kind, tears in its eyes before they've had time to open, no, no more stopping and wondering, about that or anything else, nothing will stop it any more, in its fall, or in its rise, perhaps it will end on a castrato scream. True there was never much talk of the heart, literal or figurative, but that's no reason for hoping, what, that one day there will be one, to send up above to break in the galanty show, pity. But what more is it waiting for now, when there's no doubt left, no choice left, to stick a sock in its death-rattle, yet another locution. To have rounded off its cock-and-bullshit in a coda worthy of the rest? Last everlasting questions, infant languors in the end sheets, last images, end of dream, of being past, passing and to be, end of lie. Is it possible, is that the possible thing at last, the extinction of this black nothing and its impossible shades, the end of the farce of making and the silencing of silence, it wonders, that voice which is silence, or it's me, there's no telling, it's all the same dream, the same silence, it and me, it and him, him and me, and all our train, and all theirs, and all theirs, but whose, whose dream, whose silence, old questions, last questions, ours who are dream and silence, but it's ended, we're ended who never were, soon there will be nothing where there was never anything, last images. And whose the shame, at every mute micromillisyllable, and unslakable infinity of remorse delving ever deeper in its bite, at having to hear, having to say, fainter than the faintest murmur, so many lies, so many times the same lie lyingly denied, whose the screaming silence of no's knife in yes's wound, it wonders. And wonders what has become of the wish to know, it is gone, the heart is gone, the head is gone, no one feels anything, asks anything, seeks anything, says anything, hears anything, there is only silence. It's not true, yes, it's true, it's true and it's not true, there is silence and there is not silence, there is no one and there is someone, nothing prevents anything. And were the voice to cease quite at last, the old ceasing voice, it would not be true, as it is not true that it speaks, it can't speak, it can't cease. And were there one day to be here, where there are no days, which is no place, born of the impossible voice the unmakable being, and a gleam of light, still all would be silent and empty and dark, as now, as soon now, when all will be ended, all said, it says, it murmurs.

Translated by the author

From an Abandoned Work

UP BRIGHT AND EARLY that day, I was young then, feeling awful, and out, mother hanging out of the window in her nightdress weeping and waving. Nice fresh morning, bright too early as so often. Feeling really awful, very violent. The sky would soon darken and rain fall and go on falling, all day, till evening. Then blue and sun again a second, then night. Feeling all this, how violent and the kind of day, I stopped and turned. So back with bowed head on the look out for a snail, slug or worm. Great love in my heart too for all things still and rooted, bushes, boulders and the like, too numerous to mention, even the flowers of the field, not for the world when in my right senses would I ever touch one, to pluck it. Whereas a bird now, or a butterfly, fluttering about and getting in my way, all moving things, getting in my path, a slug now, getting under my feet, no, no mercy. Not that I'd go out of my way to get at them, no, at a distance often they seemed still, then a moment later they were upon me. Birds with my piercing sight I have seen flying so high, so far, that they seemed at rest, then the next minute they were all about me, crows have done this. Ducks are perhaps the worst, to be suddenly stamping and stumbling in the midst of ducks, or hens, any class of poultry, few things are worse. Nor will I go out of my way to avoid such things, when avoidable, no, I simply will not go out of my way, though I have never in my life been on my way anywhere, but simply on my way. And in this way I have gone through great thickets, bleeding, and deep into bogs, water too, even the sea in some moods and been carried out of my course, or driven back, so as not to drown. And that is perhaps how I shall die at last if they don't catch me, I mean drowned, or in fire, yes, perhaps that is how I shall do it at last, walking furious headlong into fire and dying burnt to bits. Then I raised my eyes and saw my mother still in the window waving, waving me back or on I don't know, or just waving, in sad helpless love, and I heard faintly her cries. The window-frame was green, pale, the house-wall grey and my mother white and so thin I could see past her (piercing sight I had then) into the dark of the room, and on all that full the not long risen sun, and all small because of the distance, very pretty really the whole thing, I remember it, the old grey and then the thin green surround and the thin white against the dark, if only she could have been still and let me look at it all. No, for once I wanted to stand and look at something I couldn't with her there waving and fluttering and swaying in and out of the window as though she were doing exercises, and for all I know she may have been, not bothering about me at all. No tenacity of purpose, that was another thing I didn't like in her. One week it would be exercises, and the next prayers and Bible reading, and the next gardening, and the next playing the piano and singing, that was awful, and then just lying about and resting, always changing. Not that it mattered to me, I was always out. But let me get on now with the day I have hit on to begin with, any other would have done as well, yes, on with it and out of my way and on to another, enough of my mother for the moment. Well then for a time all well, no trouble, no birds at me, nothing across my path except at a great distance a white horse followed by a boy, or it might have been a small man or woman.

This is the only completely white horse I remember, what I believe the Germans call a Schimmel, oh I was very quick as a boy and picked up a lot of hard knowledge, Schimmel, nice word, for an English speaker. The sun was full upon it, as shortly before on my mother, and it seemed to have a red band or stripe running down its side, I thought perhaps a bellyband, perhaps the horse was going somewhere to be harnessed, to a trap or suchlike. It crossed my path a long way off, then vanished behind greenery, I suppose, all I noticed was the sudden appearance of the horse, then disappearance. It was bright white, with the sun on it, I had never seen such a horse, though often heard of them, and never saw another. White I must say has always affected me strongly, all white things, sheets, walls and so on, even flowers, and then just white, the thought of white, without more. But let me get on with this day and get it over. All well then for a time, just the violence and then this white horse, when suddenly I flew into a most savage rage, really blinding. Now why this sudden rage I really don't know, these sudden rages, they made my life a misery. Many other things too did this, my sore throat for example, I have never known what it is to be without a sore throat, but the rages were the worst, like a great wind suddenly rising in me, no, I can't describe. It wasn't the violence getting worse in any case, nothing to do with that, some days I would be feeling violent all day and never have a rage, other days quite quiet for me and have four or five. No, there's no accounting for it, there's no accounting for anything, with a mind like the one I always had, always on the alert against itself, I'll come back on this perhaps when I feel less weak. There was a time I tried to get relief by beating my head against something, but I gave it up. The best thing I found was to start running. Perhaps I should mention here I was a very slow walker. I didn't dally or loiter in any way, just walked very slowly, little short steps and the feet very slow through the air. On the other hand I must have been quite one of the fastest runners the world has ever seen, over a short distance, five or ten yards, in a second I was there. But I could not go on at that speed, not for breathlessness, it was mental, all is mental, figments. Now the jog trot on the other hand, I could no more do that than I could fly. No, with me all was slow, and then these flashes, or gushes, vent the pent, that was one of those things I used to say, over and over, as I went along, vent the pent, vent the pent. Fortunately my father died when I was a boy, otherwise I might have been a professor, he had set his heart on it. A very fair scholar I was too, no thought, but a great memory. One day I told him about Milton's cosmology, away up in the mountains we were, resting against a huge rock looking out to sea, that impressed him greatly. Love too, often in my thoughts, when a boy, but not a great deal compared to other boys, it kept me awake I found. Never loved anyone I think, I'd remember. Except in my dreams, and there it was animals, dream animals, nothing like what you see walking about the country, I couldn't describe them, lovely creatures they were, white mostly. In a way perhaps it's a pity, a good woman might have been the making of me, I might be sprawling in the sun now sucking my pipe and patting the bottoms of the third and fourth generations, looked up to and respected, wondering what there was for dinner, instead of stravaging the same old roads in all weathers, I was never much of a one for new ground. No, I regret nothing, all I regret is having been born, dying is such a long tiresome business I always found. But let me get on now from where I left off, the white horse and then the rage, no connexion I suppose. But why go on with all this, I don't know, some day I must end, why not now. But these are thoughts, not mine, no matter, shame upon me. Now I am old and weak, in pain and weakness murmur why and pause, and the old thoughts well up in me and over into my voice, the old thoughts born with me and grown with me and kept under, there's another. No, back to that far day, any far day, and from the dim granted ground to its things and sky the eyes raised and back again, raised again and back again again, and the feet going nowhere only somehow home, in the morning out from home and in the evening back home again, and the sound of my voice all day long muttering the same old things I don't listen to, not even mine it was at the end of the day, like a marmoset sitting on my shoulder with its bushy tail, keeping me company. All this talking, very low and hoarse, no wonder I had a sore throat. Perhaps I should mention here that I never talked to anyone, I think my father was the last one I talked to. My mother was the same, never talked, never answered, since my father died. I asked her for the money, I can't go back on that now, those must have been my last words to her. Sometimes she cried out on me, or implored, but never long, just a few cries, then if I looked up the poor old thin lips pressed tight together and the body turned away and just the corners of the eyes on me, but it was rare. Sometimes in the night I heard her, talking to herself I suppose, or praying out loud, or reading out loud, or reciting her hymns, poor woman. Well after the horse and rage I don't know, just on, then I suppose the slow turn, wheeling more and more to the one or other hand, till facing home, then home. Ah my father and mother, to think they are probably in paradise, they were so good. Let me go to hell, that's all I ask, and go on cursing them there, and them look down and hear me, that might take some of the shine off their bliss. Yes, I believe all their blather about the life to come, it cheers me up, and unhappiness like mine, there's no annihilating that. I was mad of course and still am, but harmless, I passed for harmless, that's a good one. Not of course that I was really mad, just strange, a little strange, and with every passing year a little stranger, there can be few stranger creatures going about than me at the present day. My father, did I kill him too as well as my mother, perhaps in a way I did, but I can't go into that now, much too old and weak. The questions float up as I go along and leave me very confused, breaking up I am. Suddenly they are there, no, they float up, out of an old depth, and hover and linger before they die away, questions that when I was in my right mind would not have survived one second, no, but atomized they would have been, before as much as formed, atomized. In twos often they came, one hard on the other, thus, How shall I go on another day? and then, How did I ever go on another day? Or, Did I kill my father? and then, Did I ever kill anyone? That kind of way, to the general from the particular I suppose you might say, question and answer too in a way, very addling. I strive with them as best I can, quickening my step when they come on, tossing my head from side to side and up and down, staring agonizedly at this and that, increasing my murmur to a scream, these are helps. But they should not be necessary, something is wrong here, if it was the end I would not so much mind, but how often I have said, in my life, before some new awful thing, It is the end, and it was not the end, and yet the end cannot be far off now, I shall fall as I go along and stay down or curl up for the night as usual among the rocks and before morning be gone. Oh I know I too shall cease and be as when I was not yet, only all over instead of in store, that makes me happy, often now my murmur falters and dies and I weep for happiness as I go along and for love of this old earth that has carried me so long and whose uncomplainingness will soon be mine. Just under the surface I shall be, all together at first, then separate and drift, through all the earth and perhaps in the end through a cliff into the sea, something of me. A ton of worms in an acre, that is a wonderful thought, a ton of worms, I believe it. Where did I get it, from a dream, or a book read in a nook when a boy, or a word overheard as I went along, or in me all along and kept under till it could give me joy, these are the kind of horrid thoughts I have to contend with in the way I have said. Now is there nothing to add to this day with the white horse and

white mother in the window, please read again my descriptions
of these, before I get on to some other day at a later time, nothing to add before I move on in time skipping hundreds and even
thousands of days in a way I could not at the time, but had to get
through somehow until I came to the one I am coming to now,
no, nothing, all has gone but mother in the window, the violence,
rage and rain. So on to this second day and get it over and out of
the way and on to the next. What happens now is I was set on
and pursued by a family or tribe, I do not know, of stoats, a most
extraordinary thing, I think they were stoats. Indeed if I may say
so I think I was fortunate to get off with my life, strange expression, it does not sound right somehow. Anyone else would have
been bitten and bled to death, perhaps sucked white, like a rabbit, there is that word white again. I know I could never think,
but if I could have, and then had, I would just have lain down
and let myself be destroyed, as the rabbit does. But let me start as
always with the morning and the getting out. When a day comes
back, whatever the reason, then its morning and its evening too
are there, though in themselves quite unremarkable, the going
out and coming home, there is a remarkable thing I find. So up
then in the grey of dawn, very weak and shaky after an atrocious
night little dreaming what lay in store, out and off. What time of
year, I really do not know, does it matter. Not wet really, but
dripping, everything dripping, the day might rise, did it, no, drip
drip all day long, no sun, no change of light, dim all day, and
still, not a breath, till night, then black, and a little wind, I saw
some stars, as I neared home. My stick of course, by a merciful
providence, I shall not say this again, when not mentioned my
stick is in my hand, as I go along. But not my long coat, just my
jacket, I could never bear the long coat, flapping about my legs,
or rather one day suddenly I turned against it, a sudden violent
dislike. Often when dressed to go I would take it out and put it
on, then stand in the middle of the room unable to move, until

at last I could take it off and put it back on its hanger, in the cupboard. But I was hardly down the stairs and out into the air when the stick fell from my hand and I just sank to my knees to the ground and then forward on my face, a most extraordinary thing, and then after a little over on my back, I could never lie on my face for any length of time, much as I loved it, it made me feel sick, and lay there, half an hour perhaps, with my arms along my sides and the palms of my hands against the pebbles and my eyes wide open straying over the sky. Now was this my first experience of this kind, that is the question that immediately assails me. Falls I had had in plenty, of the kind after which unless a limb broken you pick yourself up and go on, cursing God and man, very different from this. With so much life gone from knowledge how know when all began, all the variants of the one that one by one their venom staling follow upon one another, all life long, till you succumb. So in some way even olden things each time are first things, no two breaths the same, all a going over and over and all once and never more. But let me get up now and on and get this awful day over and on to the next. But what is the sense of going on with all this, there is none. Day after unremembered day until my mother's death, then in a new place soon old until my own. And when I come to this night here among the rocks with my two books and the strong starlight it will have passed from me and the day that went before, my two books, the little and the big, all past and gone, or perhaps just moments here and there still, this little sound perhaps now that I don't understand so that I gather up my things and go back into my hole, so bygone they can be told. Over, over, there is a soft place in my heart for all that is over, no, for the being over, I love the word, words have been my only loves, not many. Often all day long as I went along I have said it, and sometimes I would be saying vero, oh vero. Oh but for those awful fidgets I have always had I would have lived my life in a big empty echo-

ing room with a big old pendulum clock, just listening and dozing, the case open so that I could watch the swinging, moving my
eyes to and fro, and the lead weights dangling lower and lower
till I got up out of my chair and wound them up again, once a
week. The third day was the look I got from the roadman, suddenly I see that now, the ragged old brute bent double down in
the ditch leaning on his spade or whatever it was and leering
round and up at me from under the brim of his slouch, the red
mouth, how is it I wonder I saw him at all, that is more like it,
the day I saw the look I got from Balfe, I went in terror of him as
a child. Now he is dead and I resemble him. But let us get on and
leave these old scenes and come to these, and my reward. Then it
will not be as now, day after day, out, on, round, back, in, like
leaves turning, or torn out and thrown crumpled away, but a
long unbroken time without before or after, light or dark, from
or towards or at, the old half knowledge of when and where
gone, and of what, but kinds of things still, all at once, all going,
until nothing, there was never anything, never can be, life and
death all nothing, that kind of thing, only a voice dreaming and
droning on all around, that is something, the voice that once was
in your mouth. Well once out on the road and free of the property what then, I really do not know, the next thing I was up in
the bracken lashing about with my stick making the drops fly
and cursing, filthy language, the same words over and over, I
hope nobody heard me. Throat very bad, to swallow was tor-
ment, and something wrong with an ear, I kept poking at it without relief, old wax perhaps pressing on the drum. Extraordinary
still over the land, and in me too all quite still, a coincidence,
why the curses were pouring out of me I do not know, no, that is
a foolish thing to say, and the lashing about with the stick, what
possessed me mild and weak to be doing that, as I struggled
along. Is it the stoats now, no, first I just sink down again and
disappear in the ferns, up to my waist they were as I went along.

Harsh things these great ferns, like starched, very woody, terrible stalks, take the skin off your legs through your trousers, and then the holes they hide, break your leg if you're not careful, awful English this, fall and vanish from view, you could lie there for weeks and no one hear you, I often thought of that up in the mountains, no, that is a foolish thing to say, just went on, my body doing its best without me.

The Image

THE TONGUE GETS CLOGGED with mud only one remedy then pull it in and suck it swallow the mud or spit question to know whether it is nourishing and vistas though not having to drink often I take a mouthful it's one of my resources last a moment with that question to know whether if swallowed it would nourish and opening of vistas they are not bad moments tire myself out that's the point the tongue lolls out again rosy in the mud what are the hands at all this time one must always see what the hands are at well the left as we have seen still holds the sack and the right well the right after a while I see it way off at the end of its arm full stretch in the axis of the clavicle if that can be said or rather done opening and closing in the mud opening and closing it's another of my resources this small gesture helps me I know not why I have such little devices that assist me along even when hugging the walls under the changing skies already I must have been quite shrewd it mustn't be that far a bare yard but it feels far it will go some day by itself on its four fingers thumb included for one is missing not the thumb and it will leave me I can see how it throws its four fingers forward like grapnells the ends sink pull and so with little horizontal hoists it moves away this I do appreciate to go like that piecemeal and the legs what are the legs doing ah the legs and the eyes what are the eyes doing closed to be sure no since suddenly there in the mud I see me I say me as I say I as I would say he because there's the chuckle I look to me about sixteen and to top it all glorious weather egg blue sky and scamper of little clouds I have my back turned to me and the girl too whom I hold by the hand the arse I have judging by the flowers that deck the emerald grass we are in April or in May I don't know and how glad I am to ignore the reason why I abide by these stories of flowers and seasons I abide by them and that's all judging by certain accessories amongst which white rails and a grandstand of exquisite red we are on a racecourse heads thrown back we gaze I imagine before us still as statues save only the swinging arms with hands clasped in my free hand or left an undefinable object and consequently in her right the extremity of a short leash leading to an ash coloured terrier of fair size askew on its hunkers its head sunk stillness of these hands and of corresponding arms question to know why a leash in this immensity of verdure and emergence little by little of grey and white spots which I promptly name lambs among their dams I don't know the reason why I abide by these stories of animals I abide by them and that's all on a fair day I'm able to name dogs belonging to four or five completely different breeds I see them let us first and foremost not try and understand the bluey bulk closing the scene on a rough estimate three or four miles of a widespread mountain of modest elevation our heads overtop the summit as though propelled by a single spring or to be more accurate by two synchronised we let go our hands and turn about I dextrogyre she sinistro she transfers the leash to her left hand and I the same instant to my right the object now a little pale grey brick-shaped parcel maybe sandwiches perhaps for the mere sake of mingling hands anew which we do the arms swing the dog has not moved I have the silly impression we are looking at me I pull in my tongue close my mouth and smile

seen full face the girl is less ugly it's not with her I am concerned
me pale staring hair red pudding face with pimples protruding
belly gaping fly spindle legs wide astraddle for greater stability
knocking at the knees feet splayed thirty-five degrees minimum
fatuous half smile to posterior horizon figuring the morn of life
green tweeds yellow boots cowslip or such like in the buttonhole
again about turn introrse of a kind to bring us fleetingly not
rump but face to face at ninety degrees transfers of things mingling of hands swinging of arms stillness of dog the rump I have
three two one left right off we go chins up arms swinging the
dog follows head sunk tail on balls no reference to us it had the
same notion at the same instant Malebranche less the rosy hue
the humanities I had then if it stops to piss it will piss without
stopping I feel like shouting plant her there and run cut your
throat three hours of measured steps and here we are on the
summit the dog askew on its hunkers in the heather it lowers its
muzzle to its black and pink penis too tired to lick it we on the
contrary again about turn introrse transfers of things mingling of
hands swinging of arms silent relishing of sea and isles heads
pivoting as one to the city fumes silent location of steeples and
towers heads back front as though on an axle brief fog and here
we are again eating sandwiches alternate bites I mine she hers
and exchanging endearments my sweet girl I bite she swallows
my sweet boy she bites I swallow we don't yet coo with our bills
full my darling girl I bite she swallows my darling boy she bites I
swallow brief fog and here we are again as we dwindle again
across the pastures hand in hand arms swinging heads high towards the heights smaller and smaller out of sight first the dog
then us the scene is shut of us some animals the sheep like gran-
ite outcrops a horse I hadn't seen standing motionless back bent
head sunk animals know blue and white of sky April morning in
the mud it's over it's done the scene is empty a few animals still
then goes out no more blue I stay here way off on the right in the

mud the hand opens and closes that helps it's going let it go I realize I'm still smiling there's no sense in that now been none for a long time now the tongue comes out again lolls in the mud I stay like this no more thirst the tongue goes in the mouth closes it must be a straight line now it's done I've done the image.

Translated by Edith Fournier

All Strange Away

IMAGINATION DEAD IMAGINE. A place, that again. Never another question. A place, then someone in it, that again. Crawl out of the frowsy deathbed and drag it to a place to die in. Out of the door and down the road in the old hat and coat like after the war, no, not that again. Five foot square, six high, no way in, none out, try for him there. Stool, bare walls when the light comes on, women's faces on the walls when the light comes on. In a corner when the light comes on tattered syntaxes of Jolly and Draeger Praeger Draeger, all right. Light off and let him be, on the stool, talking to himself in the last person, murmuring, no sound, Now where is he, no, Now he is here. Sitting, standing, walking, kneeling, crawling, lying, creeping, in the dark and in the light, try all. Imagine light. Imagine light. No visible source, glare at full, spread all over, no shadow, all six planes shining the same, slow on, ten seconds on earth to full, same off, try that. Still his crown touches the ceiling, moving not, say a lifetime of walking bowed and full height when brought to a stand. It goes out, no matter, start again, another place, someone in it, keep glaring, never see, never find, no end, no matter. He says, no sound, The longer he lives and so the further goes the smaller they grow, the reasoning being the fuller he fills the space and so on, and the emptier, same reasoning. Hell this light from nothing no reason any moment, take off his coat, no, naked, all right, leave it for the moment. Sheets of black paper, stick them to the wall with cobweb and spittle, no good, shine like the rest. Imagine what needed, no more, any given moment, needed no more, gone, never was. Light flows, eyes close, stay closed till it ebbs, no, can't do that, eyes stay open, all right, look at that later. Black bag over his head, no good, all the rest still in light, front, sides, back, between the legs. Black shroud, start search for pins. Light on, down on knees, sights pin, makes for it, light out, gets pin in dark, light on, sights another, light out, so on, years of time on earth. Back on the stool in the shroud saying, That's better, now he's better, and so sits and never stirs, clutching it to him where it gapes, till it all perishes and rots off of him and hangs off of him in black flitters. Light out, long dark, candle and matches, imagine them, strike one to light, light on, blow out, light out, strike another, light on, so on. Light out, strike one to light, light on, light all the same, candlelight in light, blow out, light out, so on. No candle, no matches, no need, never were. As he was, in the dark any length, then the light when it flows till it ebbs any length, then again, so on, sitting, standing, walking, kneeling, crawling, lying, creeping, all any length, no paper, no pins, no candle, no matches, never were, talking to himself no sound in the last person any length, five foot square, six high, all white when light at full, no way in, none out. Falling on his knees in the dark to murmur, no sound, Fancy is his only hope. Surprised by light in this posture, hope and fancy on his lips, crawling lifelong habit to a corner here shadowless and similarly sinking head to ground here shining back into his eyes. Imagine eyes burnt ashen blue and lashes gone, lifetime of unseeing glaring, jammed open, one lightning wince per minute on earth, try that. Have him say, no sound, No way in, none out, he's not here. Tighten it round him, three foot square, five high, no stool, no sitting, no kneeling, no lying, just room to stand and revolve, light as before, faces as before, syntaxes upended in opposite corners. The back of his head touches the ceiling, say a lifetime of standing bowed. Call floor angles deasil a, b, c and d and ceiling likewise e, f, g and h, say Jolly at b and Draeger at d, lean him for rest with feet at a and head at g, in dark and light, eyes glaring, murmuring, He's not here, no sound, Fancy is his only hope. Physique, flesh and fell, nail him to that while still tender, nothing clear, place again. Light as before, all white still when at full, flaking plaster or the like, floor like bleached dirt, aha. Faces now naked bodies, eye level, two per wall, eight in all, all right, details later. All six planes hot when shining, aha. So dark and cold any length, shivering more or less, feeble slaps want of room at all flesh within reach, little stamps of hampered feet, so on. Same system light and heat with sweat more or less, cringing away from walls, burning soles, now one, now the other. Murmur unaffected, He's not here, no sound, Fancy dead, gaping eyes unaffected. See how light stops at five soft and mild for bodies, eight no more, one per wall, four in all, say all of Emma. First face alone, lovely beyond words, leave it at that, then deasil breasts alone, then thighs and cunt alone, then arse and hole alone, all lovely beyond words. See how he crouches down and back to see, back of head against face when eyes on cunt, against breasts when on hole, and vice versa, all most clear. So in this soft and mild, crouched down and back with hands on knees to hold himself together, say deasil first from face through hole then back through face, murmuring, Imagine him kissing, caressing, licking, sucking, fucking and buggering all this stuff, no sound. Then halt and up to position of rest, back of head touching the ceiling, gaze on ground, lifetime of unbloody bowed unseeing glaring. Imagine lifetime, gems, evenings with Emma and the flights by night, no, not that again. Physique, too soon, perhaps never, vague bowed body bonewhite when light at full, nothing clear but ashen glare as imagined, no, attitudes too with play of joints most clear more various now. For nine and nine eighteen that is four feet and more across in which to kneel, arse on heels, hands on thighs, trunk best bowed and crown on ground. And even sit, knees drawn up, trunk best bowed, head between knees, arms round knees to hold all together. And even lie, arse to knees say diagonal ac, feet say at d, head on left cheek at b. Price to pay and highest lying more flesh touching glowing ground. But say not glowing enough to burn and turning over, see how that works. Arse to knees, say bd, feet say at c, head on right cheek at a. Then arse to knees say again ac, but feet at b and head on left cheek at d. Then arse to knees say again bd, but feet at a and head on right cheek at c. So on other four possibilities when begin again. All that most clear. Imaginable too flat on back, knees drawn up, hands holding shins to hold all together, glare on ceiling, whereas flat on face by no stretch. Place then most clear so far but of him nothing and perhaps never save jointed segments variously disposed white when light at full. And always there among them somewhere the glaring eyes now clearer still in that flashes of vision few and far now rive their unseeingness. So for example as chance may have it on the ceiling a flyspeck or the insect itself or a strand of Emma's motte. Then lost and all the remaining field for hours of time on earth. Imagination dead imagine to lodge a second in that glare a dying common house or dying window fly, then fall the five feet to the dust and die or die and fall. No, no image, no fly here, no life or dying here but his, a speck of dirt. Or hers since sex not seen so far, say Emma standing, turning, sitting, kneeling, lying, in dark and light, saying to herself, She's not here, no sound, Fancy is her only hope, and Emmo on the walls, first the face, handsome beyond words, then deasil details later. And how crouching down and back she turns murmuring, Fancy her being all kissed, licked, sucked, fucked and so on by all that, no sound, hands on knees to hold herself together. Till halt and up, no, no image, down, for her down, to sit or kneel, kneel, arse on heels, hands on thighs, trunk bowed, breasts hanging, crown on ground, eyes glaring, no, no image, eyes closed, long lashes black when light, no more glare, never was, long black hair strewn when light, murmuring, no sound, Fancy dead. Any length, in dark and light, then topple left, arse to knees say db, feet say at c, head on left cheek at a, left breast puckered in the dust, hands, imagine hands. Imagine hands. Let her lie so from now on, have always lain so, head on left cheek in black hair at a and the rest the only way, never sat, never knelt, never stood, no Emmo, no need, never was. Imagine hands. Left on ball of right shoulder holding enough not to slip, right lightly clenched on ground, something in this hand, imagine later, something soft, clench tight, then lax and still any length, then tight again, so on, imagine later. Highest point from ground top of swell of right haunch, say twenty inches, slim woman. Ceiling wrong now, down two foot, perfect cube now, three foot every way, always was, light as before, all bonewhite when at full as before, floor like bleached dirt, something there, leave it for the moment. Waste height, sixteen inches, strange, say some reason unimaginable now, imagine later, imagination dead imagine all strange away. Jolly and Draeger gone, never were. So far then hollow cube three foot overall, no way in imagined yet, none out. Black cold any length, then light slow up to full glare say ten seconds still and hot glare any length all ivory white all six planes no shadow, then down through deepening greys and gone, so on. Walls and ceiling flaking plaster or suchlike, floor like bleached dirt, aha, something there, leave it for the moment. Call floor angles deasil a, b, c and d and in here Emma lying on her left side, arse to knees along diagonal db with arse towards d and knees towards b though neither at either because too short and waste space here too some reason yet to be imagined. On left side then arse to knees db and consequently arse to crown along wall da though not flush because arse out with head on left cheek at a and remaining segment knees to feet along bc not flush because knees out with feet at c. In dark and light. Slow fade of ivory flesh when ebb ten seconds and gone. Long black hair when light strewn over face and adjacent floor. Uncover right eye and cheekbone vivid white for long black lashes when light. Say again though no real image puckered tip of left breast, leave right a mere name. Left hand clinging to right shoulder ball, right more faint loose fist on ground till fingers tighten as though to squeeze, imagine later, then loose again and still any length, so on. Murmuring, no sound, though say lips move with faint stir of hair, whether none emitted or air too rare, Fancy is her only hope, or, She's not here, or, Fancy dead, suggesting moments of discouragement, imagine other murmurs. In dark and light, no, dark alone, say murmurs now in dark alone as though in light all ears all six planes all ears when shining whereas in dark unheard, this a well-known thing. And yet no sound, well say a sound too faint for mortal ear. Imagine other murmurs. So great need of words not daring till at last slow ebb ten seconds, too fast, thirty now, great need not daring till at last slow ebb thirty seconds on earth through a thousand darkening greys till out and incontinent, Fancy dead, for instance if spirits low, no sound. But see how the light dies down and from half down or more slow up again to full and the words down again that were trembling up, all right, say mere delay, dark must be in the end, say dark and light here equal in the end that is when all done with dead imagining and measures taken dark and light seen equal in the end. And indeed how stay of flow or ebb at any grey any length and even on the very sill of black any length till at last in and black and at long last the murmur too faint for mortal ear. But murmurs in long dark so long that longing no but need for light as in long light for dark murmurs sometimes as great a space apart as from on earth a winter to a summer day and coming on that great silence, She's not here, for instance if in better spirits or, Fancy is her only hope, too faint for mortal ear. And other times to imagine other extreme so hard on one another any order and sometimes when all spent if not assuaged a second time in some quite different so run together that a mere torrent of hope and unhope mingled and submission amounting to nothing, get all this clearer later. Imagine other murmurs, Mother mother, Mother in heaven, Mother of God, God in heaven, combinations with Christ and Jesus, other proper names in great numbers say of loved ones for the most part and cherished haunts, imagine as needed, unsupported interjections, ancient Greek philosophers ejaculated with place of origin when possible suggesting pursuit of knowledge at some period, completed propositions such as, She is not here, the exception, imagine others, This is not possible, there is one, and here another of exceptional length, In a hammock in the sun and here the name of some bewitching site she lies sleeping. But sudden gleam that whatever words given to let fall soundless in the dark that if no sound better none, all right, try sound and if no better say quite speechless, imagine sound and not till then all that black hair toss back into the corner baring face as about to when this happened. Quite audible then now for her and if other ears there with her in the dark for them and if ears low down in the wall at a for them a voice without meaning, hear that. Then further quite expressionless, ohs and ahs copulate cold and no more feeling apparently in hammock than in Jesus Christ Almighty. And finally for the moment and then that face the tail-away so common in untrained speakers leaving sometimes in some doubt such things as which Diogenes and what fancy her only. Such then the sound roughly and if no clearer so then all the storm unspoken and the silence unbroken unless sound of light and dark or at the moments of change a sound of flow thirty seconds till full then silence any length till sound of ebb thirty seconds till black then silence any length, that might repay hearing and she hearing open then her eyes to lightening or darkening greys and not close them then to keep them closed till next sound of change till full light or dark, that might well be imagined. But at the same time say here all sound most doubtful though still too soon to deny and that in the end that is when all gone from mind and all mind gone that then none ever been but only silent flesh unless with the faint rise and fall of breast the breath to whip up to a pant if too faint alone and all others denied but still too soon. Hollow cube then three foot overall, full glare, head on left cheek in angle a and the rest the only way and say though no clear image now the long black hair now scattered clear of face on floor so clear when strewn on face now gone some reason, come back to that later, and on the face now bare all the glare for the moment. Gone the remembered long black lashes vivid white so clear before through gap in hair before all tossed back and lost some reason and face quite bare suggesting perhaps confusion then with errant threads of hair itself confused then with long lashes and so gone with hair or some other reason now quite gone. Cease here from face a space to note how place no longer cube but rotunda three foot diameter eighteen inches high supporting a dome semi-circular in section as in the Pantheon at Rome or certain beehive tombs and consequently three foot from ground to vertex that is at its highest point no lower than before with loss of floor space in the neighbourhood of two square feet or six square inches per lost angle and consequences for recumbent readily imaginable and of cubic an even higher figure, all right, resume face. But a, b, c and d now where any pair of right-angled diameters meet circumference meaning tighter fit for Emma with loss if folded as before of nearly one foot from crown to arse and of more than one from arse to knees and of nearly one from knees to feet though she still might be mathematically speaking more than seven foot long and merely a question of refolding in such a way that if head on left cheek at new a and feet at new c then arse no longer at new d but somewhere between it and new c and knees no longer at new b but somewhere between it and new a with segments angled more acutely that is head almost touching knees and feet almost touching arse, all that most clear. Rotunda then three foot diameter and three from ground to vertex, full glare, head on left cheek at a no longer new, when suddenly clear these dimensions faulty and small woman scarce five foot fully extended making rotunda two foot diameter and two from ground to verge, full glare, face on left cheek at a and long segment that is from crown to arse now necessarily along diagonal too hastily assigned to middle with result face on left cheek with crown against wall at a and no longer feet but *arse* against wall at c there being no alternative and knees against wall ab a few inches from face and feet against wall bc a few inches from arse there being no alternatives and in this way the body tripled or trebled up and wedged in the only possible way in one half of the available room leaving the other empty, aha.

Diagram

Arms and hands as before for the moment. Rotunda then two foot across and at its highest two foot high, full glare, face on left cheek at a, long black hair gone, long black lashes on white cheekbone gone, glare from above for features on this bone-white undoubted face right profile still hungering for missing lashes burning down for commissure of lids at least when like say without hesitation hell gaping they part and the black eye appears, leave now this face for the moment. Glare now on hands most womanly clear and womanly especially right still loosely clenched as before but no longer on ground since corrected pose but now on outer of right knee just where it swells to thigh while left still loosely hitched to right shoulder ball as before. All that most clear. That black eye still yawning before going down to former to see what all this squeezing note how the other slips a little way down slope of upper arm then back up to ball, imagine squeeze again. Loose clench any length then crush down most womanly straining knuckles five seconds then back lax any length, all right, now down while fingers loose and in between tips and palm that tiny chink, full glare all this time. No real image but say like red no grey say like something grey and when again squeeze firm down five seconds say faint hiss then silence then back loose two seconds and say faint pop and so arrive though no true image at small grey punctured rubber ball or small grey ordinary rubber bulb such as on earth attached to bottle of scent or suchlike that when squeezed a jet of scent but here alone. So little by little all strange away. Avalanche white lava mud seethe lid over eye permitting return to face of which finally only that it could be nothing else, all right. Thence on to neck in health by nature blank chunk nearer to healthy natural neck with even hint of jugular and cords suggesting perhaps past her best and thence on down to other meat when suddenly when least expected all this prying pointless and enough for the moment and perhaps for ever this place so clear now when light at full and this body hinged and crooked as only the human man or woman living or not when light at full without all this poking and prying about for cracks holes and appendages. Rotunda then as before no change for the moment in dark and light no visible source spread even no shadow slow on thirty seconds to full same off to black two foot high at highest six and a half round good measure, wall peeling plaster or the like supporting dome semi-circular in section same surface, floor bleached dirt or similar, head wedged against wall at a with blank face on left cheek and the rest the only way that is arse wedged against wall at c and knees wedged against wall ab a few inches from face and feet wedged against wall bc a few inches from arse, puckered tip of left breast no real image but maintain for the moment, left hand most clear and womanly lightly clasping right shoulder ball so lightly that slip from time to time down slope of right upper arm then back up to clasp, right no less on upper outer right knee lightly clasping any length small grey rubber sprayer bulb or grey punctured rubber ball then squeeze five seconds on earth faint hiss relax two seconds and pop or not, black right eye like maintain hell gaping any length then seethe of lid to cover imagine frequency later and motive, left also at same time or not or never imagine later, all contained in one hemicycle leaving other vacant, aha. All that if not yet quite complete quite clear and little change likely unless perhaps to complete unless perhaps somehow light sudden gleam perhaps better fixed and all this flowing and ebbing to full and empty more harm than good and better unchanging black or glare one or the other or between the two soft white unchanging but leave for the moment as seen from outset and never doubted slow on and off thirty seconds to glare and black any length through slow lightening and darkening greys from nothing for no reason yet imagined. Sleep stirring now some time add now with nightmares unimaginable making waking sweet and lying waking till longing for sleep again with dread of demons, perhaps some glimpse of demons later. Dread then in rotunda now with longing and sweet relief but so faint and weak no more than weak tremors of a hothouse leaf. Memories of past felicity no save one faint with faint ripple of sorrow of a lying side by side, look at this closer later. Imagine turning over with help of hinge of neck to bow head towards breast and so temporarily shorten long segment unwedging crown and arse with play enough to writhe till finally head wedged against wall at a as before but on right cheek and arse against wall at c as before but on right cheek and knees against wall a few inches from face as before but wall ad and feet against wall a few inches from arse as before but wall cd and so all tripled up and wedged as before but on the other side to rest the other and within the other hemicycle leaving the other vacant, aha, all that most clear. Clear further how at some earlier more callow stage this writhe again and again in vain through weakness or natural awkwardness or want of pliancy or want of resolution and how halfway through on back with legs just clear how after some time in the balance thus the fall back to where she lay head wedged against wall at a with blank face on left cheek and arse against wall at c and knees against wall ab and feet against wall bc with left hand clutching lightly right shoulder ball and right on upper outer knee small grey sprayer bulb or grey punctured rubber ball with disappointment naturally tinged perhaps with relief and this again and again till final renouncement with faint sweet relief, faint disappointment will have been here too. Sleep if maintained with cacodemons making waking in light and dark if this maintained faint sweet relief and the longing for it again and to be gone again a folly to be resisted again in vain. No memories of felicity save with faint ripple of sorrow of a lying side by side and of misfortune none, look closer later. So in rotunda up to now with disappointment and relief with dread and longing sorrow all so weak and faint no more than faint tremors of a leaf indoors on earth in winter to survive till spring. Glare back now where all no light immeasurable turmoil no sound black soundless storm of which on earth all being well say one millionth stilled to mean and of that as much again by the more fortunate all being well vented as only humans can. All gone now and never been never stilled never voiced all back when never sundered unstillable turmoil no sound, She's not here, Fancy is her only, Mother mother, Mother in heaven and of God, God in heaven, Christ and Jesus all combinations, loved ones and places, philosophers and all mere cries, In a hammock etc. and all such, leaving only for the moment, Fancy dead, try that again with spirant barely parting lips in murmur and faint stir of white dust or not in light and dark if this maintained or dark alone as though ears when shining and dead uncertain in dying fall of amateur soliloquy when not known for certain. Last look oh not farewell but last for now on right side tripled up and wedged in half the room head against wall at a and arse against wall at c and knees against wall ab an inch or so from head and feet against wall bc an inch or so from arse. Then look away then back for left hand clasping lightly right shoulder ball any length till slip and back to clasp and right on upper outer knee any length grey sprayer bulb or small grey punctured rubber ball till squeeze with hiss and loose again with pop or not. Long black hair and lashes gone and puckered breast no details to add to these for the moment save normal neck with hint of cords and jugular and black bottomless eye. Within apart from fancy dead and with faint sorrow faint memory of a lying side by side and in sleep demons not yet imagined all dark unappeasable turmoil no sound and so exhaled only for the moment with faint sound, Fancy dead, to which now add for old mind's sake sorrow vented in simple sighing sound black vowel a and further so that henceforth here no other sounds than these say gone now and never were sprayer bulb or punctured rubber ball and nothing ever in that hand lightly closed on nothing any length till for no reason yet imagined fingers tighten then relax no sound and to the same end slip of left hand down slope of right upper arm no sound and same purpose none of breath to the end that here henceforth no other sounds than these and never were that is than sop to mind faint sighing sound for tremor of sorrow at faint memory of a lying side by side and fancy murmured dead.

Imagination Dead Imagine

NO TRACE ANYWHERE OF LIFE, you say, pah, no difficulty there, imagination not dead yet, yes, dead, good, imagination dead imagine. Islands, waters, azure, verdure, one glimpse and vanished, endlessly, omit. Till all white in the whiteness the rotunda. No way in, go in, measure. Diameter three feet, three feet from ground to summit of the vault. Two diameters at right angles AB CD divide the white ground into two semicircles ACB BDA. Lying on the ground two white bodies, each in its semicircle. White too the vault and the round wall eighteen inches high from which it springs. Go back out, a plain rotunda, all white in the whiteness, go back in, rap, solid throughout, a ring as in the imagination the ring of bone. The light that makes all so white no visible source, all shines with the same white shine, ground, wall, vault, bodies, no shadow. Strong heat, surfaces hot but not burning to the touch, bodies sweating. Go back out, move back, the little fabric vanishes, ascend, it vanishes, all white in the whiteness, descend, go back in. Emptiness, silence, heat, whiteness, wait, the light goes down, all grows dark together, ground, wall, vault, bodies, say twenty seconds, all the greys, the light goes out, all vanishes. At the same time the temperature goes down, to reach its minimum, say freezing-point, at the same in-

stant that the black is reached, which may seem strange. Wait,
more or less long, light and heat come back, all grows white and
hot together, ground, wall, vault, bodies, say twenty seconds, all
the greys, till the initial level is reached whence the fall began.
More or less long, for there may intervene, experience shows,
between end of fall and beginning of rise, pauses of varying
length, from the fraction of the second to what would have
seemed, in other times, other places, an eternity. Same remark
for the other pause, between end of rise and beginning of fall.
The extremes, as long as they last, are perfectly stable, which in
the case of the temperature may seem strange, in the beginning.
It is possible too, experience shows, for rise and fall to stop short
at any point and mark a pause, more or less long, before resuming, or reversing, the rise now fall, the fall rise, these in their turn
to be completed, or to stop short and mark a pause, more or less
long, before resuming, or again reversing, and so on, till finally
one or the other extreme is reached. Such variations of rise and
fall, combining in countless rhythms, commonly attend the passage from white and heat to black and cold, and vice versa. The
extremes alone are stable as is stressed by the vibration to be
observed when a pause occurs at some intermediate stage, no
matter what its level and duration. Then all vibrates, ground,
wall, vault, bodies, ashen or leaden or between the two, as may
be. But on the whole, experience shows, such uncertain passage is
not common. And most often, when the light begins to fail, and
along with it the heat, the movement continues unbroken until,
in the space of some twenty seconds, pitch black is reached and
at the same instant say freezing-point. Same remark for the reverse movement, towards heat and whiteness. Next most frequent is the fall or rise with pauses of varying length in these
feverish greys, without at any moment reversal of the movement.
But whatever its uncertainties the return sooner or later to a temporary calm seems assured, for the moment, in the black dark or

the great whiteness, with attendant temperature, world still proof against enduring tumult. Rediscovered miraculously after what absence in perfect voids it is no longer quite the same, from this point of view, but there is no other. Externally all is as before and the sighting of the little fabric quite as much a matter of chance, its whiteness merging in the surrounding whiteness. But go in and now briefer lulls and never twice the same storm. Light and heat remain linked as though supplied by the same source of which still no trace. Still on the ground, bent in three, the head against the wall at B, the arse against the wall at A, the knees against the wall between B and C, the feet against the wall between C and A, that is to say inscribed in the semicircle ACB, merging in the white ground were it not for the long hair of strangely imperfect whiteness, the white body of a woman finally. Similarly inscribed in the other semicircle, against the wall his head at A, his arse at B, his knees between A and D, his feet between D and B, the partner. On their right sides therefore both and back to back head to arse. Hold a mirror to their lips, it mists. With their left hands they hold their left legs a little below the knee, with their right hands their left arms a little above the elbow. In this agitated light, its great white calm now so rare and brief, inspection is not easy. Sweat and mirror notwithstanding they might well pass for inanimate but for the left eyes which at incalculable intervals suddenly open wide and gaze in unblinking exposure long beyond what is humanly possible. Piercing pale blue the effect is striking, in the beginning. Never the two gazes together except once, when the beginning of one overlapped the end of the other, for about ten seconds. Neither fat nor thin, big nor small, the bodies seem whole and in fairly good condition, to judge by the surfaces exposed to view. The faces too, assuming the two sides of a piece, seem to want nothing essential. Between their absolute stillness and the convulsive light the contrast is striking, in the beginning, for one who still remembers having been struck by the contrary. It is clear however, from a thousand little signs too long to imagine, that they are not sleeping. Only murmur ah, no more, in this silence, and at the same instant for the eye of prey the infinitesimal shudder instantaneously suppressed. Leave them there, sweating and icy, there is better elsewhere. No, life ends and no, there is nothing elsewhere, and no question now of ever finding again that white speck lost in whiteness, to see if they still lie still in the stress of that storm, or of a worse storm, or in the black dark for good, or the great whiteness unchanging, and if not what they are doing.

Translated by the author

Enough

ALL THAT GOES before forget. Too much at a time is too much. That gives the pen time to note. I don't see it but I hear it there behind me. Such is the silence. When the pen stops I go on. Sometimes it refuses. When it refuses I go on. Too much silence is too much. Or it's my voice too weak at times. The one that comes out of me. So much for the art and craft.

I did all he desired. I desired it too. For him. Whenever he desired something so did I. He only had to say what thing. When he didn't desire anything neither did I. In this way I didn't live without desires. If he had desired something for me I would have desired it too. Happiness for example or fame. I only had the desires he manifested. But he must have manifested them all. All his desires and needs. When he was silent he must have been like me. When he told me to lick his penis I hastened to do so. I drew satisfaction from it. We must have had the same satisfactions. The same needs and the same satisfactions.

One day he told me to leave him. It's the verb he used. He must have been on his last legs. I don't know if by that he meant me to leave him for good or only to step aside a moment. I never asked myself the question. I never asked myself any questions but his. Whatever it was he meant I made off without looking back. Gone from reach of his voice I was gone from his life. Perhaps it was that he desired. There are questions you see and don't ask yourself. He must have been on his last legs. I on the contrary was far from on my last legs. I belonged to an entirely different generation. It didn't last. Now that I'm entering night I have kinds of gleams in my skull. Stony ground but not entirely. Given three or four lives I might have accomplished something.

I cannot have been more than six when he took me by the hand. Barely emerging from childhood. But it didn't take me long to emerge altogether. It was the left hand. To be on the right was more than he could bear. We advanced side by side hand in hand. One pair of gloves was enough. The free or outer hands hung bare. He did not like to feel against his skin the skin of another. Mucous membrane is a different matter. Yet he sometimes took off his glove. Then I had to take off mine. We would cover in this way a hundred yards or so linked by our bare extremities. Seldom more. That was enough for him. If the question were put to me I would say that odd hands are ill-fitted for intimacy. Mine never felt at home in his. Sometimes they let each other go. The clasp loosened and they fell apart. Whole minutes often passed before they clasped again. Before his clasped mine again.

They were cotton gloves rather tight. Far from blunting the shapes they sharpened them by simplifying. Mine was naturally too loose for years. But it didn't take me long to fill it. He said I had Aquarius hands. It's a mansion above.

All I know comes from him. I won't repeat this apropos of all my bits of knowledge. The art of combining is not my fault. It's a curse from above. For the rest I would suggest not guilty.

Our meeting. Though very bowed already he looked a giant to me. In the end his trunk ran parallel with the ground.

To counterbalance this anomaly he held his legs apart and sagged at the knees. His feet grew more and more flat and splay. His horizon was the ground they trod. Tiny moving carpet of turf and trampled flowers. He gave me his hand like a tired old ape with the elbow lifted as high as it would go. I had only to straighten up to be head and shoulders above him. One day he halted and fumbling for his words explained to me that anatomy is a whole.

In the beginning he always spoke walking. So it seems to me now. Then sometimes walking and sometimes still. In the end still only. And the voice getting fainter all the time. To save him having to say the same thing twice running I bowed right down. He halted and waited for me to get into position. As soon as out of the corner of his eye he glimpsed my head alongside his the murmurs came. Nine times out of ten they did not concern me. But he wished everything to be heard including the ejaculations and broken paternosters that he poured out to the flowers at his feet.

He halted then and waited for my head to arrive before telling me to leave him. I snatched away my hand and made off without looking back. Two steps and I was lost to him for ever. We were severed if that is what he desired.

His talk was seldom of geodesy. But we must have covered several times the equivalent of the terrestrial equator. At an average speed of roughly three miles per day and night. We took flight in arithmetic. What mental calculations bent double hand in hand! Whole ternary numbers we raised in this way to the third power sometimes in downpours of rain. Graving themselves in his memory as best they could the ensuing cubes accumulated. In view of the converse operation at a later stage. When time would have done its work.

If the question were put to me suitably framed I would say yes indeed the end of this long outing was my life. Say about the last seven thousand miles. Counting from the day when al-luding for the first time to his infirmity he said he thought it had reached its peak. The future proved him right. That part of it at least we were to make past of together.

I see the flowers at my feet and it's the others I see. Those we trod down with equal step. It is true they are the same.

Contrary to what I had long been pleased to imagine he was not blind. Merely indolent. One day he halted and fumbling for his words described his vision. He concluded by saying he thought it would get no worse. How far this was not a delusion I cannot say. I never asked myself the question. When I bowed down to receive his communications I felt on my eye a glint of blue bloodshot apparently affected.

He sometimes halted without saying anything. Either he had finally nothing to say or while having something to say he finally decided not to say it. I bowed down as usual to save him having to repeat himself and we remained in this position. Bent double heads touching silent hand in hand. While all about us fast on one another the minutes flew. Sooner or later his foot broke away from the flowers and we moved on. Perhaps only to halt again after a few steps. So that he might say at last what was in his heart or decide not to say it again.

Other main examples suggest themselves to the mind. Immediate continuous communication with immediate redeparture. Same thing with delayed redeparture. Delayed continuous communication with immediate redeparture. Same thing with delayed redeparture. Immediate discontinuous communication with immediate redeparture. Same thing with delayed redeparture. Delayed discontinuous communication with immediate redeparture. Same thing with delayed redeparture.

It is then I shall have lived then or never. Ten years at the very least. From the day he drew the back of his left hand linger-ingly over his sacral ruins and launched his prognostic. To the day of my supposed disgrace. I can see the place a step short of the crest. Two steps forward and I was descending the other slope. If I had looked back I would not have seen him.

He loved to climb and therefore I too. He clamoured for the steepest slopes. His human frame broke down into two equal segments. This thanks to the shortening of the lower by the sagging knees. On a gradient of one in one his head swept the ground. To what this taste was due I cannot say. To love of the earth and the flowers' thousand scents and hues. Or to cruder imperatives of an anatomical order. He never raised the question. The crest once reached alas the going down again.

In order from time to time to enjoy the sky he resorted to a little round mirror. Having misted it with his breath and polished it on his calf he looked in it for the constellations. I have it! he exclaimed referring to the Lyre or the Swan. And often he added that the sky seemed much the same.

We were not in the mountains however. There were times I discerned on the horizon a sea whose level seemed higher than ours. Could it be the bed of some vast evaporated lake or drained of its waters from below? I never asked myself the question.

The fact remains we often came upon this sort of mound some three hundred feet in height. Reluctantly I raised my eyes and discerned the nearest often on the horizon. Or instead of moving on from the one we had just descended we ascended it again.

I am speaking of our last decade comprised between the two events described. It veils those that went before and must have resembled it like blades of grass. To those engulfed years it is reasonable to impute my education. For I don't remember having learnt anything in those I remember. It is with this reasoning I calm myself when brought up short by all I know.

I set the scene of my disgrace just short of a crest. On the contrary it was on the flat in a great calm. If I had looked back I would have seen him in the place where I had left him. Some trifle would have shown me my mistake if mistake there had been. In the years that followed I did not exclude the possibility of finding him again. In the place where I had left him if not elsewhere. Or of hearing him call me. At the same time telling myself he was on his last legs. But I did not count on it unduly. For I hardly raised my eyes from the flowers. And his voice was spent. And as if that were not enough I kept telling myself he was on his last legs. So it did not take me long to stop counting on it altogether.

I don't know what the weather is now. But in my life it was eternally mild. As if the earth had come to rest in spring. I am thinking of our hemisphere. Sudden pelting downpours overtook us. Without noticeable darkening of the sky. I would not have noticed the windlessness if he had not spoken of it. Of the wind that was no more. Of the storms he had ridden out. It is only fair to say there was nothing to sweep away. The very flowers were stemless and flush with the ground like water-lilies. No brightening our buttonholes with these.

We did not keep tally of the days. If I arrive at ten years it is thanks to our pedometer. Total milage divided by average daily milage. So many days. Divide. Such a figure the night before the sacrum. Such another the eve of my disgrace. Daily average always up to date. Subtract. Divide.

Night. As long as day in this endless equinox. It falls and we go on. Before dawn we are gone.

Attitude at rest. Wedged together bent in three. Second right angle at the knees. I on the inside. We turn over as one man when he manifests the desire. I can feel him at night pressed against me with all his twisted length. It was less a matter of sleeping than of lying down. For we walked in a half sleep. With his upper hand he held and touched me where he wished. Up to a certain point. The other was twined in my hair. He murmured of things that for him were no more and for me could not have been. The wind in the overground stems. The shade and shelter of the forests.

He was not given to talk. An average of a hundred words per day and night. Spaced out. A bare million in all. Numerous repeats. Ejaculations. Too few for even a cursory survey. What do I know of man's destiny? I could tell you more about radishes. For them he had a fondness. If I saw one I would name it without hesitation.

We lived on flowers. So much for sustenance. He halted and without having to stoop caught up a handful of petals. Then moved munching on. They had on the whole a calming action. We were on the whole calm. More and more. All was. This notion of calm comes from him. Without him I would not have had it. Now I'll wipe out everything but the flowers. No more rain. No more mounds. Nothing but the two of us dragging through the flowers. Enough my old breasts feel his old hand.

Translated by the author

Ping

ALL KNOWN all white bare white body fixed one yard legs joined like sewn. Light heat white floor one square yard never seen. White walls one yard by two white ceiling one square yard never seen. Bare white body fixed only the eyes only just. Traces blurs light grey almost white on white. Hands hanging palms front white feet heels together right angle. Light heat white planes shining white bare white body fixed ping fixed elsewhere. Traces blurs signs no meaning light grey almost white. Bare white body fixed white on white invisible. Only the eyes only just light blue almost white. Head haught eyes light blue almost white silence within. Brief murmurs only just almost never all known. Traces blurs signs no meaning light grey almost white. Legs joined like sewn heels together right angle. Traces alone unover given black light grey almost white on white. Light heat white walls shining white one yard by two. Bare white body fixed one yard ping fixed elsewhere. Traces blurs signs no meaning light grey almost white. White feet toes joined like sewn heels together right angle invisible. Eyes alone unover given blue light blue almost white. Murmur only just almost never one second perhaps not alone. Given rose only just bare white body fixed one yard white on white invisible. All white all known murmurs only just almost never always the same all known. Light heat hands hanging palms front white on white invisible. Bare white body fixed ping fixed elsewhere. Only the eyes only just light blue almost white fixed front. Ping murmur only just almost never one second perhaps a way out. Head haught eyes light blue almost white fixed front ping murmur ping silence. Eyes holes light blue almost white mouth white seam like sewn invisible. Ping murmur perhaps a nature one second almost never that much memory almost never. White walls each its trace grey blur signs no meaning light grey almost white. Light heat all known all white planes meeting invisible. Ping murmur only just almost never one second perhaps a meaning that much memory almost never. White feet toes joined like sewn heels together right angle ping elsewhere no sound. Hands hanging palms front legs joined like sewn. Head haught eyes holes light blue almost white fixed front silence within. Ping elsewhere always there but that known not. Eyes holes light blue alone unover given blue light blue almost white only colour fixed front. All white all known white planes shining white ping murmur only just almost never one second light time that much memory almost never. Bare white body fixed one yard ping fixed elsewhere white on white invisible heart breath no sound. Only the eyes given blue light blue almost white fixed front only colour alone unover. Planes meeting invisible one only shining white infinite but that known not. Nose ears white holes mouth white seam like sewn invisible. Ping murmurs only just almost never one second always the same all known. Given rose only just bare white body fixed one yard invisible all known without within. Ping perhaps a nature one second with image same time a little less blue and white in the wind. White ceiling shining white one square yard never seen ping perhaps way out there one second ping silence. Traces alone unover given black grey blurs signs no meaning light grey almost white always the same. Ping perhaps not alone one second with image always the same same time a little less that much memory almost never ping silence. Given rose only just nails fallen white over. Long hair fallen white invisible over. White scars invisible same white as flesh torn of old given rose only just. Ping image only just almost never one second light time blue and white in the wind. Head haught nose ears white holes mouth white seam like sewn invisible over. Only the eyes given blue fixed front light blue almost white only colour alone unover. Light heat white planes shining white one only shining white infinite but that known not. Ping a nature only just almost never one second with image same time a little less blue and white in the wind. Traces blurs light grey eyes holes light blue almost white fixed front ping a meaning only just almost never ping silence. Bare white one yard fixed ping fixed elsewhere no sound legs joined like sewn heels together right angle hands hanging palms front. Head haught eyes holes light blue almost white fixed front silence within. Ping elsewhere always there but that known not. Ping perhaps not alone one second with image same time a little less dim eye black and white half closed long lashes imploring that much memory almost never. Afar flash of time all white all over all of old ping flash white walls shining white no trace eyes holes light blue almost white last colour ping white over. Ping fixed last elsewhere legs joined like sewn heels together right angle hands hanging palms front head haught eyes white invisible fixed front over. Given rose only just one yard invisible bare white all known without within over. White ceiling never seen ping of old only just almost never one second light time white floor never seen ping of old perhaps there. Ping of old only just perhaps a meaning a nature one second almost never blue and white in the wind that much memory henceforth never. White planes no trace shining white one only shining white infinite but that known not. Light heat all known all white heart breath no sound. Head haught eyes white fixed front old ping last murmur one second perhaps not alone eye unlustrous black and white half closed long lashes imploring ping silence ping over.

Translated by the author

Lessness

RUINS TRUE REFUGE long last towards which so many false time out of mind. All sides endlessness earth sky as one no sound no stir. Grey face two pale blue little body heart beating only upright. Blacked out fallen open four walls over backwards true refuge issueless.

Scattered ruins same grey as the sand ash grey true refuge. Four square all light sheer white blank planes all gone from mind. Never was but grey air timeless no sound figment the passing light. No sound no stir ash grey sky mirrored earth mirrored sky. Never but this changelessness dream the passing hour.

He will curse God again as in the blessed days face to the open sky the passing deluge. Little body grey face features crack and little holes two pale blue. Blank planes sheer white eye calm long last all gone from mind.

Figment light never was but grey air timeless no sound. Blank planes touch close sheer white all gone from mind. Little body ash grey locked rigid heart beating face to endlessness. On him will rain again as in the blessed days of blue the passing cloud. Four square true refuge long last four walls over backwards no sound.

Grey sky no cloud no sound no stir earth ash grey sand.

Little body same grey as the earth sky ruins only upright. Ash grey all sides earth sky as one all sides endlessness.

He will stir in the sand there will be stir in the sky the air the sand. Never but in dream the happy dream only one time to serve. Little body little block heart beating ash grey only upright. Earth sky as one all sides endlessness little body only upright. In the sand no hold one step more in the endlessness he will make it. No sound not a breath same grey all sides earth sky body ruins.

Slow black with ruin true refuge four walls over backwards no sound. Legs a single block arms fast to sides little body face to endlessness. Never but in vanished dream the passing hour long short. Only upright little body grey smooth no relief a few holes. One step in the ruins in the sand on his back in the endlessness he will make it. Never but dream the days and nights made of dreams of other nights better days. He will live again the space of a step it will be day and night again over him the endlessness.

In four split asunder over backwards true refuge issueless scattered ruins. Little body little block genitals overrun arse a single block grey crack overrun. True refuge long last issueless scattered down four walls over backwards no sound. All sides endlessness earth sky as one no stir not a breath. Blank planes sheer white calm eye light of reason all gone from mind. Scattered ruins ash grey all sides true refuge long last issueless.

Ash grey little body only upright heart beating face to endlessness. Old love new love as in the blessed days unhappiness will reign again. Earth sand same grey as the air sky ruins body fine ash grey sand. Light refuge sheer white blank planes all gone from mind. Flatness endless little body only upright same grey all sides earth sky body ruins. Face to white calm touch close eye calm long last all gone from mind. One step more one alone all alone in the sand no hold he will make it.

Blacked out fallen open true refuge issueless towards which so many false time out of mind. Never but silence such that in imagination this wild laughter these cries. Head through calm eye all light white calm all gone from mind. Figment dawn dispeller of figments and the other called dusk.

He will go on his back face to the sky open again over him the ruins the sand the endlessness. Grey air timeless earth sky as one same grey as the ruins flatness endless. It will be day and night again over him the endlessness the air heart will beat again. True refuge long last scattered ruins same grey as the sand.

Face to calm eye touch close all calm all white all gone from mind. Never but imagined the blue in a wild imagining the blue celeste of poesy. Little void mighty light four square all white blank planes all gone from mind. Never was but grey air timeless no stir not a breath. Heart beating little body only upright grey face features overrun two pale blue. Light white touch close head through calm eye light of reason all gone from mind.

Little body same grey as the earth sky ruins only upright. No sound not a breath same grey all sides earth sky body ruins. Blacked out fallen open four walls over backwards true refuge issueless.

No sound no stir ash grey sky mirrored earth mirrored sky. Grey air timeless earth sky as one same grey as the ruins flatness endless. In the sand no hold one step more in the endlessness he will make it. It will be day and night again over him the endlessness the air heart will beat again.

Figment light never was but grey air timeless no sound. All sides endlessness earth sky as one no stir not a breath. On him will rain again as in the blessed days of blue the passing cloud. Grey sky no cloud no sound no stir earth ash grey sand.

Little void mighty light four square all white blank planes all gone from mind. Flatness endless little body only upright same grey all sides earth sky body ruins. Scattered ruins same grey as the sand ash grey true refuge. Four square true refuge long last four walls over backwards no sound. Never but this changelessness dream the passing hour. Never was but grey air timeless no sound figment the passing light.

In four split asunder over backwards true refuge issueless scattered ruins. He will live again the space of a step it will be day and night again over him the endlessness. Face to white calm touch close eye calm long last all gone from mind. Grey face two pale blue little body heart beating only upright. He will go on his back face to the sky open again over him the ruins the sand the endlessness. Earth sand same grey as the air sky ruins body fine ash grey sand. Blank planes touch close sheer white all gone from mind.

Heart beating little body only upright grey face features overrun two pale blue. Only upright little body grey smooth no relief a few holes. Never but dream the days and nights made of dreams of other nights better days. He will stir in the sand there will be stir in the sky the air the sand. One step in the ruins in the sand on his back in the endlessness he will make it. Never but silence such that in imagination this wild laughter these cries.

True refuge long last scattered ruins same grey as the sand. Never was but grey air timeless no stir not a breath. Blank planes sheer white calm eye light of reason all gone from mind. Never but in vanished dream the passing hour long short. Four square all light sheer white blank planes all gone from mind.

Blacked out fallen open true refuge issueless towards which so many false time out of mind. Head through calm eye all light white calm all gone from mind. Old love new love as in the blessed days unhappiness will reign again. Ash grey all sides earth sky as one all sides endlessness. Scattered ruins ash grey all sides true refuge long last issueless. Never but in dream the happy dream only one time to serve. Little body grey face features crack and little holes two pale blue.

Ruins true refuge long last towards which so many false time out of mind. Never but imagined the blue in a wild imagining the blue celeste of poesy. Light white touch close head through calm eye light of reason all gone from mind.

Slow black with ruin true refuge four walls over backwards no sound. Earth sky as one all sides endlessness little body only upright. One step more one alone all alone in the sand no hold he will make it. Ash grey little body only upright heart beating face to endlessness. Light refuge sheer white blank planes all gone from mind. All sides endlessness earth sky as one no sound no stir.

Legs a single block arms fast to sides little body face to endlessness. True refuge long last issueless scattered down four walls over backwards no sound. Blank planes sheer white eye calm long last all gone from mind. He will curse God again as in the blessed days face to the open sky the passing deluge. Face to calm eye touch close all calm all white all gone from mind.

Little body little block heart beating ash grey only upright. Little body ash grey locked rigid heart beating face to endlessness. Little body little block genitals overrun arse a single block grey crack overrun. Figment dawn dispeller of figments and the other called dusk.

Translated by the author

The Lost Ones

ABODE WHERE LOST bodies roam each searching for its lost one. Vast enough for search to be in vain. Narrow enough for flight to be in vain. Inside a flattened cylinder fifty metres round and sixteen high for the sake of harmony. The light. Its dimness. Its yellowness. Its omnipresence as though every separate square centimetre were agleam of the some twelve million of total surface. Its restlessness at long intervals suddenly stilled like panting at the last. Then all go dead still. It is perhaps the end of their abode. A few seconds and all begins again. Consequences of this light for the searching eye. Consequences for the eye which having ceased to search is fastened to the ground or raised to the distant ceiling where none can be. The temperature. It oscillates with more measured beat between hot and cold. It passes from one extreme to the other in about four seconds. It too has its moments of stillness more or less hot or cold. They coincide with those of the light. Then all go dead still. It is perhaps the end of all. A few seconds and all begins again. Consequences of this climate for the skin. It shrivels. The bodies brush together with a rustle of dry leaves. The mucous membrane itself is affected. A kiss makes an indescribable sound. Those with stomach still to copulate strive in vain. But they will not give in. Floor and wall are of solid rubber or suchlike. Dash against them foot or fist or head and the sound is scarcely heard. Imagine then the silence of the steps. The only sounds worthy of the name result from the manipulation of the ladders or the thud of bodies striking against one another or of one against itself as when in sudden fury it beats its breast. Thus flesh and bone subsist. The ladders. These are the only objects. They are single without exception and vary greatly in size. The shortest measure not less than six metres. Some are fitted with a sliding extension. They are propped against the wall without regard to harmony. Bolt upright on the top rung of the tallest the tallest climbers can touch the ceiling with their fingertips. Its composition is no less familiar therefore than that of floor and wall. Dash a rung against it and the sound is scarcely heard. These ladders are in great demand. At the foot of each at all times or nearly a little queue of climbers. And yet it takes courage to climb. For half the rungs are missing and this without regard to harmony. If only every second one were missing no great harm would be done. But the want of three in a row calls for acrobatics. These ladders are nevertheless in great demand and in no danger of being reduced to mere uprights runged at their extremities alone. For the need to climb is too widespread. To feel it no longer is a rare deliverance. The missing rungs are in the hands of a happy few who use them mainly for attack and self-defence. Their solitary attempts to brain themselves culminate at the best in brief losses of consciousness. The purpose of the ladders is to convey the searchers to the niches. Those whom these entice no longer climb simply to get clear of the ground. It is the custom not to climb two or more at a time. To the fugitive fortunate enough to find a ladder free it offers certain refuge until the clamours subside. The niches or alcoves. These are cavities sunk in that part of the wall which lies above an imaginary line running midway between floor and ceiling and features therefore of its upper half alone. A

more or less wide mouth gives rapid access to a chamber of varying capacity but always sufficient for a body in reasonable command of its joints to enter in and similarly once in to crouch
down after a fashion. They are disposed in irregular quincunxes
roughly ten metres in diameter and cunningly out of line. Such
harmony only he can relish whose long experience and detailed
knowledge of the niches are such as to permit a perfect mental
image of the entire system. But it is doubtful that such a one
exists. For each climber has a fondness for certain niches and
refrains as far as possible from the others. A certain number are
connected by tunnels opened in the thickness of the wall and
attaining in some cases no fewer than fifty metres in length. But
most have no other way out than the way in. It is as though at a
certain stage discouragement had prevailed. To be noted in support of this wild surmise the existence of a long tunnel abandoned blind. Woe the body that rashly enters here to be
compelled finally after long efforts to crawl back backwards as
best it can the way it came. Not that this drama is peculiar to the
unifinished tunnel. One has only to consider what inevitably
must ensue when two bodies enter a normal tunnel at the same
time by opposite ends. Niches and tunnels are subject to the
same light and climate as the rest of the abode. So much for a
first aperçu of the abode.

One body per square metre or two hundred bodies in all
round numbers. Whether relatives near and far or friends in
varying degree many in theory are acquainted. The gloom and
press make recognition difficult. Seen from a certain angle these
bodies are of four kinds. Firstly those perpetually in motion.
Secondly those who sometimes pause. Thirdly those who short
of being driven off never stir from the coign they have won and
when driven off pounce on the first free one that offers and
freeze again. That is not quite accurate. For if among these sedentary the need to climb is dead it is none the less subject to

strange resurrections. The quidam then quits his post in search of a free ladder or to join the nearest or shortest queue. The truth is that no searcher can readily forgo the ladder. Paradoxically the sedentary are those whose acts of violence most disrupt the cylinder's quiet. Fourthly those who do not search or non-searchers sitting for the most part against the wall in the attitude which wrung from Dante one of his rare wan smiles. By non-searchers and despite the abyss to which this leads it is finally impossible to understand other than ex-searchers. To rid this notion of some of its virulence one has only to suppose the need to search no less resurrectable than that of the ladder and those eyes to all appearances for ever cast down or closed possessed of the strange power suddenly to kindle again before passing face and body. But enough will always subsist to spell for this little people the extinction soon or late of its last remaining fires. A languishing happily unperceived because of its slowness and the resurgences that make up for it in part and the inattention of those concerned dazed by the passion preying on them still or by the state of languor into which imperceptibly they are already fallen. And far from being able to imagine their last state when every body will be still and every eye vacant they will come to it unwitting and be so unawares. Then light and climate will be changed in a way impossible to foretell. But the former may be imagined extinguished as purposeless and the latter fixed not far from freezing point. In cold darkness motionless flesh. So much roughly speaking for these bodies seen from a certain angle and for this notion and its consequences if it is maintained.

Inside a cylinder fifty metres round and sixteen high for the sake of harmony or a total surface of roughly twelve hundred square metres of which eight hundred mural. Not counting the niches and tunnels. Omnipresence of a dim yellow light shaken by a vertiginous tremolo between contiguous extremes. Temperature agitated by a like oscillation but thirty or forty times slower in virtue of which it falls rapidly from a maximum of twenty-five degrees approximately to a minimum of approximately five whence a regular variation of five degrees per second. That is not quite accurate. For it is clear that at both extremes of the shuttle the difference can fall to as little as one degree only. But this remission never lasts more than a little less than a second. At great intervals suspension of the two vibrations fed no doubt from a single source and resumption together after a lull of varying duration but never exceeding ten seconds or thereabouts. Corresponding abeyance of all motion among the bodies in motion and heightened fixity of the motionless. Only objects fifteen single ladders propped against the wall at irregular intervals. In the upper half of the wall disposed quincuncially for the sake of harmony a score of niches some connected by tunnels.

From time immemorial rumour has it or better still the notion is abroad that there exists a way out. Those who no longer believe so are not immune from believing so again in accordance with the notion requiring as long as it holds that here all should die but with so gradual and to put it plainly so fluctuant a death as to escape the notice even of a visitor. Regarding the nature of this way out and its location two opinions divide without opposing all those still loyal to that old belief. One school swears by a secret passage branching from one of the tunnels and leading in the words of the poet to nature's sanctuaries. The other dreams of a trapdoor hidden in the hub of the ceiling giving access to a flue at the end of which the sun and other stars would still be shining. Conversion is frequent either way and such a one who at a given moment would hear of nothing but the tunnel may well a moment later hear of nothing but the trapdoor and a moment later still give himself the lie again. The fact remains none the less that of these two persuasions the former is declining in favour of the latter but in a manner so desultory and slow and of course with so little effect on the comportment of either sect that to perceive it one must be in the secret of the gods. This shift has logic on its side. For those who believe in a way out possible of access as via a tunnel it would be and even without any thought of putting it to account may be tempted by its quest. Whereas the partisans of the trapdoor are spared this demon by the fact that the hub of the ceiling is out of reach. Thus by insensible degrees the way out transfers from the tunnel to the ceiling prior to never having been. So much for a first aperçu of this credence so singular in itself and by reason of the loyalty it inspires in the hearts of so many possessed. Its fatuous little light will be assuredly the last to leave them always assuming they are darkward bound.

Bolt upright on the top rung of the great ladder fully extended and reared against the wall the tallest climbers can touch the edge of the ceiling with their fingertips. On the same ladder planted perpendicular at the centre of the floor the same bodies would gain half a metre and so be enabled to explore at leisure the fabulous zone decreed out of reach and which therefore in theory is in no wise so. For such recourse to the ladder is conceivable. All that is needed is a score of determined volunteers joining forces to keep it upright with the help if necessary of other ladders acting as stays or struts. An instant of fraternity. But outside their explosions of violence this sentiment is as foreign to them as to butterflies. And this owing not so much to want of heart or intelligence as to the ideal preying on one and all. So much for this inviolable zenith where for amateurs of myth lies hidden a way out to earth and sky.

The use of the ladders is regulated by conventions of obscure origin which in their precision and the submission they exact from the climbers resemble laws. Certain infractions unleash against the culprit a collective fury surprising in creatures so peaceable on the whole and apart from the grand affair so careless of one another. Others on the contrary scarcely ruffle the general indifference. This at first sight is strange. All rests on the rule against mounting the ladder more than one at a time. It remains taboo therefore to the climber waiting at its foot until such time as his predecessor has regained the ground. Idle to imagine the confusion that would result from the absence of such a rule or from its non-observance. But devised for the convenience of all there is no question of its applying without restriction or as a licence for the unprincipled climber to engross the ladder beyond what is reasonable. For without some form of curb he might take the fancy to settle down permanently in one of the niches or tunnels leaving behind him a ladder out of service for good and all. And were others to follow his example as inevitably they must the spectacle would finally be offered of one hundred and eighty-five searchers less the vanquished committed for all time to the ground. Not to mention the intolerable presence of properties serving no purpose. It is therefore understood that after a certain interval difficult to assess but unerringly timed by all the ladder is again available meaning at the disposal in the same conditions of him due next to climb easily recognizable by his position at the head of the queue and so much the worst for the abuser. The situation of this latter having lost his ladder is delicate indeed and seems to exclude a priori his ever returning to the ground. Happily sooner or later he succeeds in doing so thanks to a further provision giving priority at all times to descent over ascent. He has therefore merely to watch at the mouth of his niche for a ladder to present itself and immediately start down quite easy in his mind knowing full well that whoever below is on the point of mounting if not already on his way up will give way in his favour. The worst that can befall him is a long vigil because of the ladders' mobility. It is indeed rare for a climber when it comes to his turn to content himself with the same niche as his predecessor and this for obvious reasons that will appear in due course. But rather he makes off with his ladder followed by the queue and plants it under one or other of the five niches available by reason of the difference in number between these and the ladders. But to return to the unforunate having outstayed his time it is clear that his chances of rapid redescent will be increased though far from doubled if thanks to a tunnel he disposes of two niches from which to watch. Though even in this event he usually prefers and invariably if the tunnel is a long one to plump for one only lest a ladder should present itself at one or the other and he still crawling between the two. But the ladders do not serve only as vehicles to the niches and tunnels and those whom these have ceased if only temporarily to entice use them simply to get clear of the ground. They mount to the level of their choice and there stay and settle standing as a rule with their faces to the wall. This family of climbers too is liable to exceed the allotted time. It is in order then for him due next for the ladder to climb in the wake of the offender and by means of one or more thumps on the back bring him back to a sense of his surroundings. Upon which he unfailingly hastens to descend preceded by his successor who has then merely to take over the ladder subject to the usual conditions. This docility in the abuser shows clearly that the abuse is not deliberate but due to a temporary derangement of his inner timepiece easy to understand and therefore to forgive. Here is the reason why this in reality infrequent infringement whether on the part of those who push on up to the niches and tunnels or of those who halt on the way never gives rise to the fury vented on the wretch with no better sense than to climb before his time and yet whose precipitancy one would have thought quite as understandable and consequently forgivable as the converse excess. This is indeed strange. But what is at stake is the fundamental principle forbidding ascent more than one at a time the repeated violation of which would soon transform the abode into a pandemonium. Whereas the belated return to the ground hurts finally none but the laggard himself. So much for a first aperçu of the climbers' code.

Similarly the transport of the ladders is not left to the good pleasure of the carriers who are required to hug the wall at all times eddywise. This is a rule no less strict than the prohibition to climb more than one at a time and not lightly to be broken. Nothing more natural. For if for the sake of the shortcut it were permitted to carry the ladder slap through the press or skirting the wall at will in either direction life in the cylinder would soon become untenable. All along the wall therefore a belt about one metre wide is reserved for the carriers. To this zone those also are confined who wait their turn to climb and must close their ranks and flatten themselves as best they can with their backs to the wall so as not to encroach on the arena proper.

It is curious to note the presence within this belt of a certain number of sedentary searchers sitting or standing against the wall. Dead to the ladders to all intents and purposes and a source of annoyance for both climbers and carriers they are nevertheless tolerated. The fact is that these sort of semi-sages among whom all ages are to be admired from old age to infancy inspire in those still fitfully fevering if not a cult at least a certain deference. They cling to this as to a homage due to them and are morbidly susceptible to the least want of consideration. A sedentary searcher stepped on instead of over is capable of such an outburst of fury as to throw the entire cylinder into a ferment. Cleave also to the wall both sitting and standing four vanquished out of five. They may be walked on without their reacting.

To be noted finally the care taken by the searchers in the arena not to overflow on the climbers' territory. When weary of searching among the throng they turn towards this zone it is only to skirt with measured tread its imaginary edge devouring with their eyes its occupants. Their slow round counter-carrier-wise creates a second even narrower belt respected in its turn by the main body of searchers. Which suitably lit from above would give the impression at times of two narrow rings turning in opposite directions about the teeming precinct.

One body per square metre of available surface or two hundred bodies in all round numbers. Bodies of either sex and all ages from old age to infancy. Sucklings who having no longer to suck huddle at gaze in the lap or sprawled on the ground in precocious postures. Others a little more advanced crawl searching among the legs. Picturesque detail a woman with white hair still young to judge by her thighs leaning against the wall with eyes closed in abandonment and mechanically clasping to her breast a mite who strains away in an effort to turn its head and look behind. But such tiny ones are comparatively few. None looks within himself where none can be. Eyes cast down or closed signify abandonment and are confined to the vanquished. These precisely to be counted on the fingers of one hand are not necessarily still. They may stray unseeing through the throng indistinguishable to the eye of flesh from the still unrelenting. These recognize them and make way. They may wait their turn at the foot of the ladders and when it comes ascend to the niches or simply leave the ground. They may crawl blindly in the tunnels in search of nothing. But normally abandonment freezes them both in space and in their pose whether standing or sitting as a rule profoundly bowed. It is this makes it possible to tell them from the sedentary devouring with their eyes in heads dead still each body as it passes by. Standing or sitting they cleave to the wall all but one in the arena stricken rigid in the midst of the fevering. These recognize him and keep their distance. The spent eyes may have fits of the old craving just as those who having renounced the ladder suddenly take to it again. So true it is that when in the cylinder what little is possible is not so it is merely no longer so and in the least less the all of nothing if this notion is maintained. Then the eyes suddenly start to search afresh as famished as the unthinkable first day until for no clear reason they as suddenly close again or the head falls. Even so a great heap of sand sheltered from the wind lessened by three grains every second year and every following increased by two if this notion is maintained. If then the vanquished have still some way to go what can be said of the others and what better name be given them than the fair name of searchers? Some and indeed by far the greater number never pause except when they line up for a ladder or watch out at the mouth of a niche. Some come to rest from time to time all but the unceasing eyes. As for the sedentary if they never stir from the coign they have won it is because they have calculated their best chance is there and if they seldom or never ascend to the niches and tunnels it is because they have done so too often in vain or come there too often to grief. An intelligence would be tempted to see in these the next vanquished and continuing in its stride to require of those still perpetually in motion that they all soon or late one after another be as those who sometimes pause and of these that they finally be as the sedentary and of the sedentary that they be in the end as the vanquished and of the two hundred vanquished thus obtained that all in due course each in his turn be well and truly vanquished for good and all each frozen in his place and attitude. But let these families be numbered in order of maturity and experience shows that it is possible to graduate from one to three skipping two and from one to four skipping two or three or both and from two to four skipping three. In the other direction the ill-vanquished may at long intervals and with each relapse more briefly revert to the state of the sedentary who in their turn count a few chronic waverers prone to succumb to the ladder again while remaining dead to the arena. But never again will they ceaselessly come and go who now at long intervals come to rest without ceasing to search with their eyes. In the beginning then unthinkable as the end all roamed without respite including the nurselings in so far as they were borne except of course those already at the foot of the ladders or frozen in the tunnels the better to listen or crouching all eyes in the niches and so roamed a vast space of time impossible to measure until a first came to a standstill followed by a second and so on. But as to at this moment of time and there will be no other numbering the faithful who endlessly come and go impatient of the least repose and those who every now and then stand still and the sedentary and the so-called vanquished may it suffice to state that at this moment of time to the nearest body in spite of the press and gloom the first are twice as many as the second who are three times as many as the third who are four times as many as the fourth namely five vanquished in all. Relatives and friends are well represented not to speak of mere acquaintances. Press and gloom make recognition difficult. Man and wife are strangers two paces apart to mention only this most intimate of all bonds. Let them move on till they are close enough to touch and then without pausing on their way exchange a look. If they recognize each other it does not appear. Whatever it is they are searching for it is not that.

What first impresses in this gloom is the sensation of yellow it imparts not to say of sulphur in view of the associations. Then how it throbs with constant unchanging beat and fast but not so fast that the pulse is no longer felt. And finally much later that ever and anon there comes a momentary lull. The effect of those brief and rare respites is unspeakably dramatic to put it mildly. Those who never know a moment's rest stand rooted to the spot often in extravagant postures and the stillness heightened tenfold of the sedentary and vanquished makes that which is normally theirs seem risible in comparison. The fists on their way to smite in anger or discouragement freeze in their arcs until the scare is past and the blow can be completed or volley of blows. Similarly without entering into tedious details those surprised in the act of climbing or carrying a ladder or making unmakable love or crouched in the niches or crawling in the tunnels as the case may be. But a brief ten seconds at most and the throbbing is resumed and all is as before. Those interrupted in their coming and going start coming and going again and the motionless relax. The lovers buckle to anew and the fists carry on where they left off. The murmur cut off as though by a switch fills the cylinder again. Among all the components the sum of which it is the ear finally distinguishes a faint stridulence as of insects which is that of the light itself and the one invariable. Between the extremes that delimit the vibration the difference is of two or three candles at the most. So that the sensation of yellow is faintly tinged with one of red. Light in a word that not only dims but blurs into the bargain. It might safely be maintained that the eye grows used to these conditions and in the end adapts to them were it not that just the contrary is to be observed in the slow deterioration of vision ruined by this fiery flickering murk and by the incessant straining for ever vain with concomitant moral distress and its repercussion on the organ. And were it possible to follow over a long enough period of time eyes blue for preference as being the most perishable they would be seen to redden more and more in an ever widening glare and their pupils little by little to dilate till the whole orb was devoured. And all by such slow and insensible degrees to be sure as to pass unperceived even by those most concerned if this notion is maintained. And the thinking being coldly intent on all these data and evidences could scarcely escape at the close of his analysis the mistaken conclusion that instead of speaking of the vanquished with the slight taint of pathos attaching to the term it would be more correct to speak of the blind and leave it at that. Once the first shocks of surprise are finally past this light is further unusual in that far from evincing one or more visible or hidden sources it appears to emanate from all sides and to permeate the entire space as though this were uniformly luminous down to its least particle of ambient air. To the point that the ladders themselves seem rather to shed than to receive light with this slight reserve that light is not the word. No other shadows then than those cast by the bodies pressing on one another wilfully or from necessity as when for example on a breast to prevent its being lit or on some private part the hand descends with vanished palm. Whereas the skin of a climber alone on his ladder or in the depths of a tunnel glistens all over with the same red-yellow glister and even some of its folds and recesses in so far as the air enters in. With regard to the temperature its oscillation is between much wider extremes and at a much lower frequency since it takes not less than four seconds to pass from its minimum of five degrees to its maximum of twenty-five and inversely namely an average of only five degrees per second. Does this mean that with every passing second there is a rise or fall of five degrees exactly neither more nor less? Not quite. For it is clear there are two periods in the scale namely from twenty-one degrees on on the way up and from nine on on the way down when this difference will not be reached. Out of the eight seconds therefore required for a single rise and fall it is only during a bare six and a half that the bodies suffer the maximum increment of heat or cold which with the help of a little addition or better still division works out nevertheless at some twenty years respite per century in this domain. There is something disturbing at first sight in the relative slowness of this vibration compared to that of the light. But this is a disturbance analysis makes short work of. For on due reflection the difference to be considered is not one of speed but of space travelled. And if that required of the temperature were reduced to the equivalent of a few candles there would be nothing to choose mutatis mutandis between the two effects. But that would not answer the needs of the cylinder. So all is for the best. The more so as the two storms have this in common that when one is cut off as though by magic then in the same breath the other also as though again the two were connected somewhere to a single commutator. For in the cylinder alone are certitudes to be found and without nothing but mystery. At vast intervals then the bodies enjoy ten seconds at most of unbroken warmth or cold or between the two. But this cannot be truly accounted for respite so great is the other tension then.

The bed of the cylinder comprises three distinct zones separated by clear-cut mental or imaginary frontiers invisible to the eye of flesh. First an outer belt roughly one metre wide reserved for the climbers and strange to say favoured by most of the sedentary and vanquished. Next a slightly narrower inner belt where those weary of searching in mid-cylinder slowly revolve in Indian file intent on the periphery. Finally the arena proper representing an area of one hundred and fifty square metres round numbers and chosen hunting ground of the majority. Let numbers be assigned to these three zones and it appears clearly that from the third to the second and inversely the searcher moves at will whereas on entering and leaving the first he is held to a certain discipline. One example among a thousand of the harmony that reigns in the cylinder between order and licence. Thus access to the climbers' reserve is authorized only when one of them leaves it to rejoin the searchers of the arena or exceptionally those of the intermediate zone. While infringement of this rule is rare it does none the less occur as when for example a particularly nervous searcher can no longer resist the lure of the niches and tries to steal in among the climbers without the warrant of a departure. Whereupon he is unfailingly ejected by the queue nearest to the point of trespass and the matter goes no further. No choice then for the searcher wishing to join the climbers but to watch for his opportunity among the

searchers of the intermediate zone or searcher-watchers or simply watchers. So much for access to the ladders. In the other
direction the passage is not free either and once among the
climbers the watcher is there for some time and more precisely
the highly variable time it takes to advance from the tail to the
head of the queue adopted. For no less than the freedom for
each body to climb is the obligation once in the queue of its
choice to queue on to the end. Any attempt to leave prematurely
is sharply countered by the other members and the offender put
back in his place. But once at the very foot of the ladder with
between him and it only one more return to the ground the aspi-
rant is free to rejoin the searchers of the arena or exceptionally
the watchers of the intermediate zone without opposition. It is
therefore on those at the head of their lines as being the most
likely to create the vacancy so ardently desired that the eyes of
the second-zone watchers are fixed as they burn to enter the first.
The objects of this scrutiny continue so up to the moment they
exercise their right to the ladder and take it over. For the climber
may reach the head of the queue with the firm resolve to ascend
and then feel this melt little by little and gather in its stead the
urge to depart but still without the power to decide him till the
very last moment when his predecessor is actually on the way
down and the ladder virtually his at last. To be noted also the
possibility for the climber to leave the queue once he has reached
the head and yet not leave the zone. This merely requires his
joining one of the other fourteen queues at his disposal or more
simply still his returning to the tail of his own. But it is exceptional for a body in the first place to leave its queue and in the
second having exceptionally done so not to leave the zone. No
alternative then once among the climbers but to stay there at
least the time it takes to advance from the last place to the first
of the chosen queue. This time varies according to the length of
the latter and the more or less prolonged occupation of the lad-

der. Some users keep it till the last moment. For others one half or any other fraction of this time is enough. The short queue is not necessarily the most rapid and such a one starting tenth may well find himself first before such another starting fifth assuming of course they start together. This being so no wonder that the choice of the queue is determined by considerations having nothing to do with its length. Not that all choose nor even the greater number. The tendency would be rather to join straight-way the queue nearest to the point of penetration on condition however that this does not involve motion against the stream. For one entering this zone head-on the nearest queue is on the right and if it does not please it is only by going right that a more pleasing can be found. Some could thus revolve through thou-sands of degrees before settling down to wait were it not for the rule forbidding them to exceed a single circuit. Any attempt to elude it is quelled by the queue nearest to the point of full circle and the culprit compelled to join its ranks since obviously the right to turn back is denied him too. That a full round should be authorized is eloquent of the tolerant spirit which in the cylinder tempers discipline. But whether chosen or first to hand the queue must be suffered to the end before the climber may leave the zone. First chance of departure therefore at any moment be-tween arrival at head of queue and predecessor's return to ground. There remains to clarify in this same context the situa-tion of the body which having accomplished its queue and let pass the first chance of departure and exercised its right to the ladder returns to the ground. It is now free again to depart with-out further ado but with no compulsion to do so. And to remain among the climbers it has merely to join again in the same condi-tions as before the queue so lately left with departure again pos-sible from the moment the head is reached. And should it for some reason or another feel like a little change of queue and lad-der it is entitled for the purpose of fixing its choice to a further full circuit in the same way as on first arrival and in the same conditions with this slight difference that having already suffered one queue to the end it is free at any moment of the new revolution to leave the zone. And so on infinitely. Whence theoretically the possibility for those already among the climbers never to leave and never to arrive for those not yet. That there exists no regulation tending to forestall such injustice shows clearly it can never be more than temporary. As indeed it cannot. For the passion to search is such that no place may be left unsearched. To the watcher nevertheless on the qui vive for a departure the wait may seem interminable. Sometimes unable to endure it any longer and fortified by the long vacation he renounces the ladder and resumes his search in the arena. So much roughly speaking for the main ground divisions and the duties and prerogatives of the bodies in their passage from one to another. All has not been told and never shall be. What principle of priority obtains among the watchers always in force and eager to profit by the first departure from among the climbers and whose order of arrival on the scene cannot be established by the queue impracticable in their case or by any other means? Is there not reason to fear a saturation of the intermediate zone and what would be its consequences for the bodies as a whole and particularly for those of the arena thus cut off from the ladders? Is not the cylinder doomed in a more or less distant future to a state of anarchy given over to fury and violence? To these questions and many more the answers are clear and easy to give. It only remains to dare. The sedentary call for no special remark since only the ladders can wean them from their fixity. The vanquished are obviously in no way concerned.

The effect of this climate on the soul is not to be underestimated. But it suffers certainly less than the skin whose entire defensive system from sweat to goose bumps is under constant stress. It continues none the less feebly to resist and indeed honourably compared to the eye which with the best will in the world it is difficult not to consign at the close of all its efforts to nothing short of blindness. For skin in its own way as it is not to mention its humours and lids it has not merely one adversary to contend with. This desiccation of the envelope robs nudity of much of its charm as pink turns grey and transforms into a rustling of nettles the natural succulence of flesh against flesh. The mucous membrane itself is affected which would not greatly matter were it not for its hampering effect on the work of love. But even from this point of view no great harm is done so rare is erection in the cylinder. It does occur none the less followed by more or less happy penetration in the nearest tube. Even man and wife may sometimes be seen in virtue of the law of probabilities to come together again in this way without their knowledge. The spectacle then is one to be remembered of frenzies prolonged in pain and hopelessness long beyond what even the most gifted lovers can achieve in camera. For male or female all are acutely aware how rare the occasion is and how unlikely to recur. But here too the desisting and deathly still in attitudes verging at times on the obscene whenever the vibrations cease and for as long as this crisis lasts. Stranger still at such times all the questing eyes that suddenly go still and fix their stare on the void or on some old abomination as for instance other eyes and then the long looks exchanged by those fain to look away. Irregular intervals of such length separate these lulls that for forgetters the likes of these each is the first. Whence invariably the same vivacity of reaction as to the end of a world and the same brief amaze when the twofold storm resumes and they start to search again neither glad nor even sorry.

Seen from below the wall presents an unbroken surface all the way round and up to the ceiling. And yet its upper half is riddled with niches. This paradox is explained by the levelling effect of the dim omnipresent light. None has ever been known to seek out a niche from below. The eyes are seldom raised and when they are it is to the ceiling. Floor and ceiling bear no sign or mark apt to serve as a guide. The feet of the ladders pitched always at the same points leave no trace. The same is true of the skulls and fists dashed against the wall. Even did such marks exist the light would prevent their being seen. The climber making off with his ladder to plant it elsewhere relies largely on feel. He is seldom out by more than a few centimetres and never by more than a metre at most because of the way the niches are disposed. On the spur of his passion his agility is such that even this deviation does not prevent him from gaining the nearest if not the desired niche and thence though with greater labour from regaining the ladder for the descent. There does none the less exist a north in the guise of one of the vanquished or better one of the women vanquished or better still the woman vanquished. She squats against the wall with her head between her knees and her legs in her arms. The left hand clasps the right shinbone and the right the left forearm. The red hair tarnished by the light hangs to the ground. It hides the face and whole front of the body down to the crutch. The left foot is crossed on the right. She is the north. She rather than some other among the vanquished because of her greater fixity. To one bent for once on taking his bearings she may be of help. For the climber averse to avoidable acrobatics a given niche may lie so many paces or meters to east or west of the woman vanquished without of course his naming her thus or otherwise even in his thoughts. It goes without saying that only the vanquished hide their faces though not all without exception. Standing or sitting with head erect some content themselves with opening their eyes no more. It is of course forbidden to withhold the face or other part from the searcher who demands it and may without fear of resistance remove the hand from the flesh it hides or raise the lid to examine the eye. Some searchers there are who join the climbers with no thought of climbing and simply in order to inspect at close hand one or more among the vanquished or sedentary. The hair of the woman vanquished has thus many a time been gathered up and drawn back and the head raised and the face laid bare and whole front of the body down to the crutch. The inspection once completed it is usual to put everything carefully back in place as far as possible. It is enjoined by a certain ethics not to do unto others what coming from them might give offence. This precept is largely observed in the cylinder in so far as it does not jeopardize the quest which would clearly be a mockery if in case of doubt it were not possible to check certain details. Direct action with a view to their elucidation is generally reserved for the persons of the sedentary and vanquished. Face or back to the wall these normally offer but a single aspect and so may have to be turned the other way. But wherever there is motion as in the arena or among the watchers and the possibility of encompassing the object there is no call for such manipulations. There are times of course when a body has to be brought to a stand and disposed in a certain position to permit the inspection at close hand of a particular part or the search for a scar or birthblot for example. To be noted finally the immunity in this respect of those queueing for a ladder. Obliged for want of space to huddle together over long periods they appear to the observer a mere jumble of mingled flesh. Woe the rash searcher who carried away by his passion dare lay a finger on the least among them. Like a single body the whole queue falls on the offender. Of all the scenes of violence the cylinder has to offer none approaches this.

So on infinitely until towards the unthinkable end if this notion is maintained a last body of all by feeble fits and starts is searching still. There is nothing at first sight to distinguish him from the others dead still where they stand or sit in abandonment beyond recall. Lying down is unheard of in the cylinder and this pose solace of the vanquished is for ever denied them here. Such privation is partly to be explained by the dearth of floor space namely a little under one square metre at the disposal of each body and not to be eked out by that of the niches and tunnels reserved for the search alone. Thus the prostration of those withered ones filled with the horror of contact and compelled to brush together without ceasing is denied its natural end. But the persistence of the twofold vibration suggests that in this old abode all is not yet quite for the best. And sure enough there he stirs this last of all if a man and slowly draws himself up and some time later opens his burnt eyes. At the foot of the ladders propped against the wall with scant regard to harmony no climber waits his turn. The aged vanquished of the third zone has none about him now but others in his image motionless and bowed. The mite still in the white-haired woman's clasp is no more than a shadow in her lap. Seen from the front the red head sunk to the uttermost exposes part of the nape. There he opens then his eyes this last of all if a man and some time later threads his way to that first among the vanquished so often taken for a guide. On his knees he parts the heavy hair and raises the unresisting head. Once devoured the face thus laid bare the eyes at a touch of the thumbs open without demur. In those calm wastes he lets his wander till they are the first to close and the head relinquished falls back into its place. He himself after a pause impossible to time finds at last his place and pose whereupon dark descends and at the same instant the temperature comes to rest not far from freezing point. Hushed in the same breath the faint stridulence mentioned above whence suddenly such silence as to drown all the faint breathings put together. So much roughly speaking for the last state of the cylinder and of this little people of searchers one first of whom if a man in some unthinkable past for the first time bowed his head if this notion is maintained.

Translated by the author

Fizzles

Fizzle 1

HE IS BAREHEAD, barefoot, clothed in a singlet and tight trousers too short for him, his hands have told him so, again and again, and his feet, feeling each other and rubbing against the legs, up and down calves and shins. To this vaguely prison garb none of his memories answer, so far, but all are of heaviness, in this connection, of fullness and of thickness. The great head where he toils is all mockery, he is forth again, he'll be back again. Some day he'll see himself, his whole front, from the chest down, and the arms, and finally the hands, first rigid at arm's length, then close up, trembling, to his eyes. He halts, for the first time since he knows he's under way, one foot before the other, the higher flat, the lower on its toes, and waits for a decision. Then he moves on. Spite of the dark he does not grope his way, arms outstretched, hands agape and the feet held back just before the ground. With the result he must often, namely at every turn, strike against the walls that hem his path, against the right-hand when he turns left, the left-hand when he turns right, now with his foot, now with the crown of his head, for he holds himself bowed, because of the rise, and because he always holds himself bowed, his back humped, his head thrust forward, his eyes cast down. He loses his blood, but in no great quantity, the little wounds have time to close before being opened again, his pace is so slow. There are places where the walls almost meet, then it is the shoulders take the shock. But instead of stopping short, and even turning back, saying to himself, This is the end of the road, nothing now but to return to the other terminus and start again, instead he attacks the narrow sideways and so finally squeezes through, to the great hurt of his chest and back. Do his eyes, after such long exposure to the gloom, begin to pierce it? No, and this is one of the reasons why he shuts them more and more, more and more often and for ever longer spells. For his concern is increasingly to spare himself needless fatigue, such as that come of staring before him, and even all about him, hour after hour, day after day, and never seeing a thing. This is not the time to go into his wrongs, but perhaps he was wrong not to persist, in his efforts to pierce the gloom. For he might well have succeeded, in the end, up to a point, which would have brightened things up for him, nothing like a ray of light, from time to time, to brighten things up for one. And all may yet grow light, at any moment, first dimly and then—how can one say?—then more and more, till all is flooded with light, the way, the ground, the walls, the vault, without his being one whit the wiser. The moon may appear, framed at the end of the vista, and he in no state to rejoice and quicken his step, or on the contrary wheel and run, while there is yet time. For the moment however no complaints, which is the main. The legs notably seem in good shape, that is a blessing, Murphy had first-rate legs. The head is still a little weak, it needs time to get going again, that part does. No sign of insanity in any case, that is a blessing. Meagre equipment, but well balanced. The heart? No complaints. It's going again, enough to see him through. But see how now, having turned right for example, instead of turning left a little further on he turns right again. And see how now again, yet a little further on, instead of turning left at last he turns right yet again. And so on until, instead of turning right yet again, as he expected, he turns left at last. Then for a time his zigzags resume their tenor, deflecting him alternately to right and left, that is to say bearing him onward in a straight line more or less, but no longer the same straight line as when he set forth, or rather as when he suddenly realized he was forth, or perhaps after all the same. For if there are long periods when the right predominates, there are others when the left prevails. It matters little in any case, so long as he keeps on climbing. But see how now a little further on the ground falls away so sheer that he has to rear violently backward in order not to fall. Where is it then that life awaits him, in relation to his starting-point, to the point rather at which he suddenly realized he was started, above or below? Or will they cancel out in the end, the long gentle climbs and headlong steeps? It matters little in any case, so long as he is on the right road, and that he is, for there are no others, unless he has let them slip by unnoticed, one after another. Walls and ground, if not of stone, are no less hard, to the touch, and wet. The former, certain days, he stops to lick. The fauna, if any, is silent. The only sounds, apart from those of the body on its way, are of fall, a great drop dropping at last from a great height and bursting, a solid mass that leaves its place and crashes down, lighter particles collapsing slowly. Then the echo is heard, as loud at first as the sound that woke it and repeated sometimes a good score of times, each time a little weaker, no, sometimes louder than the time before, till finally it dies away. Then silence again, broken only by the sound, intricate and faint, of the body on its way. But such sounds of fall are not common and mostly silence reigns, broken only by the sounds of the body on its way, of the bare feet on the wet ground, of the laboured breathing, of the body striking against the walls or squeezing through the narrows, of the clothes, singlet and trousers, espousing and resisting the movements of the body, coming unstuck from the damp

flesh and sticking to it again, tattering and fluttered where in tat-
ters already by sudden flurries as suddenly stilled, and finally of
the hands as now and then they pass, back and forth, over all
those parts of the body they can reach without fatigue. He himself has yet to drop. The air is foul. Sometimes he halts and leans
against a wall, his feet wedged against the other. He has already a
number of memories, from the memory of the day he suddenly
knew he was there, on this same path still bearing him along, to
that now of having halted to lean against the wall, he has a little
past already, even a smatter of settled ways. But it is all still fragile. And often he surprises himself, both moving and at rest, but
more often moving, for he seldom comes to rest, as destitute of
history as on that first day, on this same path, which is his beginning, on days of great recall. But usually now, the surprise once
past, memory returns and takes him back, if he will, far back to
that first instant beyond which nothing, when he was already
old, that is to say near to death, and knew, though unable to
recall having lived, what age and death are, with other momen-
tous matters. But it is all still fragile. And often he suddenly begins, in these black windings, and makes his first steps for quite a
while before realizing they are merely the last, or latest. The air is
so foul that only he seems fitted to survive it who never breathed
the other, the true life-giving, or so long ago as to amount to
never. And such true air, coming hard on that of here, would
very likely prove fatal, after a few lungfuls. But the change from
one to the other will no doubt be gentle, when the time comes,
and gradual, as the man draws closer and closer to the open. And
perhaps even now the air is less foul than when he started, than
when he suddenly realized he was started. In any case little by
little his history takes shape, with if not yet exactly its good days
and bad, at least studded with occasions passing rightly or
wrongly for outstanding, such as the straitest narrow, the loudest
fall, the most lingering collapse, the steepest descent, the greatest

number of successive turns the same way, the greatest fatigue, the longest rest, the longest—aside from the sound of the body on its way—silence. Ah yes, and the most rewarding passage of the hands, on the one hand, the feet, on the other, over all those parts of the body within their reach. And the sweetest wall lick. In a word all the summits. Then other summits, hardly less elevated, such as a shock so rude that it rivalled the rudest of all. Then others still, scarcely less eminent, a wall lick so sweet as to vie with the second sweetest. Then little or nothing of note till the minima, these too unforgettable, on days of great recall, a sound of fall so muted by the distance, or for want of weight, or for lack of space between departure and arrival, that it was perhaps his fancy. Or again, second example, no, not a good example. Other landmarks still are provided by first times, and even second. Thus the first narrow, for example, no doubt because he was not expecting it, impressed him quite as strongly as the straitest, just as the second collapse, no doubt because he was expecting it, was no less than the briefest never to be forgotten. So with one thing and another little by little his history takes shape, and even changes shape, as new maxima and minima tend to cast into the shade, and toward oblivion, those momentarily glorified, and as fresh elements and motifs, such as these bones of which more very shortly, and at length, in view of their importance, contribute to enrich it.

Translated by the author

Fizzle 2

HORN CAME always at night. I received him in the dark. I had
come to bear everything bar being seen. In the beginning I would
send him away after five or six minutes. Till he learnt to go of his
own accord, once his time was up. He consulted his notes by the
light of an electric torch. Then he switched it off and spoke in
the dark. Light silence, dark speech. It was five or six years since
anyone had seen me, to begin with myself. I mean the face I had
pored over so, all down the years. Now I would resume that
inspection, that it may be a lesson to me, in my mirrors and
looking-glasses so long put away. I'll let myself be seen before
I'm done. I'll call out, if there is a knock, Come in! But I speak
now of five or six years ago. These allusions to now, to before
and after, and all such yet to come, that we may feel ourselves in
time. I had more trouble with the body proper. I masked it as
best I could, but when I got out of bed it was sure to show. For I
was now beginning, then if you prefer, to get out of bed again.
Then there is the matter of its injuries. But the body was of less
consequence. Whereas the face, no, not at any price. Hence
Horn at night. When he forgot his torch he made shift with
matches. Were I to ask, for example, And her gown that day?,
then he switched on, thumbed through his notes, found the par-

ticular, switched off and answered, for example, The yellow. He did not like one to interrupt him and I must confess I seldom had call to. Interrupting him one night I asked him to light his face. He did so, briefly, switched off and resumed the thread. Interrupting again I asked him to be silent for a moment. That night things went no further. But the next, or more likely the next but one, I desired him at the outset to light his face and keep it lit till further notice. The light, bright at first, gradually died down to no more than a yellow glimmer which then, to my surprise, persisted undiminished some little while. Then suddenly it was dark again and Horn went away, the five or six minutes having presumably expired. But here one of two things, either the final extinction had coincided, by some prank of chance, with the close of the session, or else Horn, knowing his time to be up, had cut off the last dribs of current. I still see, sometimes, that waning face disclosing, more and more clearly the more it entered shadow, the one I remembered. In the end I said to myself, as unaccountably it lingered on, No doubt about it, it is he. It is in outer space, not to be confused with the other, that such images develop. I need only interpose my hand, or close my eyes, to banish them, or take off my eyeglasses for them to fade. This is a help, but not a real protection, as we shall see. I try to keep before me therefore, as far as possible, when I get up, some such unbroken plane as that which I command from my bed, I mean the ceiling. For I have taken to getting up again. I thought I had made my last journey, the one I must now try once more to elucidate, that it may be a lesson to me, the one from which it were better I had never returned. But the feeling gains on me that I must undertake another. So I have taken to getting up again and making a few steps in the room, holding on to the bars of the bed. What ruined me at bottom was athletics. With all that jumping and running when I was young, and even long after in the case of certain events, I wore out the machine before its time. My fortieth year had come and gone and I still throwing the javelin.

Translated by the author

Fizzle 3: Afar a bird

RUINSTREWN LAND, he has trodden it all night long, I gave up, hugging the hedges, between road and ditch, on the scant grass, little slow steps, no sound, stopping ever and again, every ten steps say, little wary steps, to catch his breath, then listen, ruinstrewn land, I gave up before birth, it is not possible otherwise, but birth there had to be, it was he, I was inside, now he stops again, for the hundredth time that night say, that gives the distance gone, it's the last, hunched over his stick, I'm inside, it was he who wailed, he who saw the light, I didn't wail, I didn't see the light, one on top of the other the hands weigh on the stick, the head weighs on the hands, he has caught his breath, he can listen now, the trunk horizontal, the legs asprawl, sagging at the knees, same old coat, the stiffened tails stick up behind, day dawns, he has only to raise his eyes, open his eyes, raise his eyes, he merges in the hedge, afar a bird, a moment past he grasps and is fled, it was he had a life, I didn't have a life, a life not worth having, because of me, it's impossible I should have a mind and I have one, someone divines me, divines us, that's what he's come to, come to in the end, I see him in my mind, there divining us, hands and head a little heap, the hours pass, he is still, he seeks a voice for me, it's impossible I should have a voice and I have none, he'll find one for me, ill beseeming me, it will meet the need, his need, but no more of him, that image, the little heap of hands and head, the trunk horizontal, the jutting elbows, the eyes closed and the face rigid listening, the eyes hidden and the whole face hidden, that image and no more, never changing, ruinstrewn land, night recedes, he is fled, I'm inside, he'll do himself to death, because of me, I'll live it with him, I'll live his death, the end of his life and then his death, step by step, in the present, how he'll go about it, it's impossible I should know, I'll know, step by step, it's he will die, I won't die, there will be nothing of him left but bones, I'll be inside, nothing but a little grit, I'll be inside, it is not possible otherwise, ruinstrewn land, he is fled through the hedge, no more stopping now, he will never say I, because of me, he won't speak to anyone, no one will speak to him, he won't speak to himself, there is nothing left in his head, I'll feed it all it needs, all it needs to end, to say I no more, to open its mouth no more, confusion of memory and lament, of loved ones and impossible youth, clutching the stick in the middle he stumbles bowed over the fields, a life of my own I tried, in vain, never any but his, worth nothing, because of me, he said it wasn't one, it was, still is, the same, I'm still inside, the same, I'll put faces in his head, names, places, churn them all up together, all he needs to end, phantoms to flee, last phantoms to flee and to pursue, he'll confuse his mother with whores, his father with a roadman named Balfe, I'll feed him an old curdog, a mangy old curdog, that he may love again, lose again, ruinstrewn land, little panic steps

Translated by the author

Fizzle 4

I GAVE UP before birth, it is not possible otherwise, but birth there had to be, it was he, I was inside, that's how I see it, it was he who wailed, he who saw the light, I didn't wail, I didn't see the light, it's impossible I should have a voice, impossible I should have thoughts, and I speak and think, I do the impossible, it is not possible otherwise, it was he who had a life, I didn't have a life, a life not worth having, because of me, he'll do himself to death, because of me, I'll tell the tale, the tale of his death, the end of his life and his death, his death alone would not be enough, not enough for me, if he rattles it's he who will rattle, I won't rattle, he who will die, I won't die, perhaps they will bury him, if they find him, I'll be inside, he'll rot, I won't rot, there will be nothing of him left but bones, I'll be inside, nothing left but dust, I'll be inside, it is not possible otherwise, that's how I see it, the end of his life and his death, how he will go about it, go about coming to an end, it's impossible I should know, I'll know, step by step, impossible I should tell, I'll tell, in the present, there will be no more talk of me, only of him, of the end of his life and his death, of his burial if they find him, that will be the end, I won't go on about worms, about bones and dust, no one cares about them, unless I'm bored in his dust, that would surprise me, as stiff as I was in his flesh, here long silence, perhaps he'll drown, he always wanted to drown, he didn't want them to find him, he can't want now any more, but he used to want to drown, he usen't to want them to find him, deep water and a millstone, urge spent like all the others, but why one day to the left, to the left and not elsewhither, here long silence, there will be no more I, he'll never say I any more, he'll never say anything any more, he won't talk to anyone, no one will talk to him, he won't talk to himself, he won't think any more, he'll go on, I'll be inside, he'll come to a place and drop, why there and not elsewhere, drop and sleep, badly because of me, he'll get up and go on, badly because of me, he can't stay still any more, because of me, he can't go on any more, because of me, there's nothing left in his head, I'll feed it all it needs.

Translated by the author

Fizzle 5

CLOSED PLACE. All needed to be known for say is known. There is nothing but what is said. Beyond what is said there is nothing. What goes on in the arena is not said. Did it need to be known it would be. No interest. Not for imagining. Place consisting of an arena and a ditch. Between the two skirting the latter a track. Closed place. Beyond the ditch there is nothing. This is known because it needs to be said. Arena black vast. Room for millions. Wandering and still. Never seeing never hearing one another. Never touching. No more is known. Depth of ditch. See from the edge all the bodies on its bed. The millions still there. They appear six times smaller than life. Bed divided into lots. Dark and bright. They take up all its width. The lots still bright are square. Appear square. Just room for the average sized body. Stretched out diagonally. Bigger it has to curl up. Thus the width of the ditch is known. It would have been in any case. Sum the bright lots. The dark. Outnumbered the former by far. The place is already old. The ditch is old. In the beginning it was all bright. All bright lots. Almost touching. Faintly edged with shadow. The ditch seems straight. Then reappears a body seen before. A closed curve therefore. Brilliance of the bright lots. It does not encroach on the dark. Adamantine blackness of these.

As dense at the edge as at the centre. But vertically it diffuses unimpeded. High above the level of the arena. As high above as the ditch is deep. In the black air towers of pale light. So many bright lots so many towers. So many bodies visible on the bed. The track follows the ditch all the way along. All the way round. It is on a higher level than the arena. A step higher. It is made of dead leaves. A reminder of beldam nature. They are dry. The heat and the dry air. Dead but not rotting. Crumbling into dust rather. Just wide enough for one. On it no two ever meet.

Translated by the author

Fizzle 6

OLD EARTH, no more lies, I've seen you, it was me, with my other's ravening eyes, too late. You'll be on me, it will be you, it will be me, it will be us, it was never us. It won't be long now, perhaps not tomorrow, nor the day after, but too late. Not long now, how I gaze on you, and what refusal, how you refuse me, you so refused. It's a cockchafer year, next year there won't be any, nor the year after, gaze your fill. I come home at nightfall, they take to wing, rise from my little oaktree and whirr away, glutted, into the shadows. I reach up, grasp the bough, pull myself up and go in. Three years in the earth, those the moles don't get, then guzzle guzzle, ten days long, a fortnight, and always the flight at nightfall. To the river perhaps, they head for the river. I turn on the light, then off, ashamed, stand at gaze before the window, the windows, going from one to another, leaning on the furniture. For an instant I see the sky, the different skies, then they turn to faces, agonies, loves, the different loves, happiness too, yes, there was that too, unhappily. Moments of life, of mine too, among others, no denying, all said and done. Happiness, what happiness, but what deaths, what loves, I knew at the time, it was too late then. Ah to love at your last and see them at theirs, the last minute loved ones, and be happy, why ah, uncalled for.

No but now, now, simply stay still, standing before a window, one hand on the wall, the other clutching your shirt, and see the sky, a long gaze, but no, gasps and spasms, a childhood sea, other skies, another body.

Translated by the author

Fizzle 7: Still

BRIGHT AT LAST close of a dark day the sun shines out at last and goes down. Sitting quite still at valley window normally turn head now and see it the sun low in the southwest sinking. Even get up certain moods and go stand by western window quite still watching it sink and then the afterglow. Always quite still some reason some time past this hour at open window facing south in small upright wicker chair with armrests. Eyes stare out unseeing till first movement some time past close though unseeing still while still light. Quite still again then all quite quiet apparently till eyes open again while still light though less. Normally turn head now ninety degrees to watch sun which if already gone then fading afterglow. Even get up certain moods and go stand by western window till quite dark and even some evenings some reason long after. Eyes then open again while still light and close again in what if not quite a single movement almost. Quite still again then at open window facing south over the valley in this wicker chair though actually close inspection not still at all but trembling all over. Close inspection namely detail by detail all over to add up finally to this whole not still at all but trembling all over. But casually in this failing light impression dead still even the hands clearly trembling and the breast faint rise and fall.

Legs side by side broken right angles at the knees as in that old statue some old god twanged at sunrise and again at sunset. Trunk likewise dead plumb right up to top of skull seen from behind including nape clear of chairback. Arms likewise broken right angles at the elbows forearms along armrests just right length forearms and rests for hands clenched lightly to rest on ends. So quite still again then all quite quiet apparently eyes closed which to anticipate when they open again if they do in time then dark or some degree of starlight or moonlight or both. Normally watch night fall however long from this narrow chair or standing by western window quite still either case. Quite still namely staring at some one thing alone such as tree or bush a detail alone if near if far the whole if far enough till it goes. Or by eastern window certain moods staring at some point on the hillside such as that beech in whose shade once quite still till it goes. Chair some reason always same place same position facing south as though clamped down whereas in reality no lighter no more movable imaginable. Or anywhere any ope staring out at nothing just failing light quite still till quite dark though of course no such thing just less light still when less did not seem possible. Quite still then all this time eyes open when discovered then closed then opened and closed again no other movement any kind though of course not still at all when suddenly or so it looks this movement impossible to follow let alone describe. The right hand slowly opening leaves the armrest taking with it the whole forearm complete with elbow and slowly rises opening further as it goes and turning a little deasil till midway to the head it hesitates and hangs half open trembling in mid air. Hangs there as if half inclined to return that is sink back slowly closing as it goes and turning the other way till as and where it began clenched lightly on end of rest. Here because of what comes now not midway to the head but almost there before it hesitates and hangs there trembling as if half inclined etc. Half no but on the verge when in its turn the head moves from its place forward and down among the ready fingers where no sooner received and held it weighs on down till elbow meeting armrest brings this last movement to an end and all still once more. Here back a little way to that suspense before head to rescue as if hand's need the greater and on down in what if not quite a single movement almost till elbow against rest. All quite still again then head in hand namely thumb on outer edge of right socket index ditto left and middle on left cheekbone plus as the hours pass lesser contacts each more or less now more now less with the faint stirrings of the various parts as night wears on. As if even in the dark eyes closed not enough and perhaps even more than ever necessary against that no such thing the further shelter of the hand. Leave it so all quite still or try listening to the sounds all quite still head in hand listening for a sound.

Fizzle 8: For to end yet again

FOR TO END yet again skull alone in a dark place pent bowed on a board to begin. Long thus to begin till the place fades followed by the board long after. For to end yet again skull alone in the dark the void no neck no face just the box last place of all in the dark the void. Place of remains where once used to gleam in the dark on and off used to glimmer a remain. Remains of the days of the light of day never light so faint as theirs so pale. Thus then the skull makes to glimmer again in lieu of going out. There in the end all at once or by degrees there dawns and magic lingers a leaden dawn. By degrees less dark till final grey or all at once as if switched on grey sand as far as eye can see beneath grey cloudless sky same grey. Skull last place of all black void within without till all at once or by degrees this leaden dawn at last checked no sooner dawned. Grey cloudless sky grey sand as far as eye can see long desert to begin. Sand pale as dust ah but dust indeed deep to engulf the haughtiest monuments which too it once was here and there. There in the end same grey invisible to any other eye stark erect amidst his ruins the expelled. Same grey all that little body from head to feet sunk ankle deep were it not for the eyes last bright of all. The arms still cleave to the trunk and to each other the legs made for flight. Grey cloudless sky ocean of dust not a ripple mock confines verge upon verge hell air not a breath. Mingling with the dust slowly sinking some almost fully sunk the ruins of the refuge. First change of all in the end a fragment comes away and falls. With slow fall for so dense a body it lights like cork on water and scarce breaks the surface. Thus then the skull last place of all makes to glimmer again in lieu of going out. Grey cloudless sky verge upon verge grey timeless air of those nor for God nor for his enemies. There again in the end way amidst the verges a light in the grey two white dwarfs. Long at first mere whiteness from afar they toil step by step through the grey dust linked by a litter same white seen from above in the grey air. Slowly it sweeps the dust so bowed the backs and long the arms compared with the legs and deep sunk the feet. Bleached as one same wilderness they are so alike the eye cannot tell them apart. They carry face to face and relay each other often so that turn about they backward lead the way. His who follows who knows to shape the course much as the coxswain with light touch the skiff. Let him veer to the north or other cardinal point and promptly the other by as much to the antipode. Let one stop short and the other about this pivot slew the litter through a semi-circle and thereon the roles are reversed. Bone white of the sheet seen from above and the shafts fore and aft and the dwarfs to the crowns of their massy skulls. From time to time impelled as one they let fall the litter then again as one take it up again without having to stoop. It is the dung litter of laughable memory with shafts twice as long as the couch. Swelling the sheet now fore now aft as permutations list a pillow marks the place of the head. At the end of the arms the four hands open as one and the litter so close to the dust already settles without a sound. Monstrous extremities including skulls stunted legs and trunks monstrous arms stunted faces. In the end the feet as one lift clear the left forward backward the right and the amble resumes. Grey dust as far as eye can see beneath grey cloudless sky and there all at once or by degrees this whiteness to decipher. Yet to imagine if he can see it the last expelled amidst his ruins if he can ever see it and seeing believe his eyes. Between him and it bird's-eye view the space grows no less but has only even now appeared last desert to be crossed. Little body last stage of all stark erect still amidst his ruins all silent and marble still. First change of all a fragment comes away from mother ruin and with slow fall scarce stirs the dust. Dust having engulfed so much it can engulf no more and woe the little on the surface still. Or mere digestive torpor as once the boas which past with one last gulp clean sweep at last. Dwarfs distant whiteness sprung from nowhere motionless afar in the grey air where dust alone possible. Wilderness and carriage immemorial as one they advance as one retreat hither thither halt move on again. He facing forward will sometimes halt and hoist as best he can his head as if to scan the void and who knows alter course. Then on so soft the eye does not see them go driftless with heads sunk and lidded eyes. Long lifted to the horizontal faces closer and closer strain as it will the eye achieves no more than two tiny oval blanks. Atop the cyclopean dome rising sheer from jut of brow yearns white to the grey sky the bump of habitativity or love of home. Last change of all in the end the expelled falls headlong down and lies back to sky full little stretch amidst his ruins. Feet centre body radius falls unbending as a statue falls faster and faster the space of a quadrant. Eagle the eye that shall discern him now mingled with the ruins mingling with the dust beneath a sky forsaken of its scavengers. Breath has not left him though soundless still and exhaling scarce ruffles the dust. Eyes in their orbits blue still unlike the doll's the fall has not shut nor yet the dust stopped up. No fear henceforth of his ever having not to believe them before that whiteness afar where sky and dust merge. Whiteness neither on earth nor above of the dwarfs as if at the end of their trials the litter left lying between them the white bodies marble still. Ruins all silent marble still little body prostrate at attention wash blue deep in gaping sockets. As in the days erect the arms still cleave to the trunk and to each other the legs made for flight. Fallen unbending all his little length as though pushed from behind by some helping hand or by the wind but not a breath. Or murmur from some dreg of life after the lifelong stand fall fall never fear no fear of your rising again. Sepulchral skull is this then its last state all set for always litter and dwarfs ruins and little body grey cloudless sky glutted dust verge upon verge hell air not a breath? And dream of a way in a space with neither here nor there where all the footsteps ever fell can never fare nearer to anywhere nor from anywhere further away? No for in the end for to end yet again by degrees or as though switched on dark falls there again that certain dark that alone certain ashes can. Through it who knows yet another end beneath a cloudless sky same dark it earth and sky of a last end if ever there had to be another absolutely had to be.

Translated by the author

Heard in the Dark 1

THE LAST TIME you went out the snow lay on the ground. You now lying in the dark stand that morning on the sill having pulled the door gently to behind you. You lean back against the door with bowed head making ready to set out. By the time you open your eyes your feet have disappeared and the skirts of your greatcoat come to rest on the surface of the snow. The dark scene seems lit from below. You see yourself at that last outset leaning against the door with closed eyes waiting for the word from you to go. You? To be gone. Then the snowlit scene. You lie in the dark with closed eyes and see yourself there as described making ready to strike out and away across the expanse of light. You hear again the click of the door pulled gently to and the silence before the steps can start. Next thing you are on your way across the white pasture afrolic with lambs in spring and strewn with red placentae. You take the course you always take which is a beeline for the gap or ragged point in the quickset that forms the western fringe. Thither from your entering the pasture you need normally from eighteen hundred to two thousand paces depending on your humour and the state of the ground. But on this last morning many more will be necessary. Many many more. The beeline is so familiar to your feet that if necessary they could keep to it and you sightless with error on arrival of not more than a few feet north or south. And indeed without any such necessity unless from within this is what they normally do and not only here. For you advance if not with closed eyes though this as often as not at least with them fixed on the momentary ground before your feet. That is all of nature you have seen. Since you finally bowed your head. The fleeting ground before your feet. From time to time. You do not count your steps any more. For the simple reason they number each day the same. Average day in day out the same. The way being always the same. You keep count of the days and every tenth night multiply. And add. Your father's shade is not with you any more. It fell out long ago. You do not hear your footfalls any more. Unhearing unseeing you go your way. Day after day. The same way. As if there were no other any more. For you there is no other any more. You used never to halt except to make your reckoning. So as to plod on from nought anew. This need removed as we have seen there is none in theory to halt any more. Save perhaps a moment at the outermost point. To gather yourself together for the return. And yet you do. As never before. Not for tiredness. You are no more tired now than you always were. Not because of age. You are no older now than you always were. And yet you halt as never before. So that the same hundred yards you used to cover in a matter of three to four minutes may now take you anything from fifteen to twenty. The foot falls unbidden in midstep or next for lift cleaves to the ground bringing the body to a stand. Then a speechlessness whereof the gist, Can they go on? Or better, Shall they go on? The barest gist. Stilled when finally as always hitherto they do. You lie in the dark with closed eyes and see the scene. As you could not at the time. The dark cope of sky. The dazzling land. You at a standstill in the midst. The quarterboots sunk to the tops. The skirts of the greatcoat resting on the snow. In the old bowed head in the old block hat speechless misgiving. Halfway across the pasture on your beeline to the gap. The unerring feet fast. You look behind you as you could not then and see their trail. A great swerve. Withershins. Almost as if all at once the heart too heavy. In the end too heavy.

Heard in the Dark 2

BLOOM OF ADULTHOOD. Try a whiff of that. On your back in the dark you remember. Ah you remember. Cloudless May day. She joins you in the little summerhouse. Entirely of logs. Both larch and fir. Six feet across. Eight from floor to vertex. Area twenty-four square feet to furthest decimal. Two small multicoloured lights vis-à-vis. Small stained diamond panes. Under each a ledge. There on summer Sundays after his midday meal your father loved to retreat with *Punch* and a cushion. The waist of his trousers unbuttoned he sat on the one ledge and turned the pages. You on the other your feet dangling. When he chuckled you tried to chuckle too. When his chuckle died yours too. That you should try to imitate his chuckle pleased and amused him greatly and sometimes he would chuckle for no other reason than to hear you try to chuckle too. Sometimes you turn your head and look out through a rose-red pane. You press your little nose against the pane and all without is rosy. The years have flown and there at the same place as then you sit in the bloom of adulthood bathed in rainbow light gazing before you. She is late. You close your eyes and try to calculate the volume. Simple sums you find a help in times of trouble. A haven. You arrive in the end at seven cubic yards approximately. Even still in the timeless dark you find figures a comfort. You assume a certain heart rate and reckon how many thumps a day. A week. A month. A year. And assuming a certain lifetime a lifetime. Till the last thump. But for the moment with hardly more than seventy American billion behind you you sit in the little summerhouse working out the volume. Seven cubic yards approximately. This strikes you for some reason as improbable and you set about your sum anew. But you have not got very far when her light step is heard. Light for a woman of her size. You open with quickening pulse your eyes and a moment later that seems an eternity her face appears at the window. Mainly blue in this position the natural pallor you so admire as indeed for it no doubt wholly blue your own. For natural pallor is a property you have in common. The violet lips do not return your smile. Now this window being flush with your eyes from where you sit and the floor as near as no matter with the outer ground you cannot but wonder if she has not sunk to her knees. Knowing from experience that the height or length you have in common is the sum of equal segments. For when bolt upright or lying at full stretch you cleave front to front then your knees touch and your pubes and the hairs of your heads mingle. Does it follow from this that the loss of height for the body that sits is the same as for it that kneels? At this point assuming level of seat adjustable as in the case of certain piano stools you close your eyes the better with mental measure to measure and compare the first and second segments namely from sole to kneepad and thence to pelvic girdle. How given you were both moving and at rest to the closed eye in your waking hours! By day and by night. To that perfect dark. That shadowless light. Simply to be gone. Or for affair as now. A single leg appears. Seen from above. You separate the segments and lay them side by side. It is as you half surmised. The upper is the longer and the sitter's loss the greater when seat at knee level. You leave the pieces lying there and open your eyes to find her sitting before you. All dead still. The ruby lips do not return your smile. Your gaze moves down to the breasts. You do not remember them so big. To the abdomen. Same impression. Dissolve to your father's straining against the unbuttoned waistband. Can it be she is with child without your having asked for as much as her hand? You go back into your mind. She too did you but know it has closed her eyes. So you sit face to face in the little summerhouse. With eyes closed and hands on knees. In the bloom of your adulthood. In that rainbow light. That dead still.

One Evening

HE WAS FOUND lying on the ground. No one had missed him. No one was looking for him. An old woman found him. To put it vaguely. It happened so long ago. She was straying in search of wild flowers. Yellow only. With no eyes but for these she stumbled on him lying there. He lay face downward and arms outspread. He wore a greatcoat in spite of the time of year. Hidden by the body a long row of buttons fastened it all the way down. Buttons of all shapes and sizes. Worn upright the skirts swept the ground. That seems to hang together. Near the head a hat lay askew on the ground. At once on its brim and crown. He lay inconspicuous in the greenish coat. To catch an eye searching from afar there was only the white head. May she have seen him somewhere before? Somewhere on his feet before? Not too fast. She was all in black. The hem of her long black skirt trailed in the grass. It was close of day. Should she now move away into the east her shadow would go before. A long black shadow. It was lambing time. But there were no lambs. She could see none. Were a third party to chance that way theirs were the only bodies he would see. First that of the old woman standing. Then on drawing near it lying on the ground. That seems to hang together. The deserted fields. The old woman all in black stockstill. The body stockstill on the ground. Yellow at the end of the black arm. The white hair in the grass. The east foundering in night. Not too fast. The weather. Sky overcast all day till evening. In the west-north-west near the verge already the sun came out at last. Rain? A few drops if you will. A few drops in the morning if you will. In the present to conclude. It happened so long ago. Cooped indoors all day she comes out with the sun. She makes haste to gain the fields. Surprised to have seen no one on the way she strays feverishly in search of the wild flowers. Feverishly seeing the imminence of night. She remarks with surprise the absence of lambs in great numbers here at this time of year. She is wearing the black she took on when widowed young. It is to reflower the grave she strays in search of the flowers he had loved. But for the need of yellow at the end of the black arm there would be none. There are therefore only as few as possible. This is for her the third surprise since she came out. For they grow in plenty here at this time of year. Her old friend her shadow irks her. So much so that she turns to face the sun. Any flower wide of her course she reaches sidelong. She craves for sundown to end and to stray freely again in the long afterglow. Further to her distress the familiar rustle of her long black skirt in the grass. She moves with half-closed eyes as if drawn on into the glare. She may say to herself it is too much strangeness for a single March or April evening. No one abroad. Not a single lamb. Scarcely a flower. Shadow and rustle irksome. And to crown all the shock of her foot against a body. Chance. No one had missed him. No one was looking for him. Black and green of the garments touching now. Near the white head the yellow of the few plucked flowers. The old sunlit face. Tableau vivant if you will. In its way. All is silent from now on. For as long as she cannot move. The sun disappears at last and with it all shadow. All shadow here. Slow fade of afterglow. Night without moon or stars. All that seems to hang together. But no more about it.

Translated by the author

As the story was told

AS THE STORY was told me I never went near the place during sessions. I asked what place and a tent was described at length, a small tent the colour of its surroundings. Wearying of this description I asked what sessions and these in their turn were described, their object, duration, frequency and harrowing nature. I hope I was not more sensitive than the next man, but finally I had to raise my hand. I lay there quite still for a time, then asked where I was while all this was going forward. In a hut, was the answer, a small hut in a grove some two hundred yards away, a distance even the loudest cry could not carry, but must die on the way. This was not so strange as at first sight it sounded when one considered the stoutness of the canvas and the sheltered situation of the hut among the trees. Indeed the tent might have been struck where it stood and moved forward fifty yards or so without inconvenience. Lying there with closed eyes in the silence which followed this information I began to see the hut, though unlike the tent it had not been described to me, but only its situation. It reminded me strongly of a summer-house in which as a child I used to sit quite still for hours on end, on the window-seat, the whole year round. It had the same five log walls, the same coloured glass, the same diminutiveness, being not more than ten feet across and so low of ceiling that the average man could not have held himself erect in it, though of course there was no such difficulty for the child. At the centre, facing the coloured panes, stood a small upright wicker chair with arm-rests, as against the summer-house's window-seat. I sat there very straight and still, with my arms along the rests, looking out at the orange light. It must have been shortly after six, the sessions closing punctually at that hour, for as I watched a hand appeared in the doorway and held out to me a sheet of writing. I took and read it, then tore it in four and put the pieces in the waiting hand to take away. A little later the whole scene disappeared. As the story was told me the man succumbed in the end to his ill-treatment, though quite old enough at the time to die naturally of old age. I lay there a long time quite still—even as a child I was un-usually still and more and more so with the passing years—till it must have seemed the story was over. But finally I asked if I knew exactly what the man—I would like to give his name but cannot—what exactly was required of the man, what it was he would not or could not say. No, was the answer, after some little hesitation no, I did not know what the poor man was required to say, in order to be pardoned, but would have recognized it at once, yes, at a glance, if I had seen it.

The Cliff

WINDOW BETWEEN SKY and earth nowhere known. Opening on a colourless cliff. The crest escapes the eye wherever set. The base as well. Framed by two sections of sky forever white. Any hint in the sky at a land's end? The yonder ether? Of sea birds no trace. Or too pale to show. And then what proof of a face? None that the eye can find wherever set. It gives up and the bedlam head takes over. At long last first looms the shadow of a ledge. Patience it will be enlivened with mortal remains. A whole skull emerges in the end. One alone from amongst those such residua evince. Still attempting to sink back its coronal into the rock. The old stare half showing within the orbits. At times the cliff vanishes. Then off the eye flies to the whiteness verge upon verge. Or thence away from it all.

Translated by Edith Fournier

neither

TO AND FRO in shadow from inner to outershadow

from impenetrable self to impenetrable unself by way of neither

as between two lit refuges whose doors once neared gently close,
once turned away from gently part again

beckoned back and forth and turned away

heedless of the way, intent on the one gleam or the other

unheard footfalls only sound

till at last halt for good, absent for good from self and other

then no sound

then gently light unfading on that unheeded neither

unspeakable home

Stirrings Still

for Barney Rosset

1

ONE NIGHT AS he sat at his table head on hands he saw himself rise and go. One night or day. For when his own light went out he was not left in the dark. Light of a kind came then from the one high window. Under it still the stool on which till he could or would no more he used to mount to see the sky. Why he did not crane out to see what lay beneath was perhaps because the window was not made to open or because he could or would not open it. Perhaps he knew only too well what lay beneath and did not wish to see it again. So he would simply stand there high above the earth and see through the clouded pane the cloudless sky. Its faint unchanging light unlike any light he could remember from the days and nights when day followed hard on night and night on day. This outer light then when his own went out became his only light till it in its turn went out and left him in the dark. Till it in its turn went out.

One night or day then as he sat at his table head on hands he saw himself rise and go. First rise and stand clinging to the table. Then sit again. Then rise again and stand clinging to the table again. Then go. Start to go. On unseen feet start to go. So slow that only change of place to show he went. As when he disappeared only to reappear later at another place. Then disappeared again only to reappear again later at another place again. So again and again disappeared again only to reappear again later at another place again. Another place in the place where he sat at his table head on hands. The same place and table as when Darly for example died and left him. As when others too in their turn before and since. As when others would too in their turn and leave him till he too in his turn. Head on hands half hoping when he disappeared again that he would not reappear again and half fearing that he would not. Or merely wondering. Or merely waiting. Waiting to see if he would or would not. Leave him or not alone again waiting for nothing again.

Seen always from behind whithersoever he went. Same hat and coat as of old when he walked the roads. The back roads. Now as one in a strange place seeking the way out. In the dark. In a strange place blindly in the dark of night or day seeking the way out. A way out. To the roads. The back roads.

A clock afar struck the hours and half-hours. The same as when among others Darly once died and left him. Strokes now clear as if carried by a wind now faint on the still air. Cries afar now faint now clear. Head on hands half hoping when the hour struck that the half-hour would not and half fearing that it would not. Similarly when the half-hour struck. Similarly when the cries a moment ceased. Or merely wondering. Or merely waiting. Waiting to hear.

There had been a time he would sometimes lift his head enough to see his hands. What of them was to be seen. One laid on the table and the other on the one. At rest after all they did. Lift his past head a moment to see his past hands. Then lay it back on them to rest it too. After all it did.

The same place as when left day after day for the roads. The back roads. Returned to night after night. Paced from wall to wall in the dark. The then fleeting dark of night. Now as if strange to him seen to rise and go. Disappear and reappear at another place. Disappear again and reappear again at another place again. Or at the same. Nothing to show not the same. No wall toward which or from. No table back toward which or further from. In the same place as when paced from wall to wall all places as the same. Or in another. Nothing to show not another. Where never. Rise and go in the same place as ever. Disappear and reappear in another where never. Nothing to show not another where never. Nothing but the strokes. The cries. The same as ever.

Till so many strokes and cries since he was last seen that perhaps he would not be seen again. Then so many cries since the strokes were last heard that perhaps they would not be heard again. Then such silence since the cries were last heard that perhaps even they would not be heard again. Perhaps thus the end. Unless no more than a mere lull. Then all as before. The strokes and cries as before and he as before now there now gone now there again now gone again. Then the lull again. Then all as before again. So again and again. And patience till the one true end to time and grief and self and second self his own.

2

AS ONE IN HIS RIGHT MIND when at last out again he knew not
how he was not long out again when he began to wonder if he
was in his right mind. For could one not in his right mind be
reasonably said to wonder if he was in his right mind and bring
what is more his remains of reason to bear on this perplexity in
the way he must be said to do if he is to be said at all? It was
therefore in the guise of a more or less reasonable being that he
emerged at last he knew not how into the outer world and had
not been there for more than six or seven hours by the clock
when he could not but begin to wonder if he was in his right
mind. By the same clock whose strokes were those heard times
without number in his confinement as it struck the hours and
half hours and so in a sense at first a source of reassurance till
finally one of alarm as being no clearer now than when in principle muffled by his four walls. Then he sought help in the
thought of one hastening westward at sundown to obtain a better view of Venus and found it of none. Of the sole other sound
that of cries enlivener of his solitude as lost to suffering he sat at
his table head on hands the same was true. Of their whence-
abouts that is of clock and cries the same was true that is no
more to be determined now than as was only natural then. Bring-

ing to bear on all this his remains of reason he sought help in the thought that his memory of indoors was perhaps at fault and found it of none. Further to his disarray his soundless tread as when barefoot he trod his floor. So all ears from bad to worse till in the end he ceased if not to hear to listen and set out to look about him. Result finally he was in a field of grass which went some way if nothing else to explain his tread and then a little later as if to make up for this some way to increase his trouble. For he could recall no field of grass from even the very heart of which no limit of any kind was to be discovered but always in some quarter or another some end in sight such as a fence or other manner of bourne from which to return. Nor on his looking more closely to make matters worse was this the short green grass he seemed to remember eaten down by flocks and herds but long and light grey in colour verging here and there on white. Then he sought help in the thought that his memory of outdoors was perhaps at fault and found it of none. So all eyes from bad to worse till in the end he ceased if not to see to look (about him or more closely) and set out to take thought. To this end for want of a stone on which to sit like Walther and cross his legs the best he could do was stop dead and stand stock still which after a moment of hesitation he did and of course sink his head as one deep in meditation which after another moment of hesitation he did also. But soon weary of vainly delving in those remains he moved on through the long hoar grass resigned to not knowing where he was or how he got there or where he was going or how to get back to whence he knew not how he came. So on unknowing and no end in sight. Unknowing and what is more no wish to know nor indeed any wish of any kind nor therefore any sorrow save that he would have wished the strokes to cease and the cries for good and was sorry that they did not. The strokes now faint now clear as if carried by the wind but not a breath and the cries now faint now clear.

3

SO ON TILL STAYED when to his ears from deep within oh how and here a word he could not catch it were to end where never till then. Rest then before again from not long to so long that perhaps never again and then again faint from deep within oh how and here that missing word again it were to end where never till then. In any case whatever it might be to end and so on was he not already as he stood there all bowed down and to his ears faint from deep within again and again oh how something and so on was he not so far as he could see already there where never till then? For how could even such a one as he having once found himself in such a place not shudder to find himself in it again which he had not done nor having shuddered seek help in vain in the thought so-called that having somehow got out of it then he could somehow get out of it again which he had not done either. There then all this time where never till then and so far as he could see in every direction when he raised his head and opened his eyes no danger or hope as the case might be of his ever getting out of it. Was he then now to press on regardless now in one direction and now in another or on the other hand stir no more as the case might be that is as that missing word might be which if to warn such as sad or bad for example then of course in spite of all the one and if the reverse then of course the other that is stir no more. Such and much more such the hubbub in his mind so-called till nothing left from deep within but only ever fainter oh to end. No matter how no matter where. Time and grief and self so-called. Oh all to end.

Appendix I:
Variations on a "Still" Point

Sounds

SOUNDS THEN even stillest night here where none come some time past mostly no want no not no want but never none of any kind even stillest night seldom an hour another hour but some sound of some kind here where none come none pass even the night-birds some time past in such numbers once such numbers. Or if none hour after hour no sound of any kind then he having been dreamt away let himself be dreamt away to where none at any time away from here where none come none pass to where no sound at any time no sound to listen for none of any kind. But mostly not for nothing never quite for nothing even stillest night when air too still for even the lightest leaf to sound no not to sound to carry too still for even the lightest leaf to carry the brief way here and not die the sound not die on the brief way the wave not die away. For catch up the torch and out up the path all overgrown now as more than once he must up suddenly out of the chair and out up the path by the torchlight and still no sound from the tree till nearly there when switch out and stand beneath or with his arms round it certain moods and head against the bark as if a human. Then back when enough some nights only after hours switch on and back in silence no sooner in the clear open back down the path by the torchlight as before and no sound but worse than none his feet among the weeds till back in the chair quite still as before. For clearly worse than none the self's when the whole body moves from its place as to those leaves then or some part or parts leaving the main unmoved or even at its most still as now all outwardly at rest head in hand listening trying listening for a sound. Head in hand as shown from when hand rose from rest to new pose at rest on elbow all silent the whole change so worse than none the self's as silent as if none save one faint at the end the faint creak as it gave the wicker made. Start up now snatching up the torch and out up the path no question some time past even stillest night but rather no sound hour after hour or be dreamt away better still dreamt away where no sound to listen for no more than ghosts make or motes in the sun. Room too quite still some time past and loft where such sounds once all night there by open window eyes closed or looking out never an hour but suddenly some sound room or loft low and brief never twice quite the same to wonder over a moment no longer now. Even the wind some time past so often once so loud certain nights he could pace to and fro and no more sound than a ghost or mutter old words once got by heart the very wind as though no more air to move no more than in a void. Breath itself sigh it all out through the mouth that sound then fill again hold and out again so often once sigh upon sigh no question now some time past but quiet as when even the mother can't hear stooped over the crib but has to feel pulse or heart. Leave it so then this stillest night till now of all quite still head in hand as shown listening trying listening for a sound or dreamt away try dreamt away where no such thing no more than ghosts make nothing to listen for no such thing as a sound.

Still 3

WHENCE WHEN back no knowing where no telling where been
how long how it was. Back in the chair at the window before the
window head in hand as shown dead still listening again in vain.
No not yet not listening again in vain quite yet while the dim
questions fade where been how long how it was. For head in
hand eyes closed as shown always the same dark now from now
all hours of day and night. No nightbird to mean night at least
or day at least so faint perhaps mere fancy with the right valley
wind the incarnation bell. Or Mother Calvet with the dawn
pushing the old go-cart for whatever she might find and back at
dusk. Back then and nothing to tell but some soundless place
and in the head in the hand where such questions once like
ghosts where what how long weirdest of all. Till in imagination
from the dead faces faces on off in the dark sudden whites long
short then black long short then another so on or the same.
White stills all front no expression eyes wide unseeing mouth no
expression male female all ages one by one never more at a time.
There somewhere some time hers or his or some other creature's
try dreamt away saying dreamt away where face after face till
hers in the end or his or that other creature's. Where faces in the
dark as shown for one in the end even though only once only for

a second say back try saying back from there head in hand as shown. For one or more why while at it one alone no one alone one by one none it till perhaps some time in the end that one or none. Size as seen in the life at say arm's length sudden white black all about no known expression eyes its at last not looking lips the ones no expression marble still so long then out.

Appendix II:

Faux Départs

1

Plus signe de vie, dites-vous, dis-je, bah, qu'à cela ne tienne, imagination pas morte, et derechef, plus fort, trop fort, Imagination pas morte, et le soir même m'enfermai sous les huées et m'y mis, sans autre appui que les Syntaxes de Jolly et de Draeger.
Mon cabinet a ceci de particulier, ou plutôt moi, que j'y ai fait aménager une stalle à ma taille. C'est là, au fond, face au mur, dans la pénombre, que j'imagine, tantôt assis, tantôt debout, au besoin à genoux.
Dois-je me présenter? Bah.

2

Plus signe de vie, dis-tu, dis-je, bah, imagination pas morte. Stalle, un mètre sur trois. C'est là. Par terre les Lexiques de Jolly et de Draeger. J'éteins. C'est là, dans le fond, nez au mur. Debout, assis, à genoux, selon. Toute la nuit naturelle. Me présenter? Bah. Nous tourbillonnons vers l'hiver, moi, mon coin de terre. Si ça pouvait être tout sur moi enfin. Et seuls désormais l'autre vide, le silence et le noir sans faille.

3

Le vieux je est revenu, ne sachant d'où, ne sachant où, dénué de
sens, inchangé.

Plus ou moins de syllabes, de virgules pour le souffle, un point
pour le grand souffle.

Petits pas pressés, le pied qui se pose vient de trop loin, le ferme
plus bas a trop loin à aller, il n'y a pas eu de chemin.

Il parle à part lui à la dernière personne, il se dit, Il est revenu, il
ne sait d'où, il ne sait où, il n'a pas eu de chemin.

Le pied se pose une dernière fois, l'autre monte le rejoindre, il est
rendu. Il peut lâcher son bâton blanc, il n'y a plus de bons ni de
méchants, et s'allonger.

4

Imagination dead imagine.

Imagine a place, that again.

Never ask another question.

Imagine a place, then someone in it, that again.

Crawl out of the frowsy deathbed and drag it to a place to die in.

Out of the door and down the road in the old hat and coat like
after the war, no, not that again.

A closed space five foot square by six high, try for him there.

Couldn't have got in, can't get out, did get in, will get out, all
right.

Stool, bare walls when the light comes on, women's faces on the
walls when the light comes on.

In a corner when the light comes on tattered Syntaxes of Jolly
and Draeger Praeger Draeger, all right.

Light off and let him be, sitting on the stool and talking to himself the last person.

Saying, Now where is he, no, Now he is here.

Try as well as sitting standing, walking, kneeling, crawling, lying, creeping, in the dark and the light.
Imagine light.
Imagine light.
No visible source, strong at full, spread all over, no shadow, all six planes shining the same, slow on, ten seconds to full, same off, try that.
Still his crown touches the ceiling, moving not.
Say a lifetime of walking crouched and drawing himself up when brought to a stand.
When it goes out no matter, start again, another place, someone in it, keep glaring, never see, never find, no end, no matter.

Appendix III: Nonfiction

The Capital of the Ruins

ON WHAT A YEAR AGO was a grass slope, lying in the angle that the Vire and Bayeux roads make as they unite at the entrance of the town, opposite what remains of the second most important stud-farm in France, a general hospital now stands. It is the Hospital of the Irish Red Cross in Saint-Lô, or, as the Laudiniens themselves say, the Irish Hospital. The buildings consist of some 25 prefabricated wooden huts. They are superior, generally speaking, to those so scantily available for the wealthier, the better-connected, the astuter or the more flagrantly deserving of the bombed-out. Their finish, as well without as within, is the best that priority can command. They are lined with glass-wool and panelled in isorel, a strange substance of which only very limited supplies are available. There is real glass in the windows. The consequent atmosphere is that of brightness and airiness so comforting to sick people, and to weary staffs. The floors, where the exigencies of hygiene are greatest, are covered with linoleum. There was not enough linoleum in France to do more than this. The walls and ceiling of the operating theatre are sheeted in aluminium of aeronautic origin, a decorative and practical solution of an old problem and a pleasant variation on the sword and ploughshare metamorphosis. A system of covered ways connects the kitchen with refectories and wards. The supply of electric current, for purposes both of heat and of power, leaves nothing to be desired. The hospital is centrally heated throughout, by means of coke. The medical, scientific, nursing and secretarial staffs are Irish, the instruments and furniture (including of course beds and bedding), the drugs and food, are supplied by the Society. I think I am right in saying that the number of in-patients (mixed) is in the neighbourhood of 90. As for the others, it is a regular thing, according to recent reports, for as many as 200 to be seen in the out-patients department in a day. Among such ambulant cases a large number are suffering from scabies and other diseases of the skin, the result no doubt of malnutrition or an ill-advised diet. Accident cases are frequent. Masonry falls when least expected, children play with detonators and de-mining continues. The laboratory, magnificently equipped, bids well to become the official laboratory for the department, if not of an even wider area. Considerable work has already been done in the analysis of local waters.

These few facts, chosen not quite at random, are no doubt familiar already to those at all interested in the subject, and perhaps even to those listening to the present circumlocution. They may not appear the most immediately instructive. That the operating-theatre should be sheeted with an expensive metal, or the floor of the labour-room covered with linoleum, can hardly be expected to interest those accustomed to such conditions as the *sine qua non* of reputable obstetrical and surgical statistics. These are the sensible people who would rather have news of the Norman's semi-circular canals or resistance to sulphur than of his attitude to the Irish bringing gifts, who would prefer the history of our difficulties with an unfamiliar pharmacopia and system of mensuration to the story of our dealings with the rare and famous ways of spirit that are the French ways. And yet the whole enterprise turned from the beginning on the establishing of a relation in the light of which the therapeutic relation faded to the merest of pretexts. What was important was not our having penicillin when they had none, nor the unregarding munificence of the French Ministry of Reconstruction (as it was then called), but the occasional glimpse obtained, by us in them and, who knows, by them in us (for they are an imaginative people), of that smile at the human conditions as little to be extinguished by bombs as to be broadened by the elixirs of Burroughes and Welcome,—the smile deriding, among other things, the having and the not having, the giving and the taking, sickness and health.

It would not be seemly, in a retiring and indeed retired storekeeper, to describe the obstacles encountered in this connexion, and the forms, often grotesque, devised for them by the combined energies of the home and visiting temperaments. It must be supposed that they were not insurmountable, since they have long ceased to be of much account. When I reflect now on the recurrent problems of what, with all proper modesty, might be called the heroic period, on one in particular so arduous and elusive that it literally ceased to be formulable, I suspect that our pains were those inherent in the simple and necessary and yet so unattainable proposition that their way of being we, was not our way and that our way of being they, was not their way. It is only fair to say that many of us had never been abroad before.

Saint-Lô was bombed out of existence in one night. German prisoners of war, and casual labourers attracted by the relative food-plenty, but soon discouraged by housing conditions, continue, two years after the liberation, to clear away the debris, literally by hand. Their spirit has yet to learn the blessings of Gallup and their flesh the benefits of the bulldozer. One may thus be excused if one questions the opinion generally received, that ten years will be sufficient for the total reconstruction of Saint-Lô. But no matter what period of time must still be endured, before the town begins to resemble the pleasant and prosperous administrative and agricultural centre that it was, the hospital of wooden huts in its gardens between the Vire and Bayeux roads will continue to discharge its function, and its cures. "Provisional" is not the term it was, in this universe become provisional. It will continue to discharge its function long after the Irish are gone and their names forgotten. But I think that to the end of its hospital days it will be called the Irish Hospital, and after that the huts, when they have been turned into dwellings, the Irish huts. I mention this possibility, in the hope that it will give general satisfaction. And having done so I may perhaps venture to mention another, more remote but perhaps of greater import in certain quarters, I mean the possibility that some of those who were in Saint-Lô will come home realising that they got at least as good as they gave, that they got indeed what they could hardly give, a vision and sense of a time-honoured conception of humanity in ruins, and perhaps even an inkling of the terms in which our condition is to be thought again. These will have been in France.

Notes on the Texts

Despite a pattern of errors running through the editions of Beckett's prose published by John Calder, some of the Calder texts contain Beckett's latest revisions. Beckett revised his stories of 1946, for instance, for Calder's separate edition of *First Love* (1973) and the first collection of the four stories, *Four Novellas* (1977). These texts were subsequently reprinted, with minor revisions to later stories as well, in *Collected Shorter Prose, 1945–1980* (1984). With the notable exceptions discussed below, namely *The Lost Ones*, "All Strange Away," "The Image," and "neither," the *Collected Shorter Prose, 1945–1980* texts have been adopted (and corrected) for this current volume.

For Beckett's first short story, "Assumption," the text reprinted here is that corrected and collected in *Transition Workshop* (1949, *vide* below). Two separately published stories from *Dream of Fair to Middling Women* have been included in this collection because they were published as separate stories, "Sedendo et Quiescendo" and "Text," and the texts established by Dr. Eoin O'Brien based on his editing of *Dream of Fair to Middling Women* (Dublin: The Black Cat Press, 1992; and New York: Arcade Press, 1993) have been adopted here.

As the text of Samuel Beckett's first published short story, "Assumption," suggests, editors have not always been kind to or careful with Samuel Beckett's work. It seems astonishing that for so important a publication, his first story in a journal publishing James Joyce's *Work in Progress*, (*transition* 16–17 [June 1929]: 268–71) "Assumption" should have been so poorly edited and proofread. If we except the obsolete spelling of "extasy" as indeed Beckett's (although it was revised in the reprint cited below), no fewer than five glaring typographical errors mar Beckett's first published piece of short fiction. Those errors were corrected only twenty years later in the reprint for *transition workshop*, edited by Eugene Jolas (New York: The Vanguard Press, Inc., 1949), 41–44; that text is reprinted here.

The original text for "Sedendo et Quiescendo" is even more corrupt than that for the original printing of "Assumption," except that the story has not heretofore been reprinted and so errors in the first printing have not been corrected. The number of errors in these first two *transition* stories suggests that Beckett never read proofs for either of them. For "Sedendo et Quiescendo," for instance, even the title was incorrect: the *transition* version reads "Sedendo et Quiesciendo." Like *Dream of Fair to Middling Women*, of which it finally became a part, "Sedendo et Quiescendo" is filled with the sort of Joycean wordplay that makes distinguishing error from linguistic play very difficult. Moreover, the version incorporated into *Dream of Fair to Middling Women* has been substantially revised—in places rewritten—so that the novel is not always an accurate guide to Beckett's thinking for this story version. On the whole, the ludic elements increased as Beckett absorbed story into novel. What in the story, for instance, was "a shadowy stasis between tram and sidewalk" became in the novel "an umbral stasis twixt tram and trottoir"; the "cold in the head" of the story became the "constipated coryza" of the novel; the story's "Wonderful" became the novel's "Wunnerful." The editor has, however, retained the integrity of the original story version in this printing so that readers can make their own comparisons.

The text printed in this current edition was corrected as follows:

"garden of Eden" to "Garden of Eden";

"he doesn't mush care" to "he doesn't much care";

"properties of the appropiate kind" to "properties of the appropriate kind";

"mailing his cheekbones" to "nailing his cheekbones";

"on him or to hom" to "on him or to him";

"(Nth Gt. Georges St." to "(Nth Gt. George's St.";

"a kind of contapuntal" to "a kind of contrapuntal";

"Bramaputra" to "Brahmaputra";

and finally, "he's gota bit wasted" to "he's got a bit wasted."

For "First Love" Beckett evidently made a series of revisions for the British text that never appeared in the American edition. The third paragraph of the American text begins, "Personally I have nothing against graveyards. . . ." But Beckett evidently could not resist a last-minute pun and revised the British text to "Personally I have no bone to pick with graveyards." Such late revisions were not uncommon for Beckett. Barry McGovern reports (*Independent on Sunday*, 31 December 1989), for instance, that Beckett for a time was tempted to revise the last sentence of "Dante and the Lobster" from "It is not" to "Like hell it is," but that revision never appeared in print. The revision to the British text of "First Love," on the other hand, has appeared in print as Beckett's latest revision and so has been adopted here. In the book version of "Sedendo et Quiescendo," however, Beckett changed "I don't believe it" in the first paragraph to "Like hell it does."

A number of other small changes have been made to the American text of "First Love": "But my father's yard was not among my favourite" was changed in the *Collected Shorter Prose 1945–1980* to "amongst my favourites." The first American printing missed the *g* in "grottoes," which has here been restored. And "To put it wildly" of the first British and American editions has been corrected to "To put it mildly." "They would have had to gas me out" of the American printing has been revised to "nothing less than gas would have dislodged me," as it appears in *Collected Shorter Prose 1945–1980*. Likewise, "I hate forgetting a proper name" became "I hate to forget . . ."; "*sotto voce*" became "beneath her breath"; and "even more dead than alive" became "even more dead than alive than usual."

The three British editions of "All Strange Away," including the separately published volume (London: John Calder [Publishers] Ltd., 1979), contain errors corrected only in the Grove Press edition, *Rockaby and Other Short Pieces* (New York: Grove Press, 1981), for which, evidently, Beckett read proof—at least the "toward" of the British editions, for example, is revised to the form Beckett preferred, "towards," in the Grove Press text, and "towards" is decidedly not a common American usage. (See, for example, Nicholson's *American-English Usage:* "the -s form is the prevailing one in Brit., *toward* in the US," p. 595.) In addition, all British editions print the following, "Last look oh not farewell but last for now on left side. . . ." "Left," however, was revised to "right" for the Grove edition. The Grove text, furthermore, contains a phrase missing from all British texts, ". . . better unchanging black or glare one or the other or between the two. . . ." With Beckett's revision the sentence near the end of the story then reads, "All that if not yet quite complete quite clear and little change likely unless perhaps to complete unless perhaps somehow light sudden gleam perhaps better fixed and all this flowing and ebbing to full and empty more harm than good and better unchanging black or glare one or the other or between the two soft white unchanging. . . ." Moreover, the word "head" is missing from the following sentence in all British texts: "thus the fall back to where she lay wedged against wall. . . ." The corrected Grove text reads: "thus the fall back to where she lay head wedged against wall. . . ." In all, the Grove text contains some twelve to sixteen corrections or revisions of the British text, depending, of course, on which British version is being compared. The *Journal of Beckett Studies* printing contained, for instance, typographical errors corrected for the separately published and collected printings.

When actor David Warrilow was performing the stage adaptation of Beckett's story *The Lost Ones* in Germany, a literary critic approached him after the show to suggest that the dimensions of the cylinder, "fifty metres round and eighteen high," could not be correct. If the total surface of the cylinder (or even the total wall or "mural" surface) were to be 80,000 square centimeters, as all book versions of the story have it, then the cylinder would have to be minuscule. Warrilow replied that he would see Beckett himself the following day and pose the question of the cylinder's dimensions to him directly. Beckett acknowledged that "the figure eighteen was indeed a most regrettable error." Some time later when Warrilow was making a film version of the story, he checked with Beckett a second time and Beckett confirmed the figure of sixteen meters, adding, "After all, you can't play fast and loose with pi" (see "From *David Warrilow*," *As No Other Dare Fail: For Samuel Beckett on His 80th Birthday by His Friends and Admirers* [London: John Calder (Publishers) Ltd., 1986; and New York: Riverrun Press, 1986, 87–88]).

In fact, the original French text prints the dimensions as sixteen meters high, as does the American publication in *Evergreen Review* No. 96 (Spring 1973): 41–64. The *Evergreen Review* edition, however, presents the total surface area as "twelve million" square centimeters, while the French edition, *Le Dépeupleur*, has it at "quatre-vingt mille centimètres carrés" (80,000 square centimeters), an erroneous surface area for a cylinder of either sixteen or eighteen meters high with a circumference of fifty meters. The *Evergreen Review* version seems to contain the correct figures. If one includes the area of the ceiling and floor of a cylinder sixteen by fifty meters, the total surface would be about 12 million square centimeters—eight million for the wall surface and 2 million each for the areas of ceiling and floor. Beckett, or rather the narrator, confirms these figures in the third paragraph of the story: "Inside a cylinder fifty metres round and sixteen high for the sake of harmony or a total surface of roughly twelve hundred square metres [or 12 million square centimeters, i.e., including ceiling and floor] of which eight hundred [square meters or 8 million square centimeters] mural [i.e., wall area]." All book versions of the story, however, present the total surface area on the opening page as

80,000 centimeters square. In addition, both British and American book versions of the story, the latter simply photo-offset from the British edition (London: Calder and Boyars, 1972) in which the errors above were introduced, transpose the numbers in the following: "The short queue is not necessarily the most rapid and such a one starting tenth may well find himself first before such another starting fifth assuming of course they start together" (*Evergreen Review*, p. 58). With the figures reversed, the sentence makes no sense, but the transposed figures appear in all British and American book editions. In *Le Dépeupleur* (p. 42) the figures accord with those of the *Evergreen Review* edition. The *Evergreen Review* edition, however, contains one variant. It drops the number from the following: "The more so as the two storms have this in common" (p. 56). The current publication restores the original French and American figure of sixteen meters for the cylinder's height but uses the total surface area of 12 million square centimeters for the cylinder, the figure that is mathematically accurate and that appears in the *Evergreen Review* edition. The current text as well has the queue with ten people move faster than the queue with five people as it does in the *Evergreen Review* and in *Le Dépeupleur*, and retains the number of storms at "two" as it is in all book versions. In addition, "forgo" (do without) has replaced "forego" (go before) in "no searcher can readily forgo the ladder."

"The Image," a short piece written on the way to *Comment c'est* (*How It Is*), was originally published in French in the inaugural issue of a magazine called simply *X: A Quarterly Review*, edited by David Wright and Patrick Swift. An English version first appeared in *As the Story Was Told: Uncollected and Late Prose* (London: John Calder [Publishers] Ltd., 1990), 31–40, but it was met with much suspicion by readers and scholars who argued, on the basis of internal evidence, that the unacknowledged translation could not have been Samuel Beckett's. Writing in the *Times Literary Supplement* of 26 October–1 November 1990, for instance, John Crombie points out: "Mr. Calder informs us that during the writing of *Comment c'est*, into which passages of *L'Image*, suitably reworked, were incorporated, Beckett moved from French to English and back—seeming to suggest that the text of 'The Image' is wholly by Beckett himself. But even a cursory comparison of *L'Image* and *Comment c'est* reveals that the text of 'The Image' is cobbled together from scraps taken, quite properly, from *How It Is*—i.e., using Beckett's own English—and scraps very definitely not from *How It Is*, upon which the nameless translator's skills have been brought, with disconcerting results, to bear. The resulting unevenness, to use no unkinder word, has been compounded, to put it mildly, by the fact that in many of the passages where *L'Image* and *Comment c'est* coincide and Beckett's own renderings were available, these have been disdained, or perhaps not even noticed, the translator offering his or her own approximations in place of Beckett's self-translation." "L'Image," then, was retranslated by Edith Fournier for this collection, and she notes that "Numerous similarities do occur" between "L'Image" and *Comment c'est*, "and in such cases the elements of the author's own translation of the final version as it appears in *How It Is* have here been closely respected."

The short prose work "neither" was originally published in the *Journal of Beckett Studies* No. 4 (Spring 1979) with line breaks suggestive of a poem. During the editing process, moreover, a word was dropped from the eighty-seven-word work. The omission was evidently not immediately noticed, for the correction did not appear until issue No. 6 in the Autumn of 1980, where, in his "Editorial," John Pilling noted, "It is very much regretted that the word 'neared' was accidentally omitted from the end of the fourth line of the text *neither* printed in issue 4 at post page-proof stage beyond the control of the editors" (p. 6). When the British publisher of Beckett's fiction and poetry, John Calder, was about to publish the work in the *Collected Poems*, Beckett resisted because he considered it a piece of prose, a story. As John Calder says in a letter to the *Times Literary Supplement* (24–30 August 1990), he had "originally intended to put ["neither"] in the *Collected Poems*. We did not do so, because Beckett at the last moment said that it was not a poem and should not be there" (p. 895). Subsequently, it was omitted inadvertently from *The Collected Shorter Prose 1945–1980* (London: John Calder [Publishers] Ltd., 1984), but printed in a more corrupt version in the posthumous *As the Story Was Told: Uncollected and Later Prose* (London: John Calder [Publishers] Ltd.; and New York: Riverrun Press, 1990). The printing was corrupted not only by the introduction of erroneous information (the story, identified in the *Journal of Beckett Studies* as "written by Samuel Beckett in September 1976 to be set to music by Morton Feldman," is described in *As the Story Was Told* as having been "[w]ritten for composer Morton Feldman, 1962") but when "neither" was finally collected not only was the title capitalized, but instead of including the word missing from the *Journal of Beckett Studies* printing, a copy editor's query marking the place of the lost word was taken by the printer as an addition to the text and was retained in publication; line six (in the collected edition) then reads, "doors once? gently close, once turned" instead of "doors once neared gently close, once turned. . . ." Moreover, since the piece is a work of prose, there is no question of retaining the line endings of either the *Journal of Beckett Studies* or the *As the Story Was Told* texts.

    Stirrings Still contains the misspelling of "withersoever" for "whithersoever" on page 4 of the de luxe edition. Critic Gerry Dukes pointed out the typographical error in his review of the volume in the *Irish Times* (15 April 1989). When the Irish actor Barry McGovern brought the error to Beckett's attention, the author made the correction in McGovern's copy. The error is, however, reproduced in the American trade edition by North Star Line but corrected in the version printed in *As the Story Was Told* (London: John Calder [Publishers] Ltd. and New York: Riverrun Press, 1990). The Calder edition, however, introduces a new error: "whereabouts" for the original and correct "whenceabouts" (p. 122). Thanks to Gerry Dukes for these details.

    "The Capital of the Ruins," a short piece of reportage on the Irish Hospital in St. Lô written for broadcast by Irish radio, has been shrouded in mystery, confusion, and error since its discovery amid the archives of Radio Telefis Éireann in 1983 and its publication in 1986. It was first published "in full incorporating all the manuscript changes in Beckett's hand," by Eoin O'Brien in *The Beckett Country* (Monkstown, Ireland: The Black Cat Press, 1986), 333–37. The piece was subsequently published that same year in *As No Other Dare Fail: For Samuel Beckett on His 80th Birthday by His Friends and Admirers* (London: John Calder [Publishers] Ltd., 1986), 71–76 with a brief commentary by Dougald McMillan, who also claims that the script is "published here for the first time" (p. 71). Although McMillan rightly identifies the quirky title of the piece with a booklet of photographs of the bombed-out city of St. Lô entitled *St. Lô, Capital des Ruines, 5 et 7 Juin 1944*, he claims that the piece "was read by Beckett on Radio Erin on 10 June 1946," the date in Beckett's hand on the final page of the three-sheet typescript. There is, however, no evidence for that claim. On the contrary, Dairmuid Breathnach, Chief Librarian of Radio Telefis Éireann, notes in correspondence with the editor: "The radio logs for a period of 18 months after 10 June 1946 have been examined but we have been unable to trace a date of transmission. There is no file of correspondence with Beckett in our written archives and there is no entry for Beckett in the fee cards of the period." The probability is that the piece, more than likely commissioned by Riobárd O Faracháin, general features officer at RTE (and member of the Board of the Abbey Theatre for thirty years), whose initials appear on the first page of the typescript, was never broadcast.

Both English texts cited above, moreover, include all the autograph emendations to the typed text as if they were Beckett's solely, but clearly those emendations are in several hands. I queried Beckett about the manuscript and the revisions to it in July 1983 just after the manuscript's discovery, and he wrote back on 23 July 1983: "No memory whatever of the St. Lô piece. As you say it seems to have been improved here and there by some third party—or parties." The "improvements" are stylistic rather than substantive, but nonetheless Beckett's exact prose ought to be recovered and retained wherever possible. In the first case the word "left" was added by another hand in "There was not enough linoleum left in France to do more than this." The second alteration is syntactically similar. The intrusion affects the first sentence in the second paragraph, which as published reads, ". . . and perhaps even to those of you listening to me." Beckett actually wrote the more self-deprecating, ". . . and perhaps even to those listening to the present circumlocution." The current text restores Beckett's original prose in both instances cited above.

Bibliography of Short Prose
in English

The distinction between a discrete short story and a fragment of a novel is not always clear in Beckett's work. For the purposes of this bibliography, however, if an excerpt is identified as part of a longer work in its title, it is not included. A partial list of portions of longer works is appended to the bibliography itself.

"All Strange Away," *Journal of Beckett Studies*, No. 3 (summer 1978): 19.

"All Strange Away," *Stereo Headphones*, Nos. 8, 9, 10 (1982): 3. [Facsimile typescript.]

"All Strange Away," *Rockaby and Other Short Pieces* (New York: Grove Press, 1981).

All Strange Away (London: John Calder [Publishers] Ltd., 1979).

"Assumption," *transition* 16–17 (June 1929): 268–71. [Reprinted along with the poem "Malacoda" in *transition workshop* ed. by Eugene Jolas (New York: The Vanguard Press, 1949): 41–44.]

"As the story was told," *Gunter Eich zum Gedächtnis* (Frankfurt: Suhrkamp Verlag, 1975), 10–[13]. [Reprinted in *As the Story Was Told: Uncollected and Late Prose*, 103–07.]

"As the story was told," *Chicago Review* 33.2 (1982): 76–77.

As the Story Was Told: Uncollected and Late Prose (London: John Calder [Publishers] Ltd., 1990; New York: Riverrun Press, 1990).

"The Calmative," *Evergreen Review* 11.47 (June 1967): 46–49, 93–95.

"The Capital of the Ruins," *The Beckett Country: Samuel Beckett's Ireland* (Monkstown, Ireland: The Black Cat Press [in association with Faber and Faber], 1986), 333–37.

"The Capital of the Ruins," *As No Other Dare Fail: For Samuel Beckett on His 80th Birthday by His Friends and Admirers* (London: John Calder [Publishers] Ltd., 1986; New York: Riverrun Press, 1986).

"A Case in a Thousand," *The Bookman* 86 (August 1934): 241–42.

Collected Shorter Prose: 1945–1980 (London: John Calder [Publishers] Ltd., 1984).

"Dante and the Lobster," *This Quarter* 5 (December 1932): 222–36. [One of the *More Pricks Than Kicks* (1934) stories.]

"Dante and the Lobster," *Evergreen Review* 1.1 (1957): 24–36. [As above.]

"The End," *Merlin* (Summer 1954). [Translated from the French by Richard Seaver in collaboration with the author.]

"The End," *Evergreen Review* 4.15 (November–December 1960): 22–41. [As above.]

"Enough," *First Love and Other Shorts* (New York: Grove Press, 1974).

"The Expelled," *Evergreen Review* 6.22 (January–February 1962): 8–20. [Dated 1946. Translated from the French by Richard Seaver in collaboration with the author.]

The Expelled and Other Novellas (Harmondsworth, England; New York: Penguin Books, 1980).

"La Falaise," *Celui qui ne peut se servir de mots* (Montpellier: Fata Morgana, 1975).

"Faux Départ," *Karlsbuch* 1 (June 1965): 1–5.

First Love (London: Calder and Boyars, Ltd., 1973). [First publication of *First Love* written in 1946 along with the other "Stories" or "Nouvelles."]

"First Love," *First Love and Other Shorts* (New York: Grove Press, 1974). [Includes "From an Abandoned Work," "Enough," "Imagination Dead Imagine," and "Ping" as well as "First Love."]

"Fizzle 1," *Tri Quarterly* (In the wake of the *Wake*) 38 (winter 1977): 163–67. Reprinted in *In the Wake of the Wake*, ed. by David Hayman and Elliott Anderson (Madison, Wisconsin: University of Wisconsin Press, 1978). ["Fizzle 1" designated according to the order in the original Grove Press edition, i.e., "He is barehead." See also below.]

Fizzles (New York: Grove Press, 1976). [Eight stories or "fizzles" numbered, not titled, in the American edition except for numbers 3,

"Afar a bird"; 7, the only one originally written in English, "Still"; and 8, "For to end yet again," the title story to the French and British editions, *Pour finir encore et autre foirades* and *For to End Yet Again and Other Fizzles*, respectively. In addition, the latter two each print the stories in an order different from the Grove text.]

"For to End Yet Again," *New Writing and Writers 13* (London: John Calder [Publishers] Ltd., 1975 [or 1976 as Calder says]), 9–14.

For to End Yet Again and Other Fizzles (London: John Calder [Publishers] Ltd., 1976). [Unlike the American and French editions, the British edition adopts titles for all eight of the stories: "For to end yet again," "Still," "He is barehead," "Horn came always," "Afar a Bird," "I gave up before birth," "Closed place" (mistakenly entitled "Closed Space" in this volume—"Se Voir" in French), and "Old earth." Moreover, each edition, American, British, and French, presents the stories in a different order.]

Four Novellas (London: John Calder [Publishers] Ltd., 1977). [Includes: "First Love," "The Expelled," "The Calmative," and "The End." "First Love" is then finally grouped here with the three other stories from *Stories and Texts for Nothing* or *No's Knife*.]

"From an Abandoned Work," *Trinity News: A Dublin University Weekly*, 3 (7 July 1956): 4.

"From an Abandoned Work," *Evergreen Review* 1.3 (1957): 83–91.

From an Abandoned Work (London: Faber and Faber, 1958). [First broadcast by the BBC in the Third Programme on 14 December 1957, spoken by Patrick Magee.]

"From an Abandoned Work," *Breath and Other Shorts* (London: Faber and Faber, 1971), 39–48.

"From an Abandoned Work," *First Love and Other Shorts* (New York: Grove Press, 1974).

"From an Unabandoned Work," *Evergreen Review* 4.14 (September–October 1960): 58–65. [A portion of the novel *How It Is*.]

"Heard in the Dark 1," *New Writing and Writers 17* (London: John

Calder [Publishers] Ltd., 1979). [An early extract from the novel *Company*.]

"Heard in the Dark 2," *Journal of Beckett Studies*, No. 5 (autumn 1979). [As above.]

"L'Image," *X: A Quarterly Review* 1.1 (November 1959): 35–37. ["An extract written on the way to *Comment c'est* (*How It Is*). See "A Note on the Texts" and see also James Knowlson's letter to *The Times* (23 May 1988).]

"Imagination Dead Imagine," *Evergreen Review* 10.39 (February 1966): 48–49.

"Imagination Dead Imagine," *Sunday Times*, 7 November 1965, p. 48.

Imagination Dead Imagine, (London: John Calder [Publishers] Ltd., 1965). [The "Other Works" page announces a forthcoming volume as *Stories and Texts for Nothing*, but the volume with the addition of four more stories is finally published by Calder as *No's Knife*, q.v.]

"Imagination Dead Imagine," *Evergreen Review* 10.39 (February 1966): 48–49.

"Imagination Dead Imagine," *First Love and Other Shorts* (New York: Grove Press, 1974). [Reprinted in *I can't go on, I'll go on*, ed. by Richard Seaver (New York: Grove Press, 1976), 551–54.]

"Imagination Dead Imagine," *Samuel Beckett Reader*, ed. by John Calder (London: Calder and Boyars, 1967), 186–89.

"Jem Higgins' Love-Letter to the Alba," *New Durham* (June 1965): 10–11. [Fragment of *Dream of Fair to Middling Women*.]

"Lessness," *The Evergreen Review* 14.80 (July 1970): 35–36.

Lessness (Signature Series: Signature 9) (London: Calder and Boyars, 1970).

"Lessness," *I can't go on, I'll go on*, ed. by Richard Seaver (New York: Grove Press, 1976), 555–61.

The Lost Ones (London: Calder and Boyars, 1972). [Written in 1966, between "Enough" and "Ping," final paragraph added in 1970.]

The Lost Ones (New York: Grove Press, 1972). [As above.]

No's Knife: Collected Shorter Prose 1945–1966 (London: Calder and Boyars, 1967, reprinted 1975). [Three "stories"—"The Expelled," "The Calmative," and "The End,"— the 13 *Texts for Nothing*, and four *Residua*—"From an Abandoned Work," "Enough," "Imagination Dead Imagine," and "Ping."]

"One Evening," *Journal of Beckett Studies*, No. 6 (autumn 1980). [An early version of the novel *Mal vu mal dit* (*Ill Seen Ill Said.*)]

"One Evening," *New Writers and Writing 20* (London: John Calder [Publishers] Ltd., 1983).

"One Evening," *art press*, No. 51 (September 1981): 4.

"Ping," *Encounter* 28.2 (February 1967): 25–26. [Facsimile of manuscript version of "Bing," Richard L. Admussen, *The Samuel Beckett Manuscripts: A Study* (Boston: G. K. Hall, 1979), 132–48.]

"Ping," *First Love and Other Shorts* (New York: Grove Press, 1974).

"Return to the Vestry," *New Review* (August–September–October 1931): 98–99.

"Sedendo et Quiescendo," *transition: An International Workshop for Orphic Creation* 21 (March 1932): 13–20. [Fragment of *Dream of Fair to Middling Women* printed as "Sedendo et Quiesciendo."]

Six Residua (London: John Calder [Publishers] Ltd., 1978). [Includes: "From an Abandoned Work," "Enough," "Imagination Dead Imagine," "Ping," "Lessness," and *The Lost Ones.*]

"The Smeraldina's Billet-Doux," *Zero Anthology of Literature and Art*, No. 8, ed. Themistocles Hoetis (New York: Zero Press, 1956), 56–61. [One of the *More Pricks Than Kicks* stories.]

"Sounds," *Essays in Criticism* 28.2 (April 1978): 156–57. [Along with "Still 3," a variant on "Still."]

"Still," *Signature Anthology: Signature 20* (London: Calder and Boyars, 1975).

"Still 3," *Essays in Criticism* 28.2 (April 1978): 156–57. [Along with "Sounds," a variant on "Still."]

"Stirrings Still," *The Guardian*, 3 March 1989: 25.

Stirrings Still (New York: North Star Line, 1993).

Stories and Texts for Nothing, with drawings by Avigdor Arikha (New York:

Grove Press, 1967). [Three "stories": "The Expelled," "The Calmative," and "The End." The Arikha drawings appeared in the second French edition (1958) and the first American edition. The British edition of these stories published in *No's Knife* does not reproduce the Arikha drawings.]

"Text," *New Review* (winter 1931–32): 338–39. [Poem from *The European Caravan*, to be distinguished from "Text" below.]

"Text," *New Review* 2 (April 1932): 57. [Reprinted in Ruby Cohn, *Samuel Beckett: The Comic Gamut* (New Brunswick: Rutgers University Press, 1962), 340. Fragment of *Dream of Fair to Middling Women*.]

"Text for Nothing I," *Evergreen Review* 3.9 (summer 1959): 21–24.

"Texts for Nothing VI," *The London Magazine* (New Series) 7.5 (August 1967): 47–50.

"Texts for Nothing XII," *The Transatlantic Review* 24 (spring 1967): XX.

Texts for Nothing (Signature Series: Signature 21) (London: Calder and Boyars, 1974). [The only separately published edition of these stories. See also *No's Knife* above.]

"Yellow," *New World Writing* 10 (November 1956): 108–119. [One of the *More Pricks Than Kicks* stories.]

[The following are designated as excerpts and not as separate stories: Portions of *Watt* have appeared in *Envoy: A Review of Literature and Art* 1.2 (January 1950); *Irish Writing* 17 (December 1951) and 22 (March 1953); and *Merlin* 1.3 (winter 1952–53). Portions from Beckett's "Trilogy" have appeared as follows: *Molloy*, *Transition Fifty* 6 (1950); *Paris Review* 5 (spring 1954); *New World Writing No. 5* (April 1954); *Malone Dies*, *transition* (1950), *Irish Writing* 34 (1954); *The Unnamable*, *Spectrum* 2.1 (winter 1958); *Chicago Review* 12.2 (summer 1958); *The Texas Quarterly* 1.2 (spring 1958).]

Illustrated Editions of Short Prose

All Strange Away, with illustrations by Edward Gorey (New York: Gotham Book Mart, 1976). [An edition authorized for the Estate of Jack MacGowran.]

Au loin un oiseau [*Afar a bird*], with etchings by Avigdor Arikha (New York: Double Elephant Press, 1973).

Bing (Ping), with illustrations by H. M. Erhardt (Stuttgart: Manus Presse, 1970). [8 blind-relief impressions in an edition of 50 numbered copies. Erhardt also produced illustrations for Manus Presse of "Act Without Words" I and II (1965), "Come and Go" (1968), and *Watt* (1971).]

Foirades/Fizzles, with etchings by Jasper Johns, ed. by Véra Lindsay (New York: Petersburg Press, 1976). [This edition contains only fizzles 4, 1, 6, 5, and 2 of the Grove Press arrangement.]

"Trial Proofs for *Foirades/Fizzles,*" *Foirades/Fizzles: Echo and Allusion in the Art of Jasper Johns* (Los Angeles: The Grunwald Center for the Graphic Arts, University of California, Los Angeles, 1987), 235–310. [74 plates.]

Foirades/Fizzles, Whitney Museum of American Art catalogue, 11 October 20 November 1977. [Includes the texts "I gave up before birth" and "J'ai renoncé avant de naître."]

From an Abandoned Work, with illustrations by Max Ernst (Stuttgart: Manus Presse, 1969). [A trilingual edition.]

Imagination Dead Imagine, with illustrations by Sorel Etrog (London: John Calder [Publishers] Ltd., 1977).

L'Issue, with six original engravings by Avigdor Arikha (Paris: Les Editions Georges Visat, 1968). [A passage from *Le Dépeupleur* (*The Lost Ones*).]

The Lost Ones, with illustrations by Charles Klabunde (Stamford, CT: New Overlook Press, 1984).

"The Lost Ones," illustrated by Philippe Weisbecker, *Evergreen Review*, No. 96 (Spring 1973): 41–64. [See particularly "the north," p. 59, and compare below.]

The North, with etchings by Avigdor Arikha (London: Enitharmon Press, 1972). [Excerpt from *The Lost Ones*.]

Séjour, with engravings by Louis Maccard from the original drawings by Jean Deyrolle (Paris: G. R. [Georges Richar], 1970). [A passage from *Le Dépeupleur* (*The Lost Ones*). Engravings completed by Maccard when Deyrolle died in mid-project.]

Still, with etchings by William Hayter, ed. by Luigi M. Majno (Milan: M'Arte Edizione, 1974).

Stirrings Still, with illustrations by Louis le Brocquy (New York: Blue Moon Books, 1988 and London: John Calder [Publishers] Ltd., 1988). [Collector's edition limited to 200 copies.]

Stirrings Still (New York: North Star Line, 1993). [Only trade edition with le Brocquy illustrations.]

Stories and Texts for Nothing, with drawings by Avigdor Arikha (New York: Grove Press, 1967). [First American edition and second French edition (1958) include the Arikha illustrations.]

SAMUEL BECKETT was born on April 13, 1906, in Foxrock, near Dublin, Ireland. In the late 1920s he went to Paris, where he began writing both prose and poetry. Until 1945 he wrote in English but thereafter began to write directly in French, and much of his major work was written in his adopted tongue. His translations of his own work into English are in themselves works of art. He was awarded the Nobel Prize for Literature in 1969, and his literary output, including plays, novels, stories, and poems, has earned him the reputation of being one of the most important writers of our time. He died in 1989.

About the Type

This book was set in Centaur, a typeface designed by the American typographer Bruce Rogers in 1929. Centaur was a typeface that Rogers adapted from the fifteenth-century type of Nicholas Jenson and modified in 1948 for a cutting by the Monotype Corporation.